Denise is a poet,
Protecting her heart
When she first hears the news
Her world's falling apart.

Miranda Martin
Is a registered nurse.
Who makes people feel better
When things seem at their worst.

From two different countries,
With oceans between,
Are omnipotent hands
Directing the scene?

Sometimes when we least expect it.
Hearts connect...

And nothing is ever the

same again.

By Sam Ruskin

Connecting Hearts

by Val Brown and M.J Walker

ISBN   0-9741034-1-1
First Printing 2003
Cover art and design by Anne M. Clarkson

Published by:
Dare 2 Dream Publishing
A Division of Limitless Corporation
Lexington, South Carolina 29073

Find us on the World Wide Web
http://www.limitlessd2d.net

Printed in the United States of America by
Axess Purchasing Solutions
PO Box 500835
Atlanta, GA 31150

Acknowledgements

We would like to thank Jane Wageman for her expertise in Neurology and knowledge of ALS and Monica Croatti for her insights and information. We also want to tell Di Bauden how much we appreciate her writing the foreword for the book.

No thank you would be complete without mentioning the team at Limitless. You've done much more than transfer our words to the printed page and we are grateful.

Special Notation

Please note that our authors are international. You may see spellings and some words that are unfamiliar to you. These words are not spelled incorrectly but, rather, represent the national spelling of the writer. We at **D2D** encourage international authors to submit their manuscripts to us and have elected to leave them in their original format so that you may enjoy the international flavor as much as we do.

Foreword

ALS, Amyotrophic Lateral Sclerosis, Lou Gehrig's Disease, or Motor Neuron Disease; depending on where you live the terminology will change describing this fatal neuromuscular disease. No matter which label or name it falls under, the properties of this illness are all the same and hit home all too hard. ALS has affected my family three times in my 35 years. Once with my grandmother, once with my aunt, and finally again with my mother. More times than any one family should ever experience. What is ALS? It is a silent predator that slowly steals its victim's abilities to walk, talk, move, eat and eventually breathe. No known cure has been found to treat ALS as of today. Researchers are testing many new trials to find and stop this horrific illness. Stem cell research is one of the more promising possibilities for ALS patients. Stem cells could very well develop into new nerve cells, which would replace or restore the damaged neurons in afflicted ALS victims. Many tests still have to be done before this treatment can be performed on those with ALS, but it is one of the more hopeful research developments to date. Until successful treatments can be found, my family will hold tight and pray that ALS doesn't affect any more of us. One thing that I have learned with this disease is that it absolutely doesn't care who it affects. It used to be Lou Gehrig's disease, but in all actuality, it's anyone's disease.

For more information or to make a donation to help the researchers along, please go to www.projectals.org.

--Diane S. Bauden

Chapter 1

"There's no medical evidence I can find in the literature to suggest a garlic chest rub will prevent the common cold."

Randa chuckled as she typed, knowing viruses might not stay away but most of *Herblady's* friends probably would.

Herblady was a frequent visitor to the Brightwood Information Network.com website. Her questions regarding folk medicine and herbal remedies were a welcome change of pace at the recently established Internet site.

"Thanks, dear. You're always so helpful" came the reply onto the chat screen. No, not chat screen, Randa smirked - the company preferred "consultation room".

Brightwood Pharmaceuticals Inc. had established the website six months earlier as a public service but it was more likely as a shelter against taxes and corporate guilt. Three years before, Brightwood had been researching a more effective way to de-worm dogs.

The canine project stalled, but in a case of corporate serendipity the new medicine was proved to enhance the function of several antibiotics giving doctors a new weapon against the increasing number of resistant bacteria in humans. The windfall profits from the new drug put the company on the map. Determined to be a player in the public's opinion, they established the website and hired several qualified nurses to answer questions and dispense advice 24 hours a day. Now here Randa was, dealing with people from all over the planet. The nurse marveled at how some people could have a computer and Internet access but no available medical services. "Even right here in California," she thought.

She clicked the "available" button under her name and the Internet community was made aware of the fact that Miranda Martin, RN was ready for the next question. As no new user name appeared in the consultation room, Randa rolled her chair back, ran fingers through her thick honey blonde hair and picked up her can of Diet Dr. Pepper. Taking a large drink and propping bare feet on her desk, the nurse reflected that her current job was a lot less physically and emotionally stressful than the hospital work she had done the previous six years. Randa shook her head as she realized how different this job was from her former one. In the hospital she had dealt everyday with frustrating paperwork, angry families, doctors determined to be the enemy and the never-ending bureaucracy. It made her 29 years on the planet seem so much longer.

Now Randa worked from her home using a huge database of research literature, pharmacy information and medical school expertise to supplement her natural instincts as a nurse. If Randa didn't know the answer to a question, a few keystrokes later she knew where to go to look for it. Though the nurse was still getting involved with the people who accessed the service, she didn't go to work with the dread that someone's life could literally be in her hands. If she never did CPR on a human being again in her life it would be fine with her.

Randa's reverie was broken when a too-perky electronic voice announced, "One entering from the waiting room!" She rolled her eyes and wished Derek, her friend and the site's webmaster, didn't have quite the weird sense of humor he did. She would send him an e-mail when her shift was done. It was 4 a.m. and she had three hours to go. Pulling back up to the screen Randa saw the user name *Angelsmom*. Karen Garcia was having trouble with her colicky baby again. The young woman smiled and prepared to try to soothe both the baby and the new mother.

She was a nurse; it was what she did.

There was only one bench in the park. It stood almost neglected at the far end of the public recreational area, sheltered by a thick overgrowth of coniferous trees. On one side was a single bronze plaque; a dedication to an unknown patron's loved one who had died years before. Its rusted, dull surface proclaimed its weathered age and the abundance of overgrown weeds around its legs demonstrated the park groundskeeper's lack of diligence in maintaining the bench's preservation.

Denise Jennings approached the bench with her usual long

stride. Its old, battered wood a welcoming beacon and escape from the realities of every day life. She sat down slowly, positioning herself in the centre of the seat as she looked out across the park. It seemed that everything was in the distance from this position. The children's recreational play area, the cycle stunts track for the older teens, the neglected bandstand, all far away from this little place of inner contemplation.

It was raining, not heavily, but enough to soak the ground with its continued fall. Denise was thankful that in her small place of solitude she was sheltered from the constant droplets. She breathed a sigh, a puff of condensation billowing from her lips as she exhaled. It was cold, incredibly so. Still she had been aware of this when she left the house earlier today and had remembered to put on her new dark navy parka and thickest jeans. She had tucked her long black hair up into a thick black woolly hat that brought out the colour of her vivid blue eyes. The forecast for the rest of the week looked grim and Denise knew that the British winter was fast approaching. *Maybe it will bypass autumn altogether,* she thought.

Looking down at her watch, Denise checked the time. She was only supposed to be gone for about two hours; enough time for her to run the errands that needed doing and be back for her Aunt Sara. Sara had an appointment with her local general practitioner and Denise wanted to make sure she attended the surgery with her. Sara had been feeling unwell for days now - weeks even, with a shortness of breath and the occasional trouble swallowing. It was upsetting for Denise to watch and it was she who had initially made the appointment with the doctor. Still she had a few more moments before she needed to get back to her aunt and Denise welcomed these moments of quiet contemplation.

Denise was a poet, a fact unknown to many people as she kept her identity closely under wraps. Unlike most poets in this day and age, Denise was very successful. Her expression of emotion, her beautifully sculpted wording, and her ability to bring to life each word she wrote had catapulted the name of "D Jennings" into critical acclaim and financial success. Of course she wrote under a shrouded name, the very idea of being remotely in the public eye an almost unnerving concept to imagine. She would never have considered writing for publication if it wasn't for her love of the craft and her desire to reach the people of the world with words that she hoped, in some way, would touch the heart of at least one person.

The bench was her place of contemplation where she could let her mind wander and allow the constant thoughts that stormed around in her head time to calm and flow into carefully constructed verses. Unfortunately the time she was able to spend in this clandestine place seemed to lessen by the day. Denise took her responsibilities very seriously and at the moment, one person in her life became more important above all else. Her aunt. With Sara's health taking such an unknown turn Denise devoted all her time to helping the elderly woman.

Her aunt had taken the poet under her wing at the tender age of ten years after her parents, Sara's brother and his wife, had both been tragically killed in a house fire. They had died trying to save her and although she was lucky enough to escape - her parents were not. So she had lived with Sara since that moment and for the next twenty-two years onwards.

Denise looked down at her watch once again. "Bollocks!" she muttered, realizing that she really should be on her way back to her aunt. Adjusting the collar of her thick parka, Denise stepped away from the bench and into the cold mist of rain.

Hands shaking from the cold, Denise managed to push her key into the lock and open the small double glazed, UPVC door. A wave of heat enveloped her and she shivered as the cold began to leave her body. She walked into the house she had called home for the past twenty-two years.

The dwelling was modest; what would generally be known as a "coal miners cottage". During the early nineteen hundreds the village she lived in had been a lively mining town, but when the mining pits began to shut down the workers drifted away. Although the house was small, it was still larger than the other houses on its street. Sara had an extension built on the back many years before. It served as a bedroom and study for Denise; a place where she could write in relative silence and tranquility. It was the place where she brought to life the poetry and rhymes she created with such reputed beauty and finesse.

14

She walked into the front room to find her aunt sitting quietly in her chair, rubbing the palm of her right hand. Denise frowned as she noticed the pale complexion. "Hey, Sara, are you feeling alright?"

The old woman smiled. "DJ! Yes, I am fine. I didn't hear you come in."

Denise nodded as she pulled off her black woolly hat; inky black tresses falling softly down her back. She strode over to her aunt and bent down to look into matching blue eyes. "Are you feeling short of breath again?" The concern was evident in her voice.

Sara nodded slowly, she was thankful to have her niece back home. "I wasn't doing anything strenuous though. I just don't understand this."

Denise nodded and placed her hand upon her aunt's. "That is what the appointment is for remember? We will find out what this is once and for all. Then we can get the medication or whatever it is you need to make you feel well again. Okay?" Sara had waved these symptoms off for weeks now but as they became more pronounced, Denise decided enough was enough.

Nodding, the old woman shifted to the corner of the chair. "What time is the appointment?"

"Twenty minutes." Denise replied after checking her watch. She moved to her feet. "Are you ready to go?"

With a sigh the old woman held out her hand and Denise pulled her up gently. "As I'll ever be," she replied with a weary smile.

Chapter 2

Randa stretched and forced herself from the comfortable sofa in her living room. She had been watching a taped episode of "E.R." on the VCR and relaxing before her shift on the Brightwood Information Network. It amazed her how comfortable she had become in the farmhouse since buying it less than a year ago. She never regretted the decision to leave suburbia to the young families, their lawnmowers and leaf blowers. An acre of land wasn't much but she loved the peace and the solitude it provided and she would never tire of standing on the hill behind the farmhouse to watch the blazing orange sunsets. The golden brown fields of late summer would come alive then with a fiery brilliance.

"Okay, time to stop being lazy and get ready for work but boy, if I could work with Dr. Carrie Weaver in real life it might tempt me to work in a hospital again. Or maybe that Dr. Elizabeth Corday, her curly hair and British accent knock me out!" Randa had to snicker as she thought of the picture she would present in the hospital, coming to work in the well-worn cut-off Wrangler jeans and tank top as she was going to do now.

Using the remote she flipped the television off and surveyed her work area. Database computer up and at the ready. Computer link to the website up and working, waiting for her to sign on. Supplies were handy; a large bag of corn chips, adequate supply of Diet Dr. Pepper and in the fridge a seafood enchilada and a black bean tostada awaited microwaving on her lunch break. Stopping at Miguel's Mexican Café on the way home from her workout had been genius on her part, Randa mused. There had to be some reward for the half hour on the Stairmaster and a full circuit on the exercise machines at the gym in town.

The nurse made a quick stop in the bathroom, pausing for a moment to eye herself critically in the full-length mirror on the back of the door. Though not tall, her 5 foot 5 inch frame was compact and toned from her exercise regime.

Skin clear, no wrinkles yet, Randa observed as she continued the mental inventory. *Green eyes bright, passable looks. Not bad for pushing thirty.*

She left the bathroom thinking, *No real vices if you don't count Ben and Jerry's New York Super Fudge Chunk Ice Cream, good sense of humor, wonderful personality and I'm so humble, too.* She chuckled "Not too full of ourselves now are we, Miranda? If I were that great I'd have to beat back the suitors with a stick."

In truth, Randa had many admirers, both male and female. If the nurse had given them the smallest amount of encouragement, they would have swarmed around her like bees to honey.

Randa settled in the chair at the computer desk and logged in. After she typed her name and hit the "enter" key, a voice very much like Sean Connery's intoned "Miranda Martin, RN, online." The nurse shivered in delight.

Bless you Derek for listening to me this morning.

The consultation room remained empty for the moment and Randa used the time to study the framed photograph of her parents that was sitting on the corner of the desk. The picture had been taken only a few months before Leonard Martin had suffered a massive stroke and died, leaving his wife a widow for the past two years. Janice Martin continued to live in the same house they had always lived in, but it was obvious her real joy in life was gone.

I saw what you and Dad had, Mom. That's what I want too, but it's tough being a true believer in this day and age. Randa wanted the fairy tale romance, the grand passion and the happy ending and was willing to wait for it, but oh, the waiting was hard. She resolved to call her mother first thing in the morning; she needed to hear her voice.

The nurse needed a diversion and seeing the consultation room still empty, picked up a recently purchased book and perused the cover.

Speaking of voices I love, if 'Derbyshire Dreams' is as good as this author's previous books of poetry...

Randa's thoughts were interrupted by the pseudo-Sean voice stating "One in from the waiting room, you sexy thing." The nurse burst out laughing and turned to the consultation room screen as a new user name appeared. It was time to be a true believer in earning a living.

18

The haunting melody of Beethoven's "Adagio sostenuto" drifted softly across the air of the dimly lit study. The room was of a decent size with a large mahogany desk that curved around two walls of the area. Lined up against one wall were a row of carefully constructed shelves; each one filled to capacity with an abundance of well-worn, well-read books on many different subjects. Fiction and non-fiction, history, science, reference, any type of book you could imagine - it was somewhere on those shelves, placed with pride and read with interest and enthusiasm.

The only light in the study came from the glare of a large computer screen that stood in the centre of the desk. Denise Jennings sat facing away from her computer. Sprawled out in her chair with legs crossed at the ankles, she rested her head in one hand as she gazed into space.

It's strange how life works, Denise thought. *Never an essence to grace you with the slightest of ease, it exists to test your endurance, wear your patience and force you into submission at the most unexpected of times.*

This was one of those times.

Sitting in the near darkness, Denise leaned forward and rested her elbows on her knees, still staring into nothingness, trying to organize her emotions - emotions that bordered on tearful confusion. She couldn't imagine, didn't understand how in the short space of one week the lives of the two occupants of the Jennings household had been completely turned upside down. From the moment Sara had walked into the doctor's office, things just hadn't been the same. Sara had talked with the doctor, explained her symptoms, and in doing so had realized other changes and possible symptoms that would seem to have been related. Periods of clumsiness, cramps in her muscles and a change in her normal speaking voice; these symptoms had all progressed slowly, but seemingly were all related.

So tests had been carried out, blood taken, scans recorded and results gained. Denise remembered with absolute clarity the expression on Doctor Macarthur's face as she and her aunt arrived at the hospital for the results. Sara had a disease called

Motor Neurons Disease or MND, more commonly known in the United States as ALS and although the factors of this disease had been carefully explained to them, Denise couldn't believe that Sara had just been handed her death sentence. From here on out, things could only get worse.

Rising to her feet, Denise left the confines of her study and walked out into the well-lit back hallway of the house. It was almost midday and though the day had started bright, the absence of the sun now hiding behind the white sky - broken only by darker, greyer clouds - foretold the coming of change. More rain was on its way, dark and thunderous in its descent.

Moving through the house the poet decided she would check on her aunt. The woman had still felt tired when she'd woken that morning so had decided to go back to bed. Pushing open the large white door, Denise looked into the dim bedroom; a room that had literally not changed in the whole twenty-two years she had lived there. Fresh coats of paint had been added, curtains may have been changed for ones with different floral motifs, but in essence the room was the same.

Standing between the gap of the door and its frame the tall woman studied the sleeping form resting peacefully in her bed. She took a deep breath, feeling a profound sadness swell within her chest. *Why?* It was a question that she had internally asked. *Why did this have to happen to Sara?* The woman who had selflessly given up her own space and solitude to share it with a young ten-year-old tearaway who was hell bent on making her life a nightmare. A young Denise, so hurt by the knowledge that her parents had died while saving her, had lashed out and rebelled against the prospect of getting close to another motherly figure, especially the aunt whom she did so love even then. But Sara had been patient and persisted. She had broke down the barriers that the young child had erected around her broken heart and had given her the parental love that she had so desperately craved.

Feeling a single unexpected tear fall from her eye, Denise shook her head. "This can't be it," she whispered. "I refuse to believe nothing can be done." With a shuddering sigh, Denise turned from the room, closing the door quietly behind her. She needed answers; needed to know if this really was 'terminal' as Doctor Macarthur had stated.

Returning back to her room as the last notes of

Beethoven's melody filtered through the air, Denise sat down at her computer, eager to gain some answers.

Chapter 3

Before you I would fall,
Helpless upon my knees,
My heart in my hands,
And I'd pledge my soul to you for eternity.

Randa let a small dreamy sigh escape her lips, closed the book and gently placed it on her chest.

"A pact with the devil, that's what it has to be. Nobody can write like that, touch my soul, without Satan being involved somewhere." The blonde said aloud as she shook her head.

"Get real, Randa, something that brings me so close to heaven couldn't possibly be written by anything less than an angel."

Turning the book over, Randa noted once again there wasn't the usual type of picture of the author on the dust jacket. Instead there was a picture of a tall, probably female figure in the distance, back to the photographer, apparently walking away. The figure was dressed in a heavy jacket and some sort of dark hat. Details were difficult to pick out because the picture had a blurry quality to it, as if it had been taken through raindrops. *Or maybe teardrops,* Randa thought then wondered why such an odd idea would cross her mind.

Opening the back cover, Randa read the brief note. "D Jennings lives in Great Britain with family. Previous works include the poetry collections *Without an Umbrella* and *From the Lea.* " No more details than that. The blond wondered who D Jennings was and how she could speak to a heart an ocean, a continent and a life away. Randa had read the author's two other books and had looked forward to this new volume with anticipation. The earlier books had been wondrous and this one was no exception; at times the nurse imagined she heard the voice of the poet reading to her alone.

I wish, she thought ruefully. *I hear D Jennings doesn't do readings or even book signings in public. Well, whether you're a tortured genius or disfigured or just shy, my poet, I thank you for this gift. Live your life how you want, just don't stop writing.*

Randa looked around, taking in her surroundings. She had only meant to take a short break from the list of chores she had given herself to accomplish today. Having not worked the night before, she rose from bed feeling ready to tackle all the projects that came along with being a homeowner. She had re-potted plants, hammered down a loose mopboard and cleaned the gutters in preparation for rain later in the year. The porch was littered with fall-out from her efforts. Bits of leaves, twigs and dirt needed to be swept up, but the nurse had elected to take a brief respite with her book instead. That had been an hour and a half ago.

She slipped from the hammock and found the broom where she had propped it against the porch rail. Deciding she needed a little motivation, Randa went inside the house and grabbed her CD player. Looking over her collection of music she selected the soundtrack from "The Full Monty". Flipping the track to Hot Chocolate's "You Sexy Thing", she began humming and sweeping. Soon it was impossible not to sway, and then dance, to the catchy tune. The broom was no longer a cleaning implement but a dance partner and the porch a dance floor. "Come here often?" she asked the broom. Hearing no reply she said, "Strong, silent type, huh? I can get into that. Say, you don't have much of a figure, but you've got all the right moves." Randa laughed at her own silliness and was happy to note she had worked her away across the entire back porch. As the song ended, a sexy Tom Jones tune came on and the nurse couldn't help but think of the picture on her book's back cover.

Placing a small empty terra cotta pot upside down on the broom handle Randa proceeded to croon saucily to the broom along with Tom.

"Baby, take off your coat... real slow. Baby take off your shoes...I'll help you take off your shoes. Baby take off your dress... yes, yes, yes! You can leave your hat on... you can leave your hat on... you can leave your hat on!"

Randa punctuated the last lines of the verse with a sexy bump and grind. Just as she was about to launch into a full-throated chorus a voice behind her said "Woo-hoo! You go, girlfriend!"

The blonde jumped and spun around so fast the terra cotta pot flew off the broom handle and into the back yard breaking neatly into several smaller pieces.

"Jesus, Derek! You just took a year off my life with that little stunt!" Randa shouted as she blushed furiously and clicked off the CD player.

"Sorry, babe, but you didn't answer the front door so I just came on through when I heard the music. Nice show you had going there for a minute. You know, if you're not done I can just sit here and watch until you are." Shaggy brown eyebrows wagged up and down suggestively.

"I'll show you something, Derek, and it's going to be the business end of this broom!" she growled in mock annoyance. "What are you doing here anyway?"

"Well, before I knew there was a floorshow going on I was just going to bring by this new software. It's a little program I worked up to prevent hackers from getting into our reference system by the back door."

"Got anything like that for my front door, Derek? I seem to have a problem there too." The two old friends laughed and went into the house, Randa grabbing her book as she went. As Derek was downloading the program into the blonde's computer he looked at her seriously.

"Has it ever occurred to you that if you used some of those moves somewhere beside your back porch you might not need to be dancing with a broom? Honestly, Randa, if women were remotely my cup of tea I would be on you like white on rice. Why don't you let someone have a chance with you? It would be nice to see you settled down and happy."

"I am happy, you big dope. Believe me, the rest will happen in time. Eventually I'll meet the person who can reach right into my heart and I promise then I'll do the happily ever after thing. Okay? Now that we're done discussing my life can you get this thing finished? I need a shower and a nap before my shift tonight."

Eleven o'clock came quickly and Randa was just barely in time to log on for the shift. She noticed her IM icon flashing and brought it up in another window as she kept an eye on her consultation room. Melanie Allen was one of the evening shift

RNs on the website and they frequently chatted a moment at shift change. Melanie informed her that a particularly offensive gentleman had been online and in the consultation room twice already.

"**God, not him again!**" Randa frowned as she typed. **"If he brings up Viagra one more time I'm going to scream!"** Randa had no doubt which body part "Mr. P." had gotten his user name from. It was at that moment the consultation room announcement was made. The nurse closed her eyes and crossed her fingers. Opening one eye slowly she spied the user name "DJ" on the screen. She slumped forward in relief and smiled.

"Thank you, God, I owe you one for this."

At first Denise hadn't known where to start. She had sat down at her computer, staring intently at the screen as she wondered what to type into her search engine. Of course, she knew that it was completely obvious that she should have just typed the name of Sara's disease into the search criteria and see what her server offered, but she didn't want that. They both now knew what MND was; Doctor Macarthur had more than adequately filled them in on that aspect. What Denise wanted was explanations, reasons why and basically - hope. She wanted more than just information; she wanted assistance, guidance and some form of reassurance.

It was at that point that Denise decided that there had to be something better and more personal than just the usual information sites. Somewhere that she could talk to a human being; somebody that would answer her questions in an easy and friendly manner. Not a stuffy doctor, sitting in his office as he spoke clinically about Sara's disease meanwhile checking his watch every five minutes. Overall, Denise was glad she had chosen to take Sara to a private hospital. The only drawback was getting a doctor who seemed more interested at times in his fee rather than his patient. Of course money was not an issue to the poet; she was more than covered in that department. Continuing to live with her aunt and not fond of the opulence of extravagant life styles - apart from her car, a brand new Lexus and her only vice - Denise had more than enough stashed away in several bank accounts. After all, with three best selling books under her belt and many people paying exorbitant amounts of money just to purchase a signed copy, she was definitely "comfortable". Of course there were also her other little side projects that she seldom spoke about but provided her with an average person's yearly salary every time she undertook the task. This was the odd occasion where she would write on behalf of another who would then claim her work as theirs.

It was quite by accident that Denise had come across the Brightwood Information Network.com website. She had meant to choose the site above it on the list but her rather uncooperative mouse had chosen that moment to stall and she had accidentally clicked the link below. She had initially cursed the object, annoyed at the day last week when she had accidentally dropped her infrared mouse and broken the device. She had made a mental note to go out as soon as possible and buy a new one. *Maybe one of those ones that are shaped like pens,* she thought.

Fortunately, and as fate would have it, Denise had taken a quick look at the page and had been captured by the site's boastings. It appeared to be a medical information site where you could enter a chat room, or as they had so named it in rather large bold letters, **'Consultation Room'** and talk to qualified medical personnel. Ask them questions; gain information on apparently anything you needed to know.

It was the site's pledge of privacy that had swayed Denise's decision. Never one to enjoy attention or be a subject under the microscope, she found the anonymity of it all very appealing. She had registered herself into the system, and was just about to enter the room and talk to an available Melanie Allen - RN, when Sara had entered the study.

Denise spun around in her chair and faced the woman who was holding out a bottle of mineral water. "I thought you might want a drink. How long have you been in here? Is it your new book?"

The poet shrugged. "I have been in here a while. I was trying to write a few thoughts down, but couldn't concentrate." She looked at Sara, her long grey hair hanging past her shoulders. "You didn't have to bring me anything."

"If I didn't remember to bring you something to eat and drink at times I swear you would waste away. How ever am I going to make sure you remember to feed yourself when I am gone?"

Denise bristled at her comment. "Don't say that!" She rose from her chair and took the bottle gently from Sara's hands. "Please don't speak like that."

Sara smiled sadly as she gazed upon the pleading expression in her niece's eyes. It may not have been instantaneous, but she had come to terms with the news of her sudden decline in health and just wished Denise wouldn't have to witness how her body would slowly turn against her - as she was beginning to feel a little more every day. Although Denise would never openly admit it, Sara knew she was finding it hard to deal with the news. "Alright, DJ. Listen, I am going to make myself something to eat. Are you hungry?"

Denise shook her head. "If you want something I'll make it for you… hmm?"

"I can manage," Sara replied with a smile. "You get back to your work. We don't want to keep your adoring fans waiting too long for book number four now do we?"

"Are you sure?"

"Of course."

Denise nodded. "Alright." She stepped back and sat down in her chair. "I'll be out in a little while."

Sara nodded as she smiled. With a wink towards her niece she stepped back out of the study and shut the door behind her.

Staring briefly at the closed door, Denise turned back around and faced the computer. She gazed absently at the screen until her mind moved into gear and her eyes focused on the page before her that had now turned into a series of rapidly moving blocks. With a shake of her head she pushed her mouse and the consultation room came back into view. Denise read the name on screen. It had changed and now a Miranda Martin, RN was available and waiting. Decision made, Denise entered the room, ready to speak with Nurse Martin.

Chapter 4

Okay, DJ lets see what your problem might be Randa thought.

"Welcome to the Brightwood Information Network" she typed, using her usual opening. **"I'm Miranda Martin, how can I help you, DJ?"**

Denise watched the screen carefully feeling a flutter of nervousness as the site's nurse acknowledged her presence in the consultation room. Her fingers moved slowly over the keyboard as she thought of how best to word her question. *"Miranda,"* she typed then paused. It felt too personal to use this person's first name when she didn't even know her. Denise shook her head knowing this wasn't the time to start feeling closed and reserved. *"I have a friend who has been having some problems lately and I'd like some information."*

"I'm afraid I cant help with any diagnosis on the website. I have to refer you to your own doctor for that."

The poet sighed as she typed. *"We've done that. She had been feeling a little weak but then started having occasional shortness of breath and some difficulty swallowing. Her physician said the tests show she has Motor Neurons Disease. I think you will be more familiar with it if I call it ALS."* She held her breath as she waited for the nurse's reply.

Randa heard herself let out a small "oh." She knew that Amyotrophic Lateral Sclerosis was a degenerative disease of the motor neurons that over time progressively weakened then paralyzed muscles in the body, finally affecting the respiratory system and causing death. Before nursing school she had heard it referred to as "Lou Gehrig's Disease" after the great New York Yankee baseball player. The disease had ended his playing career then ended his life. Even while thinking this, the nurse was searching the huge database for more information.

Striving to maintain some sort of professional demeanor

29

with this person who had received the devastating news was going to be difficult. **"This friend, she's close to you?"** Randa typed, hoping she wasn't prying.

Does is matter who she is? Denise thought then shook her head, knowing that this woman, whoever she was, was only trying to help. She continued to type. *"I'm her niece. I'll be taking care of her."*

A stab of sympathetic pain coursed through the blonde, knowing this woman, really both of the women, were going to have a difficult time ahead.

"I see." Randa typed. **"What kind of information can I get for you?"**

This was the question Denise had been waiting for. *What indeed,* she though with a severe frown. When Doctor Macarthur had explained the disease to her and Sara, he seemed to leave little room for the possibility of a cure. Was it really as cut and dried as the physician had led them to believe? *"Is there really no hope then?"* She typed cautiously.

That short sentence brought tears unbidden to the nurse's eyes. Glancing at the information the database had provided confirmed what Randa already remembered. The cause of the disease wasn't known and as yet there was no treatment or cure. It was always fatal; it was just a matter of time. *Damn it!* The blonde thought. *If I was in the hospital and had to tell this woman what I'm going to now, I could sit her down or hold her hand; anything to let her know someone cares.* She again cursed the impersonal computer.

"DJ, I'm so sorry. I'm not finding any effective treatment currently. There is always research in progress but at this time I'm afraid the disease is terminal."

Denise stared at the final word in the nurse's reply. She felt the breath leave her body and covered her mouth with one hand as the words on the screen blurred into a watery haze. She had known this but didn't want to believe it was true.

The nurse's shoulders slumped. She felt she had just administered the coup de grace to the other woman's hope. It wasn't a good feeling; no wonder executioners in the Middle Ages frequently asked pardon from their victims.

Letting her head fall back, Denise took a deep breath before looking back at the screen. She had to ask... *"How long?"*

No, Randa thought, *don't ask me that. Haven't I given you enough bad news? Please don't make me hurt you anymore than I have.* Biting her lower lip, the nurse typed, **"What did your aunt's doctor say about that?"**

The poet typed quickly. *"He said 'not long'. I need to know, Miranda. Please."* *Just tell me,* she pleaded in thought.

Randa sat, unsure what she should do. Technically this was overstepping her bounds. She should just refer the woman again to a doctor. She shouldn't get involved but the nurse thought she could feel the other woman's anguish through her words. Taking a deep breath, Randa touched the keyboard.

"Six months to a year."

She seemed to have waited forever for that little statement, yet when it came Denise suddenly wished she could have taken back her words. Was it really good to know? Did knowing how long Sara had left make things seem easier? *No,* she thought, *how could it?* Wiping the tear that had sneaked its way down her cheek, Denise placed her fingers back onto the keyboard yet didn't respond.

When no reply came back, Randa typed **"DJ? DJ, are you still there?**

"Yes." The poet answered, suddenly wishing she had never entered this site. "Ignorance is bliss," she mumbled to herself.

"DJ, I know you said you will be taking care of your aunt but do you have some help or support for yourself? This is going to be hard for both of you. Is there anyone you can talk to?"

"There's always just been the two of us."

"Listen, DJ, you can talk to me if you want. I'm on here 5 nights a week. Honestly, I would like it if you would talk to me, maybe let me help you out in any way I can."

"Won't that interfere with your work, Miranda?" Denise wondered why this woman would offer her services. Surely that wasn't part of the sites offerings? She didn't even know her.

Randa thought for a moment. Brightwood wouldn't appreciate their website being used for personal communication no matter what the situation. Not really understanding why she cared so much, the nurse made her decision. She typed out her personal e-mail address.

31

"Please use this e-mail to contact me at anytime, DJ. I want to help if I can. I know I might not be able to do much but I know sometimes it just helps to talk to someone. Please tell me you'll consider it at least."

As the email address appeared on the screen Denise frowned. Now this woman was giving her an obviously private e-mail address? She had never asked for help before, it wasn't in her nature, yet a deep-seated intuition told Denise that she would need this. *"I'll consider it,"* she typed; surprised as she read back her own words on the VDU.

"Thank you, DJ. And DJ? Its just Randa; really it's only my Mom that calls me Miranda anymore."

"Thanks for your time, Randa. Have a good day."

"You too, DJ. I hope to hear from you soon."

As the user name disappeared from the consultation room screen Randa shook her head. *What have you gotten yourself in for here? Wasn't this why you left the hospital in the first place? No more personal investment, no more getting involved with the patient's lives? Won't you ever learn?* She thought back to DJ's situation and her heart went out to the other woman again.

No, I guess I never will.

Looking down at the slip of paper, Denise stared at the e-mail address that she had jotted down almost absent-mindedly. She tapped her pen upon the surface of the desk, wondering why she had agreed to even consider this woman's offer. She and Sara didn't need any help - did they? Doctor Macarthur had definitely given the impression that this would be hard, but she could cope. They had always coped with everything together, why should now be any different?

Feeling a surge of anger, Denise scrunched up the slip of paper in her hand and threw it into the waste paper bin at the side of her desk. She slid further down into her chair as her mind wandered back to her conversation with Nurse Martin - Randa.

"Six months to a year." The poet muttered. Macarthur had never given a window of time. He had only stated that MND was terminal. Denise pushed herself away from her desk, the wheels of her chair rolling along the royal blue carpeted floor of the room. She leaned forward, resting her elbows on her knees. She and Sara were to go back to the hospital tomorrow, she would ask more questions then. Denise couldn't help thinking that there was just something so impersonal about the way the physician spoke to them. He didn't carry any of the warmth or compassion that Nurse Martin had shown. Unconsciously the poet's eyes strayed back to the waste paper bin and the single ball of paper in the otherwise empty container. She rolled forward and picked out the rumpled slip of paper, opening it and once again reading the address.

Getting up, Denise pulled her silver framed eye glasses from her nose and walked out of the confines of her office as she folded the address and placed it in the pocket of her jeans. Standing in the hallway she jumped suddenly as a loud smashing sound echoed through the house. With a start she set off to find Sara, instinctively heading towards the kitchen. It was the only room in the house with a hard wood floor and the sound was definitely that of something that had smashed upon the ground.

Entering the kitchen the poet found Sara on her knees attempting to pick up the remains of what looked like a broken vase. Shards of white and blue porcelain covered the pine laminate flooring.

"Whoa, Sara, what happened?" Denise asked as she moved forward to help the old woman to her feet.

Sara accepted her niece's help. "I was just going to put some fresh flowers into this vase but the thing slipped straight out of my hand." She sighed warily and pushed her long grey hair over her shoulder. She had always kept it up in a loose bun but recently couldn't find the energy to even bother.

Denise carefully escorted Sara out of the kitchen and into the living room. "You really shouldn't be kneeling when you are wearing a dress like that, you could have cut yourself."

The low hum of the television set broke the quiet of the room as Sara sat down upon her easy chair. She smiled up at her tall niece, always amazed at the striking resemblance she had to her father, Sara's brother. "So did you get anything written for me to look at? You know how much I love to be the first to read your work."

The poet shrugged slightly. "I was just looking up some

information really. I didn't get much of anything else done."
Denise bent down and noticed a slight scrape on Sara's knee
that was bleeding. She shook her head as she pulled a piece of
tissue from the box beside Sara's chair and dabbed at the blood.
"I'll go back in there and finish cleaning the floor. Did you
want anything while I was in there?"

"A cup of your wonderful tea would be nice."

Denise smiled with a nod of affirmation. "One cup of tea
coming up." Scrunching the tissue within her hands, the poet
rose to her feet and headed back out to the small kitchen. Once
out of her aunt's view she fell back against the painted
terracotta wall. Her lip trembled as she looked down at the
mess on the floor knowing this was all due to Sara's disease.
The cramping of her muscles, the clumsiness; it was all related
and served as another reminder that Sara was only going to get
worse. *Six months to a year,* Denise thought and wondered how
the disease would progress. She sincerely hoped they would
learn all they needed to know tomorrow and for Sara's sake, the
poet hoped beyond all reason this wasn't going to be in any
way painful for her aunt.

Chapter 5

The shift seemed like it would never end but 7a.m. finally came and Randa logged off the network with a weary sigh. There had been few breaks in the questions this night and the nurse's shoulders were stiff from sitting over the keyboard.

Note to self, she thought. *Remember to buy a bottle of eye drops.* Randa's eyes burned from long hours staring at the monitor's screen. Rubbing them now, she leaned back and mentally reviewed her work that night. Being honest with herself, Randa knew that the reason this night seemed more difficult than most was the first consultation of the night.

You really blew that one, girl. Randa thought. *You've barely been doing this job for six months and you went and broke your one and only rule; never get personally involved again.* The ringing of the phone interrupted the mental self-flagellation.

"For cripes sake, Randa, what were you thinking?" a voice shrieked as she picked up the phone.

"Good morning, Derek. What's happened that you feel the need to lose it so early in the day?"

"Randa, you know you're my oldest and best friend. We go way back and we've been through a lot with each other. You even let me look under your skirt in grade school, remember?"

"Yeah" the nurse replied "And I remember you didn't find anything remotely interesting to you there either as I recall."

"Petty details, Randa," Derek pouted. *"You know if you ended up hacked into pieces and buried in a shallow grave I'd still be devastated."*

"Derek, shallow grave...? What the hell are you talking about?"

"I'm talking about you giving your personal e-mail address out to a strange woman and using the Brightwood site to do it. Yeah, I know about it. I was checking the

consultations as part of the quality assurance program." the Webmaster said. *"Do you know what I could do with just your e-mail address? I'm not even a good hacker, but with that information I could learn enough about you to become a very effective stalker."*

The nurse felt a brief ripple of panic run up her spine. "God, Derek, I didn't think about...I mean I just felt...I just reacted." Randa used the heel of her free hand to beat against her forehead. "What have I done?"

"Lucky for you, maybe nothing. I ran a little tracking program on that consultation. Seems it originated in England. That would have to be a very determined stalker to want to get you from there."

Randa's panic was replaced by annoyance. "Just a cotton-picking minute! You tracked the consultation? You broke the anonymity of the process? What the hell were you thinking about?" The blonde felt her protective nature and her hackles rise.

"Randa, I was thinking about you. Thinking about protecting you and your job. You could be fired for doing something like that just like I could for running that tracking program. Look, when I ran the tracking program and found out the user came from another country, I stopped it right there. The process is still anonymous for her and as an unfortunate 'computer glitch' deleted your consultation and my tracking, I guess it is for us as well."

A wave of relief washed over the nurse. "Thanks, Derek. I appreciate it, really I do. This won't happen again."

"Sure it will; you can't help it. It's just who you are, but be careful, okay? Don't forget why you wanted this job in the first place."

"I never can, Derek"

After quick good-byes, the nurse hung up the phone and wandered over to the sofa in the living room. Lying down, she let the events of a year ago play across her mind as they had done about a million times before. Closing her eyes she could see it clearly, as if it were only yesterday.

Another night from hell, why does the full moon bring out

all the weirdos? These thoughts and more flashed through Randa's mind as she moved quickly between her patient's rooms. The Cardiology floor was busy as usual but admissions from the overflowing Emergency Room were coming almost faster than they could be absorbed. It seemed everyone was having some type of heart problem and required monitoring on Randa's unit. Each patient wore a small transmitter attached to five wires strategically placed on their chest. The boxes sent out signals to a central monitor, which was closely watched by a technician. At the first sign of a change in a patient's heart rate or rhythm the tech called a cell phone carried by the nurse responsible for that patient. Randa had already received two of those calls tonight.

Moving into the medication room, Randa entered her code to remove narcotics from the dispensing machine. This was her seventh trip into the medication room in the first four hours of her shift and each of those times was because of Mr. Johnson. Hydrocodone, Acetaminophen, Lorazepam and Morphine, Mr. Johnson had requested it all. The nurse tried not to be judgmental, but the amount of medication Mr. Johnson had taken over the last few hours would have put her in a coma for a week. Mr. Johnson had been admitted with chest pain but subsequent tests had shown he had not had a heart attack. Despite an abundance of medication, the man continued to complain of pain.

This should be the last trip for a while; this is everything he can have for a few hours. Taking the medication into Mr. Johnson's room, she noted the patient was dozing. Turning to leave, Mr. Johnson roused up. "That my medicine, nurse?

"Yes, Mr. Johnson, it is. This is everything I can give you for a couple of hours so why don't you try to get a little rest now?"

The nurse handed the small paper cup containing the pills to the elderly black gentleman. His deep brown eyes looked steadily at the young woman. "Nurse, I hurt something terrible all the time. I'm not getting any help at all from what you gave me. Isn't there something else you can do for me?"

Randa knew the day shift nurse she had received report from had already addressed the problem with the patient's physician. Dr. Stevens had refused to increase Mr. Johnson's medication noting that the patient had a history of drug seeking behavior. The doctor had practically bitten the day nurse's head off when she asked about a change in the medication regime. " I'm sorry, Mr. Johnson, but Dr. Stevens wouldn't approve any additional medication for you."

Mr. Johnson's eyes narrowed and his voice took on a coolness Randa hadn't heard before. "Listen here, nurse. I can go home and suffer like this as well as stay here so why don't you just get me my clothes out of that closet there and let me go." The patient started to get out of the bed and get dressed. The nurse stopped him with a hand to the shoulder.

"Mr. Johnson, don't go yet. Let me try to call the doctor one more time, okay? Just wait and give me a little time." The patient agreed and lay back down on the bed.

Leaving the room, Randa thought *I really needed this tonight. Now I'm stuck between a rock and Dr. Hardass.* Going to the nurse's station the blonde paged the doctor and waited for the return phone call while mentally listing all the things she needed to get done.

"Randa, Dr Stevens on line one" the unit secretary called out. Randa picked up the line and explained the situation to the physician.

"He's threatening to leave against medical advice," she concluded.

There was a moment of silence on the line and then the doctor spoke. "I'm not in the habit of having to repeat my orders more than once. There will be no increase in medication and no change to my orders, now or later. Is that perfectly clear, nurse? If Mr. Johnson wishes to leave, tell him to find a new doctor on the way out." With that, the phone was slammed down in Randa's ear. The nurse clenched her jaw tightly to prevent a string of filthy words from escaping her lips and bent to retrieve a Discharge Against Medical Advice form from the filing cabinet beneath the desk.

Randa informed the charge nurse of the problem and went back to Mr. Johnson's room. As expected, the patient got dressed, signed the form and went outside the building to wait for the friend who would give him a ride home. The nurse's night continued to be busy and approximately one and a half hours after Mr. Johnson left Janet Gayner, the Hospital Nursing Supervisor sought Randa out and asked her to step into the nurse's lounge.

"What was the deal with Mr. Johnson tonight?" Janet asked. "Why did he leave AMA?" Randa gave the supervisor the story in as concise and factual a way as possible.

"Randa, sit down." Something in the supervisor's tone of voice told the blond that whatever was going to come next wasn't going to be pleasant. Janet told Randa that Mr. Johnson had returned to the Emergency Room a short time ago. He had apparently gone home, taken a gun out of his closet and used a .38 caliber pistol to send a bullet into his brain. He came in by ambulance and under CPR but had been pronounced dead on arrival.

Randa sank to a chair and stared blankly for a moment then told the supervisor "I have charting to do and I need to re-start Mrs. Davis' IV." She moved to leave the lounge then turned back to the older nurse. The blonde felt the tears rolling down her cheeks and was helpless to stop them. "It's all my fault, Janet. It's all my fault."

Randa opened her eyes, returning to the present and her own living room. No matter how many times she had gone over the scenario of what happened to Mr. Johnson and no matter how many times she had decided she could do nothing different than she had, the nurse couldn't help but feel she had let the old man down. She thought about DJ and her aunt and came to a decision.

"It won't happen again, DJ. If you need me, I won't let you down."

At ten minutes past midnight the supermarket was almost empty. Voices tended to echo around the vacant aisles. The only other people present consisted of the store's night staff and the odd late night shopper, Denise included.

This was her favourite time to shop. The night air was peaceful and quiet, and there was no influx of agitated parents as they pushed their trolleys round the store with half a dozen children hanging off the handlebars. At this time there was only the same group of people that the poet began to recognize every time she did the shopping.

There was 'Munchies boy", a man who seemed to arrive at the store most nights heading straight to the junk food section, eyes glazed, pupils dilated. Denise didn't need to think too hard to know what his recreational past time was; presumably every night it seemed. Then there was "Waitress woman", a tall blonde with heaving bosoms who stunk of stale cigarettes and alcohol She always bought either breakfast foods or headache pills. And of course Denise couldn't forget "Stalker guy.' Not that he was exactly stalking Denise but he did have a tendency to follow her around the store whenever he noticed her. She presumed he was just too shy to talk to her, and she was damned sure she wasn't going to give him any reason to do so. The supermarket's "singles nights" were on Tuesday evenings. She hoped he would realize this and change his shopping routine. *"How much time does he need to buy his stack of microwave meals for one anyway?"* Denise often thought.

Taking her trolley, the tall woman strode down the first aisle, already spotting 'Munchies boy' as he walked along a shelf of chocolates, picking up one of each variety and chucking it into his hand-held basket. She smirked as she picked up Sara's favourite "jelly babies" and placed them into the trolley.

"I knew you couldn't hide from me forever!"

Denise turned around to see Michelle Barlow standing behind her, one hand on her hip and the other placed upon a trolley brimming with a wide variety of foods. Michelle was a small woman with long auburn wavy hair and an ever-present smile. They had known each other from the very day Denise had moved in with her aunt. They had eventually become good friends after much effort on Michelle's part. Apart from Sara, Michelle was the only person, other than the publishers, who knew the real identity of the famous poet D Jennings.

"Well I do try," Denise deadpanned.

Michelle pushed her trolley forward, smile firmly in place. "You are such a charmer, DJ. So here I am on a week shore leave and I haven't been able to get hold of you all that time. Your phone is always engaged, or I call round and nobody is in. Hell, you even drove past me two days ago and I almost jumped out in front of your damned car just to get you to notice me. You seemed a million miles away."

Denise smiled. "Must have had something on my mind at the time." She looked down into Michelle's trolley. "As it seems do you." She picked up a box of condoms and a jar of chocolate hazelnut spread. "Making the most of your last night with Brent are you, Shelly?"

The woman shrugged. "Well being as though I'm being shipped overseas for a couple of months I need to get as much in as possible until I return."

"Sure!"

"Anyway, how are you? How is Sara? I haven't seen her either this week. My mum says she hasn't been to the bridge club for almost a month now."

Denise briefly looked down into her trolley. "She is a little under the weather." She didn't want to lie to her friend but wasn't sure how to tell her the complete truth either.

"I guess it's pointless asking whether you need anything isn't it?"

She smiled. "You know me."

Michelle rolled her eyes. "That I do." She grinned before looking down into the contents of her trolley. "Okay. Well I'd better get back home." She picked up the jar of chocolate spread. "Wouldn't want this to go to waste now would we?"

The poet rolled her eyes. "Have fun."

"Oh I am sure I will. I'll see you again soon, DJ." Michelle turned to head back towards the checkout but stopped and pulled Denise into a quick hug. "By the way, DJ," she whispered. "I think the new book is wonderful."

"Thanks, Shelly." Denise said as she watched her friend stroll off towards the checkout.

Turning back to the aisle, Denise took Sara's shopping list from her pocket and opened the sheet of paper. Her aunt had already gone to bed, but knowing her niece had a fondness for midnight shopping she had prepared a list of things they needed, knowing Denise would prefer to get the chore out of the way as soon as possible. Denise picked up her pace as she headed around the store. She remembered Sara had her appointment with Doctor Macarthur at nine o'clock that morning and she was definitely going to be there.

Heavy rain fell hard upon the city streets; hitting the ground with such a force that the heavy pounding of each drop sounded out along the congested early morning traffic-filled roads. Denise squinted as she peered out through the rain blurred window screen of her black Lexus. Even the rapid pace of the car's window wipers weren't effective enough to keep the screen clear enough for easy vision. She sighed, drumming her fingers upon the black leather steering wheel with annoyance. It had been raining since they had risen that morning and showed no signs of relenting.

Holding her small brown handbag upon her lap, Sara stared out through the car's passenger side window. She smiled in remembrance. "This brings back memories, DJ."

"How so?"

Sara shook her head. "Do you remember when you were eleven?"

The poet frowned. "Vaguely, why?"

"Do you remember that spring when we had the heavy rains? It rained so much parts of the lower lands flooded." Sara's smiled widened. "Do you remember that I got up one morning to find your bedroom door missing? I went looking for you and found you in the front room with a saw, hammer and nails ready to turn your door into a raft - 'just in case' - as you so seriously stated. I only just caught you before you cut that door in half and turned it into a mini boat!"

Denise smirked at the memory.

"You stuffed your school satchel with tins of beans and mushy peas for rations. I thought that was so sweet of you."

Laughing, Denise looked over at her aunt. "Sweet? I can recall you saying something very different when you discovered I'd emptied away your bottles of homemade wine to make airtight floats around the boundaries of the 'raft'."

"Well I did come home the next day to find that you had bought, grated and juiced 30 lemons to help me make another batch of wine."

"And what a potent batch it was! It was a good job that you didn't drink because I heard that stuff could have put hairs on your chest." Denise smiled as she steered the car into the hospital car park. Turning off the engine her smiled faded. She turned towards Sara with an apprehensive look in her eyes. "Ready?"

Sara looked out through the now completely blurred window screen; the exaggerated sound of the intense rainfall hammering upon the thick glass. Sighing, she adjusted the floral scarf around her head and pulled the collar of her long winter coat around her shoulders. "As I will ever be," she replied.

The examination room, Denise observed, was of an average size and although it was typically clinical in appearance, it definitely had a much more comfortable feel to it. She realized it seemed you get what you pay for and she was suddenly very glad she hadn't stuck with the National Health System for this. Sara deserved the best as far as her niece was concerned.

Standing next to a large, grey, comfortable examination table, Doctor Macarthur took Sara's hands. He leaned forward slightly, the ends of his stethoscope hanging from around his neck. His white and blue stripy shirt was unbuttoned at the cuffs with his sleeves rolled up tight to his elbows. "Okay, Miss Jennings, Sara. I would just like you to squeeze my hands if you will."

Sara did as requested.

"As tight as you can."

Sara squeezed with all her might.

Nodding, but his expression blank, Doctor Macarthur released her hands and moved down to the bottom of the table. "Alright, Sara. Now I would like you to place your feet against my hands and push as hard as you can."

Again Sara did as bade, all under the watchful eye of her niece who sat beside the examination table observing the young blonde doctor carefully. *This guy doesn't look more than twenty-five years old,* she mused.

Sara pushed against Macarthur's hands as requested. She held a fixed expression of concentration as she pushed as hard as she was able.

"Okay." The doctor released Sara and gently laid her feet back down on the examination table. "I do have a few more things I would like to do, Sara, but first I would just like to ask you a couple of questions."

"Ask away." Sara replied.

Macarthur leaned against the table. "You have said that you started feeling periods of cramping and twitching at first. You began to have trouble swallowing at times and you felt increasingly weak and tired. These are all classic symptoms of MND. Do you feel these symptoms have progressed?"

Denise looked down at her feet, knowing the answer to the doctor's question was obviously yes. Every now and then she would hope that maybe the hospital had made a mistake and had wrongly diagnosed Sara, but as the days wore on she realized it wasn't so.

The old woman nodded. "My right hand has started cramping a lot. Sometimes I am finding it hard to pick things up, or objects just fall out of it. This morning I had trouble dressing myself and found it incredibly tiring to climb the stairs."

Denise looked up surprised. "You never said anything."

"I didn't want to worry you, DJ. I do need to be able to do these things by myself."

The poet frowned. "Maybe so but whenever you do need help, no matter what, I will always be there for you. Always." She sighed. "I know it must be hard for you, but you must understand that I want to do whatever it takes to help you."

Sara nodded quietly. It was hard, and she was positive Denise understood this. They were both very much alike: independent and private people. The notion of having to rely on somebody else for assistance was almost unthinkable. At the same time Sara knew that she would much rather have her niece helping her than anybody else.

Doctor Macarthur nodded. "We have discussed the progressive symptoms of Motor Neurons Disease and you are well aware that what you are experiencing will and is advancing." The Doctor moved over to a small desk and looked down at a small pile of different coloured folders on the surface.

Sitting rigidly in her chair, Denise watched Doctor Macarthur nervously as he picked up a large manila folder and opened it up, briefly scanning the documents inside. She then turned worried eyes to Sara who was smiling at her with a gentle understanding expression. The poet frowned wondering what her aunt was thinking.

"Okay, the purpose of this talk is because I think we need to discuss your making a living will." The Doctor turned his eyes towards Sara with a soft smile.

Sara nodded briefly.

"Living will?" Denise questioned. "Why does she need to make a living will?"

Macarthur looked at Denise, pulling small circular spectacles from his nose. "This is a standard procedure in your aunt's situation. I hope you don't mind, DJ, but I need to be blunt with you here and explain MND in its advanced stages."

Sara looked away. It was terrifying to think about how this disease was going to affect her, yet she had accepted it. What else could she do? Go into denial, cry, scream to the world that it wasn't fair? Sara knew that the only way she was going to cope with her disease was to accept that there was nothing she could do to stop it and nothing she could have done to prevent it. It may not have provided much comfort but it did help her to face her future a little easier. This was going to happen.

"MND is a neuromuscular disease characterized by a progressive deterioration of motor nerve cells in the brain and spinal cord. Basically when the motor neurons can no longer send impulses to the muscles, the muscles begin to waste away." Macarthur looked intently into Denise's blue eyes. "This is progressing rapidly in your aunt's body and for patients in the later stages of MND there is usually a complete paralysis... even though their mind will remain unaffected. Do you understand what I am saying, DJ?"

Denise nodded, stunned. "You mean..." She looked towards her aunt. "Sara will eventually become paralyzed yet still be full conscious mentally."

Sara reached out and took Denise's hand.

"Which is why we need a living will." Macarthur added. "We need to know in advance exactly what Sara's wishes are. If there comes a point that she will no longer be able to breathe, will she want a ventilator to maintain that? If her heart were to stop beating, would she want CPR? Would she want a feeding tube for nourishment if she were no longer able to ingest

45

food?"

An expression of confused disbelief crossed Denise's features. She swallowed hard as the doctor's words took shape in her mind and she realized that her worst fear was to transpire. Sara was to experience much discomfort in the later stages of her illness and the worst of it would be that she would probably not be able to communicate her thoughts, feelings and needs.

Lowering her head, Denise closed her eyes and massaged her forehead as she tried desperately to will her emotions under control. She couldn't lose herself right there and right at that moment. She couldn't. Taking a very deep breath, the poet looked back at Sara with a pleading expression in her eyes.

Clearing her throat, Denise spoke. "Um... I... Sara?"

The old woman nodded sadly. "I am aware of this, DJ, and I want you to know that when that time comes I trust you to carry out and enforce my wishes."

"Wishes?"

Sara shook her head and blinked as tears clouded her eyes. "I don't want to rely on any artificial forms of life support, DJ. When that time does come," a tear escaped Sara's eye as she watched Denise desperately trying to keep control of her emotions, "I want to die peacefully. What point would there be in prolonging the inevitable?"

"Inevitable?" She could feel her control slipping. Salty tears stung her eyes as her breathing laboured. She rose swiftly. "Excuse me a moment please?" Denise said as she fled from the room as quickly as she could.

Out in the hospital corridor, Denise stormed down the hallway passing doctors and patients alike as she desperately searched for the exit. She noticed a green sign to her left and took the turn, finding a small door leading towards the outside world. The rain was still falling fast and furious as Denise pushed open the door and walked swiftly into the heavy downpour. Leaning against the wall her head fell back against soaked masonry as she closed her eyes against the onslaught of rapid raindrops and insistent tears.

She thought of all that Sara had gone through in her life, of all the things that had happened. She thought of the woman whom she had come to love as her own mother. She thought of this terrible disease and its increasing hold upon her, the effects it was to have and the inevitable outcome. And she cried.

Two hours later Denise sat in the quiet confines of her study. She and Sara had been home a short while and Sara had retired to her room for a rest, the events of the morning leaving her drained and emotional. Denise sat at her computer, staring at an empty screen. She had hoped to take her mind off things by trying to work, but it seemed she was less than able to concentrate.

Denise hadn't been able to give her response to Sara concerning her living will and had asked for a short while to think about her request. With anything else, Denise knew she would deny Sara nothing, but this was different. She just didn't know whether she could enforce her aunt's last request for an uncomplicated and dignified death. Denise wanted it to seem an unfair request to make, but inside she knew Sara asked her because she loved, respected and trusted her. It just hurt too much and if Denise was to admit it, to herself as much as anybody else - she needed help.

Unconsciously her hand moved to her top desk drawer and she pulled out a small slip of paper. Opening it slowly she read the address. As hard as it was, Denise had to accept that she needed to speak to this nurse again and as she accessed her email account, she wondered what she was to say.

Nurse Martin,
Denise stopped and deleted the words. She started again:

Miranda,
She stopped again; didn't she say to call her Randa? Denise thought.

Randa,
I sincerely hope that you don't mind that I contact you but as you may recall you gave me your address not long ago in the Brightwood consultation room. I will admit that this is hard for me to do but I think I need your help, some advice.
Today I found out that my aunt intends to make a living will. I discovered just how debilitating and dreadful her

47

disease is and for once I am wondering how I am going to cope with watching her declining health. I accept that there is nothing that can be done to prevent this from happening, but I don't know how I am going to be able to watch as this disease slowly takes her away from this world.

She is dying. I know that, I have to accept that. I am writing to ask for any help and advice you may be able to give concerning her comfort and progression during this time. I want to do whatever I can to help her and although I am finding it very hard to accept some of her decisions concerning the later stages of her disease I know that I want her to experience as little discomfort as possible. I want to help her however I can.

I hope that I haven't imposed on you at all, and any help you can give me will be very much appreciated.

Yours faithfully,
DJ

Reading over what she had just written, Denise's hand covered her mouse as she moved to the small 'send' icon in the corner of her screen. She paused, debated cautiously as to whether she was making the right decision in taking this step and as she realized that she could no longer deal with the events alone; she clicked the icon and sent her e-mail.

Chapter 6

"Junk mail-delete, junk mail-delete, spam-delete, see Britney Spears doing *what?* Eww, delete immediately and hope my eyes haven't been permanently injured by even seeing such a thing!"

Randa continued methodically cleaning out her e-mail inbox, not overjoyed to see how much garbage had slipped past her so-called inbox protector. After removing multiple e-mails promoting get-rich schemes, claims of lower mortgage rates and websites promising "the best hardcore action on the net", Randa was left with three messages that didn't appear to be trash can material. The first was from her mother showing off the newly acquired computer skills she had picked up at the community center's adult education class. The nurse smiled and tapped out a quick reply to her mom congratulating her on transitioning to the 21st century.

"What will be next for you, Mom? Space travel?" she typed. The message was sent through the ether by a quick click of the "send" tab. The second message was from Derek giving Randa her schedule for the next month. He also included the amount of sick and vacation time she had accrued thus far as an employee of Brightwood Pharmaceuticals Incorporated. She noted with pleasure the generous fringe benefits given by the company and realized the employer was serious about retaining their nurses.

The final e-mail had a sender listed as *DJ@midengland…*

"DJ! I don't believe it! She actually wrote!" Randa was astonished as she opened the e-mail to see the English woman had indeed sent her a message. The nurse read through the text carefully then leaned back in her chair to consider her reply. The blades of the ceiling fan rotated slowly overhead stirring the still warm evening air.

"Okay, Randa, now don't blow this. You said you wanted to help so try not to mess things up." The blonde pondered how to best express her support for the woman who was dealing with some heavy emotional issues. She mentally rehearsed several approaches and rejected them all as too patronizing, too

49

trite or too somber. Honesty had always been Randa's stock in trade and she decided that wasn't going to change now. The only way to show she understood what DJ was going through was to share some of her own experience. Though she wasn't sure why, Randa wanted DJ to know her, trust her and if she was candid with herself, like her as well. That was unusual for the nurse. Oh she made acquaintances very quickly with her easy smile and slightly wicked sense of humor but friends, really good friends, were a precious few. Why was it so important to make a good impression on a person who had sent her a single e-mail? Randa didn't have a clue and yet she knew it was important somehow. Sitting back up in the chair she used the mouse to tap the "reply" tab on DJ's note.

Dear DJ,

I'm very happy you contacted me; to be truthful I wasn't sure you would. I tried to put myself in your place and all I could see was someone poking her nose in where it might not be wanted or needed. I hope your vision is better than mine and you can see someone who genuinely wants to help and support you in any way possible. I've been a nurse for over six years and though I don't know your aunt, I have known many people in her situation. Your aunt has received news that must have been damn near devastating. She now knows the manner and approximate time of her death and that can't be easy. I can tell from your e-mail you were really bothered by your aunt's decision to make out a living will. I can understand how you might feel as if she has taken the first step toward leaving you but I see it as something completely different. I see the action taken by her to be courageous and loving.

Her courage shows in the determination she has to have a say in how her life finishes. By making her wishes known she maintains a little of the decision making ability that you know she will lose soon enough. I'd be willing to bet she has been a strong willed and independent woman during her life. She shows her love by not forcing you to decide what will be done at the end. It doesn't seem like a loving gesture now but I can assure you it is.

Two years ago my father had a massive stroke. He clung to life a few days during which time my mother had to make very hard choices. Should she opt to keep him on life support when all hope of a meaningful recovery was gone? Would he have wanted to have artificial feeding when it would only prolong the inevitable? My mother didn't know because they never talked about it or made plans. They thought they had all the time in the world. I saw what my mother went through, DJ, and it was nothing short of hell. I am so happy your aunt has spared you that. She must love you a great deal.

I hope what I have told you makes it easier to understand your aunt's desire to make a living will and that it will help you accept her wishes. If I can help you by answering any questions you might have please contact me again. And DJ, if you just need someone to talk to I'd like to be here for that also.

Sincerely, Randa

Randa closed her e-mail session and shut the computer down. Feeling drained, she wandered into the kitchen and pulled a cold Corona from the refrigerator. Making short work of the cap, the nurse took a long pull of the golden brew then dragged the cool bottle across her forehead, down the side of her face and across her neck and upper chest. With a sigh she ambled out the back door to watch the remainder of the evening sunset. The sun had nearly slipped behind the hill and the red-gold rays cast a bronze color to the farmhouse and field.

Maybe next year I'll plant some wildflowers out here or maybe blanket the area with some golden poppies and let them just go wild. Randa wished, not for the first time, that she had someone to share the remarkable beauty of her home with. *One day,* she thought. *One day.*

The last fragment of sun receded from sight and a purple shadow enveloped the hillside. Not far off a young coyote yipped and barked into the early evening. Randa turned to go back inside the house when she spied the book of poetry she had once again left in the hammock. Picking up the volume she spoke to the mysterious figure on the back cover.

"I need your magic tonight, my poet. I'm afraid I've gotten myself into quite a state. Guess writing about my dad in the e-mail brought back some things I thought I was over but maybe I'm not so sure now. So, what have you got to take my mind off my problems?" The nurse strolled to the couch and made herself comfortable against the cushions. Closing her eyes, she began flipping the pages of the book back and forth. Dropping her index finger to a page, the blonde picked a poem out at random.

In the blackest of nights
I yearn for you
When the darkness takes its toll
My weeping heart cries out for love
To ease my tortured soul

Through a haze of tears
I seek you
Weighed down by my turbulent fears
My spirit blinded by loneliness
Had been searching all these years

When I close my eyes
I'm alone no more
Your arms keep me safe through the night
But as the sunshine graces the dawning sky
I'm alone in the morning light.

Randa closed "Derbyshire Dreams" and wondered again how it was that Ms. Jennings saw so clearly into her soul. "Maybe tonight I'll dream of your arms, my poet. Like you though, I'll be alone in the morning." Randa shut her eyes, meaning only to rest them for a moment but slipped away effortlessly into the arms of Morpheus and the poet.

The sudden, loud and obnoxious sound of the radio alarm clock blasted its wake up call into the darkened bedroom.

Denise jumped, releasing the empty glass that she had held in her hand all night and sent it hurtling across the bedroom. It hit the magnolia wall with a resounding smash and shattered over the carpeted floor. Doing her best to refrain from cursing, Denise reached over and slammed her hand on the 'off' button, instantly rendering the room to a peaceful quiet.

With a sigh, the poet dropped her head back to a lime pillow as she stared over at the broken glass on the floor. "Last time I take a drink of juice to bed with me." She muttered and closed her eyes. *Damn it!* She knew that she should do something about the mess her surprise knee-jerk reaction had created but her sleep filled mind refused to lighten.

Rubbing tired blue eyes, Denise looked back at the notebook on her table and the pen lying precariously upon that and the ledge of the unit. She had gone to bed with the intent of writing the night before and her mind had somehow managed to construct two poems that she was damned sure she would never release. They just felt too personal. With a sudden frown, Denise took her pen and book again. She had an urge to bring to life the remnants of a dream that she suddenly remembered having last night.

A minute later a gentle tapping drew the poet from her writing. She looked up as Sara poked her head around the corner of her door and switched on the main light.

"The sounds of breaking glass led me to believe that you were finally awake!"

Denise smiled as her eyes adjusted to the brightness. "Yeah I'll clean it up in a moment, I just have to write this down."

"Late night?" the old woman asked.

Denise nodded.

Sara nodded and walked further into the room. "The publishers called earlier. They want to talk to you about something pertaining to the sales of your latest book. Apparently they are the best yet and it's also led to further sales of your other books. That was all I could get out of Carl, he said he needed to talk to you to discuss the rest of the call."

"Fine." Denise finished her writing and placed the notebook back down on her unit. "I'll ring him later." Swinging her long legs out of the large bed Denise slipped on her boots and walked over to the scattering of broken glass. "How are you feeling today, Sara?"

"Not bad at the moment. I got up feeling quite fine so I cooked a little breakfast, yours is in the oven, and now I am or was washing some pots. That was until I heard the smashing." She shook her head and looked Denise up and down with a quirky smile. "You know, honey? You really do create quite an image. Blue and white gingham shorts, those incredibly long legs of yours and great big, black, clog-hopping boots!" Sara chuckled as Denise placed broken glass onto a sheet of paper. "You are going to create quite an impression on the person who steals your heart, love."

The dark woman narrowed her eyes. "But what if I don't want to give my heart away? I think I write my best stuff like this."

"You are not going to be a martyr to your work, DJ. I swear one day you will find that somebody who makes you want to write - as you call it, 'Through the eyes of love'." She fluttered her eyes.

Denise rose to her full height and folded her arms, tapping one booted foot on the navy carpeted floor. "Uh huh!" An eyebrow rose in scepticism.

"Don't you look at me in that tone of voice, missy. You are not too big to be put over my knee."

Trying to keep away the smirk that threatened to betray her stoic façade, the poet shook her head. The line was one of Sara's favourites that she would use in getting a young DJ to do as she was told. It had worked too, even when the young woman had reached the height of five foot five at the age of thirteen. She smirked.

"Anyway." Sara moved back over to the door, feeling weary. "I'm going to lie down for a while."

A shadow of concern clouded Denise's face. "Are you okay?"

"Fine, fine. I just feel a little tired." Sara smiled to her niece as she exited the bedroom and closed the door behind her.

Out in the hallway, the old woman sighed as she leaned against the wall. She had wanted to go back down stairs but the sudden numbness in her body and usual cramping in her right hand had returned and she felt she needed to rest. Moving away from the narrow, and somewhat steep stairway, she walked slowly into her bedroom and straight to her bed. Her throat felt suddenly very tight, yet she knew at that moment she wouldn't be able to drink anything to ease the discomfort, swallowing suddenly felt like a chore. She would have to wait it out; Sara knew it would ease eventually.

"You've got to be kidding me!" Denise said down the phone as she sat at her desk, playing her favourite game of 'Mah Jongg' on the computer.

"I kid you not, DJ. I am telling you, they are willing to pay fifty-five thousand pounds just to get an exclusive interview with D Jennings and disprove many un-substantiated and well talked about rumours!" Carl said.

Denise looked incredulously down the phone as if thinking her publisher could actually see her expression. "What kind of rumours?" She stopped playing her game.

An amused chuckle rang in the poet's ears. *"Well for a start, is D Jennings really a woman? Does she shy from the public eye due to some kind of disfigurement that she hides from the world? Are you a travelling gypsy with a tormented mind?"*

"What?" Denise laughed.

"Oh but wait this is the best one," Carl exclaimed. *"Is D Jennings really a hermaphrodite with the face of a woman yet the voice and tackle of a man? I must admit that's one of my personal favourites."*

Still laughing the poet shut down the game's screen and slumped in her chair. "Sod them. Let them think what they want, it's much more fun this way."

"It's a lot of money, DJ."

"Oh so what," she muttered. "Carl you have known me for four years now. Hell, you know what I look like. Just tell that magazine whatever you want, it makes no difference to me." The poet propped her feet up upon the corner of her desk. Still wearing her heavy boots, they clumped against the thick wood.

"DJ, I should tell you that they will up the offer if you don't accept this one. They are really serious about this."

"So the hell am I. Look, Carl, just say thanks but no

55

thanks, I don't want to be interviewed. Got it?"

"Yeah I've got it, DJ. Okay, well I better get going then. Are you coming in soon to do lunch?"

Denise bit her lip. "Um, no sorry, Carl. I've got a lot on at the moment. I'll have to take a rain check on that one okay?"

"Sure, DJ. I'll be in touch. Bye."

"See you later, Carl."

Denise placed the phone back on the receiver and rolled her eyes. She'd had requests for interviews from one source or another for some years now and she had never given in, even as the money offered rose in amount. She wondered when people would get the hint and realise that she didn't want to hear their offers. She didn't want it. She wasn't interested. It just wasn't her.

Maybe it's the same with relationships, Denise thought. She could count them without the aid of the fingers of one hand! None. She had never been in a relationship. Ever. It used to trouble her aunt, confuse her friend Michelle, but for Denise it was simple. She didn't want it. She wasn't interested. It just wasn't her. She would admit, if only to her own self, that it wasn't so much a case of wanting to live the rest of her life alone. She just didn't want the commotion of moving from one bad relationship after another - all in the quest of finding 'the one'. She had seen it with Michelle. The woman was a sailor in the navy who seemed to have a beau in every port. If she liked to live her life that way, Denise was happy for her friend, but it was not the way for her. It was that simple.

Rubbing her thigh with her right hand, Denise realised that at some point in the day she really should get dressed. Walking around looking like, as Sara put it, "A reject from the Max Wall 'looky likey' Brigade" was not productive. *Besides,* she had thought, *who the hell is 'Max Wall' anyway?*

Sara did seem much brighter today, Denise noted. *Well at first,* she thought. She had noticed that Sara did make a sudden departure and had then found her reclining upon the surface of her bed, resting. That had instantly worried Denise, but Sara had assured her that although she did feel a little tired earlier, she now felt better. The poet believed her, but also noticed that Sara did favour her left hand slightly more than her right and Denise knew it was the right hand that suffered cramping.

Turning her attention back to her computer, the poet

placed her glasses upon her nose as she accessed her inbox and scrolled down the page as she sorted through the junk and relevant mail. Denise frowned suddenly. "Who's M Martin?" she muttered, then dark eyebrows shot towards her hairline as she suddenly remembered. "Nurse Randa!" With a flutter of inquisitiveness the poet opened the link and read her mail.

Denise read over the nurse's reply, then again. She smiled slightly as she began to type her own reply.

Randa,
First of all I would like to thank you for getting back to me.

You are right in stating that it bothers me that she made a living will. It became yet another confirmation that this disease was and is a reality, and that is the hardest part to accept. Being so unexpected I don't think I reacted as well as I should have, for Sara's sake. Family-wise she is all I have left.

I also want to thank you for telling me about your father; I can imagine that it must have been a difficult time for you. Knowing how I feel now I can imagine how it must have been for you. Somehow I feel sad that you had to go through that.
It seems that you have already gained an insight into my aunt's persona. Yes she is and always has been a strong willed and independent woman and had on many occasions in my disgruntled teens kicked my sorry behind into shape! I owe her a lot.

It is a relief to finally be able to talk to somebody about this, as I have been less than forthcoming with others. I have been trying to avoid talking about it even though I know maybe some people do have a right to know. It will be a hard subject to broach.
Well I don't want to take up any more of your time, so thank you again for responding. It means a lot to know there is somebody who is willing to listen to my ramblings of woe!

DJ

Oh and by the way. I don't see somebody who is poking her nose in where it doesn't belong... Unless of course you are too subtle even for me!

Denise emerged from her study after sending her mail, to find Sara standing in the kitchen. The old woman placed her hands on her hips as she studied her niece's appearance. "DJ, it's almost lunch time. Please tell me you are planning on looking more presentable for the rest of the day?" She shook her head.

Denise held up her hands. "I'm on my way right now!"

"Good."

As Denise turned to leave the kitchen Sara picked up the tea towel that was lying on the side and coiled it into a whip before striking it across her niece's behind.

With a startled grunt Denise whirled around to see Sara diligently inspecting a large tin of mushroom soup. She looked up innocently. "I am planning on making soup for lunch so don't take too long getting ready, dear."

Narrowing her eyes the poet backed out of the kitchen. "Uh huh!" She said as she disappeared from view.

A mischievous smirk spread across Sara's lips. "Oh, DJ, you are just so much fun to tease." She said and then frowned as the cramp in her hand intensified

Chapter 7

Mushroom soup. Mushroom soup. Randa finally found the spot on the shelf where she kept the canned soups and added the can in her hand to it. Vowing to get some sort of system in place before the next grocery shopping expedition, the nurse finished putting the remainder of her purchases away and headed to the refrigerator for a bottle of water. Looking at the "to-do" list posted on the door, she noted with some satisfaction that all of her self-assigned tasks for the day had been completed. Grocery shopping, oil change on the pick-up, workout and cleaning out the tool shed had been on the list and now the last item was crossed off.

Woo-hoo, the rest of the day is mine! Randa thought. *Time to engage in a little guilty pleasure.* Randa ambled toward her computer whistling tunelessly. She pushed the master switch on the machine and as it booted the thrill of the hunt thrummed through her veins.

"By day, mild mannered nurse Randa Martin works for a major pharmaceutical company but later she's Lara Croft, Tomb Raider, who fights a never ending battle for truth, justice and the American way!" Randa was certain she had mixed her superheroes so she added "in the bat cave" for good measure. Finding the program she wanted, the nurse proceeded to dispatch bats, wolves, bears and mummies with her blazing automatic pistols. An hour later she had wreaked as much havoc as she could and Randa closed down the program. Rising, she strolled with an elegant grace through the living room and into the kitchen, her feet gliding across hardwood then linoleum flooring.

"Lady Croft returns to her manor deep in the English county of Derbyshire. Jeeves, you may bring me tea!" Randa popped open the refrigerator door and grabbed a Snapple off the top shelf. Eyeing recently purchased produce she added "and you may peel me a grape as well!" Taking her selections back into the living room the nurse had every intention of settling on the couch and devoting the afternoon to a showing of Casablanca on the classic movie channel. Passing the computer again she noted the icon for new mail was flashing.

A glance at her watch told Randa she had enough time to see what had been delivered to her inbox before the start of the film. Settling in quickly she moved the mouse to bring up her e-mail. Under "New Mail" was a single message. Green eyes twinkled with happiness when she saw the sender.

Don't get so excited, Randa. She might just be writing to tell you she thinks you're as full of crap as a Christmas goose.

As the e-mail popped up Randa became less and less sure of herself until she had read the message through at least twice. *Score!* She thought. Relief washed over the nurse and she hopped out of her chair to do a small dance of victory, arms raised in the air. She sobered suddenly, realizing the woman had practically said that Randa was the only one she was talking to about the problems in her and her aunt's lives. Feelings of responsibility mixed with something akin to pleasure at that thought. The blonde paced the floor a few minutes grasping the fact that she was something of a lifeline to the woman from England. Lifeline. *So be it then,* she thought, *I'm ready for this. I want to do this. DJ needs somebody and it's going to be me.* Randa returned to the computer and hit the compose tab.

Dear DJ,

First I want to assure you it is never going to be an imposition for you to write to me and I want you to feel free to do so at any time. I consider it an honor to be taken into your confidence. It struck me as I was reading your note that really you know nothing of me except that I am a nurse. I hope you wont think I'm too forward if I tell you a little about myself. Maybe if you know something of who I am, it will be easier to communicate with me. Well, I'm 29 years old and I was born near where I live now in Silver Valley, California. (I see by your e-mail address you live in England, someplace I've always wanted to see and one day will.) You've heard about my family; my Mom is all I have in the world since my Dad died. I moved into an old farmhouse about a year ago and its from here I do my work on the Brightwood Information Network. You know, the only thing I ever wanted to be was a nurse. Sounds stupid to some people but I knew what I wanted to do from an

early age.

I need you to know it wasn't easy to share the story of my dad's death, but I realized a few years ago if I wanted to help others then I needed to be willing to share my experiences with them. Actually I didn't come to this epiphany by myself, it was the inspiring words of a favorite poet. She said:

What you learn you must teach, give with all of your heart
Your pleasure will be your reward
And together we'll build through the faults of the past
A future for lives yet told

What an insight. I think of those lines every time I'm tempted to withdraw into myself and not give everything I know I'm capable of.

Your Aunt Sara sounds like a real firecracker. I hope this will sustain her through her illness. But what of you, DJ? What will sustain you? Do you have the support you need? If you would permit it I would like to be that support. It's my humble opinion you can't have too many friends and though I can't quite put into words why, I have a real premonition we will become great friends. So much for me possibly being subtle, huh? I sometimes think if there was an award for bluntness it would be sitting on my mantle.

So, DJ, how are you doing?

Regards, Randa

Nothing like pushing yourself on the woman, Miranda. Well, if she doesn't want me she only has to say so but until that happens I'm going to try to be the kind of friend I would want in this situation. Randa hit the send tab and sped her message on its way. As the confirmation notice appeared, the nurse felt an unfamiliar sense of loneliness spread through her, a sensation she hadn't noticed while writing to the English woman. *Maybe DJ isn't the only one who needs a friend* Randa

61

thought. Shrugging off the idea, the blonde headed to the couch to spend the remainder of the afternoon with Humphrey Bogart and Ingrid Bergman in North Africa.

The ringing of the phone woke Randa with a start. She remembered watching Bogie and Claude Raines walking off into the fog together but then things became a little foggy for her as well. Fumbling for the phone a grumpy blonde mumbled "This better be important."

"Cripes, Randa, is that anyway to talk to your best friend?"

"No, Derek, and if I had caller ID on this phone I probably never would!"

"Ouch, Randa, I'm wounded. Oh, wait let me guess, I woke Sleeping Beauty up?"

"Is it that painfully obvious? What's up, Derek?" The nurse rubbed sleepy eyes and barely suppressed a yawn.

"Well, I am just a harbinger of news, sweet thing. You know that poet you literally drool over? I just read some juicy stuff about her on the web."

"D Jennings?" Derek had Randa's attention now. "What vile gossip have you picked up about her? And I do *not* drool."

"Oh, that's right, drooling requires a moist area a little higher than where yours is. Don't lie to the best friend, you know damn good and well you hang on every word that woman has ever written. Now listen up, I read she is going to finally give an interview to some rag over in England. Maybe now you'll get all those juicy details you want."

"It would be great if it were true but I can't believe it. She's never said anything to anybody. Sorry, Derek, as far as I know D Jennings doesn't talk to anyone."

"Too bad for you then, Randa darlin,' if that's true. I was hoping you'd be able to get a few words right from the horse's mouth."

"Impossible. I just don't get that lucky, Derek. Nope, I don't get that lucky."

What Denise thought had started as a particularly decent day had pretty much gone down hill from the moment the first dark storm cloud edged its way over the bright morning sky. She had stood, looking out from her bedroom window at a small disused and abandoned mine. It's steel structure jutted up above the ground, marring the otherwise picturesque landscape. Then the clouds had come, covering the brightness of the day with a shrouded air of gloom.

It was then, as the first shower of rain fell onto the earth, that Denise had heard it; the sounds of yet another falling object hitting the floor with a heavy impact. Jumping from the window, Denise ran from her bedroom and into her aunt's room to find it empty so she turned towards the bathroom instead. She froze in the doorway, not expecting the scene that was in front of her.

Sara lay on the floor. She had obviously just had a shower, as the towel was still wrapped around her body, providing a slight amount of dignity to the fallen woman. When she realized it was in fact Sara that had fallen, the poet ran to assist the distraught woman lying helplessly on the ground.

Silent tears fell from Sara's eyes as her niece helped her to stand and assist her out of the bathroom and into her bedroom. Denise sat her carefully down upon the floral print bedspread. "Sara, what happened?"

"Oh, DJ, I am so sorry you had to see that. I have been feeling incredibly weak since I got up this morning and have only just had enough energy to get into the shower. As I was attempting to get out I wasn't able to get a grip on the shower door and I was unable to keep myself standing." Sara lowered her head, too embarrassed to look into her niece's eyes.

Denise moved to Sara's wardrobe and pulled out her thick peach bathrobe. She helped her aunt into the garment as she sat upon the bed. "I know this is hard for you, Sara…"

"Hard!" Sara interrupted, "DJ, this is damned near impossible. I have never had to rely on anybody's help before yet look at me now… too weak to even get myself dressed!" She shook her head in disgust at her own lack of abilities. "I didn't really give much thought to how bad this was going to

63

be. Not really."

Sitting down upon the bed beside her aunt, Denise placed one arm around her shoulders. "This is just a bad day, Sara. Remember Doctor Macarthur said you will have them; you will be fine later I'm sure."

"And then what?" Sara questioned. "I maybe okay for now but soon I am going to be like this permanently. It's only going to get worse, DJ, how am I supposed to deal with that? To accept what is going to happen?" Tears once again accumulated in the old woman's eyes. "You shouldn't have to deal with this, DJ. It's only going to get worse."

Denise sighed. "However bad this is going to get, Sara, I will deal with it all. I am here to look after you. Please don't feel ashamed to ask for help, I know how uncomfortable it must be for you, but I want to help you in any way that I can. I am here for you." She held her aunt closer as her own cerulean eyes clouded with tears.

"How am I to cope, DJ?" The words were whispered lightly with raw emotion.

Releasing Sara, the poet moved to kneel in front of the tearful woman. "Together, Sara. You're not alone and you will not have to cope with this alone, I will be here for you."

Sara looked deep into her niece's eyes, seeing such a familiarity with her own brother. "But I'm going to die, DJ."

Denise was still; stunned into silence. She had no idea how she was to reply to that. What could she say that would in anyway ease her aunt's words? There were none. She was going to die and as painful as it was to admit, it was a fact. With a sigh she moved to a standing position. "But not today, Sara. Today you are going to let me help you get dressed until you feel strong enough to do so yourself and let me help you down stairs and to the warmth of the living room and fire… okay?"

The old woman smiled warmly. "I don't think I have much of a choice. I can see the stubborn streak glinting in your eyes that means you are not about to take no for an answer are you!"

"Nope." Denise smiled then frowned as a sudden thought entered her mind. "Sara?"

"Hmm?"

The dark woman paused, hoping she was not being too forward in this proposal she had in mind, yet also hoping that

64

in the light of the recent events, Sara would see that what she was about to ask was for her own comfort and ease. "I know this is very sudden but I was thinking. What do you think about the prospect of me moving my study up here and your bedroom down stairs?" She held up her hand, as Sara was about to reply. "I think there could be much benefit in this. You wont have to deal with stairs if you are having a bad day. The lower part of the house is warmer as there is a fire and ground floor central heating, plus an unused fireplace in my study. It wouldn't take much to get it swept and ready for use, and there is the ground floor bathroom by the back door."

Sara was surprised and had not expected that proposal in the slightest. "What about your study and the fact that you have all your new fangled equipment set up? Plus my bed and furniture are old and heavy. The stairs will be a burden as they are so steep and narrow and I know you will not be able to do it by your self."

"Easy obstacles to overcome. A bit of drilling and threading of wires through the ceiling and as for lifting, I am pretty sure I know one such person who I will be able to convince in helping me." Denise looked at her aunt seriously. "What do you think?"

"I want to say no, but I feel that you are right."

"Does that mean yes?"

"Yes." Sara nodded. "But who are you planning on asking for help?"

The poet smiled. "Well let's just say that Carl has been badgering me to go out to lunch with him for a work related discussion. I figured that since you said you wanted to invite Diane around to talk tomorrow that I could ask him then. You did say you would like to talk with her alone." Diane was Michelle's mother; Sara's oldest friend and Denise knew that she would be the first person her aunt would tell about her illness. "Would that be okay?"

With a smile the old woman nodded. "That would be fine... thank you, DJ."

Denise looked up at the window as the rain outside turned to hail and large chips of ice began hammering upon the bedroom's windowpane. "Come on, lets get dressed and down stairs. I'll start a fire and you get warmed up, you must be cold... I know I am."

Denise helped her aunt dress and together they made their way downstairs and into the living room. Denise built a large coal fire that warmed both women and the small house within minutes.

It was the day after that found Denise walking down a sparsely crowded street on the outskirts of Matlock Bath's village centre. She turned down a narrow alleyway as she made her way towards a small popular tearoom. It was still cold and she was thankful she had chosen to wear her thick pair of black cargo pants and sweater under her parka.

As she approached the establishment she could already see Carl Lloyd sitting by the large window next to a small two-seated table. He looked up just in time to see her crossing the street and waved to the poet as she neared the small café. Denise smiled then noticed the blue folder resting upon table's surface; she knew it could only mean one thing and groaned internally as she entered the building.

"So," Carl pushed the remaining pea around his plate as he looked up at Denise. "You know what this blue folder is, don't you?"

Denise rolled her eyes. "I would guess that would be a formal offer from that damned magazine wanting an interview. Am I right?"

The editor smiled as he pushed his plate away and opened the item in question. "Sure is." He pulled out a sheet of A4 sized paper. "Here is a list of the questions they want to ask you." He ignored the glare aimed in his direction. "Oh come on, DJ. I at least have to try you know, the boss is busting my arse to get you to do this. She thinks you should finally give an interview. Imagine the scoop!"

Denise ignored the sheet of questions that was placed in front of her. "Nope."

"Oh come on, I will do anything you ask. Do you want me to strip and run around the streets naked? I think I might just do it. If you don't reply the magazine plans on dropping the article and doing one on poets and modern poetry in general. This would be so much better. Think about it." He smirked. "Or maybe I will do the strip if you don't say yes!"

Her mind working overtime, Denise thought how she would best gain from Carl's offer to do anything without actually having to give the interview. She did need his help after all and Carl was well reputed for shying away from any form of physical labour. "Look, Carl. You know I just don't want to do that kind of thing; I don't want the publicity... but... I do have an offer."

Light eyebrows framing grey eyes disappeared under blonde wavy hair. "An offer?"

"Yes and something that wont bring shame to your wife and kids when they see a picture of your naked butt in the local paper!"

"Go on."

"You said you would do anything?"

Grey blue eyes narrowed in suspicion. "Where are you going with this, DJ?"

"If you help me with a little task I have to complete tomorrow, I *will not* do the interview, but I *will* give you one," She held up a finger for emphasis, "from the horses mouth quote for the magazine's article they are doing on modern day poets and poetry. That is the best I can offer. Take it or leave it." She threw her napkin down, leaned back in her chair and folded her arms, obviously portraying the end of negotiations with only an answer pending.

The editor was quiet as he considered her offer. "What's the task?"

"Help me move a couple of things at home. I am exchanging two rooms and could use a 'big strong man' to assist me in carrying a couple of large pieces of furniture down and up the stairs. So what do you say?"

"Sounds like black mail."

"Look who's talking!"

"What about the boss?"

"You can talk her into it; you are married to her for gods sake!"

"Final offer?"

"Final offer."

"You don't want fifty/fifty or phone a friend?"

"Don't make me get physical, Carl." the poet warned.

"Aw… okay… done!" Carl held out his hand and Denise shook it with a smile of victory.

It was another two days later that Denise finally sat in her new study on the second floor of the house. She looked critically around the room. It was smaller than the old study but that didn't bother her much as she was still able to fit all her furniture into the room. *At least the walls are plain cream and it was only the ex-bedroom's accessories that are floral!*

With Carl helping her do the transfer she had managed to get the room done much quicker and had already reassembled her computer and re-connected it to the Internet. That was something she was very glad about as she dialled on line and accessed her e-mail account. Her inbox loaded onto the screen and as her eyes spied a now familiar name; she accessed the link immediately with a slight air of anticipation.

Denise read over the letter with a smile that suddenly turned to a look of surprise as she recognized the quote Randa had inserted into the mail. She smirked, *so she has read one of my works,* she thought. Denise hit the reply tab.

Randa,

How am I? Well in all honesty if I had read your mail when if first arrived a couple of days ago I would have said 'fine' but politely declined your offer of support - even though I think I would have wanted it. Believe me, Randa, if your mantle holds the award for bluntness then mind holds the award for pride and stubborn independence. Unfortunately Sara took a bad turn a couple of days ago. She had a spell of weakness and fell while getting out of the shower. For a while it was difficult for her to dress herself and as I am sure you can imagine me having to assist her was very awkward for her. I then decided to move her bedroom down stairs and my study up; needless to say a business associate and I have only just completed the task.

To be truthful, Randa, I appreciate your offer of support and would like to accept it in any way possible.

I was surprised to see that you are only 29, as you seem much wiser than that for your years. By the way - I hold you by 3 so I think I am allowed to say that. Yes I am 32, I do live in England in a small village with my aunt and I guess you would call me self-employed. I work from home, which for Sara's sake is now a great advantage.

Denise paused as she considered whether to say anything about Randa's quoting of one of her poems. She didn't consider it as one of her better works, but Denise was sure she remembered that poem being published in an American magazine a couple of years ago. *Maybe that was where she got if from.*

She continued to type…

I guess it is nice to be able to look at something in life that you can draw strength from, even if it is just some old poem.

Thank you again for telling me about your father, even though it must have been hard for you to talk about. I think that in life there are many hurdles that we all must overcome and in doing so they make us stronger and wiser in the process. I refuse to believe they are there to hold us down and break our spirit - don't you agree?

I should go and see how Sara is now.

Take care, Randa.

DJ

Chapter 8

"Elvis has left the building!" Randa announced as she wrapped up another session on the Brightwood Information Network and shut down her database. The nurse could tell the school year had commenced and wondered exactly how many questions about head lice she was going to be asked in the next few weeks. The three questions she had on that subject tonight had her feeling like she needed a long hot bath.

Randa filled the garden tub and added soft musk scented bath crystals to the water. The nurse looked around her in satisfaction; glad she had started her renovations with the bathrooms. This master bathroom was a study in cool blue and lavender, a place where the blonde could relax and recharge. Randa quickly shed her gray sweatpants and black Oakland Raider jersey and stepped into the tub.

This is so good it must be sinful she thought as she slid all but her head under the steaming fragrant water. Randa smiled and thought how good her life was at this moment. *Good job, nice home and a new friend courtesy of the Internet. A friend who needs me!* That thought made the nurse feel so good she wiggled her toes under the water. *Now if I only had someone to share this life with me.* The blonde thought back to Derek's comment earlier in the week. Okay, so maybe she did have a crush on the poet. *Maybe? All right, no maybe about it, her words touch me like nothing else can* Randa admitted. The nurse thought of the tall, dark figure on the book jacket. *She can touch me anytime* Randa smirked.

Noticing the water beginning to cool, Randa reluctantly left the tub and slipped into a green terrycloth robe. Heading out to the kitchen, she made a cup of hot chocolate and decided to use the Internet for a more pleasurable reason than to answer questions about lice. Logging onto her server she entered her user name and password to check her e-mail. DJ's name popped up on the screen and Randa ignored all other mail to go directly to the message. She read the text and her fingers flew to the keyboard in response.

Dear DJ,

I guess I can agree with your statement about hurdles in our lives making us stronger and it sounds like you definitely have a fighting spirit much like your aunt's. I think though that other things can make us stronger and wiser too without the struggle and pain of hurdles. Friendship, passion and love have given me strength in the past and though I'm not currently involved with anyone, I can see a time when I will share those things with a special person and we will learn and grow together. With that, philosophy class with Professor Martin is dismissed!

I think you were wise to move your aunt's bedroom downstairs. I've been doing some research and it appears the type of ALS your aunt has is "bulbar". This is a more aggressive form of the disease and I'm afraid it won't be long before negotiating stairs will be impossible for her. I am so reluctant to give you bad news but if I am to be your friend I have to be honest with you. Sara's ALS will progress rapidly. You should think now about making your home wheelchair accessible. I would suggest a shower chair to help her conserve energy while in there. You also need to think now about getting some help in the home for the time when Sara will require total care. I mean this, DJ, you will need to have someone you can trust to give you some time away from the situation. I know you're devoted to your aunt but for your sake you will need some time and support of your own.

One last thing about the ALS. Your aunt's type of ALS affects the central nervous system more than the other type. This may mean your aunt may experience emotional outbursts such as inappropriate crying or laughing. I want you to be prepared for that and you should tell any caregiver you bring in also. Ideally, hiring a nurse would be best as they would be ready to deal with both the physical and the emotional aspects of the disease. I'm so sorry to be the one to give you all this news; I wouldn't hurt you for the world. I hope you believe that.

Now, madam, I have to chastise you a little. I quoted you a piece of inspirational verse, which you then referred to as "some old poem". I am going to forgive you for that remark because I probably didn't make myself clear. This poetry is by an English author who in my opinion is one of the most perceptive and sensitive people on the planet. She is not *a* poet, she is *the* poet. I believe between the two of us I will have to claim to be the expert on this woman and her work because I own everything she has ever written. Her words are beautiful and poignant. I think her poetry is one of those things that I mentioned earlier, something to make us stronger and wiser without causing us pain. Okay, shall we try again?

My heart beats to the sound of your name,
Whether aloud or in unspoken thought,
I gasp air as I gaze at your face,
My eyes burn with a vision so sought.
Internal fires deep within my being,
Stir wildly out of control.
A desire so raw yet innocent,
Erupts from the depths of my soul.

Doesn't that just speak right to your heart? If that doesn't get your juices flowing you better check your pulse! Of course poetry might not be interesting to you at all and I may have just gone off on a tangent. Sorry. I'm glad you can't see me right now, I'm sure I'm blushing to high heaven. Guess I get a little defensive about my poet, huh?

I'll close now, it was a long night and sleep is creeping up on me. Be good to yourself, DJ. You need it and deserve it.

Your friend, Randa

Randa sent the e-mail off and closed her computer down. Shuffling to her bedroom, the nurse dropped the robe across the foot of the bed and slid between cool, crisp sheets. As her head hit the pillow, Randa's eyes flew open. *Did I just refer to D Jennings as* 'my poet' *in an e-mail? Oh well,* she thought, *what are the odds they know each other? Probably about the same as me winning the lotto.* With a little smile, Randa let sleep claim her.

Two days later Randa stood inside the Silver Valley Quick Stop staring at the orange and white ticket in her hand. Shaking her head in disbelief, she rechecked the results.

"6 yes, 9 yes, 24 no, 32 no, 36 no, 42 yes. I can't believe it." The nurse took the ticket to Mr. Park at the counter who checked it against the official results. The elderly Korean proprietor smiled up at Randa.

"You've been playing these same numbers twice a week for at least a year and you finally hit the ticket! Let's see, three numbers out of six, here's your five dollars."

Randa took the bill and giving it a brief kiss, dropped it in the donation bucket on the counter. Mr. Park looked surprised and said "You finally win something and you donate it to the new firehouse fund?"

"Yeah, I guess five dollars is more like a moral victory. Besides, I can still tell everyone I won the lotto!" Mr. Park nodded and chuckled along with Randa. Something in the back of Randa's mind was nagging at her, but she couldn't put her finger on it. Shrugging, she picked up her ticket for the next drawing and headed out the door to her truck.

Denise crouched down in front of a large bookshelf and pulled open it's single bottom drawer. With a furrowed brow she reached inside and started pulling out the contents. Paper, pens, and an assortment of knick-knacks were strewn all over the floor. "Where the bloody hell are you?" She muttered, growling as she continued her search.

The poet was brought out of her cursing and searching by the ringing of the phone. She reached over picked up the handset, then returned to her rummaging. "Hello?"

"Good evening, DJ, sorry it's late but I knew you would

be up."

"Well, well, well, Carl..." Denise stopped her delving and sat down upon the floor, crossing her legs. "I was just about to call you."

"Oh, I'm honoured. Well ladies first; what did you want?"

"You know when you helped me move all my stuff the other day?"

"Yeah?"

"Did you by any chance happen to see the power pack for my laptop computer? I realized that I didn't want to spend all my time on my computer in the study now that it is upstairs, so I figured I would use the laptop down stairs so I am able to keep Sara company. Trouble is that I can't find the damned power pack for the buggering thing." Denise started placing the strewn items back into the drawer. Placing them in haphazardly the drawer began to look even more disorganized than before she started her search.

"Well, let me be your knight in shining armour, DJ. You know that small red, plastic box that you keep all your coils of wire and junk gadgets inside?"

"DJ, you dopey sod!" Denise shuffled on her knees over to a small cabinet and pulled open the double doors. "I can't believe I didn't think to look in here." Grabbing the container in question, it slid to the floor with a muted thud. She yawned quietly.

"You sound tired?"

"I'm knackered actually." Denise pulled the laptop power pack out of her junk and gadgets box and attempted to uncoil the tangled wire with one hand. After little luck she balanced the phone in the crook of her neck to free her other hand.

"Well I'll make this quick then. The magazine wants the quote."

The poet placed down her unravelled wires. "Woohoo."

The editor laughed down the phone. *"DJ, do I detect a hint of sarcasm?"*

"Yes!"

"Oh, okay. Anyway so I am giving you a day's notice. They want you to give a comment on 'Passion **and drive. What motivates the poetic soul?'** *Pretty ostentatious huh?"*

"Should I just say 'privacy'?"

"You're really tired aren't you?"

"Now that I have found this thing," she waved the power pack in the air, "I am off to bed."

"Okay, DJ, I can take a hint. Listen I will ring you tomorrow evening to get the quote, okay?"

"Sure."

"Later."

"Bye." Denise placed down the phone with a tired sigh. It was past midnight and the poet was more than ready for bed.

Leaving the confines of her study she made a quick stop down stairs to make sure Sara was okay and sleeping peacefully before making her way back up stairs and to her bedroom. As she was unbuttoning her shirt, Denise realised that she hadn't even had time to check her mail for the past few days. Sitting on her bed she leaned down to undo the laces of her boots as she wondered again whether she would have a mail from Randa. Denise had wanted to check her inbox but every time she had a free moment to herself something would call her attention.

Denise frowned as she tried to examine her feelings. She suddenly realised that she actually looked forward to correspondence from the American nurse. She knew it was probably the distance but she felt like she was able to share anything with her. To be able to talk about things and not feel like she was being scrutinized or judged - it was a liberating feeling.

Kicking off her boots, Denise stood up and unbuttoned her jeans, letting them fall to the floor as she allowed her shirt to slip away from her shoulders. She briefly considered going back into her study to make a quick check on the computer but her tired body demanded that she wait until the morning. *Quick shower, brush teeth, then bed!* With that affirmation, the poet wandered off into the bathroom to commence her nightly ritual.

The next evening found Denise and her aunt sitting in the living room. Sara sat in her favourite chair watching one of the typical early evening black and white films on the terrestrial channels, while the poet sat in a single chair in the corner of the

76

room working on her laptop. Denise switched her vision between the screen of the portable computer and a large note pad. She was inputting her latest poem. She had written it that very morning; remnants of a dream she'd had that night after she had collapsed exhausted into her bed.

"Finished!"

Sara looked across from her viewing of 'Some Like it Hot'. "Is that the poem you wrote this morning, DJ?"

"Yep." Denise smiled as she closed the pad and attached the phone line to side of the laptop. "I wanted to get it on disk while remembered, but I don't think I shall be including this one in my next book."

The old woman frowned. "Why not?"

"I don't know." Denise shrugged. "This one just feels different." It wasn't the first time that the poet had written a poem and decided it wasn't for public viewing. She had a whole manuscript of such works that she kept private, away from prying eyes. She knew that some day, somebody would see these poems. But it would be somebody special.

Sara looked back towards the television. She smiled to herself as she thought of all the different ways her niece would try and convince herself as well as others that she was not looking for love. That happiness and affection were things that you could feel and achieve within oneself, and for her writing was the contentment she so desired. Sara was not fooled. She could see, if not read the yearning not only in Denise's writing but also in her eyes.

"What are you doing now?" the old woman asked, a hoarseness evident in her voice and a clear symptom of her disease.

"Just checking my e-mail box."

Sara shook her head. "Never will I understand today's modern technology. The Internet and e-mailing." She shrugged. "I still don't understand how that little thing you have shoved into your back pocket, almost invisible to the naked eye could actually be a telephone."

The poet shrugged. "Times are changing, Sara."

"You're telling me!"

Denise beamed as she looked back down at her screen and saw a mail from Randa in her inbox. A slither of excitement fluttered in her stomach as she selected the link. With a slight smile she started reading.

The woman's eyes flowed over every sentence closely. *Emotional outbursts!* Denise thought, *well she sure did have one of those this morning!*

The poet had awoken with a jolt to the sound of laughter coming from the lower part of the house. Frowning, she emerged from the cocoon of thick quilt and into the cold stark reality of the new day. The clock on her wall stated that it was half past eight, so with a disgruntled sigh she slid from the warmth of her bed to investigate what it was that seemed to be causing her aunt so much obvious hilarity.

She did think that maybe Sara was watching one of her old favourite comedies. She was an avid fan of both 'Porridge' and 'Open all hours' and in her younger days had thought, "Mr. Barker was one of the most dashing young men on the television" as she had often quoted to a bemused Denise.

She had entered the front room to find Sara sitting in the chair she herself was now sitting in laughing uncontrollably. The television was not on and in Denise's opinion there was nothing that she thought would cause such hysterics. It was then that she remembered what Doctor Macarthur had said concerning Sara's MND and the symptoms that would follow.

To see these symptoms playing out first hand and knowing there was nothing she could do to help her aunt caused a certain amount of anxiety within the younger woman. She was unsure what to do or how best to help the woman. Eventually Sara did calm down though, much to Denise's relief.

As Denise continued reading through the mail one dark eyebrow began a slow rise followed by a gradual smile. She chuckled lightly to herself. *Juices flowing? I don't believe it!*

Sara looked towards her niece confused as she witnessed her unreserved smile. "What is amusing you so, DJ?"

Denise looked up at her aunt. "Um… you remember how I said I wanted to look for some more information on err… MND."

"Yes."

"I found a site in which I was able to talk on line with a nurse from America. She answered all my questions and helped me see things a little clearer. You know… put things in perspective. Well anyway she gave me her e-mail address and we have been corresponding." Denise scrolled back and began reading Randa's words again.

"Modern technology at work once again!" Sara twisted in her chair until she was facing her niece. "So you have been talking with somebody who lives on the other side of the world. Interesting. What's her name?"

Denise smiled once again. "Miranda but she prefers Randa. She's twenty nine and works as an on-line nurse answering questions over the net on a medical site."

"And what amused you so?"

Licking her lips, Denise looked back down at the laptop balancing upon her knees. "The other day she actually quoted a couple of lines from one of my poems and I just blew it off. Well she has written back and chastised me for belittling her favourite poet."

An expression of surprise crossed Sara's features. "Really? So she is a fan?"

Denise wasn't sure why but she felt an inner delight at that prospect. "Apparently."

"In that case this woman has already gained a few extra notches in my book. So what are you going to say?"

That was the big question. The fact that Randa was obviously a fan of her work had brought a whole new facet into their sudden friendship. In any other case she would feel the need to back away from her correspondence, *it's not like we have known each other that long anyway.* But with sudden recognition Denise realised that she really didn't want to end this - *What ever it is.* She frowned. "What am I going to say? I'm not sure. I mean... I want to know her and I want her to know me. Does that sound strange?"

"Not at all, DJ." The old woman said as she witnessed an expression that she had never before seen in her niece's eyes. "You want to tell her who you are?"

"I think I do!" Denise replied seriously as she began to compose her reply. Knowing honesty was always a positive presence in any friendship, Denise wanted it to stay that way.

Randa,

I am so glad you agree that me moving the bedroom downstairs was a good idea. I didn't want it to seem

79

overbearing or forceful at all.

Thank you for your advice. I suppose I am going to have to start making the house a little more accessible for a wheelchair. I honestly don't know how Sara will react to that though for her the slow loss of her independence is becoming the hardest aspect to accept.

As for her emotions, I am afraid I have already experienced one such outburst. I think you are right and I may have to start looking for a nurse soon. I had hoped it would never have to come to that though.

Okay I feel I must apologise for my remarks concerning the poem. You seem quite a fan of the author. That is a surprise. I guess maybe I thought I had some insight, being as though it was I who wrote it. But then again you do seem quite versed in my works. Thank you for your words; though I bet you don't own everything I have ever written!

So tell me, did that poem really get your juices flowing? (I'm joking, but I bet you're looking cute if you are blushing again)

Faithfully yours

DJ

PS... Although it feels good to be able to tell you this, as I am sure you are aware what I have just told you is very confidential. I feel I can trust you. I don't know why I feel this way but I do.

Have a good day Randa.

Denise Jennings

Denise stood in the kitchen, leaning against the work surface, one elbow resting on the worktop as she waited for the kettle to boil. Her chin rested squarely within the palm of her hand and she drummed her fingers upon the side of her face. The sound of a slow bubbling began to rise as steam made its assent from the kettle's spout.

As the appliance switched itself off, Denise lifted the kettle off its base and proceeded to pour the boiling water into two cups. One contained dried instant tea, the other contained coffee granules. She stirred both infusions thoroughly before lifting the cup of tea and carrying it into Sara's bedroom.

"How are you feeling, Sara?"

The old woman sat rigidly in her bed. "Tired. My body feels stiff and achy and as usual my hand feels like I have been lying on it all night." With a grimace she attempted to flex her right hand.

Approaching the bed, Denise placed Sara's cup of tea down upon her bedside table before sitting beside her aunt. "Here let me have a go." The poet took a hold of the old woman's hand and began massaging her thumb over Sara's palm. She worked her own thumb and fingers over each one of Sara's as she tried to ease the cramp. "Feel any better?"

Sara smiled sadly.

"I guess not huh?" Denise didn't release her hand. Looking down she studied the peach and cream floral bedspread unsure of what to say. "Um... will you be able to hold your tea alright?"

"I'll manage."

Denise picked up the yellow mug and held it out for her aunt. "Try."

With a nod Sara reached out, taking the cup with her left hand. She held the handle as firmly as she could but a visible tremor moved down her arm, ending in her hand and the cup shook precariously. Golden tea lapped perilously around the rim of the mug and Denise placed her hand around Sara's steadying the motion. Sara smiled her thanks as together they moved cup to her lips and the old woman was able to take a drink.

Keeping her expression neutral, Denise hid the turmoil that was whirling around inside of her.

Sitting despondently in the silent gloominess of the living room, Denise was startled out of her dark thoughts by the ringing of the phone. With a slight jump she jogged over to the telephone and picked up the shrilling handset. "Hello, Carl."

"Hey how did you know it was me?"

Denise shrugged. "I knew you were calling some time this evening. So are you after my 'quote'?"

Carl could detect the downhearted tone in the poet's voice. "Are you alright?"

"Fine. So I was thinking about what to say and I have something that I think will correspond with what they are wanting and is also something that came to mind after a comment by a friend. I think it would work well."

"Okay, go for it, DJ."

"Right, this is it… **Not long ago somebody said to me that reading poetry was a way to make us stronger and wiser without causing us any pain. For some people that may be true but as I stated in one of my poems, 'You must learn from the errors that eventuated past'. I basically mean that the hurt and pain or even desire does come from somewhere and if that can be expressed through verse then maybe you can touch others. To show people that they are not alone or give others strength and the ability to learn through the errors or pain of the past; it can only make us stronger. So I would like to think this person was right."** She paused briefly. "How was that?"

"Great!" Carl enthused. *"I liked it. I've recorded it so I will get it written down and send it into the magazine… thank you, DJ."*

"No problem, Carl. Now if you will excuse me I really do have to go as I need to check on Sara."

"How is she?"

Denise sighed. "Not too good at the moment."

"I'm sorry, DJ. If there is anything we can do just let me know okay?"

"Thanks, Carl. Well I'll see you soon."

"Bye, DJ."

"See you later." Placing the handset back down on its charger, Denise leaned against the wall in the dark hallway. Closing her eyes she slid down to the floor and let her head fall onto her knees. Randa had stated that she should think about getting a nurse for Sara. The problem was that Denise didn't want some unknown person helping her aunt when she thought it was her responsibility to take care of the woman who had done the same for her for many years. *Maybe it isn't my decision to make,* Denise thought *Sara should have her say in this as this is all in her best interests.* The trouble was that Denise was very much like Sara, far too independent when it came to personal issues. The poet had already experienced how Sara had reacted to being dressed by her niece. How would she react to being looked after by a nurse constantly? And what of the wheelchair?

With a sigh, Denise let her head fall back against the wall. At that point, she knew inside she wanted to express her thoughts and feelings with the one person that she knew would understand. Yet she didn't move, stubborn independence, and if she was honest, an inner uncertainty, kept her immobile. It was some moments later before the poet left the murky hallway and headed back to her aunt's bedroom.

Chapter 9

Monday Night Football droned on in the background as Randa finished up the dusting in the living room. Her beloved Oakland Raiders had a comfortable lead and Randa was feeling good.

A day off, a football victory and I've got all my chores done. Does life get any better? She thought. Clicking off the television, she flipped her computer on. A quick check of her e-mail and then a little reading with a glass of wine was in the nurse's plan. The computer booted up and connected to the Internet without problem and Randa saw the flashing of the new mail icon.

Of course I have new mail, she thought, *junk mail has still not been outlawed* Randa scanned the list of senders with anticipation and was rewarded with the sight of her friend's name. Opening the message, Randa started reading DJ's note but when she had finished, the smile so noticeable earlier had fallen from her face completely.

Stunned. Stunned was the only word for it. Randa blinked her eyes rapidly and realized she was staring at she screen with her mouth hanging open. Picking her jaw up off the floor where she was sure it had dropped, she swallowed hard and began mumbling to herself.

"What the...DJ...D Jennings. DJ is D Jennings? DJ is my poet?" Randa realized she had used those very words in her e-mail to DJ earlier. She dropped her head into her hands and felt the heat rising in her face.

"Oh my god, I am so mortified! I can't believe I said all those things about her poetry. I am so embarrassed!" Randa's eyes returned to the e-mail and re-read DJ's question about "juices flowing". The blush returned with renewed vigor as the nurse let out a strangled groan. She stood and began pacing the living room running her fingers through her hair.

"Now what am I gonna do? My idol is my new friend? What is this, life's little cruel joke?" Randa stopped short as a new thought popped into her mind. A joke. It had to be a joke.

Warming to the idea, Randa came up with a whole new scenario.

Sure, that's what this has to be. DJ must have recognized the poetry I sent and because of the coincidence of the initials, she took the opportunity to jerk my chain a little. A sigh of relief escaped her lips. *I'm not worried that I'm wrong mind you but maybe I'll just do a little research.*

Randa returned to her computer and exited her e-mail. Accessing her favorite search engine, she entered "D Jennings, poet". As the results popped up the nurse was determined to check out every link until she found the proof that DJ was just joking with her.

An hour later, Randa sat back in her chair and rubbed her eyes. She hadn't found any proof DJ wasn't D Jennings, but she had found out one important thing; D Jennings was a master at protecting her privacy.

"This is getting me nowhere fast. I need something else, the most recent information I can find. Maybe I'll find out D Jennings is married with five kids and never had an Aunt Sara. Think, Randa, think." Frowning, she put her mind to the task and after a few moments she had an idea. Snatching up her cell phone she hit #2 on the speed dial.

"Hmmphh?" was the muffled response to her call.

"Derek! Derek, wake up, it's Randa."

"Of course it is. Who else calls me during my beauty rest?" he yawned. *"So, what's up?"*

"Can you remember the name of the magazine that D Jennings was supposed to give an interview to? You told me about it a week ago."

" Oh Lord, Randa. You expect me to remember what happened a week ago? I barely remember yesterday. Listen, you can get that information yourself. Go to celebgab.com and do a search there."

"Thanks, Derek. I owe you another one." Randa hung up before her friend could respond and turned her attention back to the computer. Bringing up the website Derek had told her about, the nurse began a patient search for the article. When she found the item she was looking for, it referred to a literary magazine called "The Word". Tracking down the website for the magazine, Randa selected "Poetry" from the websites offerings. She didn't have to look any further than that. In a teaser, the magazine fairly trumpeted its excitement about having a quote from reclusive poet D Jennings. Randa's spirit fell. *Only a quote she thought, not the in depth interview I was hoping for. I guess it's better than nothing though.*

The nurse started reading the quote that was featured prominently in bold type. For the second time in the space of a few hours, Randa was speechless but this time when she sat back she was smiling. *She used my words, she used what I said.*

Randa realized that DJ wasn't joking; she really was the poet D Jennings. *D Jennings is my friend. Wow. Derek is never going to believe this!*

Randa could only sit quietly and be amazed at how her life had suddenly changed in the space of a few hours on a Monday evening in autumn. *A Monday I won't forget as long as I live.*

Randa brought up her e-mail again, found DJ's note and hit the reply button.

Dear DJ,

I'm a little bit lost here as you can probably imagine. I don't even quite know what to call you. DJ? D Jennings? Denise? Do you have a preference?

I hardly know what to say; you've thrown me for a loop here. I have a lot of feelings rolling around inside me right now so if it's okay I'll just spill them a little and maybe I can get things straight in my mind. First, let me say something and get it over with. I am so embarrassed to have said I know you better than you know yourself, even though I didn't know you were you at the time. Does that sound as jumbled to you as it does to me? I have been a huge fan of yours since I first read one of your poems in a magazine several years' back. I have all your published works and I'm sorry to have said I have read everything you have ever written and for saying you might not be interested in poetry. Its obvious I couldn't have read everything you might have and it's equally clear you do have a poetic soul. Now that I have apologized and eaten enough crow to last me a lifetime, can you forgive me?

I hope you don't mind having a fan as a friend because if you think for a second that this changes our friendship in

the slightest, you are sadly mistaken. So you are my favorite poet and you are someone whose friendship has grown increasingly important to me; I can handle that. If you truly are my friend though, I have one request. Can you forget I ever mentioned juices flowing? Yes, I was blushing and I'm sure it didn't look cute, but thanks for thinking it might have been so. I am going to attach a picture of myself to this e-mail. It was taken on a ski trip to Lake Tahoe. You will see by my wind burned cheeks that a blush doesn't become me. By the way, the other woman in the picture is my Mom.

How is Sara? You and she are in my thoughts often and I wonder how you are coping. I'm glad you're giving consideration to the idea of a nurse.

I want you to rest assured on one point. I see how important your privacy is to you and I will never reveal anything you have, or ever will tell me, not even if they shove lighted bamboo shoots under my fingernails. However, if they threaten to take away my chocolate, I may have to let a few details slip.

You know, I have DJ who I have known as my friend and I have D Jennings, a brilliant poet. Do you think I might just call you Denise? I think she is going to be a combination of both.

Your friend and fan, Randa

Randa sent the e-mail on its way. She closed down the computer and allowed the news of the day to wash over her again. *Denise. Yeah, I like that.* The nurse stood and stretched, then ambled toward the bedroom. *Enough excitement for one day, Miranda, time to put your head on a pillow. Bet I know what I dream about tonight.* Randa went to the bed and turned down the covers revealing freshly laundered sheets. Spying her copy of "Derbyshire Dreams" on the bedside table she looked for the thousandth time at the figure on the back cover.

"Hey there, don't I know you? Oh, that's right, you're my friend. Good night then, friend."

A few minutes later Randa slept and in her dreams she was walking with a tall, dark poet in the rain.

Since early morning a heavy fog had drifted over the land. Dense in its presence, it covered the semi crowded streets like a misty curtain. It forced those who braved the city's roads to drive carefully upon the icy surfaces, their vision impaired and car lights illuminated brightly, reaching out like beacons through the thick fog.

Although it was lunchtime, the street was barely populated. Many people opted instead to stay inside, away from the precarious weather conditions that were both cold and dank. Denise walked down the long road of New Street, ungloved hands pushed deep into the pockets of her thick parka to ward off the chill. A black scarf was wrapped around her neck that matched her woolly hat perfectly. Sara had knitted them both.

Only being able to see no more than twenty yards ahead of her, Denise walked carefully listening out for cars that may have been on the road. The odd echo of footsteps would signal the presence of another pedestrian even before her eyes could pick up the sight. The day was miserable and as such, it in turn was beginning to affect the poet's own mood.

It appeared out of nowhere, due mainly to the murky conditions, and Denise soon found herself standing outside of the DIY store. It was 'Jacob and Sons'; a large family run hardware store; the kind of place where the owners knew you by name and vice versa. Pulling her hands from her coat pockets Denise pushed the door open and stepped into the warmth of the shop.

Instantly a strong smell of paints and varnishes, natural woods shavings and the recognizable aroma of packaged soils besieged her senses. Denise scanned the shop, searching out the items she needed along the rows of heavy stocked shelves.

"Denise, how wonderful to see you again. It has been a while."

The poet turned to the left where a small middle-aged woman with curly brown hair and a navy tabard stood behind the till. She smiled at the friendly woman. "Hi, Julia, how are you and the family?"

"Oh you know, the same. My eldest has just finished college and he is back at home for a while until he decides what to do with the rest of his life. He is helping me out in the mean time. How are you and Sara?"

Denise nodded and looked back into the shop. "Okay." She turned back towards Julia. "I am on a mission, Julia. I am widening a doorframe at home and need a list of items, you know... wood, plaster, and I'll need a new light switch. Do you have those remote control ones?" She asked and after receiving a nod Denise continued. "A large spirit level, cables for rewiring... oh and a hawk and wood float. I'm sure I have everything else I will need. Oh and of course I will need gloss, emulsion and sandpaper."

Julia nodded as she stepped out from behind the counter and approached a set of stairs that led down to the gardening area of the shop. "I'll get my Jamie to help you, then he can assist you on carrying these things to your car!"

The poet shook her head. "Would it be okay if he delivered them, Julia? I don't think my car would be big enough for the lengths of wood I will need etcetera."

The woman nodded. "Of course that would be fine. We will work out the when and where's later."

Denise smiled her thanks. She had gone through the whole of the lower house, the day before and had worked out what needed to be done in order to make the building more accessible for a wheel chair. She had discovered that the door that led into Sara's bedroom, which was in fact part of the extension to the house had a different sized doorframe. It was not as wide as the rest of the house's doors and she instantly realised she needed to resize the frame. So while Diane had arrived to visit Sara that morning, Denise had decided it was perfect time to purchase all the items she would need. The tall woman wanted to get her work started and finished as soon as possible.

Thirty-five minutes later, Denise stood at the till with a trolley loaded down with tools and materials. She watched as each item passed over the scanner then waited patiently for the total.

"Well, Denise, that all comes to one hundred and eleven pounds, seventeen pence. Add the delivery charge that is an extra four pounds."

"Okay." The poet dug her hands into her back pocket and pulled out a handful of notes. She began counting.

Julia shook her head. "Still walking around with money in your pocket? Don't you ever get nervous about carrying cash around like that? You could use a check book or credit card, surely it would be much more convenient... and safer."

Denise shook her head. "Hmm, maybe but I like it this way." She handed the small woman one hundred and twenty pounds and waited for her change. She did have a reason for not wanting to carry around credit cards or check books and it was purely because it would have her name on. She didn't want that and besides - she had been carrying money around in her pocket since she was a teenager. It was a habit she had never grown out of.

Once the transaction was complete, Denise left the shop with the understanding that her materials would be delivered just as soon as the fog had lifted.

The next day Denise walked into the living room with a sigh as she wiped her hands on the corner of her red and black tartan shirt, leaving behind a dusting of powdered plaster. Sara narrowed her eyes as she studied her niece, her face covered in speckles of dirt. "You are not going to come in here and make a mess, young lady."

Poking out her bottom lip, Denise looked down at her appearance. "What's wrong with me?" She brushed her hands over her clothes. "I'm not covered in grime."

"But you are covered in dust and if you sit in here you will get it all over the settee." Sara pursed her lips as she noticed Denise's pout. She pulled down the cream throw that covered the back of the chair and placed it upon the seat beside her. "Sit here then, Miss Sulky."

Denise grinned as she ambled over to her aunt and fell into the chair beside her. A small cloud of dust rose from her clothes. She smiled sheepishly. "Sorry."

Rolling her eyes the old woman looked out of the doorway to where she could just see through the kitchen and into the back passage where the dark green-carpeted ground was covered with a thick sheet of clear plastic. "So how is your destruction of my bedroom doorframe coming along? I think you have brought most of it in with you."

The poet nodded. "Well fine thank you. Considering I have never done it before, that 'Weekend builder' book Carl lent me is coming in great use. I don't think that book has even been opened. I'm sure his wife brought it hoping to get him to try his hand at something other than constructing buildings out of matchsticks." Denise smiled. "There isn't even a crease down the spine."

"Just as long as you are putting it to good use. And by that I mean that you are following all those instructions carefully. When you came in from the garden with that great big hammer I think my heart skipped a beat." Sara watched Denise as she picked up the laptop that was placed upon the side coffee table. "You will have to teach me how to play with that thing."

"It's not a toy, Sara!"

"Oh like I don't see you playing card games on it."

"Oh okay." Denise smiled impishly. "After I have finished I will show you the games then you can use them while I continue with the doorframe. I need to cut the electric soon and this has a battery so it will keep you occupied if you want." Denise tapped her password into the computer; her fingers flew over the keyboard with swift efficiency.

Sara smiled. "Okay."

Denise nodded as she accessed her emails and went straight to Randa's link with a smile. She read through with Sara looking over her shoulder.

Sara beamed. "Is that her? The younger one I mean. Is that Randa the nurse?"

With an expression of complete surprise, Denise nodded. "Yeah. Wow, huh?"

"I'll tell you what, DJ." Sara twisted the laptop around to gain a better look at the picture. She waggled her brows. "If I were thirty years younger!"

Jaw falling as she stared at her aunt in disbelief, Denise shook her head. "Sara! I will tell her you said that!"

"You wouldn't dare."

Two sets of blue eyes stared at each other in a duel of wits. Denise folded. "Okay, you are right I wouldn't dare!"

"Chicken."

Denise grinned as she looked back at the screen. "No, I just don't want to scare her off by thinking I am living with a letch. She might think it runs in the family."

The old woman chuckled. "It does, you just haven't reached your zenith yet. Wait until you do because I may have to start sending out warnings."

"Funny!" Denise said as she began to compose her reply.

Randa,

First of all let me apologize for throwing you. I didn't mean to shock you but I needed to be truthful and if we were to continue to be friends that was important to me.

As for forgiving you, I don't think there is anything to forgive. I didn't mean to tease you about what you said. I think I found it hard to resist because I'd never found myself in this situation before and I guess I didn't know how to react.

By the way, just for you I will forget about the juices remark; but it will be hard.

Sara is doing as expected. Yesterday I started making alterations to the house to make it more accessible for a wheel chair and tomorrow she has an appointment at the hospital.

Thank you for understanding my need for privacy. It means a lot and you can rest assured that I will not let anybody take away your chocolate without a fight. It is in both our interests after all. Either that or I will send you over some of mine; I am well aware of the supremacy of Brit chocolate!

Thank you for the picture I was very surprised to receive it. Sara was sitting next to me while I opened it and she says you are very attractive. I would have to agree. I would send you a picture in return but they are in short supply around here. Neither Sara nor myself own a camera, and we are both a little shy of the lens. Well there is a box full of pictures of me as a child with a chocolate smeared mouth or as a rebel teen in my punk phase! Instead I am attaching a poem, one that has never been published but I hope you will like.

If you want to use Denise then that is fine. I have been known as DJ for so long that I tend to use it as habit now. Whatever you feel comfortable with is okay with me.

Anyway I better get back to my demolition and rebuilding of the doorframe; it needs widening by five inches.

Can I ask how long you have worked on the Brightwood site?

Faithfully yours
Denise.

Chapter 10

For Randa, the two months that had passed since Denise had sent the unpublished poem were busy but nearly perfect. She had a job she loved, a home she was proud of and a friendship that bordered on so much more. Communication between the two women was easier and frequent. Daily e-mails found their way across the wide gulf separating them and brought them closer. Family histories, amusing stories and the little dramas of everyday life filled their messages. Always there as an undercurrent was the specter of the increasing debility of Sara. Randa felt the increasing stress and dismay within Denise. Not that the poet ever complained, but the tone of the e-mail would change on one of Sara's bad days. And the bad days were becoming much more frequent.

Randa had tried to the best of her ability to be supportive of her friend. She consulted with physical and occupational therapists, nutritionists and researchers in order to give Denise the latest and best medical advice. In addition, she tried to give Denise a sense of normalcy also. The nurse filled her e-mail with little anecdotes from her life and slowly was gifted the same from the rather private Brit. Every revelation about the other woman's life was precious to Randa, instinctively feeling none were easy to make. The nurse gently teased the poet, using several monikers for the woman all in the same e-mail. Randa would call her Denise, then DJ, then D Jennings and then the Artist formerly known as DJ. They also continued their ongoing debate of American versus British chocolate.

And she is so wrong! thought Randa. The nurse was curled up comfortably on the couch in a sweat suit and large fluffy slippers with the growling countenance of the Tasmanian Devil popping up from each toe. She carefully extracted a silver foil wrapped chocolate from the *Ethel M* box and popped it into her mouth. The rich flavor draped like chocolate silk on her tongue. Biting slowly into the center, Randa tasted the rum laced sweet cream and felt the warmth of the alcohol in her mouth provide the perfect balance for the cream and chocolate. *Oooh, DJ, it's a pity you are missing out on this!*

On the coffee table were the remains of her opened

Christmas gifts from Derek. Her friend was leaving for Atlanta to spend the holidays with his family and insisted Randa open her gifts though there was a still more than a week left before Christmas. Now gift paper and open boxes littered the floor as surveyed her booty. Derek had always been generous with his friends and this year was no exception. Randa had received the Taz slippers; two tickets to the Oakland Raider's last home game of the season, the chocolates and a thick volume of British poetry with a bookmark at the four poems written by D Jennings.

As Randa's mind wandered to the poet, she wondered if her Christmas package had arrived yet. To make the Christmas deadline for overseas packages she had selected her gifts weeks ago and mailed it out soon thereafter. A cream-colored hand crocheted shawl was sent for Sara and two presents were included for DJ. The antique cameo locket was simple yet elegant and opened to reveal an area for a small picture. On the card with the package Randa wrote she hoped Denise might find a photo of Sara suitable for that space. The other item was a small teddy bear wearing a sweater of the nurse's design. Cross-stitched onto the white sweater were the words "American chocolates rule!" Randa chuckled to herself, knowing this would be another salvo in the Great Transcontinental Chocolate Debate.

She glanced over to her Christmas tree and the box that had arrived from England the day before. Randa was surprised Denise had found the time to send her a gift. The nurse knew how much time Sara's care took now and knew the poet had little enough time for herself. The nurses DJ had interviewed so far were found lacking for one reason or another but Randa felt the real issue was probably how uncomfortable the poet and her aunt were with giving up that independence and privacy they cherished so much. The blond felt a stab of pain at the thought of the struggles her friend was going through. She stared at the twinkling lights on the fragrant pine tree through vision slightly blurred with tears.

Your friend? Randa thought. *Why don't you just admit it? You've been half in love with the woman for weeks and it wouldn't take much encouragement for you to fall completely.* With a clarity that comes with confession, she knew the words to be true. She couldn't put a finger on the moment it had happened, but there it was. Miranda Leigh Martin was totally besotted with a person she had never met in person and of whom she had never even seen a picture.

Maybe it was when she sent me the poem, mused Randa. The nurse moved from the couch to the opposite side of the room where the orange flames crackled in the fireplace. To the right of the fireplace was a document hand printed in calligraphy and encased in an oak frame. The poem had no title that she was aware of, but it had touched Randa so deeply she had trembled a little at the very first reading. It was immediately after the first reading she knew the poem had to have a special a place in her home as it had in her heart. Randa read the words again, though by now she knew them by heart.

Last night I saw you
Through my minds eye
Though I've never seen your face
And when you smiled
You stole my heart
With dignity and grace

I saw your depths
When I gazed upon
The windows of your soul
Through an ocean green
I saw your light
To which my heart took hold

A honeyed halo
Of purest gold
Framed your physical shell
Waking my heart
A yearning called
And instantly I fell

Yet when morning came
Your vision faded
To the magic of the night
And my heart did weep
For the presence that only
Fills my somnolent sight

As the days now pass
I only live
For the nights when I can sleep
Just to see you
And feel your touch
Build the memories I keep.

Randa sighed at the unrestrained beauty of the words and felt a delicious chill pass through her. A part of her wanted to boot the computer and dash off another e-mail to Denise just to feel that sense of connection that was present every time they communicated.

Don't be an idiot, Randa. Two e-mails in the space of a dozen hours? She'll probably think you are obsessed or...something. The blonde walked back over to the couch, turning off the room lights as she went. She pulled a quilt up over her legs and settled back against the cushions, just watching the small twinkling lights of the tree jump and flash. She looked again at the securely wrapped package from Denise again, *yeah...or something.*

Denise could never have imagined just how the events of the past two months would change so rapidly. She had given up writing altogether, a higher purpose taking precedence over even the most cherished aspect of her life. Sara. Her aunt had declined at a rate much swifter than even the doctors had expected. During the first few weeks after Denise had widened the doorframe to Sara's bedroom the old woman had begun to lose all strength in her ability to walk. It wasn't long before the need of a wheelchair became a high priority.

It had been a hard transition to make, neither Denise nor her aunt were prepared for the loss of independence that it entailed. Not only had Sara's lower body strength departed but her upper body's strength too. There were the occasional good days when Sara did manage to complete the odd task by herself, but for the most part it became impossible and she declined a little more every day.

To say that Denise hadn't felt the strain would have been a lie. Even the poet would admit to herself that some nights when she had finally made her way to bed - if she hadn't fallen asleep on the sofa first - she would pass out as soon as her head hit the pillow.

It wasn't just looking after Sara that took it out of Denise. There were many times while she would be dressing Sara or brushing her teeth that the old woman would just sit and cry. Not that Denise minded in the slightest, she was adamant about taking care of her aunt. She would do whatever she had to and whatever it took. Denise had also made many alterations to the house. She had converted the down stairs bathroom, installing a lift-able seat into the shower to make it easier for Sara to still enjoy the luxury of taking a warm shower. She had constructed a higher frame for her bed to make lifting from the wheel chair to bed and vice versa much more convenient.

Days would alternate between good and bad. Between days when Sara would seem stable to days when her emotions would overwhelm her, or her disease would advance further and she would lose a little more strength and independence. Denise did know that she needed somebody and had gone through the motions of interviewing several nurses. But deep down inside something was missing. She felt none of these men or women would look after Sara the way she wanted. Denise also knew that as much as Sara had insisted that they hire a nurse the old woman hated the idea of having a complete stranger look after her in ways that she was finding difficult enough allowing her niece to undertake herself.

Through it all Denise had managed to keep her resolve with the help of one person. Randa. Though thousands of miles away, the nurse had provided help and emotional support to Denise when she needed it most. The friendship had grown, and even Denise would acknowledge that. Never did she expect that she would be able to share aspects of her life with anybody the way she had done with this woman.

Sometimes when the day had been especially draining, Denise would retreat to her room and look at the picture of the woman who unknowingly gave Denise the emotional strength she needed to carry on when times were rough. Never had she felt the ability to be so open with another individual and never had she thought she would come to care for somebody as much

99

as she found herself doing with this woman. She enjoyed their correspondence, their contention on the superiority of British or American chocolate and their easy friendship.

As Christmas approached she had no doubts about the fact that she would send Randa a gift and Sara had wanted to do so as well. Denise had told Sara about their constant chocolate debates and so Sara had asked her niece to send the nurse a selection of her favourite chocolates. Denise on the other hand found the prospect of purchasing a gift slightly more difficult. She wanted to give Randa something that echoed her appreciation and sentiment towards the woman, but she found it hard to recognise exactly what that was. Fortunately it didn't take long for her unconscious mind to make the decision and she just hoped Randa would remember exactly what this object was.

Denise had ventured into her bedroom and had crouched down under her bed to retrieve a small shoebox. Inside this box she kept the trinkets and memorabilia of her parents. Her fathers silver hip flask, cuff links, and a single cigar that was a constant reminder of his aroma. Her mother's earrings, bottle of perfume that had long since spoiled, lace handkerchief embroidered with her initials and an antique bracelet. It was the bracelet that Denise was looking for. A simple golden charm bracelet with one charm, a golden capsule that unscrewed to reveal a small scroll of paper. Upon this scroll in very small print was Shakespeare's sonnet, number 116. As a child the charm and sonnet inside had fascinated Denise. She had explained to Randa that it was this poem that had sparked her desire for the lyrical verse.

Hoping Randa would appreciate and comprehend the raison d'être behind the gift; Denise had placed it into a small, red velvet inlaid wooden box and had wrapped it in silver paper with a light blue ribbon. She had mailed the package a day later.

The door to the living room thrust open and Denise walked slowly inside. Pale and gaunt, she dragged her feet over to the nearest chair and fell onto the cushioned surface with little thought as to exactly where she was. Hands trembling the poet looked aimlessly around the room yet she noticed nothing. Emotions bombarded her senses.

Unable to stop them, tears came unbidden. Vision clouding, her lip trembled as her composure broke and heavy sobs wracked her frame. Denise slumped forward, elbows upon on her knees, head resting upon her clenched fists. Her shoulder shook with a release of distraught emotion and fear.

She cried for long minutes, heavy tears running down pale cheeks, and when at last she was able to take a much-needed breath and gain her composure, Denise needed the presence of one person.

Reaching for the laptop that she now kept permanently on standby upon the sofa she lifted the lid and began to write with shaky hands.

Randa,
I'm sorry for the unexpected mail but I just needed to talk to somebody - to you.
I nearly lost her, Randa.

Denise took another calming breath as she felt her eyes once again sting with tears.

We were eating lunch when suddenly she couldn't swallow. What she was eating got stuck in her throat and it must have blocked her windpipe because she started to choke. I was so scared because for an instant I didn't know what to do. She was gasping and choking, and I did the only thing I could think of and that was to hit her on the back, then try and do that Heimlich manoeuvre to stop her choking. I managed to clear it but it was so close and I was so scared.
I don't know how much longer I can keep this up, Randa. I know now that there is no question that I do need help but I don't know where to turn for the best. I know she needs me but I don't want to do something thoughtlessly that could cause anything like that to happen again. I could see the fear in Sara's eyes and afterward she just cried herself to sleep. All I could do was hold her. I can't bear to see this happen to her, it hurts so much to see her suffer like this. I'm not enough for her and I have to admit this.

I'm sorry to spring this on you but I just needed to talk to you. I trust you implicitly and value any help or advice you can give me more than you could imagine.

Yours,

Denise.

Randa slumped back in her chair, tears filling her eyes as she felt the hurt and despair of her friend coming through from her words. The nurse had never in her whole life wanted to hold and comfort anyone as much as she wanted to right now. It was intolerable that she was so far from the person who needed her. Randa left her chair and walked straight over to the present Denise had sent her.

I don't give a damn if it isn't Christmas yet; I need to feel close to her while I try to come up with something to say that can help her. Randa opened the box and removed the packages within. Randa opened the first package and found a collection of chocolates. *British chocolates,* she noted with a soft smile and saw that Sara had sent them. *The woman is so ill but took the time to think of me. Amazing.* Then she removed a small package and unwrapped it to find a wooden box. Randa gasped as she opened the box to find the lovely bracelet with its unusual charm. Looking closely at the charm, she saw that it was in actuality a small capsule. A tiny scroll fell from the capsule and the blonde read the sonnet written there. Randa remembered DJ saying how touched she was by the sonnet, how it had inspired her, how it had basically been the beginning of her life as a poet.

Let me not to the marriage of true minds
Admit impediments: Love is not love
Which alters when it alteration finds,
Or bends with the remover to remove.
Oh, no! it is an ever-fixed mark
That looks on tempests and is never shaken;
It is the star to every wandering bark,

102

Whose worth's unknown, although his height be taken
Loves not time's fool though rosy lips and cheeks
Within his bending sickle's compass come
Love alters not with his brief hours and weeks
But bears it out even to the edge of doom.
If this be error and upon me proved,
I never writ and no man ever loved.

Randa wasn't sure quite what to make of the gift. The jewelry was lovely but what was Denise trying to tell her with the sonnet? *True minds. No matter what misfortunes happen, true love can never be shaken; it has a fixed place like the North Star. Time can cut down youth and beauty but it can't alter or destroy true love, which is immortal.* Was Denise reaching out to her? Did she feel the connection?

True minds, that's got to be the key. Our minds do seem to be in harmony. Okay then, if I were the one with the sick aunt, what do I think Denise would do?

Randa placed the bracelet on her wrist and walked to the phone. She crossed the fingers on her left hand while dialing the toll free information number.

"Can I have the number for British Airways?"

Chapter 11

As the wheels touched down at Heathrow Airport, Randa reflected back on what had surely been the busiest three days of her life. After she managed to get a ticket to London she had wrangled two weeks leave from Brightwood. They hadn't been too pleased but another nurse had just completed her training so a temporary replacement wasn't hard to find. Then Randa had to arrange for someone to watch the house, get travelers checks and change some dollars to pounds. She packed one large duffel bag and a small carry on for her purse, tickets and important papers. It wasn't until the night before she departed that the blonde remembered to call her mother. Randa recalled the conversation and how her mom had played Devil's Advocate.

"But what if she already hired a nurse?"

"Then I'll have a good visit and come on home in two weeks."

"What if she really is an axe murderer or one of those Internet psychopaths?"

"Mom, I've been talking to her for months. I think I would have picked up on something by now. She's my friend and she needs me."

"What if she doesn't want you there?" For that question the nurse had no answer.

Maybe I should have e-mailed Denise and told her what I was planning. Maybe following my heart wasn't the smartest thing to do. I'm not the sharpest knife in the drawer sometimes, I guess. Any further speculation was cut short by the flight attendant welcoming the passengers to London.

The nurse deplaned and headed with the other passengers to bag claim and Customs. As she stood in line, Randa silently thanked her mother for the previous year's three-day cruise to Ensenada, Mexico. Her mother had been under the mistaken impression that a passport was needed instead of the driver's license that actually was. If that error hadn't been made, Randa would never had been able to make the trip on such short notice or be standing here in line with a pristine passport. After she was beckoned forward to the Custom's clerk she was asked several questions and received her first passport stamp ever.

Given leave to enter the United Kingdom, Randa couldn't quite keep the grin off her face. Finding a traveler's information kiosk, the nurse found out which of the many train stations would take her north to Derbyshire as well as the timetable for the trains themselves. Exiting the airport she found the line, a *queue* as she learned, for a taxi. She shivered as she met the chilly, humid day. *Good thing I paid attention to Denise when she said how cold and wet the weather was. She wasn't kidding.*

Climbing in the back of a black cab, Randa gave the driver her destination and sat back to stare outside at the first European country she had ever been in. *I can't believe I'm really here. The land of kings, queens and amazing history, but all I can think about is seeing a poet and her aunt.* She felt the jet lag and fatigue start to catch up with her and her eyes drooped closed. The voice of the cab driver, a curious mixture of English and East Indian, woke her as the cab pulled up to St. Pancras station. The blonde paid the fare, thanked the driver and walked into the train station. Purchasing her ticket, Randa used the forty-five minute wait until departure to freshen up in the station restroom. Reflected in the mirror was a slightly haggard young woman with the beginning of dark circles under her eyes. *Looking good, Randa, who wouldn't welcome you with open arms looking like this?* She thought sarcastically.

Making her way to the correct platform, Randa boarded the train and settled in a seat by the window. Leaving London and heading out into the green countryside, she began to relax with the rhythm of the train. The conductor came by and inspected her ticket then left her to her thoughts. *Okay, I know the town is Bakewell and I suppose I can get a taxi there to Denise's house, but then what? Will she ask me to stay? Would she have room? Can I find a bed and breakfast? Guess I didn't quite think this whole thing through. This is just great; I'm going to be on tenterhooks the whole way there.* Mentally kicking herself, Randa leaned her head back and closed her eyes. The moment of darkness was enough though and she slipped easily into a dreamless sleep.

"Miss? Miss?" Randa opened her eyes in temporary bewilderment. Seeing the face of the conductor looming over her, she put together the pieces of her whereabouts.

"Didn't want you to miss your station. Bakewell is next, about 10 minutes." The nurse thanked the conductor and checking her watch was surprised to see two hours had gone by. She felt somewhat refreshed, but thought she probably didn't look it. She gathered her belongings together and in a few minutes the train glided smoothly to a stop. Following the few passengers out of the station, Randa found a lone cab waiting at the curb. She gave the driver Denise's address, an action that met with two raised bushy eyebrows.

"That would be Haversham Road, you said? Not many fares to that address." The driver looked at her expectantly in the rear view mirror as he pulled out into the sparse afternoon traffic.

"Really." Randa made no other comment, knowing how private a person Denise was. The journey was not long and the taxi soon pulled up in front of a house slightly larger than the others in the area, but similar in design. The yard was well planned, but seemed somewhat neglected. Heaving her duffel bag to her shoulder, she made her way up the steps and stopped at the door.

The coward dies a thousand times, the brave man dies but once. With those words running through her head, Randa rapped sharply on the door four times. She waited a moment and was about to knock a second time when the door swung open sharply. Standing in the doorway was unquestionably the most attractive woman Randa had ever laid eyes on. The nurse's breath stilled, as she was held transfixed by impossibly blue eyes. Randa swallowed hard and worked to find the words to form a coherent sentence. Finally she held up her right hand revealing the charm bracelet dangling from her wrist.

"Denise?" she managed to croak. "Thank you for the Christmas present."

Denise was standing in the kitchen in front of the wide sink; holding a potato in one hand and a knife in the other as she carefully peeled the large vegetable. She was preparing dinner for Sara and herself after deciding to make a large cottage pie. It would last them two or three days and would help to lessen the amount of chores Denise had to get done during the following days. Looking after Sara had turned into a full time job and although she wouldn't have it any other way or complain in the slightest, Denise was hard pressed to accomplish everything she needed to during the day.

There was also the point that Carl had been badgering her over the past week, reminding her she had a deadline for a new book to meet. Writing had taken a back seat while Denise was looking after Sara and although she desperately needed to fulfill that desire to write, Sara would always come first. She had explained the situation to Carl and he was in the process of trying to push back her deadline to allow more time.

Denise winced as she felt again the knot in her back, the result of sleeping in Sara's vanity chair all night. The constant need to be there for Sara just in case she needed anything throughout the night had forced Denise to spend the last three nights sleeping in Sara's room. Sara wasn't aware of this of course as Denise wouldn't go to sleep until Sara was herself asleep and she would always wake up well before her aunt.

Dropping the white potato back into the bowl of warm water, Denise swirled her hands around the container until she located another large potato. She commenced peeling.

With a particular frown that had frequently graced her features over the last three days, Denise thought again of Randa. She had received no word from the woman since she had sent her last message after Sara's choking incident. If she was to admit it, Denise was feeling a little anxious. The fear that she may have scared the woman off with her seemingly desperate plea for help or advice wouldn't leave her mind. *Maybe she has just been really busy with work,* thought Denise, *or isn't bothered?* The poet shook her head, doubting that somehow. She thought back to the parcel that had arrived only yesterday. She had recognized the return address immediately and knew it was a package from Randa. Denise would usually have placed it under her tree but she hadn't even had time to purchase one, so she had placed it in her study.

Suddenly an unexpected knocking from the front door caused her to jump. The sharp knife that she held tightly in her

107

left hand slipped across the potato and into her thumb.

"Oh for crying out loud... damn it!" she muttered and dropped the knife into the sink as she grabbed a tea towel and wrapped it around her hand to stop herself from getting any blood upon her blue denim shirt. She moved through the house to answer the door.

Denise pulled the door open swiftly and paused as a seemingly familiar face confronted her. She frowned again as she looked down at the blonde haired woman who portrayed an expression to that of a deer caught in the headlights.

Moving her right hand slightly behind her back to hide the blood that she could feel seeping into the material she waited for the woman to speak. *Why do I know that face?*

"Denise?" The blonde woman said in a nervous voice. "Thank you for the Christmas present."

Cerulean eyes travelled down to the wrist that was held out in front of her. Denise noticed and recognised her mother's charm bracelet and she quickly looked back up to her visitor. The blonde hair and green eyes suddenly looked very familiar and her heart hammered anxiously in her chest. "Randa?"

The nervous nod followed by a shy smile helped to pull the poet from her shock. *Oh my god!* She blinked once and came to her senses. "Um... I err..." Looking past the woman she noticed the heavy bag swung over her shoulder. A slight pulling her to the side gave away the weight of the hefty carrier. She moved forward. "Here let me take that." Denise held out her free hand.

"No that's..."

The poet noticed Randa pause as she debated her request.

"Okay, thanks." Randa relented and Denise smiled as she accepted the bag from Randa then moved to the side to allow the smaller woman into the house.

"Come in."

Both women remained silent as Denise closed the front door and motioned for Randa to move into the front room. They walked quietly into the living room and Denise shut the door, blocking the chill of the hallway from entering the warm room. The open coal fire was blazing in the hearth.

Denise placed the large duffle bag down beside the nearest chair and looked nervously up at her most unexpected visitor. She watched, as the blonde took in her surroundings, hardly able to believe this was happening. *If this is a dream then let me sleep a while longer.* Moving from one foot to another Denise kept her hand slightly behind her back. She looked intently at Randa as their eyes met and held.

Randa was the first to break the silence. "I know this is really unexpected."

Denise shook her head quickly. "No… well yes but… I mean… it's okay." She smiled self-consciously as she noticed the peculiar way in which Randa was looking at her. "I can't believe you came all the way from America. Is this… um… a passing visit? Are you on holiday or on your way to somewhere in particular?"

The nurse paused momentarily before speaking. "I got your e-mail. You sounded pretty upset and you said you needed my help." She held out her arms. "And well… here I am." She smiled. "It's wonderful to meet you."

She came all the way over here for me, because I needed her? "It's wonderful to meet you too. I can't believe you flew over here." Suddenly remembering her manners, Denise motioned towards the couch. "Please, sit."

Randa backed up slightly but didn't sit down. "I debated all the way here whether I was doing the right thing. I assure you I don't normally act so impulsively, it's just that… well…" She shrugged, seemingly not knowing what else to say.

"Thank you." Denise said with a smile.

There was a moment of silence as both women studied each other.

"How's Sara?"

"Sleeping," Denise replied, "at the moment. I thought while I had the time I would make the dinner." She held up her covered right hand. The blood was visible as it soaked into the towel. "I had a bit of an accident while I was peeling the potatoes."

Eyes wide with shock, Randa stepped forward. "Why didn't you say something? Are you all right? Let me take a look." Awkwardness all but forgotten, Randa took a hold of Denise's hand and gently peeled away the blue and white checked cloth. "Where is your nearest sink?"

Feeling slightly bewildered, Denise looked toward the door that led into the kitchen. "Um… through there, in the kitchen. It is okay you know."

109

They walked into the kitchen. Denise internally cursed the fact that she had made such a mess while preparing the dinner. The bowl full of water and half peeled potatoes was out upon the draining board. The work surfaces were covered with raw vegetables, pots, pans, mince and a selection of herbs.

"Hey, I'm a nurse, it's what I do. You should have said you were hurt sooner."

Denise smirked as Randa turned on the tap and held her still bleeding thumb under the slow stream of water. "Well I was going to tell whoever it was at the door to sod off." She smiled. "That was until I realised it was you. I didn't want you to then be confronted by a crazy woman with blood all over her hands." Denise chuckled. "I swear there is no horse's head in the freezer!" She paused. "Well there may be a trout complete with head but I swear that is all." Realising she was babbling, Denise closed her mouth. She looked down into Randa's smiling eyes.

"If I thought you were the kind of person to keep heads in your freezer then I don't think I would have even considered coming here."

"I can't believe you came at all."

To Denise it felt almost surreal to be standing in the same room as the woman who she had been thinking about no more than ten minutes before.

Randa inspected the wound closely. "It's a little deep, but I think you'll live." She smiled up at Denise. "Do you have a band-aid?"

Denise froze as she looked into dark green eyes. "Um… if you mean plasters then yes, in here." She moved over to a small drawer in the corner of the kitchen and pulled it open. Denise rummaged around the clutter of lint, cotton buds and empty paracetamol boxes. "Here's one." She pulled a plaster from the drawer and handed it to Randa then observed as the blonde opened the packaging and wrapped the flesh coloured tape around her thumb.

A sudden thought occurred to her. "Randa, do you have a place to stay?"

"Well…"

Denise noticed the hesitation in Randa's eyes.

"Not yet. I thought I could get a room in a local bed and breakfast or something like that."

The poet shook her head. "Oh believe me you don't want to get a hotel or B and B room in this part of the country. It's around the peak district; people come here for holidays and weekend breaks. I don't know what you consider reasonable but I can't have you paying when there is a bed here you are more than welcome to use."

Neither woman realised that Randa was still holding Denise's hand.

"I don't exactly have a spare room so to speak but I do have a spring action fold away bed chair in my study. It is comfortable; I know that as I have used it myself. If you would like you are welcome to stay here with us."

"If it's okay with Sara too then that would be great."

"She wouldn't mind in the slightest." Denise paused and nervously bit the corner of her lip. "So... what do you say?" she asked hopefully and waited, as green eyes looked up at her in what she thought was consideration to her offer.

Randa nodded. "Absolutely... yes."

"Great."

They smiled at each other until both became aware that they were still holding hands. Simultaneously the women pulled away.

Denise studied the cold floor. "Um..." *What's wrong with me?* Looking back up the poet caught Randa's eye. "Do you want to get settled in? I have some wardrobe space you can use for your clothes. I'll show you around this humble abode," she smirked, "and if you want you could actually take your coat off. It maybe cold outside but it's bloody warm in here."

"I was beginning to feel it." Randa stated as she started to unzip her jacket. "It must be your open fire... it's nice."

As Denise led the way back into the front room she looked down at the smouldering hearth. "It's a different story when it comes to sweeping the chimney though. Then it is a big pain in the arse."

"But worth it?" Randa asked.

Denise smiled warmly. "To feel its heat while sitting in the darkness with only the flames as a point of illumination and feel the solitude and tranquillity it instils as your mind wanders. Burning in the darkest night... a time for lovers. Emitting heat like a passionate embrace." Denise shrugged. "Yeah, it's worth it." She bent down and picked up Randa's large bag. "Are you

111

ready for the grand tour?"

The blonde nurse nodded mutely.

"Okay then." Denise opened the door to the hallway. "Let's go."

Chapter 12

Randa blinked rapidly a few times as she followed Denise through the house. *My God, did she just make up a poem on the spot? That woman has more romance in her little finger than most people have in their whole bodies.* The nurse shook herself mentally and struggled to regain the equilibrium that had been lost the moment the door was opened. *Get it together for Pete's sake! You've been staring at her like an idiot! Do you want her to think you're some sort of slack jawed fool?*

She brought her attention back to Denise who was taking them upstairs and entering a comfortable looking room with antique furniture and an overly large bed. Denise flipped the duffel bag onto the bed and Randa noticed the ease with which her friend handled the heavy object. Actually Randa had been noticing Denise all the way up the stairs having an excellent view as she trailed behind the older woman.

"This is it except for Sara's room downstairs," Denise was saying. "There should be enough extra space in the wardrobe there for your things. Let me know if you need more hangers or anything." The tall woman seemed to hesitate a moment then said "Would you like to meet Sara now or would you like to freshen up a bit first? You've had a long trip."

"Is that your way of telling me I'm a bit over ripe?" Seeing the other woman's look of discomfort she immediately said "I'm just teasing, honestly. When I'm tired my sense of humor gets a little odd. Truthfully, I could use a quick shower before I meet Sara. If she gets as shocked as you did by my arrival, the least I can do is look presentable when it happens."

Denise mumbled something the nurse couldn't quite hear. "What was that, Denise?"

The poet straightened and cleared her throat. "I said it was a nice kind of shock." The women smiled at one another as the friendship that had started out electronically became cemented a little more in the physical world. Denise broke the silence by pointing out the small upstairs bathroom and shower then fetching Randa a large bath towel and washcloth.

"If there's nothing else you need I'll just go downstairs and finish dinner preparations. Just come down whenever you're finished and we'll go in to see Sara. I know she'll enjoy meeting you." She turned to leave but was halted by the sound of Randa's voice.

"Denise?"

The brunette turned and lifted her eyebrows in question.

"Be careful down there, okay?" She gave a thumbs up sign to Denise and was rewarded with a blush and a small smile from the woman. The door closed and Randa was left alone for the first time since meeting DJ. A happy smile made its way across her face as she realized she was in England and in the company of someone who was rapidly becoming one of the most important people in her life. Her subconscious rebelled at that thought, challenging her to come up with somebody who was more significant to her, but the nurse stomped down on that idea.

Don't get carried away, Miranda. Remember why you're here. You came because Denise needed a friend and possibly a nurse. If there were anyone she would want to get carried away with though, it would be Denise. With a sigh, Randa started putting her clothes away in the wardrobe. It was so strange to feel this way especially in light of her checkered social history. She had dated a few men, experimented with sex and yet found herself oddly unmoved. She wondered if she might be gay and gave in to the desire to be with a woman in a physical way. She admitted to herself that the sex was far more pleasurable, but no one had come close to capturing her heart. From that point, Randa just figured she would wait for the right person rather than wasting time with the wrong ones.

Finishing her task, Randa made her way to the bathroom and stood under the warm stream of water in the shower. As the water cascaded down her frame, the nurse felt the tension in her body release. She closed her eyes and allowed herself to see once again the incredibly blue eyes of her friend. *They're just the color of Lake Tahoe in the summer; so very blue and inviting.*

Randa stepped from the shower, dried off and dressed quickly in black jeans and an emerald green turtleneck sweater. Finding her way back to the kitchen, Randa was able to watch Denise unobserved from the doorway for a few moments. She

114

noticed things about the poet she had missed earlier. The woman looked positively exhausted. There were small dark lines under the blue eyes and she unconsciously stretched her back as she worked, as if trying to work out a kink. Denise stilled suddenly and looked up as though she had felt Randa's eyes on her.

Neither woman spoke for a moment until Randa entered the kitchen and said, "You look tired."

Denise's shoulders seemed to drop a little. "I suppose I am...a bit. Sara's been increasingly ill lately. She doesn't rest well and I don't feel as if I can leave her at those times." The poet dropped her eyes.

Randa's heart went out to the brunette and she laid her hand on Denise's arm. "You've done everything you could by yourself, but I can see you're getting worn out." When the poet would have protested, Randa stopped her saying "Don't bother to deny it, I know what too many shifts look like. I've seen it on myself often enough to know."

Denise said nothing so Randa asked "Do you think we could go see Sara now?"

The taller woman nodded and said "She's up in the wheelchair now and I've told her of your arrival. She's anxious to meet you." The pair made their way to Sara's room and found the woman sitting quietly looking out the window. Denise went immediately to her aunt's side.

"Sara? This is Randa Martin, my friend from America I told you about. Randa, this is my aunt, Sara Jennings." The older woman in the chair turned striking blue eyes on the nurse, eyes so very similar to those of her niece. The nurse tried to suppress the need to look at DJ's aunt from a professional viewpoint as she greeted the woman, but found her training taking over in spite of her best intentions. Several things immediately brought themselves to Randa's attention but she ignored them for a moment to take Sara's offered hand. The grip was weak but Randa had an impression of strength from this woman that had little to do with her physical being.

"Welcome to England, Miss Martin. I hope you'll enjoy your stay here. I was very happy when DJ told me you would be spending time with us. Between you and I, she doesn't see nearly enough of her friends these days, not that she's ever been much for socializing a great deal anyway." She gave the blonde a conspiratorial wink. Randa could feel herself warming to this woman who had obviously not lost her sense of humor along with her muscle strength.

"It's a pleasure to meet you, Ms. Jennings and please call me Randa. I'll see what I can do about Denise's lack of socializing while I'm here." She returned Sara's wink and the two women laughed.

Denise pretended affront and said "I see my life is being planned well enough without me so I shall remove myself to the kitchen to sulk and check on the progress of dinner." She left to the continued chuckles of the other two women.

"She's a lot of fun to tease, isn't she?" said Randa. Sara laid a frankly speculative gaze upon the blonde.

"You know, Randa, that's just what I said not too long ago. That very same thing."

A little later, Randa found Denise in the kitchen placing a large cottage pie into the oven. "I like your aunt a lot. It's obvious why you love her like you do, she's pretty remarkable."

"She likes you too, I can tell. Why do I have the feeling things are going to be interesting around here for a while?"

Randa chuckled at her friend's pretended discomfort but then sobered. "Denise, I'd like to speak to you seriously a minute. I'd like you to call Sara's doctor today and arrange to get her an oxygen tank and nasal prongs. I noticed her nail beds were a little dusky when I shook her hand and she has slight difficulty finishing her sentences with a single breath. Her respiratory muscles may have weakened and I think she isn't getting enough oxygen to her system. It may be why she's restless at night too. Some low flow oxygen should help."

DJ looked devastated. "I can't believe I didn't see those things! I'm supposed to be her caregiver, how could I have missed those signs? How am I going to tell Sara?"

"You aren't trained to look for them in the first place and it's probably come on so gradually you wouldn't have noticed yet. Didn't you tell me she's only not been sleeping well for the past few days?" At Denise's nod the nurse continued. "Well,

116

there you go then, there's no reason to be upset. By the way, Sara took the news well when I explained it to her a few minutes ago."

"You told her she would need oxygen?"

"Well I figured if I could explain the reason for it to her she wouldn't be as frightened by the prospect of needing the oxygen. It didn't seem right to make the observation and then just dump it in your lap. Sara's an intelligent woman, she understood completely." Randa paused, noticing Denise staring at her. "Um, Denise…I'm afraid my jet lag is catching up with me again. Do you think I have enough time before dinner to get a nap? My eyelids feel like they're made of lead."

"Oh, of course. I haven't made up the fold away bed yet but you could sleep on my bed for now. You'll find an extra blanket in the chest near the window. I'll wake you when dinner is ready."

"That sounds great, Denise, I really appreciate it." Randa turned and exited the kitchen looking over her shoulder briefly to see Denise watching her as she went. Randa gave her a brief smile then continued on upstairs. Finding a soft quilt in the cedar chest, Randa settled herself on Denise's bed. The faint scent of herbal shampoo and something that must have been unique to Denise lay lightly on the pillow. Randa clutched the fragrant object to her and slipped into a weary slumber.

"Thank you, Doctor Macarthur… Yes I will…. Okay I will see you first thing in the morning. Good bye."

Denise replaced the receiver onto the phone's base and frowned. She felt terrible. No matter what Randa had said, she had still missed a vital need of her aunt's welfare and general comfort and ease. *If it weren't for my own selfish procrastination she would have had a nurse by now who would have known and recognised Sara's needs.* "Damn it."

Walking back into the kitchen Denise once again checked on her dinner. It was cooking slowly. She had turned down the heat in order to slow its baking and give Randa some extra rest. Denise had noticed Randa's fatigued look and thought the blonde nurse would appreciate a little extra time to relax. They were in no rush to eat. Sara had stated that she could wait a while longer and Denise ate whenever she remembered or had the time.

It was almost a surreal feeling, knowing that Randa was actually in their home. That morning the poet had woken wondering whether she would hear anything from the American nurse. She never would have entertained the possibility that the blonde would actually appear most unexpectedly on her doorstep. *And now she is sleeping in my bed!* Denise was unsure what to make of that little fact. For the past twenty-two years she had been the only person to sleep there and always considered the bed her own private island of relaxation. The bed was large, incredibly comfortable and had belonged to her parents. She had never wanted to share that privacy with anybody. *Why now?* She wondered.

Opening a wall cupboard, Denise pulled out a large, half empty jar of strawberry jam. She unscrewed the lid and dipped her index finger inside, scooping out a small amount of the fruity preserve before sucking it off her finger. She exited the kitchen and wandered back into the living room where Sara was watching television. The older woman looked up as her niece entered the room. She shook her head as she watched Denise suck more jam from her finger. "I hope you put that away before that nice young lady comes back..." she took a breath, "...down stairs. You don't want her to be privy to all of your bad habits... so soon, do you?"

"What you see is what you get, Sara."

Sara rolled her eyes with a smile. She knew her niece well enough to see that something was different. She was seeing something she had never seen before. "She's nice isn't she? I bet it was a... surprise for you to find her upon the doorstep. Why do you think she came all the way... over here?"

The poet shrugged. "She said she was responding to my last mail. I feel a little uncomfortable about that, Sara. I mean not that she is here because I am very happy to meet her, but the fact that she more or less pulled herself from her own life because I needed help. I'm not doing my best in looking after you. To have somebody come all the way over here to point out where I am failing... it's just..."

"Hey!" Sara interrupted; she took a shallow breath. "Do you think she thinks that way?"

118

Denise looked down into the jam jar. "Honestly… no… but you needed oxygen and I didn't realise that."

"And you are trained to know these things?" Sara asked.

"Well no, but…"

"But nothing, DJ, you have been wonderful. We have both done… things that in hindsight could have been done better or different." Sara smiled as she breathed slowly. "Are you sorry that she… came?"

Denise looked up suddenly. "No, not at all."

"So you did want to meet her?"

"Yes."

"Well that is good because I have a feeling… that woman had more than one reason for… travelling all the way over to England, DJ." Sara was sure that deep down inside the blonde nurse knew this too.

The poet looked at her aunt in confusion.

Sara decided a change of topic was in order. "So what time… is Doctor Macarthur arriving in the morning?"

Screwing the top back onto the sticky jar, Denise shrugged. "Between nine and half past he said." She looked down at the black leather strapped watch on her right wrist. "Do you think Randa will be awake yet? Dinner will be ready soon and if she sleeps too long she won't rest well during the night."

The older woman looked up as her niece disappeared swiftly into the kitchen to deposit the jam jar before returning empty handed. The poet seemed to be massaging her side with one hand.

"I think maybe you should go and see whether she is awake yet."

"You think?" Denise asked feeling slightly unsure. She didn't want to encroach on the other woman's privacy. Being a woman who treasured such isolation she knew how it felt to have one's seclusion threatened and intruded upon.

"Of course."

Denise nodded hesitantly. "Okay."

The upper level of the house was quiet. Even the sound of

the television from down stairs echoed like a distant hum. Denise walked along the landing as she approached her bedroom door. It was pushed to but not completely shut.

Denise approached the barrier and stood quietly by the wide wooden door. After a small inner debate she gently tapped on the light wood. There was no answer. She tried again and rapped her knuckles a little harder but still there was no answer. "Randa?" She whispered lightly.

Nothing.

Hell! Denise stood at the door as she debated what to do and realising she had no other alternative; she crept slowly into the room.

The curtains had only been half drawn but it was already dark outside and only the light from the landing provided illumination in the darkened room. The poet walked tentatively toward the bed and looked down upon the sleeping form resting peacefully on her side. Randa had her head on one of the pillows and was clutching another closely to her chest. The sound of deep even breaths filled the air. The hall light shone directly onto her slumbering features.

Denise reached the side of her bed and bit the inside of her mouth nervously as she wondered how best to wake the sleeping blonde. She leant forward resting one hand upon the surface of the bed and whispered again. "Randa?"

There was still no response.

From down the stairs Denise heard the sound of the cooker's timer buzz twice, indicating that the dinner was ready. She looked briefly out into the hallway before looking back at the sleeping woman. She decided to try again.

"Randa." She placed a hand on her arm and shook her softly as she whispered, "Randa. You shouldn't sleep too long, you...?"

She froze as two sparkling green eyes shining in the landing light regarded her unexpectedly. Denise smiled nervously. "Um... I thought that maybe you shouldn't sleep too long otherwise you would disrupt your sleep pattern for tonight. I'm sorry if I startled you but the dinner is ready if you would like some?"

Randa blinked several times before pushing herself to a sitting position and rubbing her eyes sleepily. Denise couldn't help but find the sight strangely endearing.

"Are you okay?"

The blonde nodded with a smile. "Yeah, I'm fine." She looked down at the pillow resting in her lap and nervously placed it back at the head of the bed. "And no you didn't startle me; thank you for waking me up. You're right, I wouldn't want to sleep for too long now and then be awake all night."

The women stared at each other in the semi darkness. Denise suddenly looked down at the bed self-consciously. "I want you to know that I really am happy that you are here." She looked back up into smiling green eyes. "You know, I do feel like I know you well enough that I don't feel that need to distance myself from you like I do with people I meet for the first time. You are very easy to talk with." She paused. "I... I'm just happy to finally meet you." She stammered awkwardly.

Randa placed her hand upon the larger one resting upon the surface of the bed. "Me too, Denise. Listen... if it's okay with you I'd like to help out with Sara while I'm here. You know... do the nurse thing? Would that be alright?"

Denise looked down at the hand resting upon her own before moving back and standing tall. The connection just felt a little too disconcerting for her to deal with at that moment. "Sara and myself are both honoured that you came all the way over here, Randa. Any help that you can give us would be very much appreciated, though I really want you to know that it is not expected."

Randa chuckled almost awkwardly. "I want to help you, Denise. I was more than a little nervous you'd think the only reason I came here was because I've always been a fan of your work. That truly isn't the case, though you do know what I think of your writing."

Denise was sure she noticed a blush and was almost tempted to mention Randa's 'juices flowing' comment, but she remained quiet.

"I came here because you were in need and I wanted to help you. I still do and I hope you'll consider me qualified for the position while I'm here."

Holding out her hand, Denise watched an expression of confusion cross Randa's features. The poet raised her eyebrows and indicated for the blonde to imitate her. When she did, Denise took her hand in a firm shake. "For as long as you desire, you are hired."

Randa smiled. "It's a deal."

They released hands and Denise took a step backwards. "I better go and get the dinner finished. You did say you were hungry right?"

"After eating the airline's poor excuse for food I am more than ready for some good old fashioned home cooking." Randa replied.

Denise backed her way towards the door. "Let's go and eat then. I can't promise you proper home cooking, but it is food, it's cooked and I did prepare it at home. The resemblances end there I'm afraid."

Randa chuckled as she followed Denise back down the stairs. "Let me be the judge of that."

Denise loaded the dirty dishes into the dishwasher and closed the door. She leaned forward and selected a washing cycle before turning the machine on. There was a gentle hum as the device activated and whirled into life.

Dinner had been a pleasant affair. Sara had insisted that because they had company they had to use the dining room and not sit in the living room like they had a tendency to do while eating. The older woman would be the first to admit that she and DJ were a little lax when it came to etiquette. They had nobody to impress after all. So while Denise dished up the food, Randa took Sara into the dining room where the old woman instructed the nurse on where to find the cutlery and condiments for setting the table.

It had been decided and agreed upon by all that while Randa was visiting she would take an active part in taking care of Sara and would be present during Doctor Macarthur's visit the next morning. Sara seemed happy with this, as she knew her niece had been wearing herself out. Sara had decided on first meeting that she liked the American nurse. She also knew the moment she saw the way in which the young blonde looked at Denise that Randa felt for her more than friendship - even if Denise was yet to recognise that fact. Over dinner Sara had reminded Denise about her new book's deadline for the publishers and Randa stated that she was more than happy to sit with Sara while Denise worked. She winked at the older woman and remarked on how she would enjoy their 'chats'. Denise noticed the looks the women were passing each other and stared at them both suspiciously. Two innocent faces smiled back.

Denise switched off the kitchen light before picking up the glass of Diet Dr Pepper and bottle of water and walking into the living room. She found Randa sitting peacefully on the couch after settling Sara into bed.

"How's Sara?" Denise asked as she sat down on the opposites side of the chair and handed Randa her drink.

Randa accepted the glass with a smile. "She's fine. Fell asleep more or less as soon as her head hit the pillow. She was tired." Randa took a large drink of her Dr Pepper and sighed. "Oh, I love this stuff."

Denise scrunched her nose. "'Each to their own' I guess," she replied as she unscrewed her bottle cap. "It's a good job Sara likes that drink too. I always thought she was insane though."

"Hey!" Randa feigned hurt. "I don't suffer from insanity... I revel in every moment of it."

The poet laughed as she looked into sparkling green eyes shining in an orange glow from the roaring fire. "So I see!" She smiled and turned darkened blue eyes back to the fire. "I still can't believe we are sitting here like this. That you came."

"I was a little scared that you wouldn't want me here; that you may already have help for Sara. I had my mom playing devil's advocate but something told me I just had to do it. Besides, Christmas in England... aren't you guys supposed to get snow or something?"

The poet shrugged. "If we are lucky. It depends on where you live but we can get it here. In fact Sara and I have a tradition on Christmas Eve. In the evening we go to this small place where we stand on the hill and look over the land at all the colourful lights. It started when I first moved here and we have continued the tradition every year since then. Maybe you would like to come with us?" She turned back to look at Randa and found the woman staring at her.

Randa blinked and looked away briefly before turning back. "I'd love to."

123

Denise nodded. "Good."

"Speaking of Christmas," Randa started, "I noticed you don't have a tree up yet!"

"We usually would have bought one by now but… you know. Maybe we could all go out tomorrow afternoon and purchase one?"

Randa smiled. "Sounds like fun."

Looking down at her untouched bottle of water the poet said, "I am too tired to even drink this. We should go and get your bed set up."

The nurse nodded her agreement with a yawn. "I am still tired."

"Okay." Denise held out her hand and accepted Randa's empty glass. "Lets go to bed." She felt the sudden need to correct herself. "I mean, lets go and get your bed set up." Lowering her head, Denise blushed and disappeared into the kitchen to discard the glass and bottle of water. She re-emerged empty handed to find a smirking Randa waiting for her by the door.

"Ready?"

Randa nodded and headed out of the living room and towards the stairs. Denise followed, turning off the lights as she went and rendering the lower part of the house into total darkness. *I know I was blushing then. Jesus what is wrong with me?* Shaking her head Denise followed Randa up the stairs.

Chapter 13

Morning brought clear skies, colder temperatures and Dr. Macarthur. The visit went smoothly with the physician agreeing that Sara would benefit from wearing oxygen. After a brief examination of the patient, he returned to his surgery to arrange for the necessary supplies to be delivered. Randa closed the door behind the doctor and leaned against it for a moment thinking how perfectly at ease Denise and Sara had been in allowing her to participate in the older woman's care. In fact, it seemed they were at ease with her in the house and in their lives as well.

Randa thought back to the wonderful breakfast the women had shared. They had traded stories about themselves and their homes. More than once Sara had made DJ uncomfortable by revealing some of the poet's teenage escapades. While Denise thought the stories were embarrassing, the nurse found them endearing. It amazed her to realize the rebellious teen of years ago was the sensitive, warm woman of today. There was one moment of awkwardness though that puzzled the nurse. Randa had been complimenting Sara on her homemade strawberry jam.

"This is so delicious! I hope you don't think this is crude, but if I were at home I would probably eat the stuff right out of the jar. Knowing me I wouldn't use a spoon either." There was a weird moment of silence then as Denise and Sara exchanged glances. Denise blushed and Sara smiled then said, "Do whatever makes you comfortable, dear, we don't stand on ceremony here." They all laughed but Randa still felt something had been odd.

Shaking off the feeling, she went into the living room and rejoined Denise and her aunt. As she entered the room the conversation revolved around the upcoming holiday.

"We surely need a bit of the Christmas spirit around here, DJ. Why we haven't a single decoration up anywhere, not even a tree. It doesn't feel like Christmas somehow without our usual trimmings."

"I'd like to do all those things Sara, but with the deadline for my book coming up I just don't seem to have enough hours in the day."

Randa overheard the words and decided to take a chance. "You know, Sara, if you would like it, I could take you out this afternoon and we could look for a tree. We could come back here and decorate afterward and give Denise time to work on her book. I think we should wait for the oxygen to be delivered but then I would be willing to go if you want."

DJ looked surprised. "You'd want to do that? It wouldn't be too much of an imposition?"

"Imposition? How can it be an imposition? Look, this is a win-win situation for me. I get to spend the afternoon with your aunt hearing more adorable stories about your misspent youth and I get a little closer to a new book by D Jennings. What's not to love about that?"

Sara chuckled and said, "This is the best offer I've had all day. I think it works out perfectly for everyone so let's do it."

Denise smiled and raised her hands in surrender. "I can see you two are going to do this no matter what I say anyway so I'll just go along with the plan and say I think it's a lovely idea. Thank you, Randa."

"Anything for you, Denise…and you too of course, Sara." Randa and Denise matched blushes as Sara watched them both with a knowing look.

The afternoon had been fun for both Sara and Randa. The older woman had blossomed with the trip outside and her breathing was much improved with the oxygen coming from the small tank attached to the back of her wheelchair. The pair had visited two lots full of Christmas trees with Sara inspecting each tree carefully and pronouncing them unsuitable. Finally, reaching the very back of the second lot, Sara spied a tree. She gave it little more than a cursory glance before turning to Randa.

"That's the one."

"You're sure? You've given every other one the tree version of the Spanish Inquisition and this one you barely look at and pronounce worthy? How can you be so sure?"

"It's a gift, young woman. Take me to tea and I'll tell you

126

all my secrets. No sense letting all this knowledge die with me." The two women sobered for a brief time. Randa leaned over and hugged the older woman close. Eventually, Sara pulled back and blinked away the moisture that had accumulated in her eyes.

"Let's go now before I make a fool of myself. Maybe we'll get a small something for Denise as well; she has a weakness for chocolate you know."

"Yeah, I know, it's a weakness I share."

"Oh, I think you'll end up sharing much more than that," Sara said under her breath then smiled at Randa as they found the salesman and paid for their purchase.

It was close to midnight and Randa and Denise were sitting in the living room admiring their work. The Christmas tree had been delivered in the early evening and set up according to Sara's instructions. The three women had started the decorating but Sara had soon succumbed to happy exhaustion and had let herself be put to bed. The nurse and the poet worked in an easy harmony stringing lights, hanging ornaments and putting out Sara's collection of porcelain Christmas angels. Finally they were seated with steaming cups of tea in the room illuminated only by the fireplace and twinkling lights of the tree. Denise gazed at the tree apparently lost in her thoughts. Randa studied the poet wondering what was on her mind and marveling yet again at how attractive the brunette was.

Stop it, Randa. You've got to keep remembering that Denise is just your friend and stop thinking that she's so...

"Lovely."

Randa snapped out of her reverie and realized Denise was speaking to her. "What did you say, Denise?"

"The tree, the tree is lovely. It's always been a point of pride for Sara to have a lovely tree at Christmas. Even though it's almost always been just the two of us she always took the time to make our Christmas celebrations special." Denise turned her head to face the nurse. "I was just thinking about how many Christmases I've had here with her. It's almost more than I can bear to know this will be the last one. She won't have another, will she?" A single tear freed itself from Denise's eye and traced a silent pattern down her cheek.

"I'm afraid not, Denise. I wish the answer could be different, but..."

"I know," said the poet. "It was just wishful thinking on my part. If this is to be her last Christmas though I am determined to make it the very best I can. While you were gone, I made a few phone calls as well as worked on the book. I've arranged to have all of Sara's favorite holiday things delivered. Food, friends and treats. Anything Sara might want she is going to have."

Randa nodded, thought a moment, and then spoke. "We talked at tea today. She said the same thing as you did. She wants this to be the best Christmas for you as well. She loves you very much, Denise. I've known her only two days and can see what a truly terrific woman she is. You've been a very lucky woman to have had her in your life. She's a wonderful role model and a loving guardian. If there is anything I can do to help you make this holiday special, you have only to ask."

Randa left her seat and moved to kneel by Denise's chair. She reached out her hand and gently wiped away the rogue tear, letting her hand linger momentarily on the poet's cheek. Denise brought her hand up to cover Randa's briefly then moved to rise from the chair.

"I suppose we should turn in now if we are going to get more preparations done for the holiday. Randa, what little task was Sara talking about you doing for her tomorrow?" The pair moved toward the doorway.

"None of your business there, Miss Jennings. Your aunt and I have a few plans of our own." Earlier in the day Sara had asked Randa to pick up Denise's Christmas present for her. Shortly after her diagnosis, Sara had commissioned an oil painting by a local artist. It showed a much younger Sara with Denise at the age she was when she first came to live with the older woman. Photographs and talent were bringing to life a portrait of the two Jennings women that they had never thought to have done before.

Denise paused at the light switch and gazed back once again at the tree. "I think I'll leave the lights on tonight. For some reason I don't want to turn them off." Giving a little sigh, she looked at the pine. "Lovely," was all she said then turned and left the room.

You certainly are Randa thought and followed her friend from the room.

The days past quickly during the run up to Christmas and the lives of Denise, Randa and Sara fell into an ease of comfort and familiarity. A natural routine was soon established and one that revolved around Sara and her growing need for support and assistance.

The women would spend time together in the morning before Denise would disappear to her study to work on entries for her fourth anthology of poems. It felt good to get back into the routine of spending a few hours a day just devoted to writing. She was beginning to miss the feeling of allowing her mind to wander as she constructed a multitude of verses from lyrical tales to structured sonnets. And thanks to Randa, Denise was regaining her much needed flow.

What was more, since Randa's arrival the spirit of Christmas had finally made an appearance in the Jennings household, from the beautifully decorated tree to the excitement of the impending day.

However, there was one problem that had Denise puzzling in deep thought. Since Randa had already opened her present she now needed and wanted to get her something else. Through the days leading up to the big day itself Denise had searched her mind for the perfect gift. It wasn't until the day before Christmas Eve that she finally had her epiphany.

Waking up early Christmas Eve morning, Denise realised it was the sound of the shower door closing that had jolted her from a dreamless sleep. Rolling onto her back she gazed at the clock on the wall, waiting for her blurry eyes to ease into focus.

Realising it was still rather early but knowing she would gain no more sleep, Denise decided she might as well go and start their breakfast. Though she knew Sara would not yet be awake, the prospect of spending any time alone with Randa just to talk was an opportunity she was finding hard to pass upon.

Slipping from the warmth of her bed and into the chilled

129

air, Denise approached her door and pulled it open. As she stepped out into the hallway she came face to face with Randa who was making her way from the steam filled bathroom to the poet's study where she slept.

Denise gulped as she gazed down at the woman who was wearing nothing but a thick navy towel wrapped around her torso.

"Hi." Denise said, trying desperately to keep eye contact.

"Morning." Randa replied, watching blue eyes move nervously around the landing before returning to her own green orbs. Randa looked down at Denise's short tee shirt and smirked as she read the quote on the front of the red garment. "So is that true?"

With a creased brow Denise cocked her head to the side. "Is what true?"

Randa motioned towards Denise's chest. "That."

Looking down, the poet realised what Randa was referring to. Written across her tee shirt in bright white letters was the phrase: *'Poets do it in their heads.'*

Denise thought she should have blushed but instead she felt a mischievous streak spark inside of her. "Well you know I do spend a lot of time up there!" As she noticed a pink tint grace the smaller woman's cheeks, Denise was quick to amend her words. "No I'm joking. Sara bought me this as a joke. She has a tendency to give me tops with odd quotes upon them. Like… *'Out of my mind; back in five minutes.'* … *'Friends help you move; real friends help you move bodies.'* And my favourite… *'Monday. A shitty way to spend one seventh of your life.'*

"She has a great sense of humour," Randa laughed.

Denise nodded for she knew it was true. Sara would often buy her quirky tops to see whether her niece would wear them in public.

Looking down at her barely covered form, Randa remembered her state of dress. "Umm… well I better go and get some clothes on."

"Oh… yeah… sorry." Denise moved towards the bathroom as Randa passed her and continued her journey toward her makeshift bedroom. Her eyes never left the nurse until she had disappeared from view.

Entering the bathroom, Denise closed the door and leaned

against the white barrier. Her eyes fluttered shut. "Oh god!" She muttered as the image of Randa's scantily clad form remained in her mind's eye. *What's wrong with me?*

While Randa helped Sara dress, Denise made the women their breakfast. She pulled her favourite jam out of the cupboard and smirked as she recalled Randa's comment a few days before. Denise had been sure Sara was going to divulge her niece's own eating habits when it came to her famous homemade preserve, yet she didn't. That had slightly surprised her. Denise could plainly see how well her aunt and friend got along and was aware of their conspiratorial glances and conversations with one another. Although she acted suspicious and self-conscious, Denise was actually thrilled to know they had warmed to each other so quickly.

"Denise?"

The poet looked up from her task of slicing bread to find Randa standing in the doorway. "Hmm?"

"Sara is ready to go into her chair."

"Right." Wiping her hands over her black jeans, Denise followed the nurse into Sara's bedroom. Together they helped the older woman into her chair. Then the three women headed out into the dining room for breakfast.

After breakfast Randa volunteered to do the dishes while Denise took Sara into the living room. The poet needed to talk to her aunt without the nurse's presence.

"Sara?" Denise whispered.

"Yes?" Sara asked, almost amused by her niece's cloak and dagger attitude.

"I want to talk to you about Randa. I was thinking about what to get her for Christmas and I had this idea. I want your opinion."

Sara took a sneak peak towards the door before turning back to look inquisitively at Denise. "Oh, do tell?"

"I had this idea about getting something made with Blue John. Something unique you know. I know a guy who could make something from the mine, maybe in the form of a necklace?" She looked at Sara in question; knowing her aunt had a flair for choosing appropriate gifts. "What do you think?"

The older woman looked impressed. "I like it."

"Really?" Denise asked hopefully, her eyes wide with excitement. "You think she will like it?"

"Absolutely I do, I know I would." Sara affirmed. "Denise, you do realise that Christmas day is tomorrow. If you want to give her this you better be quick."

"Yeah…" Denise paused as she twisted her head to the side listening. "I thought I heard her coming back." She said, "Anyway… I made a phone call to a contact that I know could help. It's already under way, I just need to go down there and make my choice of stone and wait for it to be completed." Denise shrugged. "I'm glad you think it was a good idea. I was beginning to feel a little nervous about it."

Both women jumped suspiciously as Randa walked into the room. The blonde looked between the two women. "Am I interrupting? I can leave if…"

"No!" Denise rose to her feet. "No we were just talking. I have to go out soon. I was just making sure I could trust you both alone together." She winked at the blonde.

Randa arched her brows as she said, "Oh I'm sure you can trust us."

Denise narrowed her eyes. "Uh huh!" Approaching the door she looked back at the women. "Why do I feel the need to leave supervision?"

Both Randa and Sara shrugged with innocent expressions.

Denise stood in a large well-used garage, hands pushed tightly in her pockets as she tried in vain to ward off the chill of the frigid winter air. A strong aroma of oils and the precise cutting machinery's heated smell of warm metal friction assaulted her senses. She looked over the shelves at the mass of tools and intricate looking equipment before turning her vision toward the young man who was bent over a well-used wooden workbench. Unruly strands of dark blonde hair fell over his face as he diligently buffed a small shiny object.

She had heard of this man by reputation. He worked at the Blue John Caverns as a guide but in his spare time made unique pieces of jewellery out of the distinctive purple blue stone. His work was of outstanding quality, highly sought after by those who could afford it, and very exclusive.

The young man looked up from his work. "If you look in that unit over there you can find a chain for the pendent. I have many different varieties, all in solid silver of course."

"Sure." Denise wandered over to the large wooden unit and opened the glass doors. She began to look through the selection for the appropriate chain. It had to be delicate looking yet at the same time strong and hardwearing.

"It's always a last minute rush at Christmas isn't it? Especially when you forget a loved one's present." He started fiddling around a small translucent box seemingly searching for something.

"Huh?" Denise frowned in question.

"I was just saying that... when you forget a loved one's present?"

Denise didn't answer but she looked at the man in confusion.

"Well I thought... you know... this must be for somebody special. Not many people can afford to pay the price of getting me to work on Christmas Eve so I presumed that this must be for a loved one. Boyfriend? No maybe not, this design is a little too feminine for a guy. Mother, maybe? It really is a lovely creation by the way. It was a good job you faxed me a sketch of what you wanted this to look like."

"Somebody special?" Denise looked back at the selection of silver chains. A frown of confusion creased her forehead as she tried to understand what 'Jamie the Jeweller' had just said. *What does Randa mean to me?*

It was a question she had fervently avoided from the moment Randa had appeared on her doorstep. She didn't want to acknowledge thoughts that she felt were futile, but with the unexpected question, Denise was forced to confront her situation.

Denise had never given much thought to her sexual preferences, but she had also never entertained the prospect that she may indeed be attracted to women. It wasn't an uncomfortable thought to her, just one she had never considered. Her one sexual encounter with a male friend had left her wondering what all the fuss was actually about. She had even expressed her feelings on this subject to Sara and her aunt had just said that when the right person came along it would be different. Denise had hoped that it was true but felt no desire to search for that so called right person. Instead she built up a world of passionate romance in her head. Creating a whole new dimension to what she perceived as the ultimate magnetism of the passionate encounter and expressing that world through her poetry.

Do I have feelings for her?

"Have you found a chain?"

Denise looked up at Jamie. "Oh... um yes I have." Picking up her choice she carried it over to the blonde man who was once again polishing the stone.

"So what do think?" Jamie asked hopefully.

Intrigued, Denise picked up the unique pendent and held it up to the light. The purple translucent stone was alive with white and light blue coloured veins and was cut into a small crystal held by a sturdy silver fob, shaped into the Celtic symbol of eternity. "It's beautiful, just how I hoped it would look."

"It was your design."

"You did a good job, Jamie." She handed the pendent back to the young man and he threaded the chain through the loop.

"Well there you go." He placed the necklace in a velvet box. "Definitely worth the money wouldn't you say?" Jamie smirked.

"You would say that," Denise retorted, "but yes it is definitely worth all nine hundred pounds of it." She pulled a large amount of notes from her back pocket. "Thanks for accepting cash by the way."

Jamie's eyes shone. "At this time of the year the more cash you have the better!"

"I guess." Denise looked down at her watch. It was half past one. It would take her a good forty minutes to return home and then they were to go out tonight for their annual pilgrimage to the lookout. "Well I better go. Thanks again, Jamie."

They shook hands.

"Any time, DJ. It was nice to meet you. And next time you see Carl, tell him he still owes me a Christmas drink from last year!"

The poet smirked. "I will." She approached the small side door of the garage, black velvet box in hand and walked back out into the cold afternoon atmosphere.

Opening the front door Denise stepped into the hallway and instantly noted the lack of sound in the quiet house. With curiosity the poet walked into the front room but found it empty. *Hmm!* Walking further through the house she checked the kitchen back passage and Sara's bedroom. There she found her aunt resting peacefully upon the surface of her bed. To her side, in the large vanity chair was Randa who also appeared to be sleeping.

Knowing from personal experience just how uncomfortable that chair could be for one's back; Denise strode forward and knelt by the sleeping blonde. She didn't want Randa to suffer the same discomfort that still bothered her.

"Randa." She whispered, not wanting to wake Sara.

There was no response as Denise looked upon relaxed slumbering features. *What do I feel for you?* She thought.

Unexpectedly, green eyes fluttered open and regarded her with interest.

Denise smiled self-consciously wondering with slight paranoia whether Randa may have actually heard her thoughts, as unlikely as it was. "That chair really isn't the most comfortable piece of furniture to sleep upon. Trust me," she whispered.

Moving from her slumped position, Randa followed Denise's lead and slowly rose to her feet. "Sorry. I didn't hear you come in. How long have you been back?"

Denise looked down at her watch. "Oh about..." she poked her lip out as she pretended to work the time out in her head, "two minutes." She smiled. "Come on."

It wasn't until she felt Randa's skin within her own that she realised she had absentmindedly taken the nurse's hand. Not wanting to appear fazed by the act she didn't let go until

135

they entered the living room. Both women sat down on the large sofa.

"So, did you get your shopping done?" Randa asked.

"How did you know I went shopping?"

The nurse shrugged. "Sara said that was where you went."

Denise arched her brows. "Oh yeah? And what else did she say?"

"Just that you were out shopping, but I wasn't allowed to know what for!"

Shaking her head the poet chuckled. "I swear when that woman gets excited she has about as much discretion as a parrot with too many secrets!"

Randa looked at Denise uncomfortably. "Denise she did lead me to believe that… well… that you went shopping for a present for…"

"You." Denise said.

Randa nodded. "Yes. I guess I feel I shouldn't have opened this now." She held up her wrist showing the charm bracelet.

"It suits you."

"It's beautiful, Denise."

"It was my mother's."

Shocked green eyes looked at Denise in surprise. "I didn't know that. I mean I knew the sonnet was a favourite of yours and you did say that it was your mother who introduced you to the poem, but I had no idea this was her bracelet. Denise I can't…"

"Yes, you can," Denise stated firmly and took Randa's wrist in her hands, holding the bracelet. "I loved this, but all it has done for the past ten years is sit in an old shoe box under my bed. As you may have noticed, I am not the kind of person to wear excessive amounts of jewellery and never around my wrist. I only wear this watch because it's tight and I hardly know it's there. I gave it to you because I knew you would appreciate how much it means to me. I wanted you to have it, Randa."

They stared at each other silently until the taller woman smiled; she felt the need to lighten the mood. "Are you ready for our little excursion tonight?"

"Yes, Sara has been looking forward to it all day."

"I hope we can get Sara into the car alright, but I see you

managed to get her onto the bed without my help earlier."

Randa nodded. "I bet we'll mange fine. How far away is this clandestine place?" She asked moving her eyes from side to side in a show of mock paranoia.

"Twenty minutes by car," the poet replied amused by the nurse's antics. "I would suggest you wrap up warm tonight as well, it's cold out there and it's only going to get colder."

"Right."

Denise released Randa's hand, realising she was still slightly holding the bracelet around her wrist. She looked away from curious green eyes to the pine tree twinkling softly in the corner. The jeweller's words echoed again in her head and with clarity she realised that she did feel an attraction to the blonde nurse. Looking back at Randa, Denise observed the woman starting intently at the tree; its colourful lights shone in the silky sheen of her hair. *Now what do I do?*

The inky darkness of night surrounded the black Lexus as it made its way up a long steep hill toward the shrouded look out. Surrounded by a thick crop of trees, the only light around emanated from the beaming fog lights of the powerful vehicle.

Denise followed the barely distinguishable route guided only by memory. The darkness that surrounded them was nothing new but never failed to give her the same unsettled feeling she got whenever she traversed this well used dirt track. The Lexus juddered and bumped over the rocky ground as the poet carefully steered her way to the top of the tor.

Inside the vehicle an intense heat blasted from its internal system and warmed the passengers. All three women were dressed in their warmest clothes and jackets, knowing just how cold the night indeed was. Sara sat in the front of the car with Denise while Randa sat in the back.

As Denise reached the top of the tor she steered near to the edge of the rocky ledge and shut off the engine.

Sara smiled as she looked out onto the scenery ahead. "Beautiful."

Randa tried to look from her position but found she was unable to distinguish much of the view.

"DJ, why don't you take Randa out for a better look. I will stay here."

Denise looked over to her aunt concerned. "Are you sure? Are you alright?"

"I'm fine, DJ. I am quite happy here, but Randa needs to get out to fully appreciate the view so you take her. I'll stay here in the warmth."

Turning towards the back seat, Denise looked at Randa in question. "Do you want to?"

The blonde nodded. "I would love to."

"Okay." Denise turned back to her aunt. "We will only be a couple of minutes, besides you will be able to see us from where you are sitting."

"Don't worry about me, I will be fine."

Randa rolled her eyes with a smile as she opened the back door and climbed out into the freezing night air. Denise followed, wrapping her parka jacket around herself as she firmly shut the driver's door, keeping the car's heat in and the cold temperatures out.

They walked to the ledge of the tor adequately illuminated by the car's lights. Randa looked out over the land.

"My God!" She exclaimed, her breath releasing in thick clouds of vapour as she spoke.

DJ nodded mutely as she followed Randa's sight.

Stretching out as far as their eyes could see and well into the horizon was a wide expanse of coloured and patterned lights. There were long rows of orange lights that gave away the position of many roads travelling across the land but all seemingly connected in some structured way. Then there were the Christmas lights. Hundreds of houses, most of them decorated with a multitude of colourful fairy lights. Some blinking and some were not, some large and powerful, and some small and hardly visible. It was almost like looking at a colourful version of the night sky upon the land below.

"It looks magnificent." Randa said as she shivered in the intense cold.

Denise looked at the blonde concerned. "You're cold. Do you want to go back inside the car?"

Shaking her head, Randa's vision never strayed from the view. "Not yet." She shivered again.

It was a swift debate and one Denise was not conscious of

making, but without much reasoning she stepped closely behind the woman and placed her hands upon her arms. "I don't want you to get a chill now!" she reasoned as she rubbed her hands over Randa's arms and created a soothing friction of heat underneath her jacket. "Feel any better?"

Randa was silent.

"Randa?" she asked again, feeling the soft strands of blonde hair tickle her nose.

"Hmm." The blonde replied. "Wonderful."

Denise smiled as she remained behind the woman. Her hands had stopped moving as they both looked out upon the magnificent view below.

"Sara..." Randa began, "she said that the first time she took you up here you saw a shooting star in the sky and was adamant that you had just spotted Santa Claus." She chuckled lightly.

The poet laughed quietly, a deep rumble in her chest. "I am not surprised she told you that! Did she also tell you that I demanded we go home quickly to make sure I was in bed before he arrived?"

The nurse nodded. "Yep. And that you insisted on putting out a whole packet of chocolate cookies to make sure you were in his good books!"

Denise shook her head. "I see nothing is safe around you two. It's a good job I have no reputation to protect otherwise I should be mortified."

"Don't worry." Randa assured as she turned around and looked into eyes so close to her own. "Your secrets are safe with me."

From inside the car Sara was more interested in the display directly in front of her. She smiled brightly hoping the women were beginning to see or acknowledge what she had sensed from the first moment they had met. *DJ, I think you may just have found that one special person.*

Chapter 14

The cold wind lashed Randa as she stared into blue eyes more magnificent than the view from the crag on which they stood. Denise didn't remove her hands when Randa turned and now the taller woman's arms draped comfortably over the blonde's shoulders. The nurse reached up and pushed a wind blown strand of hair from Denise's face and let her gloved hand linger on the cheek beneath.

"Denise, I…"

"Randa," Denise interrupted, "Let me say something to you. I've been alone for a long time now. That was by my choice, but now I see I have other options in my life. I wasn't sure how I felt when you first arrived, but now I am sure of one thing. I'm sure I'm falling in love with you." Randa was speechless with happiness, only able to give Denise a brilliant smile in return for those heartfelt words.

Then Denise's head was lowering, bringing her mouth so close to Randa's that the vapor of their breaths mixed, making them seem to breathe as one. Randa looked quickly to the car that held Denise's aunt.

"Sara is…"

"…A grown woman." Denise finished and closed the last gap between their lips. Randa felt the incredible power of Denise's warmth and love in that single kiss. The only thing to mar the sensation at all was daylight.

Daylight?

Randa opened her eyes and groaned at the intrusion of light into her wonderful dream, for that's all it had been. She was holding tight to her pillow and her body still hummed with the sensual feelings evoked by the sleep-generated fantasy. Just fantasy, not the reality of the evening before when nothing like that had happened.

No. No way. I'm not getting up, I'm going to close my eyes and get right back to my dream. Same spot, same kiss, same everything. Randa closed her eyes and waited for her mind to catch up with her libido. After a few moments she knew it wasn't going to work and she let out another groan, this one in frustration.

141

"Damn it, damn it, damn it..."

"Randa?"

The nurse's eyes popped open. That velvet voice could belong to no one but Denise. Randa cut her eyes slowly to the right and sure enough the poet's head was peeking around the door of the study, blue eyes regarding her with curiosity.

"I was going to let you sleep but then I heard your voice in here so I thought you must be awake." She looked at the pillow still clutched tightly in the nurse's arms.

Randa blushed deeply and fumbled with an explanation. "I was having a dream and I, uhm...I was..."

"You were having a confrontation with someone?" asked Denise, eyeing the pillow still crushed in Randa's arms.

The blush deepened and Randa said "Sort of."

"I see. Well, it appears you were really letting them have it," Denise observed.

You have no idea thought the blonde.

"Well, I just wanted to come by because I think there's something you should see." Denise gave a small jerk with her head indicating the window and reached down to help Randa out of the foldaway bed. Together they walked to the window where Denise drew back the curtains. "England says 'Happy Christmas', Randa."

Randa stared out the window as giddy as a child. "Snow! Oh, Denise, it's snow!"

"Sure is. It started about 4 a.m. I was up getting the turkey ready for the oven and it just started coming down. Its been going strong since then." An accumulation of almost 6 inches was on the ground and the town looked like a Currier and Ives picture.

"Can we go out there for awhile, Denise? I know there's a lot to do but at home we had to drive up into the mountains to see snow at Christmas. This is just so wonderful!"

Pure joy settled in the nurse's eyes and Denise didn't seem to want to do anything to extinguish it. "I think we could go out for a short time. Sara isn't awake yet and everything is under control in the kitchen. Get some warm things on and I'll meet you downstairs in ten minutes." The nurse let out a quiet whoop of happiness and DJ turned to leave the room. At the door she stopped briefly and looked back into the room as Randa was already fishing around for her heavy socks. The nurse's movement stilled as she looked up at the poet and smiled.

"I almost forgot. Merry Christmas, Denise."

The smile was returned full force. "Happy Christmas, Randa."

Randa and Denise played in the snow for about half an hour, making snow angels and building what had to be the world's ugliest two-foot tall snowman. As DJ cleared the walk with a shovel, Randa fought, but couldn't resist, the impulse to lob a snowball at the broad back of the poet. Denise dropped the shovel, turned toward Randa and the battle was on. There might have been a winner in the battle if the women weren't laughing so hard as to make most of the throws go astray. Finally the pair called a truce and went inside to warm themselves. Randa suggested Denise shower first while she assisted Sara with her morning routine and got her dressed. Denise agreed and turned for the stairs.

"While you're in the shower, you might want to wash this off," said Randa as she deftly removed snow from her pocket, slipped it down the back of DJ's sweater and took off for the safety of Sara's room. Denise was hot on her heels as the nurse burst into Sara's room and shrieked "Save me!"

Sara took in the sight of the two happy and playful women and exploded in laughter. Soon all three women were laughing and Christmas day in the Jennings' household was underway.

True to her word, Denise had arranged the day to provide Sara with the best Christmas she could. No expense had been spared, no detail overlooked. There were fresh imported fruits and flowers. There were treats of every variety imaginable, both traditional and exotic. If Denise could remember Sara saying she had ever liked something at Christmas, it made an appearance in the house during the day. Then there were the friends. Randa and DJ had arranged a schedule for the visits of

Sara's dear friends from the town and surrounding area. The pair made sure Sara had enough time between guests to rest and preserve her fragile strength. Finally the door closed on the last visitor and it was just the three of them again.

Sara and Denise sat at the table waiting for Randa before starting on the mouth-watering turkey dinner DJ had prepared.

"DJ, I want you to know I appreciate all the work you and Randa did to make this Christmas so special for me. I'll remember it for as long…well, let's say I'll never forget it." She raised her hand toward her niece who grasped it in her own. Sara's grip was weak but full of the love she had for the younger woman. Denise knew from the look on her aunt's face that it had been worth every ounce of the work.

Randa came into the room in time to observe the tender moment between Denise and Sara. She felt privileged to have been able to see it. She blinked back tears and smiled brightly at the women.

"How is your mum, dear?" asked Sara. Her voice was a little thick with emotion yet.

"She's fine and on her way to spend the day with my father's sister in the San Francisco Bay area. They're both widowed now and try to spend holidays together. It was good to talk to her. She said to thank you for the hospitality to me and wish you a Merry Christmas from her."

"It's no chore to provide hospitality to you, Randa." She took Randa's hand with her free one. "We love having you here, don't we, DJ?"

Denise looked deeply at the shining green eyes across from her and simply said "Definitely."

Sara cleared her throat and said, "Shall we?" She indicated the two younger women should join hands as well. In a weak but clear voice Sara gave the blessing.

"Lord, we thank you for your bounty which has placed food on this table and for your blessing which has placed friendship and love in this house. Amen."

Randa and Denise looked up at the same time and echoed the "Amen." Randa gave Denise's hand a squeeze and released it to assist Sara with her meal. She missed the look on DJ's face, but Sara didn't. She looked at her niece, gave a little wink then turned to her dinner.

The women were settled in the living room around the tree. Christmas music played softly in the background from the system Denise had installed there. The three had agreed to wait until the end of the day to exchange their gifts. Sara had received a new television with a built-in DVD player and extensive collection of her favorite movies from Denise. No one acknowledged the fact that this gift was in anticipation of the time when Sara's disease would progress to the point that mobility would be very difficult.

Denise opened the box from Randa for herself and Sara. Sara was delighted with the shawl and Denise laughed at the bear. When the poet opened the small box containing the locket and read the accompanying card she was touched at the thoughtfulness of the nurse.

"I found it at an estate sale. An Englishwoman who had emigrated with her husband brought it to California in the 1800's. It just seemed right that it should come full circle back to England. Now for a picture for the inside. You told me you were both a little camera shy but for now I'm telling you to get over it." Saying that, Randa produced a disposable camera and took several pictures of Sara and then Denise and Sara together. At Randa's request, Sara agreed to a picture with the nurse as well.

Sara gave Randa a nod and the blonde left the room and brought back a large flat package.

"This one is for you from Sara, Denise." The brunette removed the bright wrapping paper and looked at the portrait in astonishment. There in the picture were the two Jennings women as they had been twenty-two years before. Denise even remembered the dress she had on in the portrait as one given to her by Sara on their first Christmas as a family. For Denise, who had maintained bright spirits during this holiday for her aunt's sake, it was the final straw. She went to Sara and held her as the tears flowed freely down her cheeks. Sara tried to comfort Denise but was losing the battle on maintaining her composure as well. Finally, identical sets of blue eyes looked into one another and gave each other the strength to get through the emotional moment. Sara gave a weak smile to the younger women.

"This day has been a little overwhelming for me. I really

feel the need to rest now. Randa, would you help me to bed?"

Randa nodded and took Sara from the room as Denise's red-rimmed eyes followed. The nurse knew Sara was giving DJ time to regain the control she usually held with such ease. As she helped the older woman dress for bed she took extra time in brushing the silver laced hair. Finally covering Sara with the quilt, Randa leaned over and kissed the other woman's forehead.

"Goodnight, Sara. It was a wonderful thing you did for Denise."

"I won't have her remember me this way, Randa. I want her to think of me the way we were for the past twenty-two years, not what I will be in the next few months. You'll help me in that, won't you?" Randa could only nod, not trusting her voice as she could only marvel at the courage of the woman before her.

"Good girl, then. Now you've helped me enough tonight. Maybe you could help my niece a little?" The women smiled at one another and Randa left Sara to rejoin DJ in the living room.

Denise was sitting on the sofa, looking at the tree. She had pulled herself together and even gave Randa a smile as she settled next to the poet.

"It was a lovely Christmas, wasn't it, Randa?"

"The best, Denise. You made Sara so very happy."

"She deserved it. She's very special."

On impulse, Randa leaned over and kissed Denise on the cheek. "So is her niece."

Denise blushed and reached behind her to pull out a small wrapped package. "I guess Santa left one more thing and I'm pretty sure it's for you."

Randa opened the package carefully and, with a small gasp, brought out the striking necklace. "Oh Denise, it's stunning. I don't think I've ever seen a stone like this before. The color is just beautiful and the design is so unusual. It seems familiar somehow, though, like I've seen it before."

"It's Celtic. The gem is Blue John. It comes from mines not very far from here but the stones are pretty rare."

"Will you help me with it? I'd love to see it on."

The women went to the small mirror at one end of the living room. Randa gave the necklace to Denise and turned to face the mirror. The poet placed the necklace around the nurse's neck, closed the clasp and rested her hands on the other woman's shoulders. Randa stared at the radiant gift and Denise stared at Randa. Finally their eyes met in the mirror.

"I don't know if I can find the words to thank you properly for this, Denise. It's just exquisite."

"It doesn't compare," whispered the brunette softly.

Blue eyes held green for a long moment. Suddenly Randa turned and wrapped her arms around Denise's waist. Denise slowly brought her arms up and drew the nurse in closer. No words were exchanged; none were needed.

Finally, Randa drew back and looked up at the poet. "I have to agree with Sara, this day has been a little overwhelming. I think I'm going to turn in too. Thank you so much for this gift, Denise. I'll treasure it, and you, for an eternity."

Eternity. Randa realized it as soon as she said it. *That's what the symbol is, eternity.*

That realization was too much for the blonde and she turned with a hasty, "Goodnight" and fled up the stairs.

The house was deathly quiet. The only sound coming from a small carriage clock sitting upon the mantel as it ticked away a second in time. Denise thought it strange how only at this early time of the morning did she ever hear the clock's consistent ticking.

It was five a.m. and the poet had been awake for an hour already. Her sleep that night had been sporadic at best and by four o'clock Denise had finally given up the hope of dozing back off and had decided to make herself a warm drink. She remembered Sara stating how a mug of hot milk could relax your mind and help a person to sleep. Unfortunately for Denise, it didn't work.

Randa's sudden change in behaviour had bothered her from the moment she watched the blonde's retreating form disappear up the stairs. She thought they had been getting along just fine, and then unexpectedly Randa's demeanour had changed. The poet was at a loss to understand why and she thought that maybe she had offended her in some way. Maybe she just wanted some time alone. The call to her mother could have made her homesick. With a sigh she looked into her third mug of cooling milk and then froze. A chill of terror slithered through her spine. *Did I seem to come on too strong? Did she sense my attraction toward her?* Rubbing a suddenly aching forehead Denise groaned in distress. "Damn it!" *What if she hates me? What if she feels uncomfortable around me now?*

Getting up swiftly Denise walked into the kitchen and deposited her mug in the large sink. She then moved through the back of the house and on towards the extension. She stopped when she reached Sara's bedroom. Placing her ear upon the door's shiny surface she listened carefully hoping there was a slim chance Sara was actually awake. When she heard nothing she opened the door and walked into the dim room anyway.

The sound of deep somnolent breathing filtered to her ears as she walked quietly over to Sara and sat down beside the large bed. She sat quietly for a moment, placing her elbow upon the arm of the chair and the left side of her face in her palm.

Eventually she spoke.

"I wish you were awake."

"Like I could sleep through your constant sighs of woe." Sara said in a sleep filled voice.

The poet looked up surprised. "Sara! Did I wake you?"

Sara refrained from rolling her eyes and instead looked at Denise in suspicion. "Okay, what is wrong?"

"What makes you think something is wrong?"

"Oh I don't know." Sara began. "It's what?" She checked her digital clock, "half past five in the morning and you are up mooching and sighing with a face liked a smacked arse!"

Denise smiled slightly.

"So I ask again, what's wrong, honey?"

The poet's shoulders fell in defeat. "It's Randa."

Sara quirked an eyebrow in suspicion, "What is it? You know there is nothing you could tell me that would change my opinion of either of you, DJ." The old woman prodded hopefully.

Denise gazed at her aunt in confusion. "Huh?" She shook her head. "I think I may have offended or upset her last night."

"How so?"

148

"Last night I gave her the gift. At first I thought she liked it, she seemed to. Then all of a sudden she more or less fled out of the room."

Sara pursed her lips in thought. "How can you be sure she seemed upset?"

Denise shrugged. "The way she just up and left the room so suddenly, like she wanted to get away from me. There was a look in her eyes that seemed... uncomfortable maybe?" Sliding slightly down the chair, Denise placed her bare feet upon the bed. "What if she wants to leave?"

Shaking her head, the old woman gazed at her niece. "You are being a little melodramatic, DJ. What happened before she left for bed?"

"Well," Denise started, "I gave her the necklace and she asked me to help her put it on. I did. She said she liked it and hugged me. Then unexpectedly her demeanour changed and she high tailed it out of the room. I haven't seen her since."

Sara smiled and decided it was time to take a leap. She hoped she was about to make the right choice. "DJ, if I ask you something, will you answer me honestly?"

"Of course."

"DJ, how do you feel about Randa?"

Denise looked away.

"DJ?"

The poet sighed and turned her vision back towards her aunt with a serious statement. She pulled her feet from the bed and sat up straight. "I um... I like her. I more than like her, Sara. I feel an attraction towards her." She lowered her eyes. "Do you... are you uncomfortable by that?"

Sara shook her head. "No, honey, I did kind of think that."

"You did?" DJ asked surprised.

She nodded.

"Sara, what if Randa somehow sensed it and got spooked? What if she felt uncomfortable?" The poet rose from her chair and moved to sit on the bed facing Sara. It felt good to be able to talk about her feelings.

"DJ, I very much doubt that was the case. Randa doesn't seem like the kind of person to judge somebody like that. She is a lovely young woman," Sara insisted.

"But then what..."

"Talk to her." Sara interrupted. "Thinking destructive

149

thoughts like this will do no good. I bet you've hardly slept all night have you?"

Denise's vision moved to down to a close inspection of the floral bedspread.

"That is what I thought!"

"What shall I do?" The poet asked.

Sara reached out and placed her right hand over her niece's. "Just wait and see how she is today. You may be surprised to find she is fine."

"No… I mean what about what I told you… about how I am feeling?"

The older woman smiled tenderly; she was happy to hear that DJ was acknowledging the way she felt about the American nurse. For a long time she had worried that her niece may never find that somebody special. Now she hoped that Denise's insecurities wouldn't hamper her opportunity to express herself. Sara was well aware that Randa did appear to harbour her own feelings for Denise but she didn't feel it was her place to point that out.

"Your feelings aren't wrong, DJ. Maybe you and Randa just need to sit and talk?"

The poet shook her head. "No I don't think so. Not about this."

"DJ, you may be surprised."

"So may she! No, I cant." Denise rose from the bed, needing to change the subject. Even the thought that she may have scared Randa away was enough to make sure she never acted upon those feelings. "I think I might as well go and get ready. It is Boxing Day after all! Can I get you anything before I go and shower?"

"Oh no." Sara declined, "I think I'll try and get a few more hours of sleep!"

Denise gazed at her aunt sheepishly. "Um… okay." With a shy grin she exited Sara's room and closed the door softly behind her.

The house was still relatively dark as Denise made her way toward the stairs. When she reached the first step she became aware of the definite sounds of movement coming from the upper part of the house. That could mean only one thing; Randa was up and about.

Taking a deep breath Denise ascended the stairs slowly.

Standing on the semi-dark landing, Denise could see a sliver of light beaming underneath her study's door. Knowing with certainty that Randa was awake and feeling there was no point in delaying the inevitable, Denise slowly approached the door. Tentatively she knocked lightly. There was a slight moment of silence before she heard Randa's voice allowing entrance to her makeshift bedroom.

Looking down at her red and black checked pyjamas and deciding she was presentably attired, Denise cautiously pushed open the door. The brightness of the room caused her to squint slightly but the poet's eyes soon adjusted to the increase of light. She looked down with a measured amount of surprise to see Randa's smiling face greeting her.

"Morning, Denise."

Randa sat upon the opposite end of the fold away bed with her legs crossed. She held a small leather bound book in one hand that she placed down upon the surface of the bed, open on a particular page. The poet noticed how the blonde nurse had changed nightwear and now wore a pair of red pyjamas similar to her own.

Denise smiled, still filled with trepidation. "Hi."

"I see neither of us were able to sleep much last night." Randa chuckled and patted a space on the bed in front of her. "Sit down... it is your room after all! I was just looking through your book collection. I hope you don't mind. You have some impressive first editions here! I feel almost clumsy touching them." Randa paused as she watched Denise lower herself to the bed. "Denise, are you alright?"

DJ looked down at her fingers that were busy tracing the patterned surface of the thick quilt. *Am I all right? I don't know anymore.* With a frown she looked up at Randa and asked self consciously, "Are you okay?"

Perplexed, Randa leaned forward and Denise noticed the necklace fall out from over her fleecy bedtime top. "What do you mean?"

"Last night, you left in a kind of a rush. I thought that maybe I had offended or upset you in some way." Denise bit

151

the corner of her lip as she waited for Randa to speak. The look of confusion then horror in the blonde's eyes left her with mixed feelings.

"No!" Randa exclaimed. "No you didn't upset me in the slightest. Denise, I'm really sorry if you thought that but I think I was just overwhelmed by it all. The day, the people I met, the special gifts, this." She pulled at the pendent around her neck.

"You really did like it then." Denise said, more as an affirmation of relief to herself.

"Denise, it's the most unique thing I have ever seen!" Randa said with conviction.

"I should hope so!" The poet replied with a smile. "Designed it myself!"

Smile falling from her lips, Randa looked down at the stone still within her grasp. "You did? Denise it's..." She stopped seemingly at a loss for words.

A profound sense of relief flowed through DJ; she didn't think she had ever felt so reassured in her life. Still there was one more fear that coursed her mind and one she knew she wouldn't be able to reveal. She wondered if Randa had any idea just how beautiful she thought she was and how she was only just able to resist the impulse to lean over and continue the contact from the night before. Feeling Randa's arms wrapped around her waist with her head resting upon her shoulder was to Denise, the most wonderful feeling she had ever experienced. It felt entirely too good to hold the woman within her arms and feel the body so close against her own. It produced sensations she had never felt before but knew, beyond a shadow of a doubt, that she wanted to feel again.

Randa rose from the bed and walked to the window and looked out upon the snow-covered land. "I guess I see no need in sitting around here doing nothing. Why don't you introduce me to the British custom of Boxing Day and all the wonderful traditions I'm sure it entails?"

Denise couldn't help but smile as she headed toward the study's exit. "Of course. Though if you call eating day old turkey in sandwiches, or sitting in front of the television watching the same old Christmas movies while eating chocolate a tradition, then I suppose it is!"

"Bring on the Brit chocolate!" Randa exclaimed with a laugh and Denise followed suit.

As if often seemed with Christmas, the days passed quickly. Denise had given herself a week off work during which she vowed not to pick up a pen or turn on her computer the whole time. Sara's good friend Diane had visited the day after Boxing Day and Sara insisted that the two women take a few hours off so Denise had taken Randa shopping to look around the sales that had more or less started the day after Christmas.

The poet enjoyed the unreserved expressions of excitement Randa had portrayed as she led the nurse around her favourite places. A shop dedicated to exotic foods from around the world, craft shops, second hand book shops and her favourite - sports shops! The poet did have a weakness for buying training shoes and had enough pairs to wear a different style, per day, for a whole month. Randa had declared her insane, but Denise laughed if off stating that she herself had seen Randa's personal collection of novelty socks sprawled all over the fold away bed! Then as a joke she bought her a pair of Christmas socks that played the tune 'Jingle Bells' as you walked!

Unfortunately Denise had one nagging thought in the back of her mind, that of Randa's departure. She knew the nurse had arrived on a fortnight visit but as the days slowly came to an end she wondered how she would cope without her. Not only due to her growing feelings of affection but because of the assistance the nurse provided for Sara. Randa's help had been invaluable and although she had never mentioned returning to the States she was sure it must have been on her mind. It was on Denise's - constantly.

Chapter 15

The morning of New Year's Eve came much quicker than Randa wanted. She was scheduled to return to the States in two days, her vacation time being used up. Standing in the shower she ran over all the possibilities in her mind again. Sleep had been elusive the last few nights as the problem and potential solutions drifted across her mind time and time again.

The problem was simple; she didn't want to leave Denise and Sara but she was out of time and options. The potential solutions were not as easy. She felt she had two ways to go. First, she could stay. She could quit her job and help Denise with Sara for whatever amount of time the older woman had left. Randa wasn't sure what poets got paid these days but she thought it couldn't be much. Except for the Lexus, Denise didn't lead an extravagant lifestyle. The nurse had some savings and she figured if she stretched it carefully, she might be able to contribute her fair share to the household. The second option was to help Denise find a nurse quickly to take her place and go back home. She could continue to correspond with Denise and give her any help she could from a distance.

But distance isn't what you want with Denise, is it? In the few days after Christmas she had found a peace and an ease with the poet she had never had with another living soul. Randa wasn't a fool; she knew she was deeply and totally in love with Denise. This wasn't the adoration of a fan and it wasn't the casual warmth of friendship. This was the true, deep love and grand passion she had waited her entire life for. She could have kicked herself for not recognizing it sooner. Denise wasn't given to the open expression of her innermost feelings except through her poetry. Randa could respect that, but it made knowing what to do very difficult.

The water was cooling rapidly so Randa finished rinsing and quickly left the shower. She toweled herself dry and pulled on a clean pair of sweats. She had made sure to bring clothes into the bathroom since the morning she met Denise in the hall wrapped in only a towel. A warm sensation rushed through her

156

as she remembered the way Denise had blushed and had not quite been able to keep her eyes from Randa's body. *I wonder what would have happened that day if the towel had 'accidentally' slipped?*

Randa pushed those thoughts aside and resolved to make a decision about her plans. She finished dressing and went downstairs to the kitchen where she met Denise pulling the ingredients together for French toast.

"Morning, Randa," the poet said. "There's juice and tea ready. I checked and Sara isn't awake yet but it shouldn't be much longer so I decided to start breakfast."

"Tea sounds great, I could use a little caffeine boost this morning. Denise, I wanted to talk to you about something." The brunette's eyebrows rose as she waited for the nurse to continue.

"You know my plane is scheduled to leave in two days and I think some arrangements have to be made."

Denise dropped her eyes and turned to the breakfast preparations. "Yeah, I know. It's been on my mind recently as well. Look, Randa, I want you to know how much I appreciate you taking time out of your life to come here." The poet's eyes returned to the blonde. "I'm not sure how this could have been one of the happiest times of my life what with Sara ailing and all, but it has been. I want you to know how much I'll…we'll miss you, but I guess it couldn't last forever."

The women looked at one another and Randa's fingers found their way to the necklace Denise had given her on Christmas. *Forever? Well, why not? I'm never going to know unless I give it a chance.*

"Actually, Denise, what I was going to say was it seems to me I just got to know the Jennings women and it would take a while to train somebody in Sara's care and I've really come to care for her and…Oh hell, if you'll have me I'd like to stay. I have some money put aside so you wouldn't need to worry about paying anyone a salary and I could contribute to the running of the household and…" She hesitated a moment as the poet remained silent. *Did I make a mistake here? Did I misread the situation?*

Finally Denise spoke. "Well, Nurse Martin, if that's how you feel about the situation I believe I have no choice but to accede to your wishes. I think I might just manage the finances though." A bright smile broke across her features then and she let out a whoop of joy. She reached forward to hug the nurse and swung her around the kitchen. Setting Randa back down, the poet leaned forward and whispered "Thank you." The blonde shivered at the words and the look in Denise's eyes. *Oh yeah, right decision.*

"Okay. Well, that was...yeah, uhm...I'm glad you're happy about it." Looking at her watch, Randa figured the time to be about midnight at home. "I've got to make some arrangements so could I use your computer to.." The nurse stopped mid-sentence. "Your computer to..."

"Randa?" asked Denise, starting to worry about the nurse. Randa merely broke into a huge grin.

"Denise, I'm scathingly brilliant! Can I use your computer?"

"Of course, but what's going on?"

"I'll tell you after I check a few things out. By the way, do we have some champagne?" Thrown by the sudden change in conversation, the poet could only nod.

"Good, if things work out we may have reason to celebrate."

At supper that night, Randa told the Jennings women what she had been working on for the better part of the day.

"So Mom is going to move into my house until I come home. She'll look after things for me and go home on the weekends to check out her place. That was the easy part. Derek was a tougher nut to crack but we worked out that I'll work from here 3 nights a week. The company will send me up a database computer from their London offices in three days. By cutting down to part-time, I keep my benefits and still have a salary coming in so you won't have to worry about supporting the three of us by yourself, Denise. That was a worry to me, that I would be putting a burden on you."

Denise and Sara exchanged glances, but Sara only said "That's so wonderful, Randa. I'm happy you'll be staying with Denise and I. Perhaps we could have a little of that champagne now? I'm afraid I haven't stayed up to see in the New Year for

158

a few years now. Denise could use the company I would expect though. I know the last few years she just went to her study to write on New Year's Eve."

Randa wrinkled her nose in distaste. "Working on New Year's Eve when you didn't have to? Nope, not this year, young lady. You can just teach me about English tradition and not worry about writing anything tonight."

It was nearing midnight at the house in Derbyshire. Sara had stayed up later than usual but had eventually requested to be assisted to bed. She kissed each of the young women and wished them a Happy New Year. Now the poet and the nurse sat in the living room talking quietly. The fire warmed the room and the television was turned down showing soundless celebrants from various areas around London.

"So what would you be doing tonight if you were at home?" asked the poet.

"If this was a year ago I probably would have been working. Ringing in the New Year with sparkling non-alcoholic cider. I didn't mind working New Year's Eve, no matter what I said earlier. I guess I always figured that day belonged to couples and I haven't been involved with anyone for a while."

"If it isn't too personal, can I ask why? Randa, you are an attractive woman. You're funny and smart so why aren't you involved with someone?"

Randa shrugged. "Guess I haven't found that right person yet. What about you?"

"Oh I suppose the same. Besides, who would want to spend time with a reclusive old poet?"

"You mean, who would want to spend time with a beautiful, intelligent woman whose poetry could melt a glacier? No, I can't think of a single person." Randa waited the space of a heartbeat before she added in a soft voice, "Except me."

Denise blushed. "Well, thank you, Randa. You're a good friend." She reached over and squeezed the nurse's hand.

Randa looked intensely into Denise's deep blue eyes and felt herself becoming lost in their depths. Taking a steadying breath she asked, "Is that all I am to you, Denise? A friend?" She held perfectly still, waiting for the answer that would mean everything.

Denise gazed back into Randa's green eyes and whispered, "You're much more than that. So much more."

Randa closed her eyes briefly in utter happiness. She opened them again to find Denise still watching her.

"It's almost midnight," the poet said. She turned the sound up on the television as a shot of Big Ben came on the screen. Helping Randa up, both women stood to greet the New Year.

"Uhm, Denise... in the States we have a tradition at midnight..."

"We have the same one here," Denise replied. Randa reached out to the poet and drew her near as the chimes of Big Ben began to sound. Sweet anticipation began to hum in Randa's veins as she melted into Denise's embrace. The feeling of completeness was near over-whelming as they stood together. As Big Ben began to toll the hour, Randa tipped her head back to look directly at the poet.

"I'm in love with you, Denise. For the first time in my life I'm truly in love." Randa felt Denise take in a small sharp breath then release it as she gave the nurse a small smile. Without comment, she lowered her mouth to Randa's. The first sweet contact of lips left Randa shaken. The kiss had transmitted all the love unspoken between them and surpassed any fantasy and dream they may have had about this moment. When the brief encounter ended they clung together, hearts beating rapidly and breathing quickened.

"Happy New Year, Randa."

"It is now," was the reply.

Randa reached up and settled her hand in the dark tresses of the brunette. Standing on tiptoes she brought the other woman's head down again for a searing kiss. If the first kiss was a warm fireplace, this one was a volcano. Randa's tongue reached out and lightly licked across Denise's lower lip. With a moan, Denise opened her lips and allowed Randa's tongue entrance. A loving exploration followed which ended only with the need for breath.

By unspoken agreement the women returned to the couch, never losing contact with one another. Randa moved to nestle herself in Denise's embrace. Small kisses and caresses were exchanged and in those tender moments Randa knew nothing in her life would ever be the same again.

Sitting in the corner of the large three-seated couch, Denise looked down at the woman almost sitting in her lap. Hands joined and their fingers laced together, Randa's blonde head rested peacefully upon her shoulder. Although the nurse wasn't asleep her eyes were closed in peaceful relaxation.

Just over an hour had passed since the beginning of the New Year and neither woman had moved from their original positions. Lifting her hand, Denise studied the fingers wrapped around her own. She noticed a small scar running across the middle finger and wondered how it had happened.

Internally, Denise's body still hummed with the sensual feelings invoked from the moment Randa's lips had touched her own. She would never have imagined them to feel so soft, so addictive that even now she still felt the strong desire to continue kissing the woman in her arms.

She loves me, the poet thought; *she said she is in love with me!* Although Denise had hoped Randa did indeed mirror some of her affections, never did she expect the nurse to declare her heart so openly. That wasn't to say Denise wasn't thrilled by the nurse's declaration for she was. Even now she could still recall the very words and look upon Randa's face as she spoke. The poet in her knew that image would be etched into her mind forever.

Blue eyes moved to the carriage clock on the mantle as she studied the time. DJ was surprised to discover that it had just gone half past one.

She looked back down at Randa and whispered, "Hey?"

Jade eyes opened and regarded her with a content smile.

"It's getting late and although most people will still be up and partying the night away, I think for Sara's sake we should probably turn in." Denise lifted Randa's hand and kissed her fingers softly with a smile. "What do you think?"

Randa lifted her head from the comfortable shoulder. "However much I would be happy in just staying right here, I know you're right."

Decision made, the women rose together and set about securing the house for the night, turning off the television and all the lights before heading up the stairs.

Once both Randa and Denise were standing on the landing they gazed at each other awkwardly. As if feeling the magnetic pull, Denise stepped forward. She looked down into welcoming green eyes and smiled before Randa closed the distance and sealed their lips together. Denise closed her eyes. The acknowledgement that this was a feeling she would be happy to revel in forever didn't disturb her in the slightest.

Moments later she pulled away and looked back into questioning eyes. She pushed her right hand through Randa's light blonde locks in an adoring nature. "I'm so happy you are staying longer, Randa." She bent forward and placed a single kiss on her lips.

"Me too," Randa replied thickly.

They gazed at each other a while longer before simultaneously moving away.

"Well," Denise began, "I guess I will see you in the morning."

"Yes." Randa stepped back towards her door. "Goodnight, Denise, sweet dreams."

I'm sure I will. "You too, Randa. Night."

The women parted and went to their separate bedrooms. Once behind the door of her own room, Denise fell to her bed on her back. A smile graced her lips as she whispered, "She loves me!" *My god, I think I know what an infatuated teenager feels like!* With a chuckle, Denise laced her fingers behind her head and started at the ceiling, *how am I ever going to sleep tonight now?* She wondered.

Chapter 16

Randa woke up late on New Year's Day. She hadn't intended to sleep so long but the combination of the late night and the delicious warmth of being in love caused the nurse to slumber peacefully into late morning.

Randa lay quietly, reviewing the events of the night before. Denise had seemed pleased with her confession of love, but hadn't said anything in return. *I take that back, she said plenty with her kisses and I heard her loud and clear. She may not have said she loves me but I sure felt it. That will have to be enough...for now.*

Slipping from the bed, Randa grabbed her towel and headed out to take a shower before going downstairs. As she exited the study she nearly ran headlong into Denise who was on her way to the staircase. Both women stopped short, staring at the other and blushing.

"Good morning," the blonde offered. "I was just on my way to the shower. I didn't mean to sleep in. I'll hurry and help you with Sara."

"Sara is fine. We've been up for a while and have already had breakfast so take your time. I probably would have slept longer also, but something was on my mind it seems."

"Something good I hope?" the nurse probed.

"Oh, very good," Denise returned. The eye contact held until Randa came to herself and started again for the bathroom.

"Well, I guess I...uh...I should be getting in the...uh...shower and..."

A hand reached out to capture the nurse's arm as she passed. "Randa," was all Denise said, but the low sensual tone of her voice caused the blonde to turn into the taller woman's embrace and immediately seek the heat they generated so strongly together. Strong arms pulled the smaller woman in close as Randa turned her face up to Denise. Blue eyes blazed into green briefly before lids lowered and lips met. The fire of the previous night was rekindled instantly as the women deepened the kiss and hands wandered increasingly familiar territory.

Randa broke off the kiss and settled herself against Denise while trying to slow her rapid breathing. She felt the taller woman press a soft kiss against her hair then rest her cheek against that same spot. The blonde let a contented sigh escape her lips and enjoyed the marvelous physical contact a minute before stepping back.

"Me...shower...cold...now!"

Denise chuckled as Randa made her way into the bathroom. Closing the door, the nurse leaned back against it. *I feel like I've been branded and it was just by a kiss! Kisses never did this to me before.* She knew the difference was the poet. *The songwriter who said 'a kiss is just a kiss' never got one from Denise Jennings!*

Randa turned on the water and proceeded to shower, barely suppressing the urge to sing show tunes.

A short time later Randa entered the kitchen to find Denise and Sara lingering over a cup of tea. The radio was on and they were listening to the morning program Sara favored, a mixture of local news, weather and music.

"Good morning, Sara," she said as she gave the older woman a brief peck on the cheek.

"Good morning," Sara returned. "You must have slept well. What would you like for breakfast?"

"I think I'll just have some tea and toast with your delicious strawberry jam. You have to remind me to get your recipe for my mom." The nurse moved behind Sara to the cupboard where the jam was kept.

"Let me help," said Denise as she rose to her feet. "I'm afraid I returned it to a higher shelf than usual when I put it back earlier."

"Well, the President of the Vertically Challenged Club thanks you, oh tall one." Randa placed two slices of bread into the toaster as the brunette pulled the jar from the shelf. The blonde found the butter in the refrigerator and Denise opened the jam. Absently, the brunette stuck a finger in the jar and brought some of the sweet, red mixture to her lips but paused just short of her goal as she noticed Randa staring at her. The blonde was dumbstruck by the near erotic image of the sweet jam approaching even sweeter lips. Denise appeared to be embarrassed until she saw the heated look on Randa's face. The poet extended her hand to the nurse and silently offered the jam to the blonde's partially open lips. Never losing eye contact, Randa opened her lips wider and took the offered digit into her mouth. She used her tongue to swirl around the fingertip, transferring the jam to her mouth. Denise gulped audibly, but her eyes never left the blonde's. The moment ended as the toast popped from the toaster.

Pulling her hand back, Denise moved back to her aunt. "I'm...I'm going up to my study to work for a while. You'll be okay?"

"Of course, DJ. Randa and I will be fine, don't worry about us." Denise gave her aunt's shoulder a squeeze and gave Randa a look that clearly said, "Later."

Randa brought her tea and toast to the table and the two women sat in companionable silence for a moment before Sara said, "How long?"

Puzzled, the nurse looked at Sara. "How long what?"

"How long do I need to pretend I don't see what is happening between you and DJ? Probably for DJ's sake it should be a few days, I suppose. She does tend to embarrass rather easily I'm afraid," Sara said nonchalantly.

Randa was incredulous as she asked, "How did you know?"

"Now Randa, as a nurse you should know this disease doesn't affect my eyesight at all." Sara nodded at a place directly in front of her. The blonde turned to see the kitchen window with the curtains open. The sky outside was overcast and with the light on Randa realized Sara, by reflection, had an excellent view of everything happening in the kitchen. The nurse blushed a bright pink and let out a small, strangled groan.

Sara chuckled at the blonde's discomfort but said, "It's alright, Randa. I've been so worried that DJ would be alone after I'm gone. I'm glad that's not going to be the case and I'm very glad the person she found was you."

166

The nurse felt tears gathering in her eyes and she moved forward to hug the older woman. "You're the most remarkable person, Sara Jennings. I hope you know that."

Randa felt Sara smile and say, "I have my moments. Now, finish your breakfast and we won't speak any more about this. Well, not at the present anyway."

Another small groan emanated from Randa as she moved back to her tea. *This is going to be a long day.*

Two days later, Brightwood delivered the database computer. Randa showed Denise how the system worked with the regular computer and the two worked as a team to get the components set up in the study. They used the new line the phone company had installed earlier in the day and sent out test messages insuring the system would be functioning and ready for Randa's use on her first shift back to work the next night.

Two hours had passed before the pair realized it. Randa looked at her watch with a worried frown. "Denise, we should go downstairs and check on Sara. I didn't notice how the time had gotten away from me." The poet glanced at her watch as well and followed the nurse from the study. They were only halfway down the stairs when they heard a faint "DJ! Randa!" The poet took the last four steps as one and raced into the living room. Sara was slumped forward in her chair unable to raise herself back up due to badly weakened limbs. Denise eased the older woman up into a sitting position as Randa entered the room.

The nurse saw the stricken look on Denise's face but moved first to Sara. She checked the woman over and after determining there was no injury, she asked, "Sara, what happened?"

The older woman tried to cover her fear by pretending annoyance. "I forgot to ask you to place the remote control for the television in my lap and as I knew you both were busy upstairs, I tried to reach it myself. I leaned forward but when my hand was on the bloody thing I couldn't push myself back up. I've been slumped over for the last quarter of an hour."

Denise was appalled. "I'm so sorry, Sara. I should have

been here. This never should have happened. We won't leave you again."

The annoyance in Sara's voice was real this time. "DJ, this was my fault. I know better than either of you what my body is capable of and I made a serious misjudgment today. You most certainly will not spend every moment minding me as if I was a child."

A child Randa thought. *That's it, a child.*

Randa offered to help Sara to her bed, as it was close to the time she usually took her afternoon nap and Randa wanted to give her another brief check for any injury she may have missed. When she returned to the living room she found Denise with her head in her hands, rocking slightly back and forth. The nurse settled on the couch next to the brunette.

"Denise? Denise, she's fine. She was a little shook up but she's okay now." The poet refused to be comforted and continued to blame herself for the incident.

"If we're looking for blame I think there's enough of it to go around." Randa took Denise's larger hand in her own and leaned to the side to place her cheek against Denise's arm. "We both were wrong in this, but placing blame isn't going to prevent this from happening again." Denise brought her free hand up to caress the blonde's cheek.

"Randa, what am I going to do? I feel like I have let Sara down."

"*We* are going to make sure it doesn't happen again. You're not in this by yourself anymore, remember?" Turning her head, she placed a soft kiss into Denise's palm. "I have an idea about this problem and Sara is the one who gave it to me. Let's buy a baby monitor. No matter where we are in the house we can hear what is happening with Sara and we would know right away if she needed anything. You know as well as I do that Sara wouldn't be comfortable with us hovering over her every minute so I think this would be a good compromise."

"It's not a bad idea. If you'll stay here with Sara, I'll go and have a look in the stores. If we could get this thing set up today I would feel much better."

"Of course I'll stay with her. I'll be right here when you get back." Denise and Randa stood up and moved to get the brunette's hat, jacket and gloves from the closet.

"I'll try not to be gone long." She bent to give the nurse a

168

brief kiss before making her way out the door.

As Randa watched the poet move down the snowy sidewalk she felt her heart ache just a little. *Oh Denise, I love you so much and this is going to be so hard on you. You are hurting terribly already and this is just the beginning.* The nurse closed the door and moved back into the warmth of the house.

Denise had decided - due to the snowy weather and precarious driving conditions - that she would be much safer travelling to the local shop on foot. She was glad that the general store, which was no more than a mile away, seemed to stock the most unimaginable of items. Still she did hope a baby monitor would be among their varied stock. *They sell pet rabbits for god's sake!*

Walking at a rapid pace, icy snow crunched loudly under her booted feet as Denise moved down the street. As she turned a corner onto the main road she was annoyed to see another fall of brilliant white flakes begin to make their descent onto the frozen land below. *Just great,* she thought, *bloody typical.*

Speeding up her gait, Denise pushed herself to reach the general store faster. Feelings of guilt still laid heavy in her mind and just the thought of Sara's plight was upsetting to recall. To be confronted once again by the growing severity of Sara's disease brought home the reality of her suffering. And it was only going to get worse.

Folding her arms against the increasing cold, Denise sighed; her warm breath released as a dense cloud of vapour. She could feel her emotions rising but pushed them deep down. *If I start bloody crying now no doubt the damned tears will turn to icy droplets on my face,* she thought, trying to lighten her mood with internal humor.

It was going to be a long cold trek!

By the time Denise returned home the snow was falling at

a rapid pace. As she reached the front door, Denise felt the need to shake herself off and remove the large amount of flakes that had taken residence upon her head and shoulders. Hands shaking with the intense cold, DJ grappled around her pocket with her free hand - the other holding a large carrier bag - looking for her keys. Once found, she rammed the appropriate key into the lock and pushed the door open, almost falling with relief into the warm house.

"Jesus, it is cold out there," she muttered with a shiver.

Keeping a strong hold of the bag in her left hand, Denise wandered into the front room, too cold to even remove her outdoor coat. She entered to find Randa sitting by the fire reading a book. Denise could tell it was one of hers.

"Want to swap places?"

Randa looked up in surprise. "Denise! Look at you; you're freezing!"

She got up and the poet handed her the plastic carrier bag as she moved towards the roaring fire. "I need some heat. Did you know it has started snowing again?" Denise pulled the black woolly hat from her head.

"I do now!" Randa replied, placing the bag down and helping a still cold Denise out of her coat. "The snow is pretty treacherous in these parts isn't it."

"Looks better from the window, too." Denise replied with a smirk as she rubbed her hands together and held them out in front of the fire. "How's Sara?"

"Still sleeping."

Nodding, Denise turned to face Randa. "I was really glad you were here earlier, Randa, thank you. I would have been too freaked and guilt ridden to have even thought about checking for possible injuries. You were great." She smiled fondly. "I loved the way you took control so efficiently."

Randa stepped forward and took Denise's hands, warming them with her own. "It's just instinct and training." She shrugged lightly.

Denise moved her hand over Randa's arm and said, "You were still great."

With a slight blush, the blonde looked down. "Thank you." She then looked to her side at the grey carrier bag slightly covered with droplets of melted snow. "So you managed to get a monitor?"

"Yep." Kneeling down, Denise settled herself on the rug in front of the fire and Randa followed suit. "They had two, so I chose the best. It has a longer range, is off-white in colour and the cool thing is that it's two-way - only you have to press a button on the 'parents' end to talk. Obviously that part isn't entirely necessary but I wanted to get the best they had."

The nurse frowned. "You know, Denise, this was my idea. I feel I should contribute to the cost."

"Hey, no, it's fine honestly."

"I know but..."

"Randa." Denise insisted, "believe me, money is of no issue to me."

"I just thought that maybe...well... I've never really noticed..."

Denise smiled as she realised what Randa was trying to say. "Look," she licked her lips slowly in thought, "money will never be a problem, Randa. I understand what you are trying to say but believe me when I say that I am more than covered in that department."

Randa looked up, she seemed slightly uncomfortable. "I wasn't sure. You don't really seem... Well, apart from your car and sneaker obsession!"

In thought, Denise looked into the fire. She wondered whether she should explain to the nurse something that only Sara and Carl knew. After all she had signed contracts to ensure her silence in the deal, but she did trust Randa.

"Look, I um... I earn money from more than just the poetry that you know about."

The nurse frowned.

"Do you know just how much some people want to be famous?"

Randa shrugged, not entirely sure she knew what the poet was implying. "I guess... maybe?"

"Did you know that some people will do anything to be famous, even if it means paying somebody else for their work and the right to put their own name against it?"

Slowly understanding sunk in. "You mean like ghost writing and things like that? So you've written poetry for somebody else and they've called it their own?"

"Well, not just poetry." Denise stated.

"What else?"

171

The poet smirked. "Well, I also write for a greeting card company but what I was actually referring to was a couple of err... novels."

Randa's mouth fell. "You've written a novel?"

"Two actually and because the first did so well the woman paid me five times as much for a sequel." Denise still found it hard to believe that those novels had done as well as they had.

"I don't believe it!" Randa shook her head and stared at Denise in wonder. "I don't suppose you can tell me what they were? What they were called, or who the so called author is?"

"Well," Denise scrunched her nose in thought. "Let's just say that they were a couple of period novels set in the early sixteen hundreds that were adapted into television dramas."

Randa stared at Denise flabbergasted. "Wow, I'm speechless," she chuckled. "It's lucky I love you for you and not your money then, isn't it?"

Denise leaned forward. "For me, yes." She stared into clear green eyes. The flickering flames from the fire blended their orange hues with the light emerald orbs creating a vision of what Denise considered poetic perfection. "You are so beautiful, Randa."

The blonde smiled as she caressed Denise's face. The poet could tell she wanted to respond but she seemed to have a nagging thought on her mind.

"Doesn't it bother you to have somebody else taking the credit for your work like that? I mean it appears to be something very successful. This woman must be quite famous and supposedly just as successful now."

"It's what she paid for," Denise replied. "It's her conscience. She wants the fame and she now has it. I don't want it. In both cases all parties are happy."

"You really are, aren't you?"

"What?" Denise asked.

"Happy."

Taking Randa's hand, Denise looked deep into her eyes. "I was as happy as I thought I could be. Then something happened to change all of that forever and I thought things would never be the same again." She looked down at the smaller hand within her own and ran her fingers over the soft flesh. "Then through something that I thought would leave such devastation in our lives, you came along. Though I do still see

172

and feel that devastation every day you have brought a new aspect of joy into my life that I have never before felt. Randa, your presence is the reason I feel the way I do." Denise looked back up into misty green eyes. She delivered a wry smile. "That was the long winded answer to your question." The poet realised it was the first time she had ever really voiced any aspect of her feelings to Randa.

It appeared to have been the right move as the nurse leaned forward and initiated a gentle kiss, which ended far too quickly as far as Denise was concerned. Randa looked over to the baby monitor still in the shopping bag and said, "Do you want to test it out?"

With a nod of approval, Denise rose to her feet and pulled Randa with her. "Let's go and play with the new toy!"

After discovering that Sara was still sleeping, Denise and Randa decided to try the monitor themselves. Taking the main transmitter, Denise disappeared up stairs leaving Randa and the receiver downstairs. She wandered down the landing while deciding which room to enter. She eventually chose the bathroom. Denise passed through the door and pushed it to as a wicked thought crossed her mind. Sitting upon the edge of the bath, Denise turned on the transmitter. "Testing, testing one two three. This is..." she paused in thought, "lyrical lady, requesting..."she paused again. *Name, damn my mind has gone blank.* "Err, requesting um... Raunchy Randa?"

There was silence.

Denise chuckled. "Randa, press that little grey button on the top right hand corner."

There was a slight pause before Randa's electronic voice filtered through the main transmitter. "Raunchy Randa?"

"So I choked!" Denise said with a chortle. "Anyway ladies and ladies it is time to play '*Guess whose room I am in.*' Are you ready to play?"

There was a short laugh before Randa asked. "Do I get a prize if I win?"

Denise thought for a while. "Um, sure... anything you want. Okay ladies and ladies. Right, this room is used by the two younger members of this very household." The poet had to roll her eyes at her own terrible version of a game show host's voice.

"Is it a bedroom?"

"Invalid question I'm afraid… sorry." An evil glint sparkled in her eyes. "This room contains a bed that they have both slept upon."

"Well that helps a lot."

Denise sniggered. "Well then, let me venture a little further into the room, shall I?" She crossed her legs and placed one hand by her side upon the white porcelain bathtub. "Okay… let me check out the clothing. How about underwear?"

"What!"

"Oh yes, that is a good idea."

"Denise?" Randa's electronic voice questioned.

"Well this lovely lady wears some… oh some veeeeery nice black panties. Lacy… and WO HO… g-string."

There was a short silence before Denise heard the unmistakable sound of a certain blonde nurse coming up the stairs. She chuckled as she opened the bathroom door just in time to see Randa reach the top step and disappear briefly into the study before returning with a frown. Her eyes soon located Denise leaning against the bathroom doorway with a grin.

Denise smiled innocently as she gazed back at Randa who stalked towards her. *Oh am I in trouble?*

"You, Denise Jennings, were in the bathroom the entire time. You cheat!"

Denise placed a hand over her chest in shock. "Me? A cheat?"

The nurse chuckled. "Yes, you. So… was that just a lucky guess about the underwear?"

Shrugging Denise placed her arms over Randa's shoulders. "Doesn't every girl's drawer contain at least one black, lacy, thongy type underwear?"

"Do they now?" Randa wrapped her arms around the poet's waist. "Well, I still say you cheated so I demand my prize. 'Anything you want' if I recall."

"Okay," Denise conceded, "what do you desire?"

"Well my desired prize consists of two parts. First I would like at some time in the future for you to prove your statement about what every girl has in her drawer!" She wiggled her eyebrows. "And secondly, I think a kiss will do just fine for the present moment."

Denise pursed her lips appearing to be considering the request before she replied, "Deal." And slowly leaned forward, sealing their lips together.

Later that afternoon, Denise entered her aunt's bedroom to find Sara watching the television. Randa had not long ago selected a DVD for her to watch but as Denise knew it was Sara's favourite film and had seen it a dozen times, she wouldn't mind the interruption.

Carrying the baby monitor box under her arm she walked through the room and sat in the vanity chair beside Sara's bed. Propping her socked feet upon the floral cover she gazed briefly at the screen watching Audrey Hepburn's transformation as she blossomed from common flower girl to beautiful lady.

Sara looked to her right at Denise. "So what do you have under your arm?"

Biting the inside of her cheek, Denise looked at her aunt in thought. Neither she nor Randa had yet told Sara about the monitor and she hoped Sara wouldn't take it the wrong way. "We had an idea and well, we thought it might help to make sure nothing like what happened earlier today happens again."

A shadow of fear crossed Sara's eyes. "What is it?"

"This." Denise placed the box upon the bed and looked at Sara nervously.

The old woman looked down and read the label. "A baby monitor? Are you serious?"

Denise winced inside. "Well technically yes, but we just thought it could be used more as a monitor in general." She desperately wanted to explain herself. "It's um... just something to make sure that if you ever need anything, no matter where we are one of us will always be on hand and you only have to speak. It's not meant to intrude on you **or** treat you in anyway less..." she groaned; this was not going as she expected.

"I do understand, DJ."

With a sigh, Denise looked at Sara and said, "You liked watching me squirm, didn't you?"

Sara smiled warmly, but Denise could see the remnants of fear still in her eyes. "When I realised I was unable to push myself back up, DJ, I was so frightened."

Denise nodded and moved off the chair to sit on the bed beside her aunt.

"I tried so hard to push myself back to my sitting position but my limbs just refused to cooperate. I never felt helpless before that incident, DJ. It gave me a glimpse of just how this disease is progressing and it frightens me so."

"It scares me too, Sara."

Blue eyes so like her niece's filled with tears. "I feel like such a burden to you, DJ. How long before I can no longer lift a beaker or simply turn the page of a book?"

Denise tried to hold her composure but she felt her lip tremble as tears rolled down Sara's cheeks. "You will never be a burden, Sara, please believe that. You have been more than just my aunt for these past twenty years, you have been like a mother to me and I feel so very blessed for every second that you have been a part of my life." She wrapped an arm around Sara's frail shoulders and drew her in close. "I will always be here for you, you will never be alone through any of this, and that is what we want to make sure of. Both Randa and myself will always be here for you. You will **not** be alone."

Denise held Sara until her silent tears ended. The old woman moved back slightly and looked at her niece. "And neither will you."

The poet frowned.

"I am aware of how your relationship with Randa has progressed and I am very happy for you, DJ."

Her cheeks flushed and Denise lowered her eyes. "Did she tell you then?"

"Well let us just say that I got it out of her." Sara smiled. "I am happy for you both. Randa is a lovely woman." The older woman looked into her niece's eyes as she said, "So have you two…"

"Sara!" Denise blushed profusely, "I might have known you would ask me that!" She covered her cheeks with warm hands. "But no, we haven't. I don't feel ready for that just yet,

176

you know. It also doesn't help that I get the feeling that Randa is a lot more experienced at this kind of thing than me. Makes me feel a little like a clumsy novice." She shrugged with a wry smile.

"You know things will work themselves out, DJ, they always do." Sara placed her fingers under Denise's chin indicating that she wanted to look her niece in the eyes. Denise looked back up at her aunt and the old woman beamed. "You are happy?"

"She makes me very happy."

"Then that is all that matters," Sara said as she kissed her niece's cheek before turning back to the television with a smile.

Denise gazed at her aunt steadily. *But is it right to feel this happy when you are going through so much?*

Chapter 17

The next afternoon Randa was sitting on the front steps. Though the sky was overcast, no snow had fallen since the previous day. The temperature had dipped again overnight but the nurse, lost in thought, seemingly didn't notice. The door opened and Denise emerged from the house bundled up snugly in her heavy jacket and wool hat.

"Hey there, everything okay?" the poet asked. You said you were just coming out to sweep the steps so when you didn't come back in right away I thought I should come out and investigate."

Randa reached for the brunette's hand and urged her down to the step along side of her. "I'm glad you came out here with me, but I'm really alright. I was just thinking."

"About what?"

The blonde thought a moment before speaking. "I was thinking about the last few months and how my life has completely changed. If you had told me three months ago I would be sitting in England next to someone I love with all my heart, I would have said you were 'a few ants short of a picnic'. Crazy as that notion would have seemed at the time, nonetheless here I am."

"I am glad you're here, Randa," Denise said as she placed the hand still linked with Randa's into her pocket for warmth.

The nurse turned a little to look into the poet's eyes. "It's not just the being here that's been on my mind. I want to tell you a few things, have wanted to for a few days now actually." She fidgeted a little, but felt Denise squeeze the hand still tucked in her pocket.

"You can tell me anything," the brunette said softly.

"Okay then," Randa started, "but just let me stumble through this as best I can. Right about now I wish I had your gift with words because this wouldn't be so difficult for me to tell you. I want to explain to you how I feel, what has happened

178

to me. When I first arrived and saw you at the door I thought you were the most astonishingly beautiful person I had ever seen. I'm sure you've had people react like that to your looks before; you're a very attractive woman. I just wanted you to know though, that it wasn't your external beauty that made me love you. Your internal beauty captured me a long time ago. I²m not sure I could ever make you understand how you've touched me with your words. Even though I had never seen your face, I felt as if I had seen your soul and it was breathtaking. I came to England and met a visually striking woman. Yesterday you told me you were…let's call it comfortable, financially. I want, no, I need you to know that none of that means anything to me. I loved you long before I met you, you had me way *before* 'hello'." The nurse paused for a moment.

"I can't deny I've been involved with other people. I've had a few relationships but I've never felt the way I feel now. I used to think having someone care for me would make me feel good, but now I know that the feeling good part is all because I care about someone else. I'm so in love with you, Denise. For the first time, and I know the last time, I'm in love."

The poet sat quietly, absorbing the honest words. She was near to a response when a voice came from the pocket not containing the conjoined hands.

"Oh Lord, who I hope is the only one listening to me, please answer my prayers. Please let my niece DJ receive the wisdom she so obviously needs not to push down on the gray button when she is carrying the receiver to this monitor because then I would have to overhear more personal conversations, not that I just overheard one." Denise removed the receiver of the baby monitor from her pocket and showed it to Randa. The nurse just shook her head and groaned, "Not again."

"And Lord," Sara's voice continued, "Let my niece and her friend, Randa, also have the wisdom to know when to come inside out of the cold and make a cup of tea for themselves and a very nice older woman as well." Denise and Randa laughed and the poet pushed the gray button. In as deep a voice as she could muster, she said "Granted."

The two women stood up, hands finally releasing but hearts closer together than ever.

179

That afternoon Randa went upstairs to the study for her first shift back on the Brightwood Information Network in over two weeks. Denise went with her to watch the process that had allowed the pair to first meet. While the poet was no stranger to technology, the Brightwood system was fascinating. After watching Randa field the first two questions, the poet excused herself to head downstairs to make supper. Earlier, the two women had agreed on days Randa worked the brunette would cook and help Sara get ready for bed. On Randa's evenings off she would do the cooking and assisting for Sara.

As Denise turned to leave the room, Randa called, "I'll miss you."

The poet smiled and told Randa she would bring a plate of food up for her later. Working undisturbed for a couple of hours, the nurse realized she would be busier on her new shift. Being online in the evening in England meant daytime in the States and the consultation room was rarely empty. She was involved with a possible case of appendicitis when Denise came up behind her with a steaming plate of roast beef, mashed potatoes and peas. Randa finished the consultation by suggesting the client go to an emergency room as soon as possible. She then logged off for her lunch break.

Turning to her supper, the blonde eyed the meal appreciatively. "Mmmm, looks good. Occasionally though, I like to have dessert first." She reached up to Denise and pulled her head down for a lengthy kiss. "Oh yeah, you can put that on the menu every day if you like."

"Very lucky for you that it is the specialty of the house," Denise replied. "Maybe you would care for a second helping later?"

"Most definitely." Randa started to eat and was impressed by the poet's cooking skills yet again. "Please send my compliments to the chef."

"Thank you, madam," said Denise, "but all compliments must go to Sara. She insisted I learn to cook when I was a teenager. I may have hated it then but it has come in quite handy recently."

180

"How is Sara tonight?" the blonde asked.

"Tired, I think, but not too tired to tease me about her accidental eavesdropping earlier. Right now she is watching one of those Bob Hope and Bing Crosby movies on the television. She said she wanted to retire after it was done. When I get her to bed, would it bother you if I came up here and did a little writing? I could lie on the foldaway bed and work. I promise not to distract you."

"Um, sure, I'd like that." *Denise... in this room... on my bed; what could possibly be distracting about that?* Randa finished the plate of food and gave her thanks once again to the poet.

It was another two hours before Denise reappeared. Randa felt her presence immediately. It was as if someone has turned on a radiator in the room, causing there to be comfortable warmth around the blonde. Between consultations, Randa would sneak peeks over at the poet. Many times her head would be over a writing tablet, brows furrowed in concentration, but just as many times the nurse would look up to see blue eyes trained upon her. Finally, the shift was over and Randa rolled her head and shoulders, trying to loosen the knots accumulating there.

The nurse nearly jumped when she felt Denise's magic hands start working on the stiff areas. Her heartbeat picked up as strong fingers worked on sensitive spots. Randa closed her eyes and lost herself in a fantasy of Denise and herself on the poet's large bed, touching and caressing.

"Randa? You still with me?" Denise asked.

"No, but I'd like to be," replied the blonde under her breath.

"What was that?"

"Oh, nothing, just mumbling to myself. Thank you for the massage, you have very talented hands." Randa stood up and wrapped her arms around the taller woman's waist. "How about that second helping now?"

Denise smiled and brought their lips together in a kiss that left both women feeling as if their whole world was inside that one small room. They held one another for several minutes until a small cough was heard on the portable monitor set up near the bed.

"I guess we should call it a day, Denise. Let me just take a

181

quick look in on Sara then I'll be ready for some sleep."

"Well, I'll say goodnight then and I'll see you in the morning," said the poet as she laid another quick kiss on the nurse's lips then turned to leave the room.

"Goodnight, love."

Randa said the words aloud before she realized she had used the term of endearment. She knew she was blushing as the brunette turned and fixed the nurse with a gaze from her warm blue eyes.

"I love...that," said Denise and left Randa in the study with her thoughts.

The nurse looked down at the foldaway bed that still held the imprint of Denise's body. *Was that really what you wanted to say to me, Denise? I wonder...*

Chapter 18

From her bedroom window, Denise watched silently as the sun rose elegantly into the early morning sky. Higher above, the moon was still visible, creating a magnificent contrast between the amber sun and the marble moon hanging like majestic bodies in the atmosphere.

Leaning forward with both hands planted upon the natural wood of her windowsill, the poet's eyes moved lower as she studied the picturesque scene of the frozen landscape. No snow had fallen in over four weeks yet the air was so cold as to not allow the frozen flakes to melt away. Roads and pathways may have long since been cleared, either by pedestrian travelers or mobile gritters, but the untouched land of the countryside still held a blanket of icy white snow.

Turning away from the window, Denise moved over to her wardrobe and pulled open the double doors. Looking out at the winter scene had left her feeling colder than usual, though the fact that she was only wearing a pair of faded blue jeans and her bra could have also accounted for that. Denise slid a sweater and tank top from their respective hangers and closed the doors. She pulled the black tank over her head and sat down upon her unmade bed, holding the sweater. That too was black and one Sara had knitted just over a year ago. Denise ran her fingers over the complex design knowing her aunt would never again be able to create such intricate patterns.

Sara's strength had taken a rapid decline to the point where she was no longer able to move her legs and had only limited movement in her arms and upper body. She was still able to speak relatively well although she had lost more strength in her voice and it no longer sounded the same.

Both she and Randa had taken to spending more time with Sara. Sitting and watching films, television or just reading from a book or doing daily puzzles. Denise had to admit it; Randa had been wonderful with Sara. The nurse just seemed to know and understand what Sara needed better than the poet could and she was eternally grateful for that. Randa was a godsend, not only in Denise's life but in Sara's too, making the older woman's last few months a joy and comfort to experience. Of course the joy part did half span from the fact that she never did get tired of teasing the poor blonde about catching her in embarrassing situations and often stated that it was a good job she wasn't able to venture up stairs for fear of what she may find.

It always amused Denise but the truth of the matter was that their relationship hadn't progressed from the early stages. For many reasons it seemed they had not moved from what Randa had called *'first base'*. Looking after Sara who in both their eyes always came first, often feeling tired at the end of long days and of course the poets own self-consciousness dictated the need to move slowly. Randa was happy with that and had stated that jumping into bed with somebody after the first date was an experience she had learned from. Denise never did admit it, but that also contributed to her feelings of inadequacy. She had no idea where they had sprung from, but Sara had told her during one of their conversations while the nurse was working that it was more than likely due to her lack of experience. She had to agree that maybe Sara was indeed right.

Lifting the sweater, Denise pulled it over her head and pushed her arms through the sleeves. Once she was dressed she pulled her long hair back into a loose ponytail and rose to her feet. Today the three women had decided to go out for a walk around the outskirts of the village. It was obvious that Sara was beginning to feel stagnant due to being cooped up inside for so long and she needed a change and some fresh air.

Randa had risen long before Denise and had already got Sara and herself ready for the day before the poet had even made an appearance. She had ambled downstairs in her shorts and tee shirt to find the women dressed in their warmest clothing, sitting with hot drinks and waiting for her to show. Denise was literally ushered back up stairs to go and get ready for the excursion.

Opening her bedroom door, Denise stepped out into the landing now fully dressed and ready to face their forthcoming trek. She approached the stairs and took them two at a time as she made her way to the lower level of the house. Reaching the bottom step she was greeted by Randa who was looking for her and Sara's coats.

"Do I now pass Lady Randa's inspection?" Denise asked with arched eyebrows.

Randa looked the poet up and down. "You'll do, I suppose."

With a very pronounced pout, Denise folded her arms. "And after I spent the last five minutes scrubbing and buffing... that is all you have to say?"

"Oh I don't know." Randa stepped a little closer as she asked, "What exactly does buffing involve?"

Denise let her arms fall to the side as she noticed the playful yet heated look in the blonde nurse's eyes. She stepped even closer until they were almost touching. "Well I guess if scrubbing means getting clean then buffing would mean getting dry!"

"And that only takes you five minutes?" Randa asked, "Are you that quick at everything?"

"Hey, you were the one who told me to get my arse into gear if I recall. But no, I am not always that quick. Besides, I like to take my time with certain tasks." She lowered her voice an octave. "Believe me!" Denise smirked lazily as a flush covered the nurse's cheeks. She was getting the hang of this whole flirting game.

"Oh I don't know; I think I may need a little more than that to believe you."

"Really?"

Randa nodded her head.

"Well, I have it on good authority that there are certain activities that I do prefer to... take my time in!"

"And on whose authority would that be?" Randa asked.

"Um... me!"

Blonde eyebrows disappeared under equally blonde hair. "Oh so you are **that** familiar with yourself are you?"

Denise shrugged. "Occasionally."

"No help from outside sources?"

The poet leaned forward as she whispered into the blonde's ear. "A certain person does come to mind - so to speak." She moved back and looked into Randa's eyes for as long as she could before both women could no longer hold out and they started laughing.

"You are so evil," Randa stated as she fanned her flushed cheeks.

Denise chuckled. "It must be these bad influences around me!" She took a deep breath, feeling the familiar heat that surrounded her whenever she was in such close proximity to the nurse.

"You mean it isn't true?"

"Are we all ready to go yet?" Came Sara's voice from the receiver hooked upon Randa's belt.

Without replying, Denise leaned forward and kissed Randa softly before winking and exiting the hallway.

Walking across the large stone bridge, Randa - with one arm hooked through Denise's who in turn was pushing Sara in her chair - looked down into the frozen lake below. With the temperature as cold as it was the water had been frozen over for weeks and even provided entertainment for the local children. During the past three weekends skaters, eager to try out the icy surface, had accosted the area.

Wondering what the nurse was looking at, Denise peered over Randa's shoulder. "Bloody hell... there's a duck frozen into the water!"

Eyes wide Randa looked across the lake. "Where?" She looked back at Denise to gauge her line of sight and noticed her mischievous grin. "Oh you!" Randa scowled, "I think you must have gotten out of the evil side of the bed this morning."

"Sorry. I couldn't resist." Denise chuckled.

From her position in the chair, Sara rolled her eyes at her niece's antics. The woman had been in an impish mood all morning. Looking out as they neared the far end of the bridge a thought occurred to her as she noticed a specific landmark. That gave her a wicked idea. "Randa?"

The nurse turned from her glaring at Denise to look at Sara in question. "Yes, Sara?"

"You see that tree by the edge of the grassy verge, near the post box?"

Denise groaned as Randa's eyes scanned the area. "Yes."

"That is where DJ had her first kiss!"

"Is it?" Randa looked up at Denise.

"Sara!" The poet whined.

187

"Oh hush girl." Sara chewed on her lips in an effort to refrain from laughing at her niece's obvious discomfort. She continued to address Randa, "Of course she didn't tell me this until a few years later, but yes, that was the place."

"Who was it?" Randa asked with interest.

"Oh, you have asked for it now," Denise warned, "She loves talking about this."

"His name was Jeffrey," Sara replied with amusement, "and he was the most striking boy I ever do remember."

"Good looking?"

Sara laughed. "No! He preferred to be called 'Bullet Head'. He had a multicoloured Mohican hairstyle… the colours tended to change rather frequently and his jeans held more holes than actual material. After my first meeting with him I remember DJ had proclaimed that she wanted to dye her hair. Naturally I forbade it so she made a compromise and a day later she sauntered down the stairs with bright pink hair."

Randa laughed. "No! Was it real?" She looked back at Denise who was moping silently.

"Lord no. It was one of those 'spray in' dyes. The only problem was that it didn't wash out of my pillow cases and by the time she had grown out of her punk phase I had to dispose of several of those blasted cases."

"So," the nurse questioned Denise, "were you a rebel?"

"I was what you would characterize as a wannabe rebel. I may have tried to look the part, but the worst thing I ever did was graffiti my name in a text book at school."

"Wild Child."

"Oh well, it was a math book… never my favourite subject."

Randa moved closer to Denise's side for warmth. "I suppose your favourite was the English language."

"You guessed it!"

Denise smiled, as she remembered how in the beginning she had no choice but to be interested in English, especially literature. With Sara as her teacher for one term at school she was compelled to make sure she excelled in the subject.

Sara worked as a supply teacher and travelled around the local schools covering absent tutors. Denise always remembered the shock she felt while sitting in class one day waiting for their lesson to begin when all of a sudden Sara walked in. The substitute had declared that due to their usual teacher's maternity leave she was the class' temporary tutor. It wasn't long before the poet's classmates recognized the Jennings surname and the teasing began. Luckily, being one of the tallest and most imposing members of the class, Denise could usually silence them by a well-placed cold stare. *Yes, Denise remembered, sometimes it felt good to be intimidating.*

When they returned home Sara was so exhausted that Denise had taken her straight to bed, where she immediately fell asleep. After closing the curtains and assuring that the monitor was on, Denise turned around to find Randa standing in the door way. She approached the nurse and placed a hand on her right shoulder. Randa covered the larger appendage with her own hand.

"She's really… it's really taking hold isn't it?"

Randa nodded silently.

"I hardly recognise her voice any more. Everything seems like such a chore to her." Denise rubbed her forehead with a painful sigh. "God I hate this, Randa." She looked back at the silent sleeping form resting peacefully in her bed. "I really hate this."

"I know, love." Randa pulled Denise into her arms as she noticed the first tear fall from the poet's eyes.

Denise closed her eyes tight trying hard not to let her emotions get the better of her, but it was no use and her tears came anyway.

Silently, Randa led them away from Sara's bedroom door and back into the kitchen where she leaned against the work surface and pulled Denise into her arms.

"I'm sorry," the poet sniffed.

"Never be sorry to show how you really feel," Randa said as she looked at Denise with her own tearful green eyes. "Your emotions are what make you human. They craft the person that you are and help you write the way that you do. It's what makes you, **you.**"

Without replying, Denise placed her forehead upon Randa's shoulder. "Sometimes it's like I forget, you know…

189

and then suddenly it occurs to me... Sara's dying." She looked back into Randa's eyes. "She is the only family I have left now. My mother was adopted and my father had only one sister. When they died the only person I had left in the entire world was Sara, and when she dies..."

"You will have me," Randa stated.

"Will I?"

"Yes," the nurse answered seriously.

Denise brushed away the single tear that lazily made its way down Randa's own cheek. "We make a right pair, don't we?"

"I hope so."

With a smile, Denise pulled the woman closer to her, glad to have her in her arms and in her life.

Chapter 19

Randa looked at the small calendar attached to her checkbook. It amazed her that January had flown by and it was well into February already. She wrote out the payments for her monthly bills and noted with satisfaction a modest amount still left over even though she had cut her hours per week down. *Must have slipped into a lower tax bracket or something* she thought. The small excess was welcome because the nurse had spent a little of the cash on a surprise for Denise. Her mom had slipped the present in with Randa's usual shipment of bills and letters. When the poet had commented on the heavy yellow envelopes weight, Randa had nonchalantly said, "Must be my nursing journals." Denise hadn't questioned it. The nurse had saved the surprise for a day when she thought Denise would need it and it appeared that day was now.

Randa thought back to events earlier in the day. She had the receiver to the monitor with her during the night and thought she heard sounds of distress on it. Not taking time to wake Denise, she moved quickly down the stairs and into Sara's room. The older woman was weeping openly.

"Sara, what's wrong? What's the matter, sweetie? Are you in pain?"

Sara shook her head and choked out the words, "The bed."

Randa checked the bed and found the source of Sara's upset. Throwing on the internal and external nurse's mask, she brought her eyes up to the older woman.

"Don't worry Sara, I'll take care of this. I'll get you cleaned up in a jiffy and into some fresh clothing and up into the wheelchair, okay?"

"But Denise..." began Sara.

"Doesn't need to be involved this morning," Randa finished. The nurse fetched a basin with warm soapy water and proceeded to give the other woman a thorough bed bath, being sure to first place large towels between Sara and the damp linens. Randa kept up a line of general chatter as she used her professional skills of assessment. Sara's skin condition was good. Randa and Denise had taken to coming downstairs two or three times during the night to turn the older woman. Since

Sara lost use of her legs she was unable to do this on her own anymore. Sara's buttocks, hips, ankles and heels all looked good and Randa applied a fragrant lotion to these areas after rinsing and drying them. Helping Sara into her clothes was a struggle as was getting her into the wheelchair alone. Usually the poet and nurse worked in tandem at these jobs but today Randa knew Sara didn't want Denise involved.

Once Sara was safely in her wheelchair, Randa took the wet linen to the washing machine and started them on a long cycle. Returning to Sara, Randa took a seat in a chair beside her. Reaching over, the nurse took Sara's hand in her own.

"Oh, Randa, I'm so embarrassed! I could tell what was happening but I could do nothing to stop it."

"I know, Sara, I know. I'm a nurse remember? We can take care of this easily but right now I need for you to be calm so we can talk and make a few decisions. After I explain your options, you can tell me what you want to do, alright?"

Sara nodded and Randa talked to her. She was matter of fact in giving Sara her options and when the discussion was concluded, the older woman was calm and clear about her decisions.

"Okay, Sara, I'm going to wake Denise up and let her know what's happening and how you have decided to handle it. After breakfast we'll call Dr. Macarthur and have him help us with the arrangements. All this okay by you?"

"Yes. Thank you, Randa."

Randa stopped in the study just long enough to get the receiver and then headed to Denise's bedroom. Opening the door quietly, the nurse peeked in. Denise was sound asleep, her hair tousled on the pillow. Randa crept to the bedside and couldn't resist placing a tender kiss on slightly open lips. Denise's mouth curved up in a sleepy smile and said, "Jeffrey, is that you?"

Randa smacked the brunette on her arm and replied, "You better not be dreaming of Bullet Head." The two women chuckled and Denise drew Randa in for a hug. It took all of five seconds for them to realize they were both on Denise's bed in little more than sleep shirts.

"Mmmm, this is nice," Denise murmured.

"This is nicer," was the blonde's reply as she brought her lips once again to the poet's. For long moments they reveled in the pure bliss of the contact. Randa brought her hand up and lightly stroked the curve of Denise's breast. At the brunette's sharp intake of breath, Randa was brought back to the reality of why she had sought Denise out in the first place. With more than a little reluctance, Randa sat up.

Willing her breathing back under control, Randa said, "You're almost irresistible like this, but we have to talk."

Denise heard the serious note in Randa's voice and sat up quickly. "What is it? Is Sara okay?"

The nurse put a reassuring hand on the brunette's arm. "She's fine, but she had a problem this morning. Do you remember when we discussed how the course of Sara's illness would go and what problems she would have?" At the poet's nod, Randa continued. "This morning she lost control of her bladder. It was pretty upsetting for her."

Denise made as to rise from the bed, but was stopped by Randa's hands on her shoulders. "It's fine now. I got her cleaned, dressed and up in the wheelchair. She didn't want you to see her like that." The nurse waited a moment as Denise processed the information. "After breakfast we need to call the doctor, Denise. We're going to need a few things. At the least we are going to need a hospital type bed and a neck support for her wheelchair. We also need to get her a catheter. I don't want her to have the kind of embarrassment she had this morning. If they deliver it, I'll place it in today."

Denise could only nod in agreement. Randa leaned forward and placed a light kiss on the poet's nose. "Might as well get up, we've got a lot of work to do."

That had been in the morning and now it was after 9:00 p.m. Randa stood up from the desk in the study and went to the foldaway bed. From underneath it she brought forth a large shopping bag. Taking the bag she made her way downstairs to the living room. Denise wanted to stay with Sara for a while after the pair had got the older woman into bed. The new hospital bed let Sara have her head raised, which eased her breathing. A mechanical lift had also been delivered to assist with getting Sara in and out of bed. It would only be used when either Randa or Denise was not available. The catheter supplies had been delivered and Randa had inserted the device. Sara attempted to hide her dismay at losing another bodily function, but Randa saw how disappointed she was.

194

Randa heard Denise quietly close Sara's bedroom door and come down the hall to the living room.

"What's all this then?" asked the poet as her eyes took in Randa's preparations.

"What does it look like? It's an indoor picnic, of course." Denise lowered herself to the blanket as the nurse explained the setting. "We have some hot chocolate direct from the kitchen, a few tarts I picked up at the bakery yesterday and we have entertainment in this little videocassette."

The poet nodded at a bare branch sticking out of a vase at the foot of the blanket. "And that would be?"

"Well, I got that yesterday too. That's directly off the tree where you got your first kiss. I was jealous I wasn't there for it at the time, so I thought you might like to try it again now, with me."

Denise smiled and leaned forward to bring her lips flush onto Randa's. After a moment, the poet leaned back and sighed, "Much better than Jeffrey."

"Yeah? I'm better, huh? Take that, Jeffrey!" the blonde hooted.

"Definitely better. Jeffrey didn't taste like he had just nicked a tart."

"Whoops, guess I'm busted. Okay then; let's move on to the entertainment. I want to get to know everything about you, Denise, and I want you to know everything about me so I had my mom video transfer all her pictures and slides of me onto this videotape. What you have here is the Miranda Leigh Martin story in pictures in just 28 minutes."

The poet settled with her back against the couch as the nurse popped the tape in the VCR. Randa rejoined Denise and snuggled into the brunette's arms. As the pictures began to appear on the screen, Randa would explain how old she was and what was happening in the picture. All went smoothly until a particular picture popped up.

"Mom!! I said not to include that one! Oh my God, does the humiliation never end?" The nurse hid her fiercely blushing face in her hands.

Denise took Randa's hands in her own and said, "What's a picture show without a shot of a bare bottomed baby?" Randa just rolled her eyes and groaned as Denise continued. "Besides, I think it's adorable. I think you're adorable now." The poet's voice lowered with the last few words and Randa felt the surge of excitement she always felt when Denise talked to her in that tone.

"Randa, thank you for doing this. This was a difficult day for all of us, but I'm glad it's ending so much better than it started out." Denise met Randa's lean halfway and the kiss was hot, sweet and exploring. As the kiss deepened, Randa brought their still joined hands up. She placed the poet's hands on her breasts and covered them with her own. The soft touches and caresses to the blonde's body ended when the kiss did. Both women sat back, a little dazed and breathless.

"Wow, what was that?" asked Denise.

Randa just smiled and snuggled back up against the poet. "That, my friend, was second base." The women laughed, picked up their hot chocolate and resumed watching the video.

It was past midnight. Through the open curtains of her bedroom window DJ could see a multitude of ancient stars sparkling in the ebony sky. She lay on her back, hands behind her head as she stared at the random patterns and imagined making shapes out of the scattering of glimmering balls of gas.

She and Randa had retired to their separate beds over an hour ago, but she had yet to fall asleep. The unexpected changes of the day had left her feeling somewhat bemused and the stark reality of Sara's decline was slammed into her consciousness once again as she witnessed the medical equipment being delivered to their house. Deciding where to store Sara's old bed had been the biggest headache for her, but eventually she had decided on the garden shed and one of the gentlemen who assisted in delivering the medical supplies had helped her carry the heavy wooden frame, mattress and headboard outside. She did consider putting it in the study for Randa but knew it wouldn't have been a very logical move as it would have left hardly any room for them to move while working.

With a frown, Denise sat up in her bed and turned on the lamp by her bedside. She looked at the clock on the wall and was surprised to see that it had already turned one o'clock.

Sighing, she crossed her legs and looked around the room for something to do; not feeling in the least bit tired was beginning to get rather annoying. She was supposed to go down and turn Sara at around two o'clock but usually was able to get a few hours sleep before then. Tonight she was not so lucky.

Pulling the covers from her body, Denise slipped out of bed and onto the thick pile of the carpeted flooring. She looked around her minimal room. *Maybe I should just try and keep my mind busy; that could wear me out a little,* she sighed, *but I still need to go and turn Sara in a while.* Opening her bedroom door she stepped out onto the landing.

The dark space instantly illuminated with the dim light from her bedside lamp as she wandered out and into the house. Quietly she made her way downstairs and into the kitchen where she grabbed a small carton of juice from the refrigerator before heading back up stairs. As Denise reached the top step and pushed a small straw into her juice carton she was surprised to see the study door slowly open and a blonde head poke out.

"Can't sleep?" Randa asked.

DJ took a drink before she answered. "No, I had these awful nightmares about bare bottom babies coming to get me and now I am just too afraid to close my eyes."

"Oh you poor thing!" Randa pouted with false sincerity and obvious mirth. "Are there any times of the day when you do have a down period? You always seem so aware; you even wake up alert."

"Just a curse I guess."

"So what are you up to now?"

Denise looked around before her eyes moved back to Randa. "Well I was in the middle of a post midnight wandering. Care to join me? I promise not to make fun of your sleep rumpled hair."

"Such chivalry," Randa said as she emerged fully from the bedroom while pressing down her disobedient locks. "How about we turn Sara first?"

"Okay." Denise replied and together the women ventured down the stairs to check upon the older woman.

Once done and with Sara resting comfortably again, Denise walked over to the living room window. She looked up into the sky and said, "Uh oh!"

Randa quietly approached as she whispered, "What is it?"

Denise pointed up at the sky. "The stars have disappeared, my guess is that we are about to get some rain. Not that it would be a bad thing I suppose. It did feel like the temperature was lifting a little yesterday. Still it's a shame, I do love the stars... they remind me of a poem I read while I was at college."

Randa moved to stand in front of DJ and the poet instinctively wrapped her arms around the smaller body. "What poem?" the nurse asked.

"It is called, *'The Light of Stars'* by Longfellow." Denise paused as she tried to remember the first two verses.

"The night is come, but not too soon;
And sinking silently,
All silently, the little moon
Drops down behind the sky.
There is no light in earth or heaven
But the cold light of stars;
And the first watch of the night is given
To the red planet Mars"

Randa smiled. "That's nice."

Nodding, Denise buried her nose in the mass of blonde hair. "I always liked the last verse, it was so poignant." She closed her eyes as she remembered the final lines.

"Fear not in a world like this,
And thou shalt know ere long,
Know how sublime a thing it is
To suffer and be strong."

Reopening her eyes, Denise ran her hands over Randa's bare arms as she looked back into the sky. "Randa?"

"Hmm?"

Denise paused, suddenly not sure what she wanted to say. It was a familiar feeling around the blonde nurse and if truth were told, DJ was slightly unsure what exactly her feelings were. She had no doubt about what her body felt, Denise knew she wanted Randa - in every sense of the word, even with her self consciousness. Just the memory of her hands on Randa not many hours before had created stirring feelings inside of her, but the fact remained that she was still confused.

Denise had never been in love before and she would freely admit it, even though she seemed capable of writing about it. So faced with somebody who had so openly declared their love, DJ was afraid to voice her own feelings for the plain fear of not fully understanding if what she was feeling was indeed love. The weakness she felt in her knees, the way her heart fluttered in her chest whenever the blonde smiled, the way in which Randa was so capable of stealing her breath away with just a single kiss alone. Denise wanted to put a name to these feelings, but felt afraid to face something she had never before known. So instead she followed her heart and spoke with actions rather than words. For a woman who lived by the written word it was a unique experience.

"I um..."

Still standing with her back flush against Denise chest, Randa looked up and to the side. "What is it?" When no answer was forthcoming Randa turned around in Denise's arms. She looked up into clear eyes shimmering in the distant light of a street lamp. "Denise, are you alright?"

Denise gazed at Randa and nodded silently. "Do you want to sit?"

Randa nodded, seeming slightly confused by the poet's behaviour. "Sure."

Taking Randa's hand, Denise led her over to the wide three-seated sofa. She sat down quietly and pulled Randa down beside her to sit on the edge. Then she moved back and lay down on her side with her back against the couch. Randa followed suit, laying her own back against Denise as the poet wrapped her free arm around and pulled her in close.

With a deep contented sigh, Denise asked, "Are you comfortable?"

Randa nodded as she held onto the arm draped over her waist. Threading their fingers together she pulled their entwined hands up to her chest and held them just under her chin. "Hmm, comfortable."

Feeling content with the warmth of the fire and the luxurious feel of the body flush against her own, Denise began to feel the first stirrings of the slumber that had eluded her all night. Releasing her hand from Randa's grasp, Denise reached up and pulled the throw from the back of the couch, settling it over their bodies. "Is this okay?" she asked in a whisper.

"Very okay." Randa replied as she retrieved the poet's hand.

With a sleepy smile Denise closed her eyes. Within minutes both women were fast asleep.

It was the ringing of the doorbell that roused both Denise and Randa from a light sleep. Two sets of eyes opened to the bright reality of a new day as the rising sun shone into the cool living room. They had both gotten up once more during the night to see to Sara and during that time the fire had died a cold death leaving the room at a rather chilly temperature. Neither Randa nor Denise had made any vocal acknowledgement of the fact that they had spent the night together on the sofa but the poet knew that her ability to actually get to sleep had been greatly increased by a certain nurse's presence.

With a groaned, "I'll get it," Denise extricated herself from behind Randa as the nurse got up to go and see Sara.

Denise peeked through the spy hole on the door before she opened it and noticed the red Royal Mail van followed by the young man in the traditional navy uniform. With a cursed sigh to the only person who would send her mail 'next day special delivery', Denise opened the door and greeted the postman.

"Morning. Delivery for you, Miss." He handed Denise the large brown padded envelope, "If you will just print your name here then sign and date there," he pointed to a document upon a small clip board, "I'll be on my way."

"Sure." Denise took the offered pen and signed her name. She frowned in thought before asking, "What date is it?"

"Thirteenth of February!" the young man replied, "One of our busiest times of the year."

"How so?" Denise asked still not fully comprehending the postman's remarks.

"Valentines Day tomorrow!" he replied

"Oh yeah, of course." Denise dated the form and handed the clipboard back to the young man. He accepted it with a smile before turning and walking back down the pathway.

Denise closed the door quietly and walked into the living room. Randa was kneeling by the fire placing a fresh amount of coal into the hearth.

"I've already checked on Sara and she's still sleeping." Randa looked back at the lumps of coal she was placing into the hearth. "I am doing this right? This is just from memory and watching you do it all these times."

"Perfectly." Denise replied as she opened the package. Lifting the lip of the envelope she looked inside before reaching in and pulling out the contents. There was a small pile of book cover designs for her to look over. She read the accompanying letter from Carl with a measured amount of interest. There were still a couple of months before her new book was even going to be at its covers design stage, yet Carl would always send her information and ideas on the hopes of one day getting her to place a picture of herself on the back cover. It had obviously never worked.

It wasn't that Carl didn't respect her need for privacy and anonymity. The trouble was that he just wanted to see the day when the shrouded D Jennings would be revealed and he knew that time would come. Carl was her editor after all and as he often stated, he wanted the world to see the person he knew.

Randa finished re-building the fire and looked up at Denise who was in the midst of reading the cover letter from Carl's package. "Anything interesting?" she questioned, rising to her feet.

"Just more bumf from the publishers. Carl... my editor... he's just sent me a few cover ideas for the new book. He likes to keep me on my toes, and make sure I am still working away."

"Does he know about Sara?"

Denise shrugged a little guiltily. "He knows she is unwell, but I never told him just what the problem was." She looked at Randa timidly before putting the mail back inside the envelope and placing it upon the mantle. "I know I should tell him but I..," She sighed, "hell... truth be told I'm just not good at telling people things like that." Denise shook her head as she moved back over to the sofa and sat down upon the discarded throw. "Pretty awful huh? For many reasons I should say something, but I am just too damn scared. Maybe by leading people to believe that Sara is just under the weather at the moment leaves a slight air of possibility that she may get better... even though I know that possibility is in the eyes of other people. At least it means they don't act like she is dying with that air of gloom and nervous sensitivity due to making sure they don't say the wrong things. I remember when my parents died; some people would actually cross the road when they saw Sara and I walking down the street. I know it was mainly because they didn't know what to say but it still hurt."

With a sad smile, Randa sat down beside DJ. "I do know what that's like, Denise. My mom went through something similar when my dad died. Some people just don't know how to act when faced with death."

"Yeah!" Denise laughed ironically. "For such an every day occurrence and reality in life, it's the one thing we are all most afraid of. Death... the unknown... the most terrifying yet assured aspect in all our lives and the one thing with an unequivocal guarantee." Looking down at her palm, Denise's free hand traced the lifeline in the centre of her hand. "Do you believe death is the end, Randa?"

"No," she stated simply and took Denise's hand. "I've seen more than my fair share of death over the years and I could never believe it was the end. I didn't want to. Whether we all go up to heaven or return in another life, I truly believe death is not the end. The spirit is a strong force... I don't think even death can hold that back."

Feeling a surge of devotion as she listened to Randa's honest words, Denise cupped the nurse's face and leaned in, kissing her softly upon her lips. "Thank you."

"What for?"

With a shrug and tiny shake of her head, Denise kissed her again. "For always knowing what to say to make me feel better. You must have a gift. You're just wonderful, you know?" She leaned in again but froze as she heard the unmistakable sound of Sara's voice coming through the monitor. "That's our cue," she said quietly as she rose, pulling Randa with her and together the smiling women headed in to see Sara.

It was early evening and while Randa was upstairs working, Sara was in the living room watching the evening news while Denise was sitting on the floor searching through the lower cupboard of the mahogany, free standing unit.

Sara sat in her chair feeling a lot more comfortable now that she had the neck brace to keep herself upright a little better. Although she would admit to hate having to wear it, the brace did provide unquestionable relief. For that alone the older woman would happily wear the support.

With amusement, Sara looked down at her niece, wondering again what the younger woman was up to.

Denise reached inside the middle cupboard as she pulled out handfuls of compact discs. She glanced at each case one by one as she read the labels. *What the hell do you have to do to find anything in this house?*

"What are you up to?" Sara asked.

Turning frowning eyes up toward her aunt, Denise folded her arms. "I was looking for that relaxation CD, you know the one with the sounds of the countryside. Distant life, the wind, birds, rippling water... yada yada."

"The one that you used to listen to... when you wanted to relax your mind to sleep?"

"Yes!"

"Why do you need that, honey?" she asked, her voice hoarse and her speech slow.

Denise shrugged. "I've been having trouble getting to sleep and I remembered how it used to help me. Last night was so bad that I ended up wandering around the house until I think I woke Randa up. She talked with me for a while and eventually we fell sleep on the sofa together."

Sara smiled inside. "Maybe your body is trying to tell you something."

"Yeah." Denise replied as she turned back to continue her searching. She pulled out another handful of compact discs, "That if I don't find this CD, the only way I will be able to get any sleep is to wake other members of this house up and get them to talk me into unconsciousness."

Sara wanted to shake her head at her niece's lack of understanding. She sincerely hoped she would realise what was so plainly written all over her face. Sara had an idea. "You know, DJ, it's Valentines Day tomorrow."

"That was something I forgot until this morning. Unfortunately I haven't really had any time to think or do anything about it yet."

"I have an idea... if you're interested?"

Blue eyes perked up hopefully. "What?"

"Well, it will involve surprising Randa, and you taking her out tomorrow night."

The poet shook her head. "Oh no, we are not leaving you just to go out. That isn't right."

"Of course it is, silly!"

Denise arched her eyebrows.

"Diane will come around and visit me tomorrow night, it will be no problem and you know that. She will be more than happy to sit with me for a couple of hours while you take Randa to a certain place that if you remember she did mention the other day."

Denise frowned as she tried to remember what Sara was talking about - it soon came to her. Randa had suggested getting take out food and stated that she liked Mexican but Denise had told her that there was only one Mexican restaurant within sixty miles of the area and it didn't cater to the take out industry. "You mean take her out for a meal to that Mexican place?"

"Yes!"

"You think so?"

"Yes and it should be... a surprise."

"Hmm." The poet pondered thoughtfully. "Are you sure you will be alright?"

"**Yes**," Sara answered, hoping Denise would go for her idea. She desperately needed a push in the right direction.

"Okay." Denise quit her CD search and instead started looking for the Yellow Pages. "Lets hope I can get a table!"

Chapter 20

"Is your figure less than Greek?
Is your mouth a little weak?
When you open it to speak,
Are you smart?
But don't change a hair for me.
Not if you care for me,
Stay, little Valentine, stay
Each day is Valentine's Day."

Randa finished "My Funny Valentine" on a slow sweet note. *Well, it's a slow sweet note to me, but I bet cats are howling for miles around* she thought. She had always sung in the shower and the songs that flowed across her mind and past her lips could usually gauge her mood. For the weeks she had been in the Jennings household though, she had suppressed that activity. Today, however, was Valentine's Day, the most romantic day of the year, and Randa gave in to the urge to sing.

Hearing Savage Garden in her head, Randa started singing

"I want to stand with you on a mountain,
I want to bathe with you in the sea,
I want to lay like this forever,
Until the sky falls down on me…"

Randa finished up the romantic ballad and stepped from the shower. *Wonder if Valentine's Day is as big a deal here as it is in America?*

Her mind wandered back to when her father was still alive. He loved the day and always went out of his way to make it special for his wife and daughter. He sent flowers, brought chocolates and when Randa was older, always took them out for the evening. They might play miniature golf, visit an arcade or just go out for a fancy supper. Where they went wasn't important, it was the love he showed for his spouse and child that always impressed Randa. When the evening ended, her parents would tuck her in and spend the rest of the evening together. As a child, Randa thought it must have been boring for them just being together, but when she grew up she realized that time, for the two of them, was the most precious.

Dressing quickly, the nurse joined Denise and Sara in the kitchen. Denise was feeding Sara oatmeal and working on her own breakfast as well.

"Good morning again," Randa said and gave each of the Jennings women a kiss on the cheek. Denise and Randa had been up earlier in the morning, bathing and dressing Sara then assisting her into the wheelchair. Though Sara's body weakened her mind stayed sharp and she enjoyed talking and teasing with the two younger women.

Taking the spoon from Denise, the nurse said "Let me help Sara with her breakfast and you eat yours before it gets cold. By the way, Happy Valentine's Day."

Sara looked surprised and said, "Can you believe how rapidly this month is going by? We're almost halfway through already."

"I was thinking the very same thing myself," Denise said. "I need to remember to get that letter to Carl out to the post today." Sara nodded in agreement.

"So," Randa said hopefully as she spooned up another bite of the hot oatmeal for Sara, "Are there any special Valentine's Day traditions here in England?"

Denise appeared thoughtful. "No, not really. It's just not a big celebration here."

Randa tried to hide her disappointment. Her visions of a romantic day with Denise were stopped cold. *Maybe next year Denise and I can start some new traditions of our own.* The nurse felt a warmth rush through her as she contemplated a future with the brunette. *That's a first for me, but it feels wonderful.*

Outwardly, Randa asked, "So what's on the agenda today?"

Denise shrugged. "I thought I might work on the book a little this morning. This afternoon I had hoped to organize my files and my CD's. I seem to be having problems finding things I need lately."

Well, that's a romantic day thought the blonde. "Oh, Denise, remind me to return one of your CD's. I found a relaxation CD with country sounds on it and I borrowed it because I was having a little trouble sleeping. The last two nights though, I haven't seemed to have needed it." She watched as Denise blushed and knew they were both thinking of the last two nights together on the couch.

After the first night it seemed natural that both women had gravitated downstairs and to each other. Randa felt some wall between them had been breached and felt closer to Denise than ever. The emotional closeness had been mirrored by a physical closeness as sometime during the night Randa had turned in her sleep to face the brunette. The first sight Randa saw on waking was the sleeping face of the beautiful poet. The blonde had sighed softly in contentment.

Randa thought back to a fairy tale she had read as a young girl about the Light Princess. For a hundred kisses from the Prince, he received one kiss from the Princess and felt himself too well repaid. *That's what I am* she had thought. *What did I ever do to deserve the presence of this woman in my life? I am too well repaid.*

Blue eyes had opened in front of her and were studying her intently. "What are you thinking about, Randa?"

Randa smiled. "Fairy tales, and how I never believed in them until now."

Denise appeared to like that answer because she tightened her hold around the nurse that had started in their sleep. The blonde watched as blue eyes moved closer then closed as the poet kissed her tenderly. *Too well repaid* flitted through Randa's mind before she lost herself completely to the sensation created by Denise. It was only after some moments that the women became aware of their bodies being pressed together in an intimate way with Randa's leg between Denise's longer ones. The blonde felt a powerful rush of hunger for the woman before her. *I want to make love to her* she thought.

Caution warred with desire as thoughts raced through Randa's mind. *Okay, Denise seems to enjoy the kissing and touching with me but she's never showed me she's ready for the next step. I don't even know if she's been with a woman before. I've got to take this as slow as she needs. Slow it down, Miranda. You know she's the love of your life; you've got time.*

Randa moved back and slowly eased out of Denise's embrace. The brunette asked, "Is something wrong?"

The blonde laughed. "No, something is too right. We just don't have the time right now for me to show you exactly how

208

right it is. We just might be able to squeeze in a cup of tea before Sara wakes up though."

The moment had passed and now a day that started out so promising looked like it was going to turn out like the others before it.

"Sara, just because Denise is going to do the reclusive poet thing doesn't mean we're stuck here too. How about a short turn about the town? I feel like a little fresh air."

"Sounds like an excellent plan to me. If you'll just assist me with my coat and scarf, I'll be ready to go."

Randa went to fetch the older woman's things and her own jacket as well. Denise followed her into the hall.

"You're not upset with me because I'm working, are you?" the poet asked. The blonde turned to face her.

"No, of course not." Randa reached up and pulled Denise down for a steamy kiss that was punctuated by the nurse's hands moving from the poet's thighs to her breasts in a brief but passionate mapping. Pulling herself away with extreme reluctance, Randa said in a growl, "God, you have just **got** to learn how to celebrate Valentine's Day."

With that Randa returned to Sara and headed out into the cool fresh air.

While the women were out, Denise had double-checked her table at the restaurant that evening. She couldn't help but smile as she remembered the look of disappointment so obvious on Randa's face, even if she had tried to hide it. Denise hoped she would like this surprise. She had never done anything like this before so considered herself a novice in the arts of romance. *How hard could it be?* she wondered, and then had to decide how she would accomplish her plan. She did want to surprise Randa and that meant waiting until they almost had to leave the house before springing the surprise upon her. Denise thought on how to best carry out that feat.

She was still locked away in her study when she heard Randa return with Sara. Denise waited until she had finished copying a hand written sonnet onto her computer before going downstairs to ask them how their walk had been. Though it had rained yesterday the air was once again cooling and last night Denise had been sure she heard hail stones hammering against the living room window.

Descending the stairs, Denise entered the living room to find Randa helping Sara off with her coat.

"Nice walk?" she asked looking at the white box upon Sara's lap.

"Cold walk," Randa replied.

"Aww," Denise said as she placed her arm around Randa and rubbed her arms with a warmth producing friction. She looked at Sara in question. "So... what's in the box?" The poet was positive she recognized the design.

"Ah ha," Sara responded. "Not for you missy. This is for when Diane visits me tonight. It is always nice to see her so I thought I would surprise her with her favourite treat."

"Please don't tell me you have a jumbo sized chocolate éclair in there and you are not going to let me have any?"

Randa laughed as she watched the sulk forming on the poet's features.

"Okay, I wont," Sara replied, "Besides they are not the jumbo ones."

"They?" Denise asked hopefully.

"Does she always act this way when you bring cream cakes into the house?" Randa asked.

"Always," Sara replied. "If you ever want anything doing such as the chimney sweeping, the floor cleaning, the garden digging, just wave an éclair under her nose and ask away. I came across this amusing fact when she was younger and have selfishly used it to my best advantage ever since."

"Oh, maybe I'll remember that," Randa said as she watched Denise try to take a peak inside the box. She slapped her hand away with a look of warning.

"Well," Denise stated, releasing Randa and moving backwards, "I better get back to my work if you guys are not going to relent." With a sigh she turned and approached the door. "See you later."

Sara watched her niece exit the room with affectionate eyes.

"Do you think we should have told her we brought her one for lunch?"

"Nope," Sara replied. "It will be a surprise when she

comes down later. Of course you can always use it for bargaining material if you like. She is excellent with an iron. Unless you have some other completely wicked idea in mind," she winked conspiratorially.

Denise had stayed in her study all day, not even emerging for lunch. She knew they would be eating in the evening so decided to forgo food until that time, knowing she was prone to experimentation whenever she ate out at foreign eateries. Randa had emerged upstairs twice to see whether she wanted food, but Denise had declined saying she was too busy to stop and didn't want to disrupt her flow. She had, however, left her room once to assist Randa when she had asked for her help with Sara.

By early evening Denise had decided to call it a day and glanced at her watch. It was fast approaching six o'clock and she knew she needed to be ready to take Randa out by seven. The table was booked for eight and it was a forty-minute drive into the only town to have a Mexican restaurant. El Macho. She had been there once before with Carl and his wife during a meeting so she knew how best to time herself.

Denise walked out onto the landing and listened to the sounds coming from the lower part of the house. She could hear one of Sara's favourite soaps starting and knowing Randa had a tendency to sit and watch it with her, she decided she might as well get herself ready.

Forty minutes later Denise was standing in front of the full length mirror on the back of her wardrobe door. She was dressed in an ivory satin shirt that Sara had bought for her last year. The older woman said it reminded her of a '*poetic writer's style shirt*' with slightly flared cuffs and a loose fit. The blouse travelled down to the top of her legs where she wore black hipster style trousers, held up by nothing more than a small zip. Shrugging and hoping she looked presentable, Denise pulled on a pair of black-heeled boots bolstering her height by several inches. *Lets go.* She closed the wardrobe door, turned off her light, and headed down the stairs.

Denise walked into the room to find both women engaged

211

in light conversation. "Hey."

Two sets of eyes turned in her direction, one pair with hidden delight, and the other with bemused confusion.

"Um..." Denise looked again at her watch before looking up at Randa and beckoning the nurse with her index finger.

With an obvious frown Randa rose and followed Denise out of the room. Green eyes looked the poet up and down in question.

"I know this is short notice, but I wanted it to be a surprise."

"What's a surprise?" Randa asked.

"Us... going out. We have to leave just as soon as Diane arrives."

The nurse never lost her look of confusion. "Denise, what are you talking about?"

"Valentines Day." The poet smiled.

"But you said..."

Denise flapped her hands. "I say a lot of things," she smirked. "Did you really think I would forget the most romantic day of the year? It's not like your singing this morning didn't let me know just how much it means to you too. Come on, I've had this booked since yesterday."

Randa looked down at herself self-consciously. "But look at me, I'm not dressed to go out anywhere."

"You look beautiful. Hey, I only changed out of my jeans because they had a hole in the knee. You on the other hand always look presentable." The poet noted the unsure look upon Randa's face. "But okay... if you want we have about five minutes to go until Diane arrives so you better hurry."

With a bright smile, Randa leaned up and kissed Denise before taking off up the stairs two at a time.

Shaking her head, Denise walked back into the living room with a grin.

"I take it Randa was pleasantly surprised?"

Denise chuckled. "She just bounded up stairs to make sure she is presentable enough to leave the house!"

"She always looks presentable," Sara said with amusement.

"That's what I said."

"Well just remember," the older woman stated with sincerity, "Chivalry is not dead just a forgotten art. Remember to open doors for her, pull out her chair... you know all the little things us girls like."

"Whatever happened to equality? I am a girl too you know."

"Ah, but this is your surprise so you have to do the courting and the wining and dining."

"Hmm." Denise frowned in thought. "So, do you think I should wear my leather jacket? That way if we come across any puddles I can cover them for her to walk over and the jacket will still remain pretty much dry for me to wear after."

Sara narrowed her eyes. "One day that smart-alecky mouth of yours will get you into trouble young girl, you mark my words. And don't you forget what I said by the way!"

Denise smiled as she kissed Sara on the cheek. "Yes ma'am," she replied only just reining in her urge to salute her aunt.

They drove through the brightly lit city centre in companionable silence as Randa looked out the window at the nightlife - such as it was. Although there was only one nightclub, each road held at least four pubs that were all brimming with life. It seemed there was a football match and the larger pubs held large boards outside informing the public that they had the satellite link and a large wide screen television. Whenever England's first team was playing the whole country knew about it.

Denise steered the Lexus down a smaller street and pulled into a semi-circled car park. Trees lined the entire arch of the area. "Well, here we are."

"Where?" Randa looked around

"El Macho," Denise replied and pointed to the building behind them, "the only Mexican around here. I remember you said... well Sara reminded me... that you said you liked Mexican food, so I hope this is okay. I figured Mexican to you is like what Indian and Chinese food is to us."

Randa's eyes filled with delight. "Denise, this is just great."

The poet smiled affectionately. "Lets go then."

Randa placed her hand on the door to exit the car but Denise stopped her. "Whoa, nope, that's my job."

"Denise," Randa chuckled, "I can open my door!"

"I am sure you can but when Sara gives me the third degree, asking how the evening went and I tell her that you did in fact open a door yourself, she will have my hide!"

Randa laughed.

"Just play along, okay? I think Sara wants to know that I treated you with the utmost respect."

Randa leaned towards Denise. "Not too much respect I hope?" She kissed Denise softly and the poet happily responded.

"Well in that case, you're on your own if we come across a puddle!" Denise replied with a laugh and Randa frowned. "Just joking, I will explain later."

The nurse nodded. "You better," she replied and kissed Denise again.

When the two women arrived home the house was pleasantly peaceful. Denise was the first to walk into the living room to find Diane reading a book in front of the muted television. After a brief chat and update on how Sara had been while they were out, Denise offered to give Diane a lift home. Although the older woman declined, stating that she had walked there and didn't mind the trek back, the poet insisted. The night was still very cold and due to limited amounts of street lighting in the rural area, it was dark.

So while Denise was out taking Diane home, Randa went in to check on Sara. The older woman had woken up at the sound of Denise closing the front door and was eager to hear how the evening had turned out.

Randa helped Sara in adjusting her position. She smiled at the older woman as Sara asked whether she enjoyed her evening. "It was… it was wonderful," Randa replied. "Such an unexpected surprise. I really thought Denise had either forgotten or just didn't acknowledge this day."

"Oh not my little niece. She may have needed a slight kick in the right direction, but she did remember."

With a short laugh the nurse readjusted Sara's pillows before looking back at the older woman. "Little?" she asked sceptically.

"Believe it or not," Sara stated, "There was a time when I actually outranked her in height."

Randa eased Sara back down onto the pillows as she said, "And at what age was that?"

"Up until about the age of fifteen!" Sara chuckled. She looked up at Randa who was brushing a lock of her hair from her face and a tender warmth of affection filled her heart. "I am so happy you entered her life, Randa. DJ always told me that she was happy being alone… and the sad fact was that I knew it was true." Sara took a slow breath. "My only hope was that she would find somebody to share her reclusive lifestyle with. I think now she has."

"I hope she feels that too," Randa replied with meaning.

"She does," Sara assured her, "Whether DJ realises it or not; I know she does."

When Denise arrived home the house was in darkness. Venturing into Sara's bedroom she found her aunt fast asleep. She kissed her lightly on the cheek before leaving to seek out Randa; she was surprised not to find the nurse waiting for her. *She can't have gone to bed could she?*

Taking the stairs two at a time, Denise reached the landing and instantly noticed the light on in the bathroom through a gap under the door. She also noticed the monitor sitting upon the banister so she picked it up casually. With a shrug she walked into her bedroom and placed the monitor upon her unit before taking off her coat, hanging it over the top of the wardrobe door. Denise was hoping to see Randa while she still had the nerve, as she wanted to give the nurse a certain something and realised this would be the perfect time.

From the landing she heard the bathroom door open and she walked back out to see Randa. The blonde was just exiting the bathroom, already dressed for bed in blue and white striped pyjamas.

Randa look up at Denise in surprise. "Hey… I didn't hear

215

you come back."

"Only just got here," Denise replied.

"I didn't know how long you were going to be so I thought I would just take a quick shower to warm up a little before I go to bed." She bit her lip a little self-consciously. "Denise, I had a really great time tonight. Thank you."

Nodding, the poet took Randa's hand and led her into the study. Once inside she released her and looked around the room nervously as she tried to formulate a sentence. Suddenly words seemed a little lost to her. "Randa... I um... I want to give you something, a gift, something to... you know... celebrate the day." Kneeling down she pulled open the small drawer at the bottom of the freestanding shelf and removed a medium sized leather bound manuscript. Running her fingers over the black cover she rose to her feet and looked back at Randa. "Remember when you said... before we met in person I mean... that you had read everything I have ever written?"

Randa blushed as she nodded. "Yes, how can I forget? I said a lot of things that I wish I could have taken back if I recall."

Denise chuckled lightly. "Well this here is **the** everything. This is all the poetry that I thought for one reason or another was too personal for publication. This is the stuff that nobody, not even Sara, has read and I want you to have it." She held out the handwritten book with an air of apprehension. "For you."

Looking down at the leather book held in Denise's hands, Randa seemed at a loss for words. "Denise, I..." She paused.

"What?" The poet asked.

Reaching out, Randa took the manuscript from Denise's hands. Looking down, she opened the book and began to turn the pages. She ran her fingers over the precise hand written verses.

"There are over sixty poems in there," DJ supplied, "I always knew that one day somebody else would see these but it would be somebody who I hoped would appreciate it. Somebody I trusted enough to see this part of myself. Somebody special."

Randa's head was lowered as she studied the pages. With curiosity, Denise turned her head to the side and looked down at Randa with concern. *Did I make a mistake?* she wondered. With a frown she placed two fingers under Randa's chin and

216

lifted her lowered head. Misty green eyes greeted her.

"Hey, surely they are not all that bad?" she said with a smile. "I am sure there has to be at least one that you will like!"

"Do you mean it?"

"Mean what?"

Randa wiped a stray tear from her eye. "Somebody special? It's just that... I..."

With a sinking feeling Denise realised Randa felt insecure about how she felt about her and if she were honest with herself, she knew the blonde had good reason. With certainty, Denise knew that had to change. Stepping closer she took the manuscript from her hands and placed it down upon the desk. Running her fingers through blonde locks she cupped the back of Randa's head and held her close. "You are more than I can express, Randa. You've changed me forever and I could live an eternity and never be able tell you just how much you mean to me." She swallowed hard realising she was about to take the biggest step ever. "But I would like to show you."

Green eyes gazed up at Denise as understanding settled in Randa's mind. Before she could speak they met in an unyielding kiss. Their lips moved slowly against one another as they parted and searching tongues found each other with innate accuracy.

Denise felt strong hands move over her back and settle over her shoulders as she pushed her own hands over Randa's body until they covered her behind. Bending her knees, Denise lifted Randa slowly and the blonde's legs instinctively wrapped around her waist as she moved out of the study. Reaching out she shut the light off as she carried Randa into her bedroom, kicking the door to before moving toward the bed.

Gently she placed Randa back down onto her feet as their lips parted. She looked down into Randa's hesitant eyes and smiled shyly.

"Denise, are you sure?"

The poet nodded cautiously. "Of this I am sure. Of what comes next you may have to give me a little um..." she looked away bashfully but gentle fingers guided her back. "A little... You see I've only ever once... with a guy. You may have to show me." Again she looked away but Randa guided her back softly. She leaned up and kissed Denise once and let her right hand move down the front of the poets blouse where it stopped at the top button and her index finger hooked itself around the ivory fastener.

"Anything you desire," Randa replied as she released the first button from its hole.

Denise looked down and watched as each small ivory button of her blouse was released one by one and as every one was freed she felt her heart beat a little faster. Moving her vision up, Denise's eyes locked with hazy green staring at her with undisguised hunger. She swallowed hard as she felt the back of Randa's fingers move softly down her stomach, and the last button was released. A powerful heat was building inside of her and instantly she panicked, *Oh my god what am I doing?* "Wait!"

Randa's hand fell away limply as she looked up in concern. "Denise, are you all... do you want to stop?"

Internally DJ took stock of her body's reactions. Without Randa's hands upon her she felt suddenly empty. *Do I want her to stop?* She thought, and instantly knew the answer. *No!*

Taking a deep breath and shaking her head, Denise stepped forward; her expression slightly confused as she took Randa's hands and placed them upon the warm skin of her waist. "I don't think I will ever want this to stop," she whispered as she closed the distance between their lips and once again initiated an increasingly ardent kiss. Her eyes closed as she sunk into a feeling that she knew she would never tire of.

Randa moved her hands cautiously over Denise's arms until she reached the top of her shoulders. Slowly she pushed the satin shirt from the poet's body, allowing it to fall un-needed onto the carpet. Denise half expected the coolness of the upper part of the house to chill her exposed flesh but the heat Randa was creating inside, radiated outwards warming both bodies that were so closely connected.

Releasing Randa's lips Denise moved her own across the nurse's jaw, her tongue coming into play as she reached Randa's ear lobe and sucked the soft flesh into her mouth. Randa groaned as her own hands slid across Denise's back and deftly unhooked her bra. Releasing the succulent lobe, Denise grinned into Randa's neck at the apparent efficiency in which Randa was undressing her. She felt blunt nails drag across her back and groaned at the unexpected feeling it instilled within her. DJ closed her eyes in pleasure. She moved her lips down Randa's neck until they came into contact with a wildly beating pulse and there she sucked eagerly. Denise knew she would leave a mark.

With the sound of heavy breathing and light moans filling the air, Randa pushed the white bra from Denise's body, that too falling unwanted to the ground. She moved her hands around to the front of the poet's body and quickly upward to cover newly exposed breasts.

Denise's eyes flew open and she pulled away from Randa's neck with a strangled groan as warm hands moved sensually over her breast, knowledgeable thumbs circling the peaks with desired intent. A startling impact of throbbing heat streamed through her body and her knees felt instantly weak. She looked down into Randa's hooded eyes, her breathing harsh and ragged, her body beginning to pulse with an unrestrained yearning.

I need to see her was her only thought as Denise moved the hands that she was using for balance upon Randa's shoulders down to the nurse's stripy pyjama top. She unclasped the top button before Randa pulled away and her hands moved from Denise's breasts. The poet suddenly felt bereft, but the feeling soon subsided as she watched Randa begin to undo each button. Once released, the nurse slid the top from her shoulders and DJ got her first glimpse of the desired flesh. She was amazed by the physical reaction inside her as the sight alone caused her body to throb uncontrollably. Blue eyes eagerly devoured the newly exposed torso. *So beautiful,* she thought.

Randa moved her hands across her chest to rest upon the waistband of her bottoms. "Do you want me to continue?" She asked in a voice filled with deep desire.

With the realisation that Randa was only wearing one other item of clothing, Denise nodded eagerly. "Oh yes." She breathed and watched transfixed as the blonde slid the stripy bottoms down her legs and stepped out of them

Denise visually consumed the revealed body, desperately wanting to touch the sculpted flesh, and noticeably trembled as Randa stepped toward her. Drawn by an irresistible magnetic pull, they came together in an intense kiss, naked flesh meeting for the first time. The sensation alone caused both women to groan into the increasingly fervent kiss. Tongues moved lovingly around one another as hands traced along increasingly warm flesh. The poet moved her hands down to cover Randa's behind where she cupped the firm flesh within both her hands and pulled her roughly against her own body.

"Oh... God!" Randa groaned as her hands dropped to the waist of Denise's black trousers. Finding nothing more than a simple zip holding the clothing upon the poet's hips she pressed the zipper down and released the trousers. They fell soundlessly to the floor.

Randa stepped back and looked down upon the revealed body. A noticeable heat seared within her eyes as she realised the poet wasn't wearing any underwear and the obvious evidence of her arousal was clear to see. Denise blushed at Randa's blatant stare, yet her desire increased as the blonde fell to her knees and began to move the trousers away from her feet, removing leather boots as she did so.

The poet didn't think it was possible but her heart's fevered pounding increased even more as she stared down at the blonde head so close to her desire. She closed her eyes, basking in the feeling. Randa finished removing the clothing but seemed to pause as she held herself close to Denise's thighs. Warm breath caressed her fevered flesh and Denise reopened dark blue orbs, gazing down in anticipation, just in time to see Randa move forward and place a single lingering kiss to her inner thigh. She felt a soft tongue sweep across her skin before Randa pushed herself to her feet and hungry eyes stared into one another with an unrestrained craving. Harsh breathing and an aching tension saturated the still air as their lips came together with increasing urgency and Denise was positive she could taste her own passion upon Randa's lips. A groan from deep within erupted from the poet's entire being.

They moved backward, Randa steering Denise toward the bed until she felt the back of her legs hit the heavy object. Moving down, Denise positioned herself onto the bed and instinctively moved to its centre, Randa followed and she lay beside Denise's right side. For a few moments she did nothing more than move her hands over the poet's flesh, watching with obvious pleasure as little goose bumps erupted wherever her fingers travelled.

Denise looked up as Randa moved above her and gazed

into devouring jade eyes. The feel of the blonde's body lying upon her own and the warm flesh gliding against hers was nothing short of ecstasy. Again, Denise knew it was a feeling she would bask in for eternity. The sensation of Randa's breasts heavy against her own and engorged nipples pressing into her caused a surge of molten desire to flow from her own body. Her chest heaved with laboured breath.

Randa leaned forward, pushing one of her legs in between Denise's and the poet instinctively opened up, allowing her greater access. They moved against each other slowly and Denise felt the proof of Randa's passion slick against her thigh. She groaned and slid her hands down to further increase Randa's contact.

"You okay?" Randa asked in a breathless whisper as she started a slow grind against the poet, pushing her thigh a little firmer into Denise's centre.

Denise nodded as she surge her own hips against Randa's. "Oh yeah," she breathed.

Grinding slowly against each other, Randa lowered her lips to Denise's chest and kissed the rise of her breast before moving her tongue over to the poet's rigid nipple and taking it into her mouth. Her tongue moved over the stiff peak as she sucked firmly and her free hand moved up to cover Denise's right breast, rolling the neglected nipple around her fingers.

"Oh, Randa," Denise groaned and clutched the blonde head against her chest, feeling the effects of her manipulative ministrations as waves of pleasure shot throughout her body. A flush of heat coloured her cheeks. "That feels so good," she whispered and unconsciously increased the rhythm of her hips.

Freeing her right hand, Randa moved it down Denise's body and smoothed her fingertips along the poet's thigh. Releasing the breast within her mouth, Randa lifted her frame slightly and faced Denise. Her hand moved to the apex of her thighs and eased over the molten heat of Denise's passion. She groaned wordlessly and looked at the poet in question, her breathing rough and laboured, matching the brunette's. "Denise?"

The exquisite feel of Randa's fingers swirling around her centre forced Denise to close her eyes helplessly under Randa's welcome assault. Then suddenly the nurse's thumb glided over the source of her arousal and her body surged with a wild fire

221

of heated desire. Eyes shooting open, Denise cupped Randa's face and held her close.

"God yes... Randa... please."

Leaning forward the nurse kissed Denise roughly, pushing her tongue into Denise's mouth as her fingers plunged into the poet's depths.

Denise's body bucked, thrusting up against Randa with the conscious need for more and as the blonde set out a steady rhythm, Denise moved against her in synchrony.

Never before had she felt such intense feelings of want, of need, of an uncontrollable craving that she knew only Randa could fulfil.

With one hand holding Randa in a fiery kiss, her other moved down the hot perspiring body to cup her behind. Lifting her thigh she moved again between Randa's legs eager to feel the source of the nurse's arousal as it glided over her thigh. The heat was incredible.

As her breathing became increasingly laboured, Denise pulled away from Randa's lips. An uncontrollable inferno was bubbling within her and her body ached with the need for more.

"Randa," She whimpered.

"I know," Randa replied as she withdrew from Denise and entered her harder, adding a third finger.

Denise cried out at the sensation of being so utterly complete. She felt Randa was touching the deepest parts of her soul and for the first time ever she felt blissfully whole, like she had found the missing pieces to her entire being.

Moving against one another at an increasingly favoured pace, Randa ground against Denise's thigh. As they both felt the poet begin to pulse around her fingers, Randa increased her speed moving in and out of Denise with deep thrusts.

"Randa!" Denise shouted, as a tidal wave of throbbing pleasure released throughout her body. She held onto the blonde desperately, riding her fingers as Randa closely followed. Calling out the poet's name, an intense orgasm eclipsed her entire frame.

As the feeling subsided Randa collapsed upon Denise, both women breathing hard and clutching each other with a desire to never let the other go.

Endless moments later, Randa lifted her head and Denise

gazed into heavy lidded jade eyes. She raised her hand and brushed a sweat soaked lock of hair away from her forehead. Randa grinned as she leaned down and kissed Denise softly.

"Gosh," the poet breathed.

Randa chuckled.

"Now I know what was missing the first time."

"And that was?" Randa asked as she brushed her thumb over a bead of sweat rolling down Denise's cheek.

"You," Denise simply replied. Lifting slightly she rolled them over until she was above the blonde. "So, when can we do that again?"

"How about now?"

"Sounds good to me," Denise said as she initiated a hot demanding kiss, feeling a new surge of confidence swell within her.

Chapter 21

Randa woke in unfamiliar, but very comfortable warmth. Opening her eyes she saw, as well as felt, Denise's long frame next to her. Randa had snuggled in close to the brunette, wrapping an arm possessively around her middle. One of the blonde's legs was flung over the longer ones of the poet. She gazed up at Denise, watching the rhythmic rise and fall of her chest as she slept peacefully on.

This has been the most wonderful Valentines Day ever the nurse thought. *How did I live my life up to now without her?* Lifting her head further, Randa was able to see the alarm clock over Denise's shoulder. With a sigh of resignation Randa placed a tender kiss on the other woman's lips then trailed smaller kisses along her jaw line.

"Denise?" she said softly. "Denise, it's time to…"

"Okay, Randa, but I'm going to be knackered in the morning, you know," the poet mumbled as she reached for the nurse.

Randa laughed out loud at Denise's assumption. A puzzled expression crossed the brunette's features.

"Denise, it's two o'clock. Now I admit staying right here in bed with you is much a more appealing idea, but we need to get up and turn Sara."

Denise blushed. "Oh, yeah, we uh…we need to do that."

Randa laughed again at the poet's embarrassment saying, "After we're done though, may I suggest we pick up on your marvelous idea?"

"We can most definitely do that," Denise replied. She hugged the blonde to her and initiated a kiss that threatened to re-ignite the passion of previous hours. Her lips then moved to the nurse's earlobe with tantalizing nibbles.

"God, Denise, if you don't stop right now I guarantee it will be a long while before we get down to Sara."

The poet stopped abruptly and rolled from the bed. "What are you waiting for, slow coach? The sooner down, the sooner done and the sooner back to bed."

Randa laughed as she pulled her pajamas from the floor where they had been discarded hours earlier. "Uh-oh, I think

224

I've created a monster!"

Denise found a pair of boxers and a T-shirt that she put on quickly. Reaching for Randa's hand she said, "Come on, Dr. Frankenstein, let's get moving!"

The pair went downstairs, moved Sara to a new position and massaged lotion onto the areas she had been laying on. When they had completed the task, Randa addressed the brunette.

"Why don't you go back to bed? I just want to get a drink of water and then I'm going back too."

"I'll be waiting." Denise clapped a hand over her mouth and her eyes widened as she looked down at her aunt trying to ascertain if her words had been overheard. Sara's eyes were closed and apparently she had drifted back to sleep. The poet made a wiping motion across her forehead then gave Randa a grin. As the brunette turned to leave the room she heard an unmistakable snort of amusement followed by poorly suppressed giggles. She turned back to see both her aunt and her lover convulsing with barely contained laughter.

"Sara, you could have at least pretended not to hear," Denise pouted.

"Oh, no, I could not," said Sara and laughed again. Denise maintained her air of disapproval for all of three seconds before joining in the laughter. After a few moments the laughter subsided and the poet gave a visible shiver.

"I'm going to go back upstairs before I freeze." Giving Randa an adorable smile, she added, "Don't be long."

"Not a chance," replied the nurse.

Denise left and Sara looked at Randa.

"So you…"

"Yeah."

"And it was…"

Randa blushed but met Sara's gaze and said evenly, "It was the most incredible thing to happen to me in my entire life. I love her so much."

"That's good then." Sara smiled. "You best go along and if you're heading to the kitchen…"

Randa re-entered the bedroom with a tray bearing two bottles of water, a few candles and a napkin covered plate. Denise was already back in the bed, covers pulled up to her waist. Handing one of the bottles to the poet, the nurse said, "I thought you could use this."

"Hmm, I could, thanks." The brunette twisted off the cap and took a long drink as she watched Randa place the candles around the room and light them. Randa switched off the light and approached the bed.

"And what might be under the napkin?" asked Denise.

"Denise, when you gave me your book of poems, I was so touched. I know what your work means to you and how difficult it must have been to share the thing that's been so important in your life. I want to sit and read each one slowly; savor them because I know your heart and soul show through each line. I don't think I can ever tell you how much it means to me to be allowed to see that work and your beautiful heart. I know I don't have anything to compare with your gift, but I do have this." Randa removed the napkin from the plate to reveal a mouth watering chocolate éclair cut into bite sized pieces.

"I saved it for you when you didn't come down for lunch. Do you want it now?" Randa's tone made it clear she wasn't just talking about the éclair any longer.

" Oh yes…I want it now," whispered Denise.

"That's very good, Denise, because it's all for you." Randa took a small step back from the bed.

"All that I am, and ever will be, is for you." Saying that, Randa reached for the waistband of her pajamas, dropped them to the floor and kicked them away. Left in only the striped pajama top, she unbuttoned the top button and then the second one, never losing eye contact with the poet. Ample breasts were revealed again and Randa felt herself respond to Denise's burning gaze. There was no mistaking the look of hunger on the brunette's face.

"Impatient for your treat?" Randa teased. Denise could only nod. The nurse opened the remaining buttons and let the shirt fall from her shoulders. Climbing onto the bed, she straddled the poet's thighs.

"Ah, Madame, welcome to the Bare Naked Café. The specialty of the house today is éclair, which we would love to serve you, but you are in violation of our dress code. I'm truly

226

sorry but your shirt must go." Randa reached out and pulled the shirt from the poet's body, favoring her with an appreciative gaze.

"Madame, we are not crazy for your clothing but your...accessories...are outstanding!"

Denise laughed at the words in spite of the very sensual situation. "Randa, you are absolutely bonkers!"

"No, just bonkers for you, love. Ready for some éclair?" Receiving an affirmative reply, Randa picked up a piece of the pastry and brought it to Denise's lips. The poet took in the offering as well as a little of the fingers that delivered it. The nurse brought her fingers out of the brunette's mouth and up to her own. The combination of Denise and chocolate was heady stuff and Randa's heartbeat picked up noticeably. Taking another piece of the éclair, the blonde scooped the sweet cream filling out and, using her fingertips, coated Denise's taut nipples. The poet sucked in her breath as Randa leaned over and took one nipple in her mouth, working her tongue around and across until all traces of the cream was gone. She repeated the action on the other breast, eliciting a low moan from the brunette.

Randa placed soft kisses between Denise's breasts then trailed them down across the flat planes of the poet's stomach. She looked up as she reached to tug the waistband of the boxers down. The brunette's breathing was ragged now as she lifted her hips, allowing boxers and covers to be tossed to the end of the bed.

"All for you, Denise," the nurse vowed as she lowered her mouth to the poet's glistening passion. At the first touch of Randa's tongue, Denise's hips bucked involuntarily and the blonde grinned, knowing the pleasure she was giving to her partner. As Denise began moving her hips rhythmically to match the nurse's strokes, Randa brought her fingers up to the brunette's wetness. Slipping two fingers inside the poet, Randa increased the speed and intensity of her intimate caresses. Denise neared the pinnacle and her movements became almost frantic. Randa curled her fingers inside Denise and felt the contractions begin. Taking the swollen nub in her mouth and sucking firmly, Randa felt Denise's orgasm take her.

"Randa! Oh, God..." Spasm after spasm passed through the poet.

The nurse gentled her touches and slowly brought Denise back down to earth. Removing her fingers from the brunette and moving up into her embrace, Randa felt a peace settle over her that she had never known before.

"Randa, we should...for you..."

Randa smiled and held Denise tightly. "Oh, we will, but not this time. This time was for you. Sleep now. We can always have more...éclair...later."

Peeking through a small gap in her bedroom curtains, Denise gazed at the dawning sky. The abundance of textured clouds brightly lit by the rising sun created an awe-inspiring sight of orange hues. It forced the poet to feel a certain amount of insignificance when faced with the grandeur of Mother Nature.

Feeling a shiver travel down her spine as a chilly draft whistled through a gap in the window, Denise turned away and looked toward the bed. She gazed adoringly at the sleeping form resting peacefully on her stomach. Her face was turned away from Denise but the sound of deep even breaths filled the room.

Picking up the tee shirt that had been repeatedly discarded upon the floor, the poet shrugged into the extra layer of warmth before moving around the bed. Sitting upon the edge Denise studied Randa closely. Lifting her right hand she pushed her fingers through the sleep tousled blonde locks with an affectionate smile. Denise thought that maybe she should have felt a certain measure of astonishment but the poet was filled only with a happy contentment. In the space of one evening alone, Randa had changed her forever. Suddenly she was now living a whole new world of passion and sensuality that at one time she believed would always be foreign to her.

With a contented smile, Denise trailed her fingertips down Randa's back, slightly pushing down the thick quilt that covered her smaller frame. Leaning down she kissed Randa's shoulder blade before pulling back. On the bedside cabinet Denise spotted the plate containing the half eaten éclair. With a smirk she took one of the bite sized pieces from the plate and popped it into her mouth, sighing with indulgent delight. *Hmm, chocolate.* Sucking the remaining cream from her thumb, Denise leaned forward and removed the appendage from her mouth before kissing Randa's neck. She couldn't resist the urge to wake the nurse and gaze once again into those heated green eyes.

Stretching her body out beside Randa, Denise lay upon her side and propped her head in one supporting hand. In a singsong voice she said, "Randa?"

There was no response.

She tried again. "Randa, wakey, wakey." A moment later Denise was greeted by two sleepy green eyes and she smiled brightly. "Morning."

Randa blinked before replying. "Morning. What time is it?"

Denise shrugged before looking briefly at her clock. "It's just gone seven o'clock."

"In the morning?"

The poet laughed. "Of course in the morning. You haven't gone and lost all perception of time and space have you?" she asked with a look of pseudo seriousness. "Do you know what the date is? Can you tell me your name?" Denise held up her index finger and moved it in front of Randa's nose. "Look at this and follow my finger as it moves, okay?"

With a swift movement, Randa grabbed Denise's hand and rolled over onto her back pulling the poet with her. "You, as usual, are far too effervescent for such an early hour of the morning."

Denise looked down and grinned happily. "I guess I was just hyped this morning." Leaning forward she kissed Randa softly upon the lips. "I can leave if you want more sleep though?"

Randa held on to her tightly. "Don't move."

With a smirk Denise asked, "Ever?"

Randa shook her head. "How long have you been awake?"

"Not long." Lifting herself, Denise pulled the covers out from between their bodies. She looked down briefly at the span of unblemished, naked flesh before settling her body down upon Randa. "I was just indulging in one of my favourite past times."

"Which is?"

"Looking up at the sky and feeling utterly insignificant in the presence of such magnitude... and thinking."

"About." Randa's fingers moved inquisitively under Denise's shirt and travelled along the warm flesh of her back.

"You."

The nurse then separated her thighs and Denise slipped a thigh of her own between them, they fit together perfectly. "And did you come to any conclusions?" She closed her eyes briefly as Denise pressed against her.

"I did actually." Moving one hand from Randa's shoulder, Denise lowered her appendage and caressed Randa's thigh. She felt the blonde open her legs a little wider as her hand moved with curiosity.

Randa's breathing increased. "And?"

Denise smiled slightly as she lowered her head and trailed light kisses across Randa's chest. "And what?" she whispered.

The nurse clasped the back of Denise's head as a tongue moved languidly over her breast. "How... did your thoughts conclude?"

"Ah!" Denise looked up as her hand moved in between Randa's thighs. "It's a little selfish." Her heart picked up its pace as she felt the moist heat of Randa's desire.

"Tell me," the blonde pleaded and moved against Denise's caress.

"Are you sure?" Denise looked into heavy lidded jade eyes. She leaned forward and pressed soft kisses across Randa's forehead, down her nose and upon her lips where they instigated a kiss of mutual intensity.

Moments later both women pulled away breathlessly.

"Please?" Randa asked.

"I decided..." Denise sunk her fingers into an abundance of molten desire. The sheer heat that enveloped her was overwhelming. "I decided that I want you forever." She entered Randa slowly, teasingly. "I want to feel this... you... forever." Denise paused all movement and looked at Randa seriously. "Is that a selfish feeling? How can I possibly feel the way I do in the face of such... considering everything else that is happening? If it weren't for you, Randa, I would have fallen apart a long time ago. How you've changed me so!" Once again Denise initiated a slow pace as she moved in and out of Randa, desperately wanting the moment to last.

230

Placing her forehead upon Randa's, blue eyes gazed into green with absolute devotion. "Randa?" she breathed.

Randa groaned as DJ increased her speed. "Yes?" Her strong hands gripped Denise's shoulders urgently.

"I... um you're... I just...." At a loss for words that the poet deemed appropriate, and feeling that her actions could speak louder than her confused ramblings, Denise sunk into the blonde, deciding to show her what she seemingly felt unable to say.

The gentle, soothing sound of the gas cooker heating a large saucepan of milk filled the otherwise quiet kitchen. Denise stood over the stove and watched the movement of the semi-skimmed milk as it began to bubble slowly. She dipped her finger into the increasing heat and then sucked the liquid off her finger.

From her wheelchair positioned at the table, Sara watched her niece at the cooker. She couldn't help but notice how DJ had yet to make eye contact with her. She smiled inside. "So... where's Randa disappeared to?" Sara's rough strained voice broke the calm of the kitchen.

"She's gone to have a shower." Denise answered as she turned off the gas and picked up the saucepan, carrying it toward three bowls of oatmeal. She poured the hot milk into two of the bowls and stirred the mixtures together.

"Hmm," Sara replied, "she looked a little tired this morning."

"Did she?" Denise picked up the two bowls of the hot breakfast cereal and carried them over to the table. Placing the bowls down upon the surface, Denise sat down facing Sara. She picked up her aunt's spoon as she said, "I don't think it's too hot."

"DJ?"

With her head still lowered, blue eyes peeked up through the dark fringe of her hair. "Hmm?"

"Are you embarrassed?"

"No!" Denise looked back down at Sara's breakfast, stirring the spoon around the slow cooling cereal.

"Well look at me then."

Rolling her eyes, Denise looked up at Sara with a coy smile. "Okay, I admit it, it's a little embarrassing knowing you know what... well... you know what I mean." She blushed noticeably forcing Sara to chuckle.

"DJ, give me your hand."

With only slight reluctance as she wondered what her aunt had in mind, Denise reached over the tabletop and placed her hand in Sara's that rested limply upon the chairs armrest.

"Now you listen here, DJ. Nothing makes me happier than knowing you and Randa have acknowledged the special connection the two of you share. I can leave this world now, safe in the knowledge that you will not be alone." Older blue eyes stared seriously into younger ones.

Those simple words struck a deep emotional cord within the poet's heart. Shaking her head, Denise said, "I don't want you to die, Sara. This just isn't fair." Her bottom lip trembled as she held onto Sara's hand tightly.

"We have no control over fate, DJ."

"Fuck fate," Denise replied angrily. "How anyone can believe in something so cruel and ruthless is beyond me."

Though surprised by her niece's outburst - that in itself was so out of character, Sara understood from where it came. To her it was understandable that DJ would feel such anger towards something she was unable to control. Her usual calm head and mild manner disappeared in the face of utter helplessness.

Sara looked evenly into moist blue eyes and felt her heart break. She knew of no way she could make this easier for Denise and she hated the knowledge that DJ would watch her die. "DJ, ... have you ever considered..."

"No!" Denise replied firmly,

"You don't even..."

"Yes I do and the answer is no," the poet stated seriously. "You stay here with me... and Randa. She did come all the way over here to help take care of you remember?"

Sara nodded, feeling internally relieved at her niece's words although she knew the nurse travelled to England for more than just her needs. For that she was eternally thankful.

There was a moment of awkward silence as Sara decided it was time to lighten the mood. "So..." she waited until Denise looked back up. "Randa isn't the only one who looks a little on the tired side this morning, you know!"

Denise snorted as her head fell into her hands and she shook it with a groan. "You never let me get away with anything, do you?" The poet looked back with pink tinted cheeks.

"Not since you tried to blame your hamster 'Snotty' for eating the icing on that three tier wedding cake I was making when you were eleven."

Denise chuckled. "Poor Snotty. How on earth did I ever get away with calling her a name like that anyway? And why on earth did you agree to it?"

Watching as Denise pushed her spoon back into the breakfast cereal and stir around the contents of the bowl, Sara smiled slightly. "Believe me, if I recall correctly that was the most respectable of the names you had suggested. You see... even then you were far too creative for your own good."

"And I never got over the disappointment of not being able to call her after a certain part of the female anatomy!"

"Thank the lord for small mercies. I would have probably shrivelled away with mortification if I'd have told people what you did want to call her."

Denise smiled in memory as she lifted a small spoonful of cereal towards Sara's lips and said; "I think this should be cool enough by now."

Sara accepted the offering and the women fell into an easy silence while eating their breakfast.

While Sara sat peacefully in the living room, watching one of her many favourite soap operas, Denise went on a search for Randa. The blonde hadn't made an appearance since she had disappeared to take a shower over an hour ago and Denise was starting to get curious as to what was taking so long.

Ascending to the upper level of the house, Denise wandered across the landing until she reached her study door. There was no sound coming from inside the room, yet DJ knew Randa was in there. She could almost sense it. Lifting her hand, the poet rapped her knuckles on the door and waited. A moment later Randa appeared with a frown.

"Why are you knocking?" she asked.

DJ shrugged and walked into the room. "Um... I was just wondering whether you wanted anything to eat? You have been ages and I had made you breakfast."

"Oh!" Randa looked down at her watch. "I guess I have been a while, huh? I was just on the computer, I needed to do something for work and mail Derek a question concerning the site. Sorry. Did I miss breakfast?"

"You did... and after I slaved all morning over a hot stove to make you your essential nourishment... you go and ruin all my hard work." Denise folded her arms with false indignation and a hidden smile. She sniffed melodramatically as she said, "I don't think I will ever recover from the disappointment of your blatant rejection." Her bottom lip drooped into a pronounced pout.

An expression of amusement crossed Randa's features and she moved a hand to cover her growing smile. "Man, where did you learn such melodramatics? Its just breakfast."

Denise pursed her lips and arched an eyebrow as her arms fell to her sides. "Just what exactly are you implying, Miss Martin?"

"Nothing."

"Uh huh."

DJ took a step forward and Randa took a step back. She could clearly see the nefarious glint sparkle in the poet's eye.

"I'll have you know that my cooking is more than just."

"Your cooking is nice."

Denise moved another step in her advance towards Randa. "Just nice? Nice is a pretty non-descript word in my opinion. To me, nice is the colour of black socks or the flavour of warm water."

This time it was Randa who moved a step towards DJ. "Are you fishing for compliments? She who has literary critics singing her praises is digging for yet more accolades?"

"Well no... I was just..." Denise paused; *hold on a minute!* "Hey don't you go trying to turn this around! If I remember correctly you were insulting my cooking."

"I was not."

"And that is something I just cannot let slide." DJ sighed empathetically as she said, "I'm afraid I'm going to have to make you pay."

Randa's eyes widened as she took another step backwards and realised she'd hit Denise's overly tidy desk. She had almost backed herself into a corner. "Pay? What do you mean make me pay?"

"I think you have a pretty good idea what I mean."

"I'm not sure," Randa replied cautiously, watching DJ to try and gauge her next move.

Pale blue eyes narrowed and with a sudden movement, Denise stepped forward, lunging towards the blonde. Randa stepped to her left quickly, opting for her only route of escape as she shot past the poet and headed for the door.

"Oh you are not trying to escape!" DJ laughed as she spun around and followed Randa out of the room.

Randa took off down the stairs as fast was she was able but Denise was close behind, taking the steps two at a time. She was closing in on the nurse rapidly. Randa hit the bottom step and ran through the lower part of the house, bursting into the living room where a startled Sara watched her enter with bemusement.

Denise shot into the room and cornered Randa behind the sofa. "Ah... I've got you now! Surrender and I may give you a reprieve."

"Never." Randa looked towards Sara beseechingly, keeping one eye trained upon the poet. "Sara, will you please tell your niece that I did not just insult her cooking?"

Not completely sure what was happening, Sara did as requested. "Randa didn't just insult your cooking, DJ." The older woman moved her eyes back towards Randa. "You didn't by any chance use the words 'okay' or 'nice' or even 'fine' did you?"

"Well..." Randa looked at Sara then jumped as Denise made a false move to her right then stopped. "I may have said something like that."

"Oh well then I'm sorry, Randa honey, but you are on your own. DJ takes after me with her pride in cooking. Give her hell, DJ."

Randa's mouth dropped and she looked at Sara in shock.

"My pleasure," Denise said as she stepped up onto the sofa and vaulted over the back of the chair, landing in front of the nurse. In one swift movement she grabbed Randa and hoisted her over her shoulder.

"Denise!" Randa shrieked as she found herself hanging half upside down and facing the poets back. "Denise put me down!"

DJ grinned down at her aunt. "Don't worry I have this under control." She patted Randa's jean clad behind softly. "Let me go and take care of this and I'll be back in a jiffy."

"Take your time." Sara laughed as she watched Denise carry a protesting Randa out into the hallway. When they were gone she turned back to the television with a smile.

"Denise if you don't put me down this very minute I'll..." Randa suddenly found herself deposited in a sitting position upon the stairs.

"You'll what?" Denise asked with a smirk.

"You... you are a... a..."

Denise leaned forward and silenced Randa with a kiss. "You are so adorable when you are flustered."

Randa grinned as she said, "And you are a pain in my..."

Once again Denise's lips silenced Randa. The poet leaned forward, bracing her knees on either side of Randa on the stairs. She pulled away with a pout. "Do you really think I am a pain?"

"Maybe," Randa replied, "Unless you can convince me otherwise."

"Ah... and how could I do that?"

Randa pushed Denise forward until they were both standing. "Let me think about it and I'll let you know tonight." She hooked her finger around the buttonhole of the poet's denim shirt. "Don't worry too much though; I'm sure you won't be disappointed."

"Well in that case I will look forward to it."

"Me too," replied Randa with a lascivious leer. "So, is it time to eat your astonishingly wonderful... delight to my senses... treat to my taste buds breakfast?"

Denise nodded with approval. "You see; that wasn't too hard now was it?" She took Randa's hand and led her towards the kitchen. "Anything madam desires, I'll do my best to grant."

"Those may be your famous last words."

"Just this evening I hope."

"You're unstoppable."

"I learned from the best." Denise waggled her eyebrows.

236

The women entered the kitchen as Randa asked, "The best?"

"You know, that impassioned woman who kept me awake for more than half the night."

"Are you complaining?"

Denise pulled the blonde into her arms. "Never."

Chapter 22

The week after Valentines Day was blissful for Denise and Randa. Sara's condition had seemed to stabilize and the house settled into a routine that gave the younger women time to explore the new aspect of their relationship. The days and evenings were reserved for Sara and work, while the nights were reserved for each other. The exploration started on the holiday continued and they became more comfortable with each other's bodies. The long nights spent in each other's arms were the most restful either had ever spent, each finding a feeling of rightness and contentment.

Randa and Denise split the nighttime duty of repositioning Sara allowing the other to continue to sleep uninterrupted. Uninterrupted, unless the one remaining in bed chose to be a one-woman erotic welcoming committee on the other's return.

It was the middle of the night late in February when Randa made her way downstairs to turn Sara. Moving quietly, the nurse slipped into the room as she had done so many times before to look at the woman who had become almost as close to her as her own mother.

As Randa reached to gently wake Sara, her hand stopped short of touching the woman's shoulder. The training drilled into the blonde came out and she realized something wasn't right with Sara. Pulling back, Randa slipped her professional demeanor on and began an assessment of the older woman. The problem hit her almost immediately. Despite having the ever-present oxygen on, Sara was still struggling slightly for breath. Randa observed the breathing for a moment and saw what she believed was the problem. They would need to call Dr. Macarthur first thing in the morning, but it was the talk with Denise that the blonde dreaded more than that. Waking Sara,

Randa completed the repositioning and kissed the older woman goodnight.

Randa climbed the stairs slowly. *This news is going to hurt Denise. I thought it was tough to give her bad news before, but now that we've moved beyond the 'just friends' stage it's going to hurt like hell to tell her what she has to know.* Randa walked into the room she had shared with the poet for over a week and looked at the sleeping woman. *This will wait until morning; I'm not going to wake her up right now.* The nurse slipped quietly into the bed where Denise reached for her in her sleep. Randa closed her eyes, allowing the warmth and security of the brunette's embrace to temporarily banish the chill that had settled in her heart.

The next morning Randa woke to find the bed empty. She was just starting to rise from the bed when Denise walked in toweling her hair dry. Just the sight of the taller woman was enough to pick the nurse's pulse rate up pleasantly.

"Good morning, love," Randa said to the poet. Denise approached the bed and leaned over to give the blonde woman a lingering kiss.

"No doubt about it," the nurse sighed, "you absolutely know how to say 'good morning' right."

Denise chuckled. "What are you doing up so early? I thought you might sleep in as you were up with Sara last night."

Randa frowned as she remembered the conversation she needed to have with Denise this morning. "Denise, could you sit here with me a minute before you go downstairs? I want to talk to you about Sara."

Concern was evident in the poet's voice as she said, "What's the matter? Has something happened to Sara?"

"No, no!" the nurse said. She reached up and drew Denise down to sit on the bed. "Sara is okay, love. I think though that there has been a change in her condition and we are going to have to do something about it. When I went down to turn her the last time, I noticed there was a problem with her breathing. I think she's had further weakening of her respiratory muscles."

238

The nurse felt the brunette's hand tighten around her own. "Further weakening? I didn't notice anything yesterday. She seemed the same as always."

"During the day she's taking deeper breaths because she's awake but at night she breathes more shallowly and her respiratory muscles aren't strong enough to hold her lungs open fully," Randa explained. "I think we need to contact Dr. Macarthur and get a C-PAP machine for Sara."

"Whatever you think is best, Randa, but what exactly is a C-PAP?" Denise asked.

"C-PAP stands for Continuous Positive Airway Pressure. It's a machine that's connected to a mask Sara will need to wear at night. The mask is a pretty tight fit over her nose and mouth. The machine will give a positive airflow to Sara, helping to keep the lungs open even though her lung muscles are weak."

Denise thought about this a minute and chewed lightly on her bottom lip. "Her condition is deteriorating again, isn't it?"

Randa reached out and pulled the poet to her. "Oh, love, I'm so sorry. I know we had hoped she wouldn't progress to this point so quickly."

The nurse felt the brunette choke back a sob as she asked, "How long do you think she has? She won't suffer, will she? I don't know if I could stand that."

Randa pulled back to look into tear filled blue eyes. "I don't know how long Sara has, Denise, but I want you to know one thing for sure. We will not let Sara suffer. We will see her through this no matter what it takes and she will know she is loved and cared for in whatever time she has left."

Denise swallowed hard and nodded. She moved away from Randa and stood up. "I need to go downstairs and get the fire going in the living room." The nurse could only watch as the brunette left the room wiping the tears from her eyes.

You've handled everything by yourself for so long you have no idea how to let someone in, even now. Let me help, Denise. Let my love help you through this. Randa sighed and left the bed, knowing she needed to find the key to getting the poet to open up to her and let the hurt and anger out.

239

Throughout the day, Randa made several attempts to get Denise to talk about what she was feeling. The poet gently rebuffed those attempts, saying she was fine and just needed some time to think through the things that had occurred in the space of the last day. Dr. Macarthur visited and ordered the C-PAP, agreeing with Randa's assessment of the older woman's respiratory system. He asked about Sara's food intake. The pair admitted Sara's swallowing difficulties were more noticeable again and they had been forced to change her diet to only soft and liquid foods. Denise repeated the question she had asked Randa earlier.

"How long?"

Dr. Macarthur looked uncomfortable as he said, "It's difficult to say, maybe days, maybe weeks. Everything will depend on the progression of the weakening of the breathing muscles. I'm going to prescribe Sara a mild sedative. Many times patients who feel their breathing is failing have problems with panic at some point. The sedative can help her get through those times. Denise, are you sure you still want to care for Sara at home? I could arrange for a bed in hospital if you'd like."

"No!" Denise replied angrily. "No hospital! Sara is my family, she stays here in her home as I promised!" The poet walked angrily from the room and Dr. Macarthur turned to Randa.

"I didn't mean to offend her, but you and I know how difficult this is going to get. How is Denise holding up?"

"About as well as can be expected given the circumstances. She's been so independent for so long it's hard for her to accept help. She made a huge leap by letting me stay and help with Sara. I only wish it was easier for her to talk about it, she keeps the hurtful feelings bottled up and tries to deal with them on her own."

"I can see that. Well, here is the prescription. You know, you two are doing a very impressive job with Sara. Let me know if there are any more changes or if you need anything at all."

Randa saw the doctor out and wandered back into the house, finding Denise sitting on the couch staring into the fire in the living room. The nurse sat quietly next to the brunette and rested her head on Denise's shoulder. The poet said nothing, but reached for Randa's hand and held it tightly.

240

"I love you, Denise Jennings," Randa said simply. Denise turned slightly, kissed the blond woman's head and rested her cheek there.

"Thank you for that," Denise said.

The two sat silently watching the fire, no more words passing between them.

It was early evening, two days after the C-PAP had been delivered and while Randa was working and Sara was asleep, Denise sat out on the step of the back door. The days were just starting to grow longer and there was still enough light outside to provide adequate vision for Denise. Sitting with her legs stretched out upon the pathway, the poet studied the overgrown, shabby garden. It had been neglected over the winter months and now stood as a shadow of the pruned and sculpted beauty it used to be. DJ knew Sara would have tended her garden all through the winter, keeping what was almost an obsession, a sight of perfection. From the rambling rose bushes and perfect lawn, to the small orchard at the bottom of the garden. Sara dedicated much of her time tending to her passion.

Rising to her feet Denise slipped the monitor to her side and turned on the outdoor light by a switch next to the back door. She then pulled the door closed and walked out in to the garden.

Pushing her hands into her pocket to ward off the evening chill, Denise strode down the garden path. Light trousers and a short-sleeved top did not provide adequate warmth for the weather. DJ was overwhelmed by the state of Sara's garden and for once she was glad her aunt wouldn't be able to see it. *She would be heartbroken,* Denise thought.

Reaching the vegetable patch she looked down into the mass of neglect. Amongst the rubbish were weathered stray potato shrubs, rubbish that the wind had swept over the fence and even a dead mouse, obviously left by a generous neighbourhood cat. Shaking her head, the poet leaned down and picked up the empty crisp packets and sodden firework that had fallen into the garden from the last Bonfire Night. Placing the rubbish upon the path, Denise rose and studied the garden, taking in the sight in a three hundred and sixty-degree turn.

"Sara would never have allowed this to happen," the poet muttered, feeling a surge of anger towards herself for allowing the garden's deterioration. Kicking the retrieved garbage that lay by her feet, DJ strode over to the shed. Pulling the door open she stepped inside and surveyed the rows of tools. Picking up a spade, fork and pair of shears, she took them back outside. Moving over to the vegetable patch, Denise dropped the fork and shears onto the ground and began turning the soil in the vegetable patch.

It was two hours later when Randa found Denise. The sun had set and the moon shone sporadically through a mass of moving clouds in the dark sky. The poet was working in the artificial light of the garden's halogen lamp. With a noticeable frown, Randa stepped out into the cool air as Denise stood by the far fence trimming the stray branches of the rose bushes.

"Denise?" Randa called as she made her way up the garden path. "What are you doing?"

Unable to hear the nurse, Denise carried on with her pruning. Her vision was hindered as she squinted in the medium darkness. Being at the bottom end of the garden meant the light was not as bright.

Randa stepped further up the garden path and quickly approached the poet. "Denise, what is going on?"

Hearing Randa's voice Denise stopped and turned to face the blonde. "Hey!"

"What are you doing?" Randa asked again.

With a deep sigh the poet turned back to the bushes and snipped at another stray branch. "Just tidying a little."

"How long have you been out here?" asked Randa, placing her hand upon the poet's exposed forearm she instantly felt the chill of the frozen flesh.

Denise shrugged. "I don't know... a while I guess." She looked back at Randa. "This place was Sara's pride and joy. She would spend hours out here every day tending to all of this." Denise made a sweeping motion with her hand. "I can't believe I let it get so bad."

Randa shook her head. "This overgrown garden was not your fault; other things have just taken a higher priority, Denise."

"If Sara knew what this looked like."

"So what are you going to do? Stay out here all night? Denise, you're freezing; come back into the house before you catch a chill."

"I want to get this looking right again. Even if Sara can't see it at least she'll have the knowledge and peace of mind to know that I am still tending to its upkeep," DJ persisted.

Randa pulled the shears out of Denise's hands. "And are you going to stay out until you catch a chill? What help are you going to be to Sara if you're too ill to look after her? She needs us, Denise. She needs you. You know what Doctor Macarthur said."

"**Yes** I know what he said," Denise stated, "how could I forget?" She pulled the sheers back out of Randa's hands. "And what can I do about it? **Nothing!** There is nothing I can do for her." In a rush of anger Denise threw the metal tool across the garden. It landed upon the lawn in overgrown grass. "Sara's dying and there is nothing I can do."

Randa looked at DJ in silence, unsure of the poet's next move.

After a while she spoke. "Maybe you can continue with this tomorrow?"

Denise snorted. "What's the point? What's the point with anything anymore? We as humans are worth nothing in this life. We are born just to die. We live our lives for no purpose other than our own selfish gains. Why bother?"

"I don't believe that," Randa said with conviction. She reached over and pulled DJ's hand into her own. "I don't believe for one moment that you think that. Not in here." She placed one hand over Denise's heart as her eyes stung with unshed tears. "Don't let your hurt and feelings of helplessness turn into something darker." She lowered her head, trying to look into DJ's downcast eyes. "Please talk to me."

When no answer was forthcoming, Randa took a firm hold of Denise's hand and pulled her back towards the house. DJ allowed herself to be led back inside, as Randa escorted her through the building and into Sara's bedroom. They stopped at the door.

Sara was asleep in her bed, breathing much easier with the assistance of the C-PAP. The room was dark, the only illumination coming from the lighting in the hallway. Both women stood within the doorway looking at the sleeping form

243

upon the hospital bed.

"You know she needs you, Denise."

Watery blue eyes gazed down at the nurse. "What can I do for her, Randa? What possible use could I be to her anymore?" Denise whispered. "You and that machine are more beneficial to her than anything I could do." With an angry sniff, Denise wiped her eyes before any tears could fall.

Randa turned to face the poet, placing her hands on Denise's upper arms. "You're her niece, and for all intent and purpose and a lot of wishful thinking... the closest thing to a daughter she has ever had... and those were her own words."

Denise looked up at Randa, feeling slightly surprised by her statement.

"Your presence is all she will need, Denise. You can't deny her that."

Shaking her head, Denise replied in a slow whisper. "Never."

With a deep sigh, DJ closed her eyes and leaned into Randa. "I'm sorry. Sometimes I feel so angry and frustrated. I acknowledge that Sara is dying then feel glad that it isn't quick as I get to spend this extra time with her, then I resent myself for thinking and feeling that way because Sara is going through so much suffering and stress. She is like my mother too. It's not like I forget my real mother you know, I just feel extra blessed that I was lucky enough to have two."

Wrapping her arms around the taller woman, Randa lifted upon her toes and kissed Denise softly. The poet leaned into the blondes' lips and reveled in the contact a little longer before pulling away. Opening her eyes she looked down at Randa and studied the nurse's face intently. "Do you sense it?" she whispered.

"Sense what?"

"That shadow of doom looming over us? Sara calls it fate, but whatever it is, it will cause nothing but pain and heartache. I know you, Randa. In here," she placed her hand over the nurse's heart, "and here," she then moved her finger up to the side of Randa's head. "I know how you feel. I don't want that shadow of despair to hurt you too."

Randa removed one hand from Denise's back and took the finger upon her forehead. She kissed the digit gently. "What do you suggest then because I am not leaving you, Denise. I won't

244

let you face that despair alone. I love you."

DJ smiled as she cupped Randa's cheek. "And love conquers all?"

"I, for one, believe it does."

"Then I have faith in your beliefs," Denise replied, hoping beyond all hope that her words were true.

Chapter 23

Randa's curiosity got the better of her and she went up the stairs to find Denise. The blonde knew Denise was up as she had heard the shower running earlier, but that had been some time ago and she hadn't come downstairs yet. It had been the poet's night to turn Sara and she had stayed down with her aunt for a while, as had become her habit the last several nights, just watching as the older woman slept. More than once Randa had found the brunette asleep at Sara's bedside in the uncomfortable chair. The nurse would pull Denise away then and bring her back to bed, knowing her friend needed her rest as well.

Denise feels it, she knows we're coming close to the end and she desperately wants to hang on. I've seen it a thousand times, the death vigil. It doesn't make it any easier though, especially when it's Sara. I just hope Denise doesn't make herself sick and exhausted in the process. At the top of the stairs Randa turned into the study to find it empty. She smiled with pleasure at the conspicuously absent foldaway bed. It had been relegated back to its storage area, as it had not been used for the past few weeks. Randa felt a shiver of pleasure as she recalled waking up in Denise's arms again this morning. The blonde had wanted the other woman right then but, seeing the dark circles under Denise's eyes, had decided to let her sleep on and settled for a light kiss to her cheek instead.

Now Randa entered the bedroom to see Denise sprawled face down over the bed fast asleep. The poet had obviously dressed halfway before succumbing to her need for sleep again. Her blue jeans were on and Randa appreciatively noted the snug fit over hips and bottom. Up top, Denise was attired in only a black bra. Randa gazed lovingly at the well-toned body that belied a totally literary life.

Unable to resist, Randa felt herself pulled toward the bed. Sitting quietly on the edge, she reached up to stroke the brunette tresses on the head facing away from her. *So beautiful.* The nurse knew though that despite the physical beauty of her friend there was so much more to this complex, wonderful person. Heeding a sudden need to be close to the poet, Randa leaned over and placed soft kisses on the poet's back, crossing from shoulder blade to shoulder blade. Denise wriggled slightly under the gentle assault and gave a slight sigh. Moving dark hair from Denise's back, Randa trailed more kisses down the poet's spine. Reaching the bra, the nurse used both hands to unclasp the ends and move them apart. Fingertips pushed the material to the side and continued on their journey outward to the swell of Denise's breasts. Randa felt the firm muscles of the brunettes back bunch slightly at the movement. The nurse continued her southward path with her kisses, adding the tip of her tongue to Denise's skin. Her hands roamed down to the brunette's firm rear.

"Randa...stop." The nurse's movements stilled immediately. Denise turned over and fixed her amazing blue eyes on the blonde. "We can't...Sara..."

"Denise," Randa interrupted, "Sara is bathed, dressed, breakfasted and downstairs enjoying a visit with Diane. Believe me, we can." Still Denise hesitated so the nurse asked, "Love, what's wrong?"

"I'm not really sure," Denise replied. "It's just that with Sara so ill sometimes I feel almost...disloyal that I'm so happy when I'm with you. Does that make sense?"

Randa thought about it a moment. "No, it doesn't. Well, I mean I guess I can understand why you feel that way, but I think that you should try to have some happiness in your life precisely because Sara is sick. She wouldn't want you to be unhappy and she wouldn't want you to stop living. You deserve happiness; don't ever think you don't. Please." Randa reached out to caress the poet's cheek.

Denise looked into the green eyes opposite her and saw the sincerity there. She turned her head and placed a kiss on the palm of Randa's hand. Bringing her deep blue eyes back to the nurse, she gave a small smile. Never losing eye contact, she shrugged out of the black bra.

"Do you think you could do that back thing again?"

Randa felt her pulse rate jump and she leaned toward Denise to capture the poet's lips. "Oh, yeah. The back thing, the front thing and everything."

247

Randa sat with Sara in the dimly lit room. It was 4 a.m. and the only sound in the room was the hum and whooshing of the C-PAP holding open the older woman's lungs as she exhaled.

Not one of the best days I've ever had Randa thought. To be sure, the morning lovemaking with Denise had been wonderful. The completeness they found in each other was incredible as always. Almost immediately afterward, however, Denise had left the bed, washed quickly and went downstairs to check on Sara. Randa went with her but missed the feeling of holding the poet and enjoying their closeness in the afterglow of pleasure.

It was almost as if Denise regretted being with me and felt guilty about our being together. A part of Randa was hurt at those thoughts and she desperately wanted to talk to the poet about it, but held back. *She doesn't need me loading her down with my insecurities with everything she's carrying. This can wait for now.* Randa believed the words but somehow it felt like she was trying to convince herself.

I wish I could talk to you about it Randa thought, glancing at Sara. *You know that niece of yours so well and you have more wisdom than most of the people I know. I'm going to miss you so much.* The nurse thought about how Sara had taken to confiding in her recently. She told Randa stories about DJ, gave her the recipes for the poet's favorite dishes and went over her arrangements for her funeral and burial. She did all this out of the love she held for Denise.

"I'm sorry to have to lay these matters at your doorstep but I worry about DJ. Please promise me you won't let her go back to her solitary world of total self reliance." Sara's voice took on an unmistakable sound of urgency though it was little more than a whisper these days. Randa assured the older woman that it would be her honor to help Denise in any way she could and would do her damnedest to keep her from ever dealing with unpleasant things alone.

Sara's features relaxed then. "Good girl. I knew you were the right one for that headstrong niece of mine almost from the moment I met you. I am glad you came into our lives."

Tears rolled down Randa's cheeks as she kissed the older woman's head. "So am I, Sara Jennings, so very glad.

With a sigh, Randa stood to return upstairs to Denise. She didn't rush as she had on other nights when going back to her lover. Earlier in the night the poet had rebuffed the blonde's attempts to be close, saying she was exhausted. Randa hoped it was the truth but feared it was something more.

Entering the bedroom, Randa heard the slow even breathing that indicated the poet was sleeping peacefully. *Please don't back away from me, Denise. I need you and I know you need me.* Taking off her nightshirt and slippers, she slid under the covers. The brunette turned and wrapped the nurse in her arms and held her tightly.

You do need me, Denise. Please remember that when you wake up. Snuggling in even closer to the poet, Randa fell deeply asleep.

It was almost like the beat of a drum, rhythmic and consistent, that coaxed DJ from a weary sleep. Opening heavy eyes she focused on her surroundings, still slightly curious about the noise that had woken her. Instantly she realised she was resting upon Randa's chest and the constant beat was the nurse's steady heart rate. Randa was sleeping deeply due to the fact that it had been her turn to tend to Sara last night and the effects of the heavy night remained as shadows around her eyes. DJ knew she would sleep for a few more hours yet.

Rising to a sitting position, Denise turned slightly and looked down at the sleeping woman. One arm was positioned over her head and the other had been wrapped around the poet. Bending her knees, Denise pulled them up to her chest and wrapped her arms around her legs. She continued to look down at Randa. She remembered waking during the night as she heard the blonde ascend the stairs after attending to Sara. She kept her eyes closed as the blonde re-entered the room, pretending to sleep with deep even breaths. DJ lay silently and as Randa got into bed she waited for the nurse to approach her side or wrap an arm around her like she usually did, but it never happened. Denise rolled over and looked at Randa; she

249

lay on her back with her arms by her side. It was then she realised that her rebuff from the night before had obviously affected her more than she let on.

By the light of the moon shining through a gap in the bedroom curtains, DJ had been able to see Randa's eyes shimmering in the marble glow. The blonde lay silently, staring at the ceiling and seemingly thinking. Denise could just make out the faint lines of tension upon the blonde's brow.

"Hey," she called in a light whisper.

Randa had jumped unaware DJ was awake. She turned her head and looked at the poet. Denise noted the apprehension so clearly visible in her eyes. Without a word she reached out and took Randa's hand, twisting their fingers together in a light grip. Randa instantly increased the hold and pulled DJ close. The poet moved beside Randa and placed her head upon the nurse's chest. Within moments Randa was fast asleep. Denise followed close behind, content in the woman's embrace. They had stayed in that same position until DJ awoke.

Resting her chin upon her knees, the poet sighed as she gazed at Randa. Reaching out she lightly traced her middle finger across the nurse's lips. The blonde moaned and rolled onto her side. With a lingering smile Denise turned and looked at the clock, her thoughts instantly turning to Sara. With a twist the poet rolled out of bed and headed out of the bedroom, straight for the stairs. As Denise descended quickly to the ground floor, the phone began to ring.

She picked up the hand set, "Only one person would dare to call me at this time of the morning."

"That is because only one person knows you would be up and about at this time."

"What can I do for you, Carl?"

The editor cleared his throat. *"DJ, are you aware of just what time it is?"*

Denise frowned. "I thought we had already established that?"

Carl sighed. *"No I don't mean clock wise... I mean date wise. DJ, it's the 28th of February. Your deadline was yesterday and although I will admit it did temporarily skip my mind too... you never forget. So I am wondering what's up? You would have usually delivered by now. My better half is throwing a wobbly."*

A bolt of genuine surprise rushed through the poet. Not only could she not believe she had missed her own deadline, but she was also shocked by the date. *The days seem to pass in a haze. I'm not even sure I know what day it is anymore.* "Sorry, Carl, things are a little blurred at the moment."

"Well, have you finished?"

"Almost."

"Almost?"

"Yes... almost. I've had a lot on my mind, Carl. I'm sorry but work has taken second place at the moment."

There was a slight pause before Carl asked, *"Is it Sara? DJ, what is wrong with her... really?"*

Denise bit her lip as she studied the base of the phone. The fingers of her free hand trailed over the numerical digits.

"DJ?"

"She's... she's um..."

"What?"

"She has ALS... or what we Brits call Motor Neurons Disease."

After a small silence, *"What?"* Carl exclaimed, *"but that's terminal."*

A heavy stillness fell down the line, as Carl seemed lost for words and DJ tried urgently to steel herself from the hurt that besieged her emotions.

Eventually Denise spoke, "Yes... terminal."

"Why didn't you say something... anything?" Carl asked, sounding almost angry. *"DJ..."* he sighed, *"I can't believe you didn't tell me."*

The tone in the editors voice was one of hurt and Denise felt a sudden regret. "I'm sorry, Carl. I had a hard time dealing with this myself."

The sound of thoughtful tapping echoed down the receiver before Carl spoke again. *"Okay, DJ, listen. Forget about the deadline all right? We can hold off longer; you know I always like to work ahead of schedule anyway. Just you concentrate on Sara and don't worry about things on this end; I'll handle everything."*

Denise sagged against the wall. "Thanks, Carl."

"And DJ?"

"Hmm?"

"You should have told me, you know."

251

She nodded. "Talk to you soon, Carl."

"Bye, DJ."

Denise dropped the phone back onto its base. She looked at the device briefly before her body slid down the wall. She landed on the cool carpeted flooring. Without the fire warming the house the air was still uncomfortably cold.

Shaking her head, DJ let it fall to her knees. *What day is it anyway?* She wondered with confusion, *I don't know anything anymore.*

Suddenly a gentle and familiar voice invaded her musings. Looking up Denise noticed Randa standing in front of her. She hadn't even been aware of the woman's approach. The blonde looked down at her with confused green eyes, her sleep rumpled hair was tousled around her head in what Denise always considered a most endearing sight. The poet frowned, realising she was unsure of what Randa had just asked.

"Denise, are you alright?"

"Um... yes." Bracing herself upon her feet, DJ slid up against the wall as she pushed herself to a standing position. She smiled slightly and moved past the nurse. "We better go and see to Sara and start a fire."

After a few steps, she looked back to find Randa still standing by the phone. A confused expression shone in the blonde's eyes. "Are you coming?"

Randa nodded. "Yeah."

Silently she followed Denise into Sara's room.

It was later in the day, just after lunch, a lunch that Denise had been conspicuously absent from. Hunger having all but abandoned her; the poet had used any excuse possible in order to stay away from the midday ritual of eating with her aunt and Randa. Now as the two women who meant more to her than anything else sat in Sara's room talking, she stayed outside in the hallway listening. DJ could hear the muted tones of Randa's voice as she spoke to Sara but she was unable to hear Sara herself. The woman's voice was nothing more than a strained whisper.

Leaning with one shoulder against the wall, Denise looked

at the door, trying to find the courage to enter. To her confusion, an internal barrier had frozen her limbs. To make matters worse she wasn't even sure she wanted to go inside. The poet was at a loss for something to say and if she was to admit it - if only to herself - she was afraid.

As Sara's physical health rapidly deteriorated and the inevitable edged ever closer, the more DJ felt herself withdrawing from her family. She knew she was hurting them both, she could see it plainly written in Randa's eyes, but she wasn't able to fight against it. The more she feared losing her aunt and the worse Sara's suffering became the further into herself she retreated.

Denise closed her eyes and the night her parents died instantly came to mind. She remembered the smell, the acrid stench of thick smoke that filtered into her bedroom, waking her from a happy sleep. Opening bright blue eyes Denise remembered seeing the grey fumes as they filtered under her door. The ferocious roar of savage flames raged in the ground floor of their large home. Scrambling out of bed and running to her parent's bedroom she found them still sleeping and woke them hastily. Instantly she was scooped up into her father's arms and together they made their way through the burning house. Around her DJ could see the orange and yellow flames as she clung to her father. The penetrating heat engulfed her flesh as the fire ate through their home.

Reaching the door and running out into the fresh open air, her father instantly realised his wife wasn't behind him. He had let go of her hand as they reached the stairs. Placing DJ onto the ground he told her to wait while he went back to get her mummy. They could hear her shouts for help above the roar of escalating flames. Promising to be 'back in a minute' her father rushed back into the house to save his wife. It was the last time she ever saw him.

Standing alone on the front lawn, Denise trembled in the warm summer night air. She heard her mother's screams; her father's desperate shout to find her - and then there was nothing but the mounting siren of approaching fire engines.

She had watched her parents die. Saw her mother at the second floor window of their home, hearing her screams as the flames ravaged her body. The poet didn't know whether she could watch another person she loved die. Sara's disease was

253

apparent, her deterioration rapid and the fear clear in alert blue eyes. She just didn't know whether she had the strength that both Sara and Randa needed to go through it all again.

So deep in her own thoughts, DJ was unaware Randa had exited Sara's room until she was standing beside her.

"Denise, what are you doing?"

Blinking unfocused eyes the poet looked down at Randa. "Oh! Um... I was just thinking."

Randa nodded noticing the glaze in her eyes. "Are you going in to talk to Sara? I know that she really..."

"Actually no," DJ interrupted, "I just remembered something I must do and should get on with it while I still remember. I'll talk with Sara later." The poet turned and headed back toward the kitchen but stopped as Randa's gentle voice called out to her. She turned around and looked at the nurse in question.

"I just wanted to say that I think it would be a good idea if you did speak with Sara while..."

"I will... just not at the moment, okay?"

"Denise," Randa insisted, "You don't understand. I..."

"I know," the poet said. "I just..." She looked down, casting her vision away from Randa's beseeching eyes. "I just can't right now." Not looking back up, DJ turned and disappeared from sight.

Hearing muffled footsteps re-enter her bedroom, Sara knew instantly that the short light steps didn't belong to her niece. Unable to turn her head she waited until Randa moved into view.

"No DJ?" She asked with effort.

Randa shook her head. "She has something she needs to do but she'll be back later." Even to her own ears it was obvious the nurse was doubtful of her words.

"If that's what she said," Sara replied, "then she will be here... soon." Weary eyes studied Randa's expression. "You are worried about her... yes?"

The blonde nodded. "Yeah... I am. I feel like she's slipping away from us, Sara, and I don't know how to reach her."

"You will," Sara replied reassuringly. "No matter what it takes, or what you have to do, I know you will reach her."

Chapter 24

Randa closed the door to Sara's room and leaned against the frame. The face that had been composed only moments before crumbled to be replaced by a look of pure anguish. A strangled cry escaped her lips as hot tears escaped her eyes. She dropped to her knees and brought her hands up to her face.

Not now, not yet. Denise isn't ready for this. The nurse shook her head, as if wishing that the early morning's events had not happened would make them go away. But it would not go away; this was forever. *For however long that will be.*

Randa stemmed the flow of tears by sheer force of will alone. Taking a deep but shaky breath, she attempted to calm herself and tried to decide how she should deal with the problem and how she could help Denise do the same. *I have to tell her and I have to do it now.*

Rising to her feet, Randa wiped the remnants of moisture from her face and headed for the stairs. She knew Denise would be in her study working as she had been doing the past three days since her conversation with Carl. Randa hadn't minded taking over the care of Sara for those days, she knew how strongly Denise felt about keeping her word and honoring her work commitments, even if the deadline had needed to be pushed back. The nurse knew Denise also wanted to complete the next book for Sara. She had told Randa how much pleasure the older woman had in reading the poetry before it was published.

Entering the study, the nurse saw Denise at work at the computer, small glasses perched on her nose. Randa felt the strong rush of affection that coursed through her every time she looked at the poet. *I love her so much.* Walking up behind the brunette, Randa wrapped her arms around the strong shoulders and placed a loving kiss on the poet's cheek.

Blue eyes turned on the nurse and Denise smiled a welcome. "Did you need something or are you just up here providing me with inspiration?"

Randa returned the smile, but then her face became serious. "Denise, this morning I went down to Sara just like every other morning but there's a change today." The nurse felt the tension immediately in the body under her hands. Maintaining contact for support, Randa looked straight into Denise's now intense gaze.

"Love, Sara can't speak anymore. You know she hasn't had much more than a whisper for some time now but when I went into her this morning, she wasn't able to vocalize at all." Denise slumped a little in her chair and Randa could see tears brimmed the poet's eyes. Each day recently had seen a steady decline in Sara's condition. She could no longer eat solid food and had been changed to a completely liquid diet and there was nothing left of her ability to move her extremities. The ravages of her disease had left Sara with only some movement of her head and facial muscles. Her ability to speak had been her last pleasure and now that had been stripped away also. Sara was almost totally a prisoner of her own body.

Denise squeezed her eyes tightly shut and leaned into Randa, accepting the comfort briefly before moving back in the chair.

"How is she holding up?" the poet asked. "Does she need anything, should I go down to her now?"

"In just a minute, love. As you can imagine, Sara was upset. I went through her morning routine as usual though and afterward she calmed down somewhat. I talked to her and tried to keep any questions I had simple. Sara still has some head movement so she can let us know yes or no to questions, but she's not going to be able to call us when she needs help. The monitor in her room isn't going to be enough anymore. I can't think of anything else to do, one of us will need to be with her at all times. I think we should move the fold-away bed down into Sara's room."

Denise was silent and nodded, agreeing with the unspoken conclusion that this move heralded the final days for their beloved Sara. As one, the women moved into a close embrace, each feeling as if another small piece of them had been taken away. Reluctantly Randa broke the hug and moved away from

Denise.

"I suppose we should take the bed down now. We'll need to do a little rearranging in Sara's room."

As the two women moved the bed downstairs, the blonde couldn't help but look across the landing to the door of Denise's bedroom. She sighed at the pending loss of closeness, knowing they wouldn't be together in Denise's large bed for sometime to come. Denise saw the direction of Randa's gaze but said nothing. The rest of the morning was spent in changing the appearance of Sara's room yet again.

That evening, Randa sat alone in the living room with the volume of unpublished poetry Denise had given her on Valentine's Day. Sara had been cleaned and dressed for bed when DJ volunteered for the first shift in Sara's room. The nurse and the poet had agreed to split the nights on the foldaway bed while the other slept upstairs. Randa knew there was no way she could sleep in the brunette's bed without the woman herself and resigned herself to a night on the couch. She remembered the nights she and Denise spent on the couch together and smiled at the memory of warm arms around her.

Settling back, Randa continued with her reading of the unpublished works. What she had read so far had amazed her. The poetry was almost luminous in its beauty and the nurse felt near to tears as more and more of Denise's soul was revealed. *If the whole world could read these poems it would be as deeply in love with you as I am.* Randa again felt the privilege of knowing and loving the poet.

The window rattled in the living room and the nurse looked up momentarily startled. March had started out sunny but windy and the swift breeze could cut through you at night when deprived of the sun's warmth. Randa moved to the window to check on the security of the fastenings. Satisfied, she moved restlessly around the room. Randa had always trusted her instincts when it came to her patients. She had said many times that she could walk onto her nursing unit and just feel there was going to be a problem. That same feeling brushed across her now and the nurse knew the reason was

Sara. Her decline had been rapid and she had taken on a look of resignation today that was almost painful to observe in a woman so strong. That look was reflected in her niece's eyes.

Randa's heart ached for the two women destined shortly to be parted. Though Sara's nightmare would be over, Denise's would continue on. The blonde wondered again what Sara's passing would bring for Denise and herself. They hadn't spoken of any long term plans; there had been no discussion of commitment. Those things wouldn't have bothered Randa, but one other thing still loomed large in her mind. Denise had yet to say, "I love you". *I don't want to push you, love, but hearing that from you would ease my mind so much. I guess I'm still afraid that someone as wonderful as you might not be able to love someone as insignificant as me.*

The nurse drifted down the hall and peeked into the door of Sara's bedroom. Sara was apparently sleeping quietly and Denise sat cross-legged on the foldaway bed writing on a tablet. Feeling the blonde's gaze somehow, Denise looked up from her work. Blue eyes connected with green and the poet reached out a hand to Randa. Randa made her way quietly over to the small bed and sat down closely to the brunette. They leaned into one another and Randa felt a measure of reassurance about Denise's feelings for her.

Seeing the tablet in the poet's lap, Randa was struck by the title.

" 'A World of Sara', that's beautiful. Is it a new poem?" the nurse asked in a hushed voice.

"No," replied the brunette, "I actually finished up the new book of poetry a little while ago. These are some notes for an idea I had for a novel. I thought maybe I could fictionalize Sara's life in a book. I know I'm going to lose her but maybe this way I can give her a touch of immortality."

Randa turned to look at Denise. "A novel of your own, with your name on it?" At the poet's shrug, Randa smiled. "I think it's a great idea. I especially like you considering using your own name. Sara would be proud."

Denise gave a small smile. "No, she would be furious with me for invading her privacy but, I thought that after…"

Denise's words faltered as a soft sob choked off the sentence. Randa reached for the poet and drew her close.

"It's okay, love. I understand." The evening grew late as

258

the two women sat wordlessly together, hands clasped and hearts joined.

"No, no, no, no... NO!" Denise's forehead fell to the floor with a loud growl. She lay upon her stomach in front of the smouldering fire as her head slowly pounded up and down on a large writing pad. With a sigh she threw down the black pencil in her hand and looked at the sheet of paper containing a single sentence. Lifting the papers edge she ripped the sheet from the pad and scrunched it into a ball.

Randa walked into the living room in time to witness a projectile wad of paper hurtle towards her and she ducked just in time. With a frown she looked down at Denise who had started another round of head butts upon the floor.

"Denise?"

The poet looked up startled. "Oh... hey."

"What's wrong?"

"I can't think... I've got writers block... empty mind... airhead syndrome..." she paused in thought, "is that last one even conceivable?" DJ pulled silver framed glasses from her nose and placed them on the floor before rolling onto her back. Blowing out a forced sigh of annoyance through pursed lips she sat up and pushed herself to her feet. Denise looked down at the pile of crumpled paper scattered around her feet.

"Denise, why don't you take a break for a while? You've been at this since five o'clock this morning. I know you missed breakfast. Have you even eaten anything today?"

DJ shrugged.

"Are you hungry?"

She shrugged again.

Randa sighed. "Well anyway, I came out here because Sara has just woken up."

Denise looked alarmed, knowing full well what Randa was about to suggest. Nervously her eyes scanned the perimeter of the room as though she was plotting her means of escape. For the past four days she had hid away from her aunt, too afraid to face her and hating herself a little more as every day passed. DJ knew she could no longer delay the inevitable and her responsibilities. Sitting with Sara while the old woman slept was not the same and she knew it. The poet hadn't made verbal contact with her aunt for many days and the guilt alone was tearing her apart inside.

Denise looked back at Randa and nodded. She wiped suddenly sweaty palms down the front of her pullover and jeans. "Okay."

"Okay?"

"Okay I know I have to go and see her... speak to her."

With a smile of relief the nurse stepped forward. "Are you all right?"

A nervous smile was her reply.

"Do you want me to go in there with you for a while?" Randa took DJ's hand and brushed her fingers over her palm. She looked up into anxious blue eyes.

Shaking her head the poet released Randa's hand. "No, that's okay." She took a step backwards away from the nurse. "I need to do this alone. I've delayed this for too long now." Taking a deep breath to steel her confidence, Denise closed her eyes. *Just go in there, DJ. God... what if she can't forgive me for hiding away for so long. I am so stupid!*

As a look of anguish crossed Denise's features Randa closed the distance between them and lifted up onto her toes, placing a loving kiss upon her lips. Denise opened her eyes with surprise and looked down into supportive green. Within the space of one precious moment she saw her world, her future, and her only anchor right in front of her. A great emotion surged inside, filling her heart with devotion. Parting her lips, Denise attempted to speak, to vocalise her feelings but no words escaped. Stuttering clumsily she sighed with frustration and kissed Randa's forehead before stepping away.

"I'll see you in a bit." She walked away.

"I'll be here."

Denise looked back at Randa. *Always?* She thought. Winking she turned and completed her journey towards Sara's room.

The poet entered Sara's bedroom, keeping her eyes averted

from the bed in the centre of the room. Her gaze was down, studying the floor beneath her as she closed the white gloss door. Hearing only the sound of the C-PAP, Denise walked toward the bed in the centre of the room; she didn't stop until she was directly within her aunt's line of sight. Biting the inside of her cheek, DJ looked over to her aunt. Alert blue eyes gazed back. Denise smiled weakly as a sorrowful emotion swelled within her chest. She swallowed hard fighting against the lump in her throat.

After a long moment of silence DJ spoke softly. "Sara..." She waited, as though needing the older woman to acknowledge her presence. Sara's eyes narrowed in an expression that DJ could easily identify as her aunt's smile. Whenever Sara smiled her face would light up and her eyes would sparkle as their lids lowered.

Denise reached out and took her hand. She looked closely at the withered appendage as she whispered, "I'm so sorry." The motionless hand within her own was warm to her touch and DJ sat on the side of the bed, covering Sara's hand in both her own.

"I was... I just didn't... think I could..." confused and frustrated Denise rubbed her suddenly throbbing forehead and looked back at Sara. A single tear had fallen from older blue eyes and was trailing lazily down the side of Sara's face. A shuddering sigh escaped Denise's chest as she leaned forward and wiped away the stray droplet. Fighting against her own emotions was futile but she did it anyway. "I've been so selfish."

Sara's eyes widened as her head moved slightly to the left then right.

"Don't, Sara," Denise said sternly, "I know how I have been acting. I've seen the upset I've caused so clearly in Randa's eyes. I've distanced myself from you... I've pushed her away." The truth Denise acknowledged was that whenever she did have a problem and did need to talk she'd always had Sara as her sounding board and could guarantee sound advice. Now that was impossible and although within her own heart she knew she had that closeness with Randa, the poet was afraid to divulge to the blonde just how much she needed her.

Eyes glazing with reluctant tears, Denise looked back at the closed door. She blinked hard in an attempt to clear her vision. "Would you have ever believed she would have happened to us? Randa, I mean?" DJ cast her eyes back toward her aunt as she said, "She made the house feel brighter from the moment she entered." There was a pause as the poet frowned in thought. "Or maybe she just made me feel brighter."

There was another moment of quiet.

With a slow smile, DJ suddenly chuckled to herself. "Do you remember... oh it must have been about fifteen years ago now?" She rolled her eyes, "I can't believe I have only just remembered this. Anyway... it was after my rather disappointing first sexual encounter. I declared that if that was what 'it' was like then I was willing to spend the rest of my life celibate," she chuckled. "You told me one day I would meet somebody that would change my mind." She shook her head, "Then you said that it would be pretty boring if I spent the rest of my life being my 'own best friend' anyway. I can't believe I have only just remembered that. I had no idea what you were talking about at the time... it didn't quite compute!"

Sara's eyes sparkled with mirth.

"Sara Jayne Jennings!" the poet admonished, amused.

There was silence before DJ spoke again. "There are so many questions I wish I'd asked you, Sara. You know... when mum and dad died I was so afraid I'd have nowhere to go... nobody to love me. I wondered where I would live. Then I discovered you wanted me. I know I was one hell of a pain in the beginning but I want you to know that no matter what I may have said or how I acted... I knew from the start that I was in the only place I would have ever wanted to go. Sometimes I used to wonder why you wanted a tag along kid when you had such a free and exciting life style. Travelling around, teaching at schools around the country, never knowing where you would be needed next but loving every minute of it. I couldn't believe that you gave it all up to look after me." Denise paused and looked deep into Sara's eyes. "I do have one question though. How come you never settled down with anybody special?" The poet smiled shyly, "I knew about you and Diane."

Sara's eyes portrayed an expression of shock and the poet chuckled again.

"Whatever your reason was for keeping it quiet... I want you to know that I understand and respect that. Though I am sure the secrecy was mainly due to Diane, yes? She was

262

married after all."

Sara nodded shortly.

Lifting the older woman's hand Denise looked down. "Did you love her?" She paused and looked back, "no... don't answer that. I was just wondering really but... how do you know though? How do you know when you have found that one special person that you are willing to spend the rest of your life with? I want that person for me to be Randa but I'm afraid. I'm afraid of me... to look deep down within myself and acknowledge what is in my heart. She says that she loves me... and I don't know how to respond. Its like my insides freeze, my mind stutters and I'm suddenly scared to say the words. I want to tell her that she is the last person that fills my mind when I go to sleep and the first one I think about when I wake but when I look at her... its like... I think that if I say any of this it will be acknowledging that she does mean something special to me and for that I will lose her. Like mother... and father... and now you."

Biting her lip, Denise released Sara's hand and reached out, smoothing loose strands of grey hair around her head. She needed to change the subject.

"Anyway... how are you feeling... all right?"

After a moment Sara blinked once.

"Does that mean yes?" The brunette asked.

Sara blinked again.

Denise nodded. "You're surprised I knew about Diane aren't you?"

With a blink and slight nod, Sara confirmed her niece's suspicions.

"It was more of an inkling at first; like I always saw something special when you were together. The look in your eyes when she was around, it was a look that she mirrored. Then something changed between you both and it was like part of you was missing. I always wondered what happened. Sara... did you love her?"

One blink.

Denise frowned. "Do you still love her?"

Another single blink

"Have you told her that you still love her?"

At Sara's double blink and small shake of her head, DJ nodded in understanding. "Because she was married and then

263

her husband died and it didn't feel right? Like maybe she would see it as disrespectful or something like that?"

One blink

"Even though she obviously feels the same way?"

Sara nodded once.

"Life's so damn complicated," the poet sighed, "maybe I was right and it's better to stay alone."

Sara's eyes widened and she shook her head, glaring at her niece. Denise noticed her expression and grinned sheepishly. "Maybe not?"

Sara blinked twice.

Rising from the bed Denise turned and walked around its edge towards the window. Looking through the glass she gazed briefly at the garden with a critical eye. She had pruned the climbing rose bushes along the fence and tidied the vegetable patch but the rust was still an overgrown mess.

"I finished the new book," she said turning back toward her aunt and walking to the bed. She regained her position beside Sara. "I made a decision. I've decided for the first time ever that I am going to put a dedication inside the cover. I'm not sure yet exactly how I will get around to wording it but I just wanted to let you know because... well because..."

Twin sets of blue eyes locked upon each other as understanding settled between them.

Squeezing her eyes closed, Denise sighed but was determined not to lose herself in front of her aunt. She felt she needed to be strong for her but every time she so much as looked at her aunt and acknowledged the almost completely paralysed body in front of her it was difficult to keep her composure and not to seethe with anger, hurt and frustration. *The worst part is that she knows everything that's going on yet she can do nothing about it,* Denise thought, *she is a prisoner in her own body.*

Taking a deep cleansing breath the poet looked back into Sara's understanding eyes. "I'm dedicating the book to the two most important people in my life. I'm not going to tell Randa yet though... I may not use your names, but it will be obvious to the two of you. I sent the collection off to Carl and his ever impatient wife and I am sure I will hear from them within the next couple of days."

Denise looked to her left and spotted a large book lying

upon Sara's dressing table. Rising from the bed she crossed the room and picked it up.

"Les Miserables?" she asked, walking back to Sara. "Has Randa been reading this to you?"

Sara's eyes twinkled with a small nod.

Denise laughed. Sara had stated many times that she had wanted to read the novel but often said she couldn't find the drive needed to tackle the mammoth book. "You are a cunning one, Sara Jennings, I'll give you that!"

Sitting back upon the bed, Denise flipped through the pages as she said, "Would you like me to read some to you?"

Sara blinked once.

"Okay... hold on a moment." Denise dashed out of the room and quickly returned seconds later with her glasses. Placing the silver frames upon her nose she retrieved the novel and began to read aloud.

"Chapter twelve..."

Time seemed to pass quickly as DJ read to Sara and it was while the poet was half way through reading chapter fourteen that an unexpected sound forced her to stop and look up from the novel. Sara's breathing had changed. Her eyes had taken on a wide panicked expression as her breath laboured and she seemed to gasp for air.

Jumping from the bed, Sara's book fell unnoticed to the floor as Denise's full attention turned toward her aunt.

"Sara, what's wrong?"

The frail woman's eyes were brimming with fear and unshed tears.

"Is it... what... can't you breath?" Denise asked in desperation as Sara's lungs fought for oxygen. "Oh hell...RANDA!" The poet shouted as she dashed out of the room and into the main area of the house frantically looking for the nurse. "Randa, quick it's Sara, she can't..."

Suddenly the sound of rapid footsteps echoed as Randa flew down the stairs. She met the poet in the living room and instantly noticed the terror in her eyes. Without question she followed the brunette back to Sara's room. The older woman was still fighting for breath in an obvious state of alarm.

"What's happening?" DJ asked as Randa swiftly attended to Sara.

The nurse barely responded, focusing all her attention on the older woman. "She's panicking," Randa answered quickly as she continued to take care of Sara.

Standing back against the wall, Denise watched Randa at work. The look of sheer terror in her aunt's eyes haunted her thoughts and not being able to endure seeing Sara this way, she quickly left the room.

When the nurse had finished and Sara had calmed down enough to sleep, she turned around to find Denise absent. Feeling a spark of concern, Randa went in search of the poet.

Sitting silently in the living room, Denise leaned forward, her elbows resting upon her knees and her head hidden within her hands. She heard Randa as she entered the room and looked up at the nurse in question. A clear expression of apprehension shone in her worried blue eyes.

"How is she?"

"She's okay," Randa replied. "She had some difficulty breathing which made her panic. I gave her a sedative to calm her down. She's resting now."

With an anguished frown the poet let her head hang limply. "I can't take what this is doing to her, Randa. Can't even begin to understand what she must be going through or how she must feel, knowing there isn't anything anybody can do. I'm so glad you're here for her." Rising to her feet, DJ approached the blonde. "How are you?"

"I'm okay," Randa replied simply.

"You're tired."

"A little."

Denise reached out and wrapped one arm around Randa's shoulders. "Come on." Taking the lead she led them both back into Sara's room and toward the foldaway bed. "You lay down and rest for a while."

Sitting down upon the low metal action bed, Randa kicked off her shoes. "What about you?"

"I'll be right here." DJ slid down the wall until she was sitting beside Randa. Spying the book still lying upon the floor she reached out with her foot and dragged the large novel toward her. She looked back at Randa who was lying on the bed watching her. Leaning to her side, Denise pressed her lips

266

upon Randa's and they were welcomed immediately. "Just try and get some sleep for a while. I'll be here when you wake."

Re-opening the book, Denise stared blankly at the pages, neither reading nor seeing the text in front of her. She tried to close her eyes but the terror filled blue orbs of her aunt filled her mind's eye. With a heavy sigh she turned to look upon Randa and settled for watching the blonde as she slept.

Chapter 25

The early days of March were grim in the Jennings household and the weather outside seemed to reflect it. The skies were gray and opened frequently to douse the countryside with icy rain. When there was no rain, the wind blew in frigid gusts, bending trees to its will and pushing humanity along its way.

It's an ill wind that blows no good thought Randa, remembering a phrase spoken by her grandmother in times of bad weather or bad fortune. She turned away from the large window in the living room and returned to the couch where she had been resting and thinking about the bleak situation. It seemed when Sara lost her voice; her will to fight and live went with it. She had seemed slightly better after her talk with Denise but for the past two days Sara had taken little nourishment. A few spoons of soup or tea, then she would refuse to open her lips further, no matter how much she or Denise implored her.

The twinkling, always so present in Sara's eyes had disappeared, replaced with resignation and a measure of fear. The fear had led to a few panic attacks but those had been fairly well controlled with the Xanax prescribed by Dr. Macarthur. The C-PAP was in use almost continuously but Randa could tell Sara was still having difficulty getting enough oxygen. Her weak respiratory muscles left her breathing shallow, occasionally labored and just recently, somewhat irregular.

None of the symptoms Randa had seen worried her as much as when she looked into the older woman's eyes today. Sara's gaze was fixed on some distant point, as if lost in memory. She roused a little when Randa spoke to her and gave her body the care it required, but then she soon drifted off again. Having observed many patients at the end of their lives, the nurse knew Sara's passing would not be long in coming. Randa's feelings were torn about the situation. *On one hand I'm glad the torture of the last six months is coming to an end for Sara but losing her so soon after meeting her is tearing me up inside.*

Randa knew she should be resting. It was her night to be with Sara, sleeping on the foldaway bed. The nurse had abandoned sleeping in the bed upstairs altogether, preferring to sleep on the couch on the nights Denise stayed with her aunt. The bed just felt too cold without the warmth of the poet beside her, though the blonde's discomfort had nothing to do with the temperature of the room.

Randa had never needed a great deal of sleep and she had worked shifts on less, but she decided to try resting for a while. Laying back on the couch, green eyes closed and the blonde napped fitfully.

At eleven o'clock, Denise woke the nurse with warm lips pressed to her forehead and a soothing hand stroking her cheek.

"Randa?" the poet said. "Randa, you wanted me to wake you at eleven." The blonde stretched and wrapped her arms around Denise, pulling her close.

"Good evening," she murmured and brought DJ down for a lingering kiss. "I was dreaming about you, but the real thing is so much better." That made Denise smile but it wasn't enough to hide the exhaustion seemingly ever present in the poet's eyes these days. Randa gently traced the outline of the brunette's lips and asked, "How's Sara?"

"About the same. She looked at me once or twice but for the most part she just stared off into space. Do you think she could be suffering in any way?"

Randa considered her reply a moment. "I don't think so. I think she's calm now, the low oxygen levels in her body are probably responsible for that but I'm glad she doesn't seem so scared anymore." Denise nodded and seemed to accept that. Randa sat up and yawned widely.

"Sorry about that. I think I'll just take a quick shower to wake up and then go sit with Sara. I'll only be a few minutes. Why don't you lay down here and get some rest?" The women exchanged places and as Denise started to lie down she

269

grimaced. "Denise, what's the matter?"

"Nothing much, I just made the mistake of sitting too long on that chair in Sara's room instead of the foldaway bed and my back is bothering me a little. The next Bonfire Night that thing is going to be first on the bonfire pile."

Randa chuckled and said, "I'll help you toss it on myself. Right now, why don't you turn over and let me work on those knots a minute?" Denise flipped to her stomach and the nurse ran her hands under the poet's sweater feeling the tension that had settled into the muscles there. Initiating a rhythmic kneading and massaging of the area, Randa soon had DJ sighing with relief.

"Better now?" asked the blonde. Denise responded with a sleepy nod and a barely audible "Better." Randa covered Denise with the blanket and lowered the lights in the living room. She made her way upstairs, took a brief shower and was back in Sara's room in only a few minutes. She approached the bed and routinely let her eyes wander over Sara and the equipment at the bedside. The C-PAP was functioning efficiently providing Sara with as much support as it could. The older woman's body was in good alignment and limbs were supported with pillows. Satisfied everything was as it should be, Randa allowed the nurse inside her to recede a little. Now she looked down at Sara through the eyes of a friend. Randa found herself wondering what the older woman was seeing as her gaze seemed to be fixed on a spot somewhere high in the corner of the room.

"Let it be friends and family you see, Sara. Let them come and guide you. It's okay now; you go when you need to. I'm here and I'll always be here for Denise. I'll remember and keep my promise to you. I will love Denise to the end of my days and do everything I can to make her happy." If Sara heard she gave no visible sign of it. Randa leaned over and placed a kiss on the soft gray hair. "I love you, Sara. I'll be right here if you need me."

The nurse moved to the foldaway bed, took her place on it and picked up the book on the table. She saw Denise's glasses sitting next to the book and smiled. The brunette always looked so adorable with them perched on her nose, probably looking very similar to what Sara had looked like in her teaching days. *Well, if Denise grows older and looks like Sara I'll have*

270

nothing to complain about. The prospect of being with Denise until they reached a ripe old age together gave Randa a warm and secure feeling inside. *It's going to be happily ever after for us, Denise.*

Randa opened the book, found her place and began reading.

It was almost 4 a.m. when Randa finished Les Miserables. She had started reading it at Sara's request but after Sara didn't seem to comprehend it anymore she decided to complete the book to keep her mind occupied. Sara's status had been unchanged through the wee hours and Randa had checked on her breathing and repositioned her several times. As the nurse set the book down she felt a chill pass down her spine. Something had changed in the room and she sat still a moment trying to figure out what her senses had picked up that her conscious mind hadn't processed yet. Rising and heading toward Sara's bed the nurse in her took over and she methodically began assessing the situation. The C-PAP hummed properly, the connections were fine. The mask fit correctly but she soon realized the problem was Sara herself. The woman's respirations were shallow and more irregular. Randa brought her watch up and timed the respirations; Sara was only breathing 8 times a minute. The nurse reached for Sara's wrist and found her pulse to be 42. Randa's heart dropped as she thought *this is it.*

During those brief moments of clinical observations, Randa almost missed it. As the nurse brought her line of sight to Sara's face, those wonderful blue eyes looked at her with clarity for the first time all night. "Oh Sara…hang on, okay. I'm going to get Denise." Randa went to the living room and gently tugged on Denise's arm.

"Denise, you need to wake up, love. It's Sara, you should come now." DJ shook off her sleep and rose to her feet.

"Is she…?" Denise began. Randa reached out and took the poet's hand.

"Not yet but very soon I think. She needs us to be with her now." With hands still clasped the pair made their way quickly back to Sara's side. Randa didn't need her watch to tell her that the rate of Sara's breathing had slowed a little further in the bare minute she had been gone. Denise went immediately to the head of the bed and reached out to touch Sara's soft cheek. Looking up at Randa, Denise asked, "Can we remove this now?" The blonde nodded and undid the Velcro straps holding the mask of the C-PAP in place. The sudden quiet in the room as Randa turned the machine off accentuated the ragged breathing.

Denise saw that Sara's eyes were on her and she leaned over closer to her aunt. In a shaky whisper the poet said simply, "I love you. I'll never go a day without remembering you. I'll see you again on the other side." The tears came then; Denise could not stop them and did not want to try. Randa moved around the bed to stand next to the poet. Wrapping an arm around the brunette's waist, Randa saw that Sara struggled to pull in a breath now.

In a voice choked with emotion, the nurse said, "Godspeed, Sara. Safe journey, my friend." Randa held tightly to Denise and let her own tears fall as well. For one brief moment it seemed Sara looked directly at the two women then her eyes fluttered closed. There were a few short, shallow breaths then Sara exhaled and did not draw another. Sara Jennings passed from this world, guided by her brother and sister-in-law, toward a place where her physical limitations no longer mattered.

Remaining behind, Denise and Randa turned and held tightly to each other, letting their grief and their tears flow unchecked.

Chapter 26

The distant sound of the carriage clock upon the mantel echoed throughout the silent house. Suddenly it seemed every noise, not just within the house but the whole neighbourhood increased tenfold, breaking the cold stillness in the Jennings household.

The air hummed with a ghostly chill and Denise thought that if she listened hard enough she could almost hear a whispering wind rustle through the empty rooms of the house. She sat in her study, resting upon the floor with her back against the closed door. Whether DJ was keeping the rest of the house out or herself in, she was unsure and only knew she needed to distance herself from the stark realities of the coming new day.

Randa was asleep in bed and although the blonde had asked DJ to accompany her for some much needed rest, Denise had stayed only until she was sure Randa had drifted into an exhausted sleep. Upon that moment she had kissed the blonde softly before retreating from the bedroom. Now sitting alone in the confines of her study, DJ's tired, red-rimmed eyes stared blankly into space - thinking.

The four days that had passed since Sara's death had been, from Denise's point of view, a complete haze of constant preparations. Having never before faced the feat of having to deal with the events after a loved one's death, the poet had no idea where to begin. It was Randa who had taken effective control. Together, and with much guidance from the blonde, the women were able to undertake the arrangements for Sara's funeral.

Stretching out her long, red pyjama clad legs, Denise let her head fall back against the door as she looked up at the ceiling. The poet frowned as she studied the curious patterns formed by the artex designing. She had found that as long as she kept her mind occupied and away from thoughts of Sara, she could control her emotions. Every time DJ closed her eyes she could see her aunt's final days. The fear in her conscious eyes and her paralysed body, unable to utilize even her most basic communication skills. Not being able to do anything to ease Sara's suffering tormented her like a pressurised weight of guilt.

Blue eyes turned toward the window and Denise saw the full moon shining high in the sky. Rising to her feet, the poet approached the window and looked up into the glittering sprinkle of stars. Suddenly she remembered a scene from her childhood and the first week after her parents' death. It was a night very similar to the one she was looking out upon now, and as she lay in her unfamiliar room, in her unfamiliar bed, she looked out through the open curtains. To her left she remembered hearing the door open and her aunt enter her new bedroom. Sara approached the window and looked out into the sky.

"The moon is shining full tonight," she had said softly, her glittering eyes turning toward her niece.

Denise nodded mutely.

Sara smiled instinctively as she continued. "Did you know that the moon is magic?"

The young brunette shook her head and pulled the covers up above her shoulders until they covered half of her face. Blue teary eyes shone in the moonlight.

"Oh yes," Sara said, "the moon is like a big magic telescope that hangs down from heaven. Whenever the moon shines full the angels in heaven can look down upon their loved ones and see how they are. Make sure they are happy and healthy and all looking after each other."

Denise was quiet as she processed her aunt's information. After a while her timid voice asked, "Really?"

Sara smiled; glad to finally receive some response from her withdrawn niece. "I do believe so," she replied.

Cautiously the young girl pulled the covers down and rose to her knees as she shuffled across the surface of the bed. Holding onto the windowsill Denise looked up into the sky. "Do you think that mummy and daddy are watching me right now?"

"I think they will always be with you, watching over us both and making sure we are looking after one another, Denise."

"DJ."

"DJ?" Sara asked.

The brunette edged a little closer to her aunt. "Daddy

274

always called me DJ."

Sara nodded her approval. "Okay, DJ it is." She held out her arms and smiled in relief as her niece accepted her embrace.

The poet smiled in memory as a single tear escaped her eye. Wiping her face she turned away from the window and looked back at the closed door. In another room across the landing she knew Randa was sleeping alone. The poet felt a strong desire to go to the blonde and simply take comfort in her presence, but something forced her to stay away. An overpowering urge had nestled deep within her and one she felt helpless to deny. Her new book, the novel she had been compiling notes on for many days, suddenly became of high importance to her. A task that would keep her mind occupied for a long period of time.

It suddenly became apparent that if she wanted to keep her mind focused on something other than Sara's death, she should focus on her life. Not so much her own life than a fictionalised and hopefully humorous world in which Sara, the younger woman she remembered, would play a pivotal and lead role.

Taking a seat at her desk, DJ turned on her computer and waited patiently for her machine to boot up. Retrieving her glasses from on top of the CPU, Denise placed them upon her nose and began to type.

Hours passed seamlessly without any acknowledgment from Denise as she sat at her computer, oblivious to all around her. It was only when the door to her study slowly opened that Denise became aware of her surroundings. Looking over her shoulder the poet watched as Randa ambled into the room.

"You left me," the blonde said quietly. Obviously she had just woken up.

DJ looked away guiltily, turning her eyes back to the glare of the computer screen. Behind her she heard Randa continue her approach until she stood at the back of her. Uncertain hands landed upon her shoulders.

"You haven't slept all night?"

With a light shake, Denise turned back around to look up at Randa. "I couldn't."

"You haven't slept right for days." The concern was evident in the blonde's voice. "You need some rest, Denise, the funeral is tomorrow."

"I know," Denise snapped, then softened her voice, "I'm sorry." Closing her eyes she rested her forehead against Randa's chest. "I just don't want to think about things too much. Every time I lie down and close my eyes I just remember... it hurts too much, Randa. I need to keep my mind busy."

Denise felt a kiss placed upon the crown of her head. She looked up at Randa as she said, "I'm sorry I didn't stay with you but I just needed to do something... to keep active."

Randa looked over to the computer screen. "You've been writing all this time?"

"Just about."

Raising her hand Randa brushed her fingers through DJ's thick locks. She tilted her head up until they were both staring directly into each other's eyes. "It's okay to feel, Denise. To think about Sara... to mourn... to cry."

"I'd rather work," DJ replied.

"To exhaustion?" Randa studied the poet, tracing her fingertips around tired shaded eyes. "Please, Denise, you need some rest."

Denise shook her head. "No I don't need to rest, I need to work. I need to do something... anything as long as I don't have to think."

"But you haven't stopped," Randa insisted, "you don't rest, you don't sleep, you wont even eat properly. Denise you need to take time out before you burn out."

Dropping her gaze the poet let her vision fall to Randa's covered stomach. The blonde had taken to wearing the poet's thermal shirts - what she used to wear while gardening outside with Sara - for bed. Denise loved the look of her larger shirts swamping the smaller woman. Running her hands down the back of the red and black checked top, DJ buried her nose into the blonde, breathing in her scent.

"Denise."

"I can't stop."

"Of course you can." Randa grasped Denise's head and dragged the penetrating blue gaze back to look up at her. "Denise you really do need some rest; tomorrow will be a long day for both of us."

DJ rose to her feet forcing Randa to take a step backwards. "Rest later... work now."

"But..."

"No," the poet interrupted, "please, Randa... I can't at the moment."

With a sigh, Randa smiled as she caressed DJ's cheek and said, "I'll be back later... you know that right?"

The poet nodded and turned back to her computer. She sat down, facing the visual display unit, her mind already focusing on the words upon the screen. Without another thought she commenced her typing, concentrating only on the tale she was weaving.

After several short moments of silence, Randa turned and left the room. She didn't return until four hours later and when she did she found Denise slumped down over her desk, collapsed in an exhausted sleep. The sound of deep somnolent breaths filled the air.

The poet came around to the sound of a gentle voice calling her. Opening bleary eyes she found Randa leaning over her slumped form. "Is it time to get up?" she asked, confused.

Randa smiled. "No, it's time you went to bed to get some proper sleep... come on."

DJ didn't argue as Randa helped her to her feet and gently led her out of the study and into the bedroom. The bed was still unmade and the curtains were wide open. With a foggy mind and exhausted body, Denise crawled into bed as Randa re-closed the curtains.

"Randa?" Denise asked, looking at the dusky form by the window.

"Hmm?"

"Don't leave me yet."

Without a word, Randa moved towards the bed and slipped under the covers, lying behind Denise. She spooned her body around DJ and wrapped her arm over the long body, pulling her closer. "Get some sleep now."

Denise nodded as she closed her eyes. Though she felt mentally drained, the memories resurfaced, forcing the poet to re-open her eyes with a heavy sigh. "Randa?"

"Hmm?"

"Tell me a story... of your life. What is your oldest memory? What were you like at school? Tell me about your friend Derek. Tell me anything."

"Okay..."

277

Randa paused as she thought of something trivial that she hoped would lull the poet into a deep and much needed sleep.

Softly - she began.

Denise closed her eyes, concentrating fully on the sound of Randa's voice. Within minutes she fell into a much-needed slumber.

The reflection in the mirror stared back at her with an impassive visage. With her emotions buried deep within the recesses of her consciousness, Denise continued to dress with an air of forced indifference.

She had awoken that morning to find the spring sun shining brightly through her windows. As the day progressed the temperature began to rise and a flawless blue sky stretched out over the land. The happy singing of nesting birds greeted her ears as she stared out over the countryside. Unfortunately Denise was unconvinced; the forecast had predicted rain today and she knew it would soon be on its way.

Lifting the fitted black jacket from its hanger, Denise slipped her arms through the sleeves and settled the garment over her shoulders. Once finished she ran her hands over the dark two-piece trouser suit with a critical gaze. *Should I wear this white top or the blue one?* With a shrug DJ leaned down and slipped into black boots. From outside her bedroom she heard Randa ascend the stairs and she opened the door to see how the blonde was faring. Denise greeted the nurse on the landing. Randa was wearing a black two-piece skirt suit, sans shoes.

"The cars are here," said Randa as she entered the bedroom and slipped on her shoes. "Diane has just arrived and is waiting outside."

DJ let her eyes flutter shut, taking one more moment to steel away her tears. She was determined to keep her composure. The poet didn't want to lose control, especially in front of their friends. When she re-opened her eyes, Denise saw Randa standing with her back to her as she stared silently out of the bedroom window.

DJ softly approached Randa as she asked, "Are you

278

ready?" Randa turned and misty green eyes greeted Denise. "Come here," she said and pulled the blonde into her arms.

Randa choked back a sob as she clung to Denise. "I don't think I can do it."

"You can do it," Denise assured.

Drawing in a shuddering breath, the nurse pulled back and looked up at Denise.

"I'll be here for you and you'll be here for me."

Randa looked up with an expression of almost disbelief. "You're so… I don't know… you're so composed."

"I'm just trying to keep my head above the water," She answered. Leaning forward, DJ pressed her lips against Randa's, instigating a kiss of reassurance. She ran her hands over the blonde's body and cupped her face with a gentle touch. Softening her caressing lips she pulled away and looked down into Randa's closed eyes. "Ready to go?"

Green eyes re-appeared and Randa nodded. "Ready."

Denise reached down and took the nurse's hand, entwining their fingers together. "Let's go."

With a smile of support, Denise and Randa left the house confident that they could face what lay ahead of them as long as they faced it together.

Saint Bartholomew's Church was a ninth century building that was both very old and very cold. Its grey cobbled stonewalls spanned all the way up to a slatted roof that bore a network of thick wooden beams. The church was small with two rows of long wooden pews that were all filling to capacity as mourning friends entered the church. Along the walls on either side were six small stained glass windows, their colourful depictions often standing as focal points for much discussion. Running down the centre of the church laid a well-worn green carpet and in front of the dark wooden altar was a solitary gold trimmed coffin.

Denise sat between Randa and Diane, listening to the footsteps behind her as the last of Sara's friends filtered into the church. The building was filled with a hushed simple organ tune that she didn't recognise and was unsure that she had ever heard before. Against her will she turned her head and instantly spotted Carl sitting on the opposite side of the pews. The blonde man wore an obviously expensive single-breasted black suit and black trench coat, similar to the dress of many others in the church. DJ forced a smile as her friend nodded in acknowledgement and support; she then faced the altar again.

Waiting silently in front of Sara's coffin stood an elderly grey-haired priest who was both small in stature and general appearance. In his hands he held a large black bible that DJ was sure seemed out of proportion to the rest of his diminutive frame.

As the doors to the church shut and Father Brian began to announce the first hymn, Denise turned her attention to Randa. Looking to her right she was greeted by shimmering green eyes. The poet smiled reassuringly and entwined her fingers with Randa's before lifting their hands and kissing the blonde's smaller appendage.

"Are you alright?" DJ asked.

Randa nodded with a weak smile but Denise spotted the tears shining brightly in her eyes. Clutching the hand within her own in a reassuring squeeze she resisted the urge to wrap her arms around the nurse. Instead she turned back and rose to her feet as the first notes of one of Sara's favourite hymns filtered into the air. DJ's eyes turned to the coffin in front of the altar and the sudden realisation of just who was inside the small cramped box hit her like a bolt of electricity. *She hates small spaces.* With a hitched breath, DJ closed her eyes, squeezing them tight, wanting to shut out the view in front of her and concentrate only upon the sounds. She swallowed hard and took a deep breath. *Control* the poet said to herself, *got to keep control.*

Unexpectedly, Denise felt a reassuring hand move over her back in a soothing circle. She looked down to see understanding brown eyes behind small oval spectacles, glistening back at her. DJ smiled at Diane and turned her attention to the small hymnbook in the older woman's hands. She stared at the song upon the page unable to distinguish the words in front of her. *Got to keep control,* Denise thought again, the words becoming a short mantra within her mind.

As the priest once again started speaking, DJ pulled her attention away from the tiny man and moved her eyes around the old church. She looked up and studied a large crucifix upon the wall and then to her left where a small group of boys and girls sat beside the organ. Their choir robes were a contrast of maroon and white and the poet realised each child must have been no more than fifteen years old.

Denise hated funerals, she would freely admit it and did so to Father Brian when she met with him days before. She was sure the feeling was the same for most people. The poet had only ever been to one other funeral and that was her parents. She had vowed never to attend another after that. Being so young she didn't truly understand what was happening and soon became a little horrified when she discovered that her parent's bodies lay in the two long boxes at the front of the church. Sara, as always, had managed to ease her fears with a gentle explanation and a loving hug. DJ knew there was no question as to why her aunt was so popular with the children she taught; Sara had a very unique, understanding approach with them.

"… Niece DJ is going to say a few words."

At the sound of her name, Denise blinked and focused her attention back on the proceedings. Father Brian was now looking towards her as she felt a gentle coaxing hand squeeze her thigh. Denise looked down at Randa.

"That's you," the nurse whispered softly.

With understanding and a slight feeling of dread, Denise nodded and rose to her feet. Repeating the mantra under her breath the poet made her way towards the pulpit. As she stepped up and looked out upon the sea of faces, DJ realised it was the first time she had not only stood in front of a large group of people but read something out that she had herself written. Shutting off the nerves that threatened to consume her she looked momentarily at Randa, gaining comfort in her supportive gaze.

DJ cleared her throat. "I would like to read something." Her eyes drifted briefly to Carl and she knew that he and Randa were the only people who would know the truth behind what she was about to read out.

"I would like to read something written by one of Sara's favourite authors. It's something that I think portrays one's feelings in this situation."

Blinking, DJ looked down at the sheet of paper she had

just pulled out of her pocket. Unfolding its edges she stared down at her precise hand written script. Shakily she began:

"I fight the tears that accept your loss
Ignoring the void in my heart
I face the destruction that overwhelms my life
And the pain that tears me apart

For when you passed you left behind
A world full of laughter and fun
That no longer welcomes me with open arms
And I fight the impulse to run

You were my crutch, my solid ground
You rescued my childlike soul
That had wanted to fade so long ago
But you saved me you made me whole

So with my heart now shattered to infinity
And my soul facing eternal night
I pray for your wisdom to gain my stride
And for love to fill me with light."

As the final words were spoken, blue eyes glanced briefly into ocean green. A silence once again flowed over the church and not knowing what else to say, DJ forced a weak smile before stepping down from the pulpit and making her way back toward Randa and Diane. The rest of the service progressed smoothly and was over before Denise did even realise.

Rain that had started out as a light sheen had progressed during the church service into a steady downpour. Standing in the open air of the graveyard, Denise observed as Sara's coffin was lowered carefully into the ground. Around her the gentle flow of raindrops splashed against the cold ornamental gravestones. The small marble structures stretched out across the span of broken green fields, covering the once flawless countryside.

With an indifferent heart that took every ounce of will to maintain, DJ stood silently beside Randa, the blonde's hand firmly within her own. Within the other hand she held a fully blossomed red rose, Sara's favourite flower. As in the church she stood between Randa and Diane. Both other women stood under black umbrellas but DJ refused to do so, preferring instead to remain in the streaking rain as the droplets slowly soaked her through.

A light thud travelled up through the grave as Sara's coffin hit its bottom. Denise looked down at Randa to see the blonde engulfed in tears. Releasing Randa's hand DJ reached up and wiped one of the many tears that trailed the blonde's face. She smiled tenderly as Randa looked up and without warning pulled the blonde into her arms. Randa wrapped her arms around Denise's back as her head rested under the taller woman's chin. The nurse cried softly.

"Di?" Denise said as she looked down at the older women by her side.

Diane looked up at the poet as she whispered, "Yes?"

Without a word, DJ held out the rose, presenting it to Diane. The older woman looked at her in slight confusion.

"For Sara," DJ said, "I know what you meant to her."

An expression of relief flooded Diane's face. "I loved her," she confessed, "I still do." The older woman seemed almost liberated to finally be able to acknowledge that fact.

"I know," DJ replied and held out the beautifully bloomed flower once again.

Diane accepted the rose and stepped forward, looking down into the grave. Randa turned her head and watched along with DJ as the elder woman dropped the rose on top of the coffin.

Turning back, Randa caught Denise's attention. She ran her fingers through the poets soaked hair, both women no longer aware of the others present.

"Why wont you cry?" Randa asked.

Denise shook her head as an expression of confusion furrowed her brow. "I don't know," she answered, "I can't." She looked over Randa's head and into the deep grave. "I'm afraid."

Drawing Denise's head back, Randa looked deep into anguished blue eyes. "Why?" She questioned in a light

283

whisper.

"I'm afraid to accept that I am now alone."

"Do you really think that?" The hurt was clearly evident in Randa's voice.

Do I? Denise thought as she gazed searchingly into crystal green eyes that shone back at her with so much devotion. *I don't want to but what if I lose her too?* DJ smiled slightly. "I don't want to," she replied, not voicing the rest of her fears.

A sudden determination shone in Randa's expression. "You wont and you're not...ever. Please believe that."

Around them they slowly sensed that people were beginning to move away from the graveside. DJ looked up into the sky as the light rain began to ease.

"Everybody's leaving," Randa said.

"Are they all coming back to the house?"

"Quite a few of them I think."

Denise sighed. "God I can't handle that many people. I don't think there has ever been that many people in the house, Randa."

"We'll be fine," Randa assured, rubbing DJ's arm, "Are you ready?"

"I guess so." Denise looked back over to Diane who was still standing forward, looking down into the grave. "You go on, I'll be over in a moment." She inclined her head towards the elder women.

Randa nodded in understanding. "Okay, I'll see you in a minute."

As Randa headed back toward the black Rolls Royce, Denise stepped forward beside Diane. She looked down into teary brown eyes.

"Sara always said that if she was to go first then I was to make sure you never withdrew further into yourself. She was quite adamant you never do that."

DJ smiled.

"She didn't want you to play the reclusive writer part all your life. You have so much going for you, DJ."

"You know?" Denise asked. She wasn't aware Diane knew who she really was. Most people who knew DJ were all under the impression that the poet was actually a web designer.

"How could I not know?" Diane said. "Sara was always so proud of you. She had the entire collection of works by D

Jennings beside her bed. It was hard not to gain a hunch with the surname. I guessed and she never actually denied my suspicion."

"She would never lie," Denise stated and Di nodded.

"Exactly."

"So," DJ put her arm around the older woman's back, "Are you coming back to the house?"

Diane nodded assertively.

Behind her the poet heard wet slushy footsteps approach and she looked around to see Randa; an expression of need shone in the nurse's sea green eyes. The blonde stopped by DJ's right side and the poet once again found herself standing between the two women.

The rain had completely stopped and silently the three remaining women stood by Sara's graveside. Denise looked down at the light wood coffin and the single rose lying upon its rain-spoiled surface. She didn't even try to stop the lone tear that escaped her eye. "I'll miss you," she whispered softly before the three women turned and slowly walked away.

Chapter 27

Randa walked slowly down the street toward the Jennings home. Her eyes stung from the fierce March winds and her exhaustion was magnified by the emotional stress of the past few days. The loss of Sara had been difficult and tears still came easily at the thought of the older Jennings woman.

Randa had decided to take a weeklong bereavement leave from the Brightwood Information Network. Up until Sara's death she had been able to maintain the three shifts a week she had promised but this week was unlike any of the previous ones she had spent in England.

The day after Sara's funeral, the nurse sat in the living room with Denise and Sara's lawyer for the reading of the will. As expected, except for a small bequest to Diane in the form of jewellery, Sara's estate passed to DJ in its entirety. The next day Randa had the medical equipment removed and Sara's bed returned to the room from the storage shed. In accordance with her wishes, Sara's clothes had been donated to a local charity run by her church. That left only her personal things that, in the last three days, Denise had refused to deal with.

Since shedding a tear at Sara's graveside, Denise had continued with her life wrapped in a cocoon of numbness. Outwardly she appeared to be functioning normally, but Randa knew the poet was dazed and avoiding dealing with the reality of her loss.

I'll bet she's up in that damn study again, working herself ragged just like every other day. Denise, I love you and I hope you know that because this is about to become unpleasant for you. Randa arrived at the house and glanced up to see a soft glow was indeed coming from the poet's study. Giving herself a mental shake, Randa steeled herself for the upcoming confrontation. That she too would hurt while causing hurt to DJ was something she wouldn't think about.

Entering the house, Randa hung up her coat and scarf then headed with determination up the stairs. Entering the study, the nurse saw the beautiful profile silhouetted against the light from the computer screen and for a moment she hesitated in her mission. When Denise turned pained and tired eyes toward her though, the nurse knew what had to be done.

"Denise, are you still working? Before I left you promised me you would only be another 10 minutes or so and then you would quit and get something to eat. I've been at Diane's house for almost two hours and you're still at the computer."

The poet looked a little guilty but made no move to leave her project. "I was just involved in the work and I guess I lost track of time. I only need a few more minutes to finish up."

Randa had only intended to pretend to be mad at Denise, but now her temper rose in earnest. "That's what you said yesterday and the day before. You do nothing but sit up here and work all day. You won't eat and you only sleep when you've driven yourself to exhaustion. There are three boxes of Sara's things in the living room downstairs waiting for you to go through them. They've been there for days and you haven't given them a glance. You haven't given anything a glance but that computer!"

DJ sat stunned, hurt claiming the once brilliant blue eyes. "It's only been a few days, Randa. I just need time to..."

"To what?" interrupted the nurse, "To make yourself sick? To push away everybody who cares about you? To convince yourself that you'll be better off without me because that way you won't have to risk losing another person in your life?"

Denise's mouth dropped open. She looked at Randa with an unbelieving expression on her face. Randa ignored the sudden urge to throw her arms around the brunette, opting instead to press on with what DJ didn't want to, but needed to hear.

"God, Denise, look at yourself! You're haggard and losing weight. You won't allow anyone to come near you or comfort you. You won't let me touch you at all!"

"Do you think you're the only one hurting, that you're the only one who's lost someone precious? I sat with Diane this afternoon and I can tell you she's hurting! She's hurting but she's going on with her life because that's what Sara would have wanted. She isn't wallowing in self-pity or ignoring her own life because someone else's has ended. I didn't know Sara anywhere near as long as you did, but I think she had a real reverence and love for life that you're not showing. You said she taught you so much, it's a pity you didn't learn that." Randa felt her anger begin to get the best of her and she stalked to the door of the study. Denise had still not said a word since the nurse started on her rampage.

Pausing at the door, Randa turned to deliver the cruelest blow. "Denise, I love you with my whole heart. I love you with everything I am and everything I hope to be but damn it all to hell, if you wanted to die with Sara you should have thrown yourself in on top of her coffin days ago." With that she left the study, slamming the door in the process.

Closing her eyes, she murmured, "Forgive me, Denise. Forgive me and follow me, please." She started down the stairs and had just reached the bottom step when the study door flung open and an enraged poet burst forth onto the landing.

"Just a damn minute there, Randa!" DJ came down the stairs and followed the nurse into the living room.

You wanted this Randa, now you have to take it thought the nurse. *Let's see how tough you are.*

Denise's eyes blazed with anger. "You come here for a few months and you think you know me and everything about me? You don't know the first thing about me or Sara or how I feel! You didn't lose the last living relative you have, I did! You didn't stand by helplessly while the only person to give a damn about me since my parents were taken died, I did! You don't have to know what it's like to lose the person who made you what you are and gave you love unconditionally, I do!"

Tears filled Denise's eyes and slipped un-noticed down her cheeks as she continued. "You said you love me, now there is a laugh. How can you love me and then proceed to kick me when I'm down at my lowest point? What's the matter? Is my grief interfering with your plans for me? You said I never let you touch me, is that the problem here? You've not been getting enough attention? Let me rectify that situation then!"

Denise pulled the nurse to her roughly and lowered her head to place a crushing, bruising kiss upon Randa's mouth. The blonde was momentarily stunned by the hostility she felt in the kiss but willed herself to remain passive and still. Tears from Randa's eyes joined those of the poet when a moment later she felt the tone of the kiss change. The anger seeped away and was replaced with something else. Denise lifted her lips from Randa's for a moment before returning them in a kiss filled with longing, longing for reassurance and comfort and love. The nurse gave those things and more back in the kiss she was now partaking in.

Denise broke the kiss and with a ragged sob, hugged the blonde to her as she cried.

"Oh God, Randa, it should have been me! She was so strong and I could do nothing but stand by and let her die. It should have been me."

The nurse let Denise release the feelings of guilt and anger that had been like a poison in her soul for days. She led the poet to the couch and held her as Denise finally gave vent to the emotions that had paralyzed her as surely as the disease had paralyzed Sara.

Eventually Denise quieted and calmed. With her head on Randa's chest she said "Thank you for loving me enough to do this. I know it couldn't have been easy for you"

When Randa would have protested, Denise lifted her head, looked into the green eyes and smiled a little. "I'm not dense, just a little blind sometimes. Forgive me?"

Randa nodded. "As long as you forgive yourself. Denise, as much life and death as I've seen, I still don't have a clue about it. I only know the living have to go on. We'll be given the answer to the mystery soon enough."

"I suppose so," the poet replied. "Lord, I feel like I've been struck by a train. I'm really tired, Randa. I think I could sleep a little now." Rising to her feet, she held out a hand to the nurse. "Join me?"

The weight of the world dropped from Randa as she took Denise's hand.

Maybe the hurting can recede now and the healing can start the nurse thought hopefully. The pair made their way toward the bedroom turning off lights as they went. Randa heard the phone ring in the study but by unspoken mutual consent they let it go unanswered.

Whatever it is, it can wait until morning. Randa snuggled closer to the poet and they headed off together for some much needed rest.

The familiar creaks and groans of an old house as its joists and well-trodden floorboards rest against each other were the sounds that had finally awoken Denise. Lying in the darkness of her bedroom with Randa's back laying flush against her chest she came around to the recognizable sounds the old house often made. During the day these noises were almost indistinguishable, but at night - in the still silence - every creak sounded hauntingly like ghostly footsteps wandering through the darkened abode.

DJ lifted her head from the pillow and looked over to the illuminated read-out of the digital alarm clock.

"Seventeen minutes past three?" she whispered, confused as memories of the day before invaded her mind. She remembered Randa coming home after visiting Diane and she did very much remember the way in which the nurse had shouted at her. The hurt she had felt at Randa's words had quickly turned to anger as the blonde stormed back out of the room. It was an anger that she had expressed with just as much force as she released days if not months of bottled up hurt and frustration.

Afterward, when she had exhausted all emotions, Randa had accompanied her to bed for some much needed sleep. Neither woman had done anything more than remove their shoes as they crawled beneath the covers and settled into the cool sheets of the once lonely bed. Denise was surprised to discover that they had both slept undisturbed for over ten hours straight. *I guess we really did need it,* she thought.

Loosening her hold on the smaller frame in front, DJ moved away allowing Randa to slide backward until she was lying upon her back. As her eyes adjusted to the darkness of the room the poet gazed down at the relaxed slumbering features of the woman beside her. She reached out, trailing her fingertips up and over Randa's sweatshirt covered torso and on toward her lips. Denise never failed to be amazed by the silky softness of the smaller woman's lips. She found the texture positively addictive and only refrained from claiming them with her own for fear of waking the nurse.

"You have no idea, do you?" she whispered softly, "No idea of just what you do to me." Denise gently brushed stray blonde tresses across Randa's forehead. "How could I have treated you the way I have? You were right, you know..." she continued in a light murmur, "Sara would have wanted to do nothing more than kick my behind into reason for the way I was behaving!"

Her hand moved down to Randa's and she smiled in affection as she noted the way in which Randa's fingers instinctively grasped her own. Leaning forward she gingerly placed her lips upon the blonde's and kissed her softly, still not wanting to wake her. After a blissful moment she pulled back and once again rested her gaze upon Randa who was still very much unconscious to the world. Smiling, DJ backed out of the bed and readjusted the covers around Randa's form. The air was remarkably cold and she didn't want Randa to awake through a penetrating chill.

Still dressed in her old worn jeans and sweater, Denise padded out of the bedroom and onto the landing. She looked at the open doorway to her study, gazing at the blank screen of the computer but the desire that had consumed her the past few days seemed to have vanished. Surprised by the weight that had removed itself from her mind and knowing just who was responsible for that, DJ bypassed her study and moved instead down the stairs.

The cold chill of the still air enveloped her flesh causing goose bumps to rise upon its surface. Denise headed straight for the living room and began to build a roaring fire that in minutes had started to consume the frigidity of the house's atmosphere, replacing it instead with soothing warmth. The crackling sound of the flames as they bounced over the coal in the hearth was a comforting presence and DJ settled herself close to the amber blaze, luxuriating in its relaxing glow. She sighed in deep contentment - a contentment that she had not felt for a very long time.

In her left peripheral vision Denise spotted a small cluster of boxes. She knew instinctively that they were containers of Sara's belongings that had been stored away for a long period of time. These boxes were not Sara's personal effects, which for the most part still littered the house; these were her collection of 'bits and bobs', 'nicks and knacks' that she had hoarded throughout the years. Rising to her knees, DJ shuffled over to the first box that lay upon the other two and pulled it forward, dragging it back toward the fire. Biting the inside of her cheek she lifted the flaps and looked inside. An assortment of objects greeted her vision.

"Wow!" DJ muttered as one hand moved into the box and she began to pull the most original objects out.

A neatly folded silk embroidered scarf, a wooden carved figurine of a distorted form lying upon its side, a small mirror surrounded by a metallic bronze finish that had peculiar etched scrapings around it. Denise had never seen the figures before but was sure they must have been letters of some kind. Her eyes grew wide as she pulled the next item out of the box. *Wow, a Ouija board? Oh well I am sorry, Sara, but there is no way this is staying in the house!* Denise looked down at the surface, recognising its details from many films she had seen and shuddered in memory. *I sure as hell am not keeping this thing!*

Shaking her head, Denise placed the board warily beside the growing pile of goodies she was pulling out of the box as her other hand descended back inside the container. Out came an assortment of more objects. She pulled out a large pile of pages bound by a thick twine and covered by hard leather. Dark brows drew together as she opened the pages and looked inside. *Wow!* Blue eyes moved over the pages with bemused interest, *I had no idea you were once or at all interested in all of this, Sara!* She read over the inscriptions upon the pages, *Druid tree magic, tarot cards, spells and potions, runes?* DJ closed the book with a smile.

"What else is in these boxes?" she wondered.

An hour later Denise sat amongst a wide variety of objects ranging from the obscure to normal every day possessions. She had also discovered a bag of rune stones and a box of tarot cards mixed in with a collection of old teaching handbooks, spare reading glasses, a single pink baby's sock and an old china tea cup wrapped up in newspaper that dated from the nineteen seventies.

Rising to her feet, DJ placed her hands upon her hips as she studied the assortment of stash! Suddenly the poets head quirked to the side as she heard the unmistakable sound of creaking floorboards. Knowing Randa had just risen she moved into the kitchen and switched on the kettle deciding to make the nurse a cup of tea along with the coffee she had intended on making for over half an hour. Unfortunately the collection of goodies she was finding kept her glued to the floor.

While in the kitchen she was aware of Randa descending the stairs and she knew the moment the blonde entered the living room when she heard the muted gasp. With a smirk she wandered back into the front room to gauge Randa's expression. The blonde was looking around the mass of objects with bewilderment.

"Quite a little booty huh?"

"What is all this stuff?" Randa asked as her eyes moved over the floor.

"This is Sara's stash! Can you believe some of this stuff?" Denise knelt down onto the floor and started rifling through the items. She picked up a tiny box and held it out. "You may not want to look in here but this seems to be a collection of baby teeth; mine if I am not mistaken. I mean… when I was younger I did believe in the tooth fairy. My teeth always disappeared from under my pillow at night and instead I would wake to find a ten pence piece… then a twenty pence piece, but when I got older and knew the truth I did wonder as to where my teeth actually went. Seems now I know!" DJ placed the box back upon the floor and picked up another item. "This is a deck of tarot cards…" she placed the box back upon the floor and picked up an old card, "And this is an old ration book from the Second World War! Amazing huh? I am thinking it must have belonged to my grandmother."

Randa knelt down upon the floor and surveyed their surroundings. "Wow, it's a regular little treasure trove isn't it?"

"Yeah!" Denise placed down the ration book and looked back at the nurse who was kneeling no more than three feet away from her. Memories from the earlier events returned to mind. "I'm sorry, Randa."

Seeming to know instinctively what Denise was talking about Randa shook her head. "It doesn't matter, Denise. You're back now and that's all that matters."

"Thank you for giving me a little… or not so little," she smirked, "shove… in the right direction."

With a gentle smile, Randa moved forward and caressed DJ's cheek. "You look a lot better now. The darkness around your eyes has faded considerably. We were out for quite a while. What time is it anyway?"

Denise looked around to the clock on the videocassette recorder. "It's almost five o'clock. We were asleep for just over ten hours I think. It seems we both needed the rest. How do you feel now?"

"Okay."

293

"Do you want a drink? I put the kettle on for coffee so maybe you would like something too?"

"Maybe in a minute." Randa lifted her hand and pushed it through the poet's long dark hair.

DJ clearly noted Randa's intent and instinctively closed her eyes as she moved closer to the blonde. Their lips met cautiously at first as though they needed a moment to feel out the precarious ground they had both treaded for many days now. As their comfort grew so did the kiss and Denise pushed forward, moving down toward the floor as she reached out and moved some of the items out of the way before laying Randa down upon the carpeted ground.

Resting herself above the nurse, DJ released Randa's lips and looked down upon her with an open expression of affection. "Is it alright for us just to be with each other for a while? I can make the drinks in a moment but right now I just need to..." not bothering to finish her words, Denise re-captured Randa's lips, sinking into the taste and texture of the woman that she so craved. *This is what I need,* DJ thought as one hand combed through light blonde hair and the other moved down the supple body.

As she pulled away and re-captured Randa's gaze, words died on her lips as the sound of the ringing telephone echoed through the small home. *Damn it...*

Chapter 28

"Don't answer it," Randa said and reached up to bring Denise's mouth down to hers again.

Denise paused as lips moved to within a fraction of an inch from each other. "Maybe I should answer it. It might be important."

"Right now there's nothing more important than this. I need you, Denise. I need you and I want you. The phone be damned." As if on cue the ringing stopped and the women grinned at one another. "Now, where were we?" questioned the nurse. "Oh, yes, I remember now. You were just about to do this."

Randa reached up again to Denise but this time took hold of her shirt with both hands and pulled until the poet was settled on top of her and snuggled deeply between her now spread legs. Grins vanished from the women's faces, replaced with looks of open hunger.

"Make love to me, Denise," the nurse pleaded.

"Your wish is definitely my command," replied the poet as she lowered her head to place heated kisses along Randa's neck. Receiving an appreciative moan in response to her actions, Denise brought her right hand up and caressed the nurse's breast through the fabric of her shirt. Moving her hand down and back up, Denise slipped the questing appendage under Randa's shirt and resumed her sensuous touches skin to skin. The poet was lowering her mouth to follow the path blazed by her hand when the phone began to ring again.

"Oh cripes!" Randa groaned. "What does a girl have to do in order to have a little peace and quiet to get ravished in?"

Denise chuckled at that and raised her head to look at her partner. "I'll answer it and get rid of whoever it is. If I don't, we'll never have any...peace."

Realizing DJ was just as frustrated as she was, Randa released the poet who rose and moved quickly over to the phone.

Eyes never leaving the nurse's body, Denise snatched up the phone and growled an irritated "Yes?"

The poet listened a moment then her demeanor changed

completely. "No, this is the correct number. Please hold just a minute." Covering the mouthpiece, Denise whispered, "It's a woman claiming to be your Aunt Joann."

"What?" Randa rose from the floor and moved to take the phone from Denise. "Jo, what's up? How did you get this number?" The nurse listened intently and Denise moved to the couch, not wanting to eavesdrop but curious nonetheless.

The conversation lasted no longer than five minutes with Randa occasionally interjecting questions and ended with the nurse saying, "Okay, I'll let you know when. Thanks for calling me. Give her my love...Bye." Replacing the phone back on its base, Randa turned to Denise with a forlorn look.

"Randa? What is it? Is something wrong?" The nurse swallowed hard and instinctively moved to the warmth and safety of Denise who stood and took the blonde into her arms.

"It's Mom. She was driving home from the community center last night. The fog was pretty thick, the way it gets all winter in northern California. Some idiot blew through a stop sign and crashed into Mom's car."

"Oh my God, is she all right?" asked Denise.

"Pretty much. She's got a lot of scrapes and bruises and a couple of nasty fractures of her left tib-fib." At the poet's confused look, Randa clarified, "The tibia and fibula, the bones of the lower leg. She's having surgery in the morning to have hardware put in to stabilize the breaks and then she'll have to be casted."

"She won't have any permanent damage will she?" Denise questioned.

"No, she should be fine eventually but my Aunt Joann is leaving in a couple of days for a few weeks of meetings on the east coast for her job. She won't be able to stay with my mom."

Randa felt a lump form in her throat and she clung tighter to the poet. "Denise, I have to go home." For the first time in her life, the word "home" didn't have the same meaning and she quickly added, "Back to the States."

Both women were silent, contemplating the news and the impact on their lives and recently tested relationship. Randa's thoughts were a jumble of medical questions, schedules and worries about Denise.

Pulling back, the nurse looked at DJ. "This changes nothing between us, you know. I love you very, very much. I'm not leaving you, okay? This separation is only going to be temporary. We'll be together again soon and then nothing will keep me away from you again," Randa said with a confidence she didn't quite feel.

"I better go upstairs and start my packing." Looking around the room, Randa's eyes came to rest on the portrait of Sara and Denise. "You and Sara made this house a home for me, Denise. I'm not going to forget that while we're apart, I'm not going to forget that ever." The blonde reached up and placed a soft kiss on the poet's lips. She broke away reluctantly and headed for the doorway.

On an impulse she turned and looked at DJ. "Come with me, Denise. Please, I really want you to come back to the States with me."

Denise hesitated for a moment, enough time for Randa to put her own interpretation on the reason behind it. Mustering a weak smile she said, "Man, will you listen to me? All needy and selfish sounding. I'm sorry I asked you, Denise, it wasn't fair. I know you have obligations here what with the book about Sara and the new volume of poetry coming out and everything. Forget I mentioned it okay?"

Denise looked like she wanted to say something but instead nodded. The two continued to look at each other and Randa silently berated herself for pressing the poet too much. *She hasn't even said she loves me. What was I thinking, pushing her like that? Dummy! Idiot!*

Maintaining an outward calm Randa said, "I guess I'll have to dig out that return ticket after all. Could you call British Airways for me and check on a flight back?"

"Of course," Denise assured her. Randa waited only the slightest part of a second before she walked over to the poet and wrapped her arms around the taller woman's waist. Laying her head on Denise's chest, she allowed herself to be comforted by the steady heartbeat she heard there.

Moving back, the nurse took the poet's hands in her own. Mirroring Denise's actions of what were only a few minutes before, she lowered both of them to the floor. Bringing her face close to the brunette's, she gazed deeply into the impossibly blue eyes and whispered, "Love me, Denise. Love me."

The poet erased the distance between them and the lovemaking designed to temporarily banish all thoughts of a

297

painful separation, did exactly that.

Pacing back and forth in the living room, Denise continuously stepped over the assorted hoard of treasures that once belonged to Sara. Re-dressed in her jeans but wearing a clean shirt the poet swung her car keys around her index finger in anxious thought. She had done as Randa requested and had enquired about the next flight back to Randa's destination and was a little disappointed to discover that a seat was available for the nurse on the next outbound flight in five hours.

She's really going! That's it... she's going! DJ stopped in the middle of the floor and studied the white and navy training shoes adorning her feet. Above her she could hear Randa move around the upper level of the house as she packed her bags and although she knew she should at least help her, the brooding woman just couldn't bring herself to participate. *I don't want her to leave,* Denise shook her head, "But am I going to tell her how I feel? No!"

With a frustrated sigh Denise resumed her pacing. "You are a coward, Denise Jennings, that is what you are." She kicked one of the empty boxes lying on the floor as she muttered, "What the hell is wrong with me?"

It wasn't the fact that Randa was going home to care for her mother, for she completely understood and respected that. It was who Randa was and indeed what she had done when she travelled all the way over to England to care for Sara in the first place. She would have expected nothing less from the woman. It was the mere point that when Randa had asked her to accompany her, a small part of the poet had desperately wanted to think of a reason to say yes. *Then why didn't I?* Unresolved issues stampeded her mind and DJ knew that until she was able to work through them she would never be able to give herself fully to Randa. And that was something she knew the blonde woman wanted. She could see it every time she looked into longing green eyes and saw a glimmer of sadness shining back at her. Randa was the most open person she had ever met, the woman wore her heart on her sleeve and if DJ was to admit it, she was a little overwhelmed by that.

There was no doubt in the poet's mind that she saw a future for Randa and herself, but the mere speed in which their affections had escalated and Randa's confession of love was something she wasn't ready for. Quite simply, having spent the best part of her adult life up to that point steering clear of all emotional involvement, DJ was unprepared for the sheer roller coaster of feelings, both physical and emotional that would besiege her.

Taking a steady breath and releasing it slowly through pursed lips, DJ looked down at the bunch of keys within her hand. She briefly studied the black moulding around the Lexus' ignition key before ramming the entire bunch back into her pocket.

"I can't just leave her up there to pack alone," she mumbled as she exited the living room, heading for the stairs. As she reached the landing Denise stopped short of entering her bedroom as she stood face to face with Randa. The blonde stood before her, a large duffel bag in each hand containing the majority of her clothes. An uneasy silence passed between them as they faced each other and the fast approaching inevitable.

"You're packed!"

Randa looked down at the hefty carriers, "Yeah… it didn't take too long."

"So…" Averting her eyes, Denise looked desperately around the landing as she searched her mind for words that refused to grace her.

"So," Randa continued, "I guess we better get to the station?"

DJ shook her head. "Airport."

"Excuse me?"

"I'm taking you to the airport. I'm not letting you travel down to London on a train… besides you must know by now how unreliable they are at the moment. I'll take you."

"All the way down to London? Denise you don't have to do that." Randa insisted.

"Of course I do… I want to. Anyway it is a long drive so we better get moving." Denise stepped forward intending to relieve Randa of her luggage but froze. "Randa?"

"Yes?" the nurse whispered.

Denise looked down into hopeful eyes and her face

299

contorted with frustration. "We better get going."

Sighing, DJ reached out and took possession of Randa's bags. Without making eye contact she turned on her heels and headed for the stairs. Randa followed solemnly behind.

The silence in the car was palpable, so thick and heavy that you could not only cut it with a knife but was suffocating in its density. Cruising at a steady speed down the motorway, Denise kept her eyes forward, both hands gripping the steering wheel. The mounting dread that curdled her insides caused her stomach to twist with anger. All she had to do was open her mouth and speak. To say something, anything that would ease the uncertainty in Randa's eyes. Reaching forward she turned on the radio and instantly the car was filled with the monotonous drone of a local newscaster. Nervously she looked to her left and caught the jade penetration of Randa's beseeching gaze.

"How long will your flight take?" DJ asked and looked back to the road as she changed lanes.

"About 11 hours I guess. Around the same time it took to come here."

Denise nodded. "I've never flown myself," she said needing to say something in order to ease the tension between them.

"No?"

"Never." Denise's eyes left the road briefly as she gazed at Randa. "I've always wondered what it would be like, but I have never had the opportunity," she paused, "well… that and I never quite had the guts! I'm more of a boat person. When I was in my early twenties I took a few boat trips to places like Amsterdam with some friends and I took Sara to France about two years ago. She had this dream about visiting the Eiffel Tower, so I thought… what the hell!" Denise realized she was beginning to ramble. "Do you like flying?"

Randa shrugged her shoulders as her eyes veered to the view of the countryside around them. "It gets you from A to B. I have no qualms about it really," she replied.

Apart from the low drone of the radio, the uneasy silence

between Randa and DJ returned. Words - they were something that she presumably had a gift with, a belief of almost every critic and literary lover alike. It was ironic, DJ thought, that if they were to ever know this side of her they sure as hell would not believe Denise and D Jennings were indeed one and the same person. Maybe that was the reason she preferred to keep her identity a secret, because she truly believed people would be disappointed in the real DJ. Even now, as she looked at Randa, she could see that disappointment and although she knew she had the power to erase Randa's fears, in the face of reality, DJ froze. *Maybe I've just spent too long in my own little creative world that I can no longer deal with real life?* Denise would admit that it was a terrifying thought if true.

The airport restaurant was large and split into two sections, smoking and non-smoking. Unfortunately, as it so often was with the busiest airport in London, the eatery was full and it was only by chance as an elderly couple were leaving that Randa had managed to locate a small corner table. Pushing the empty teacups to one side, Denise placed down their tray and took a seat facing the blonde nurse. They had forty minutes until Randa had to leave for the departure lounge.

Lifting her large cardboard cup, Denise looked down into the clear bubbling liquid of her carbonated mineral water. She watched intently as the bubbles exploded upon the water's surface.

"Do you ever think back to the moment you woke up on any particular morning and wonder how you would have reacted if you knew what events were to unfold that day?"

Randa looked up at Denise slightly surprised by her question.

"If I had known what was going to happen today I don't think I would have wanted to wake up this morning. I would never have believed I would be sitting here with you now, waiting with you until you caught your plane to fly back to the states."

Reaching out to Denise, Randa took the poet's free hand resting upon the table. "This is only temporary, Denise. I love you and I don't want to leave you like this... especially at this moment in time. With everything that's happened."

Sensing the uncertainty hidden behind Randa's words, DJ looked down at the blonde's hand as she threaded their fingers together. For what DJ was sure was the hundredth time that hour a disembodied female voice echoed throughout the airport warning all passengers not to leave unattended luggage lying around. Looking back up at Randa, Denise spoke softly. "Let me know when you get there so I know you arrived safely, okay?"

"Okay."

"And tell your mum 'hi' from me and send her my best wishes."

"I will."

"Are you sure you don't want to stock pile chocolate so you don't have to suffer the inferior stuff when you get back home?"

Randa rolled her eyes with a grin. "I'm sure I'll survive, Denise."

Smiling, DJ shook her head. "You know, you are the only person who has ever gotten away with that. I even made my teachers call me DJ."

"How come I can get away with it then?" the blonde asked.

Denise pursed her lips in thought. "I think I just like the way it sounds coming from your lips." She winked.

"Yeah?"

That seemed to delight the nurse; *maybe occasionally I can say something right!* Denise thought. "Absolutely!" Lifting their entwined hands, DJ kissed the smaller fingers as the call for Randa's flight echoed through the speakers. *Already?* An instant wave of sadness overcame her. "I think that maybe we should get a move on!"

With a nod the nurse released their fingers. Reaching inside her pocket she pulled out her boarding pass and looked down at the printed card, seeming to study the flimsy object. "I wish..." She started then paused...

"What?" Denise asked as she looked down at Randa's lowered head.

The nurse shook her head, as she said, "Nothing."

With a frown DJ reached over the table placing two

fingers under Randa's chin as she lifted the blondes gaze. "What do you wish, Randa?" *Please tell me, I need to hear you say it.*

The blonde remained quiet as she looked into DJ's eyes. She obviously hesitated and seemed to change her intended statement. "I was just going to say that I wished this hadn't happened so soon... you know?"

Nodding, DJ knew that wasn't what Randa really wanted to say but accepted her statement nonetheless. After all she had hidden much of her own feelings, but she wondered whether Randa did indeed feel as terrible as she did?

Rising from their seats together, the women moved away from the table and ventured on through the airport.

Her steps were slow and as every second passed that they moved closer to the entrance of the departure lounge, Denise felt a little more of herself fade into nothingness. When Randa passed through the doors and disappeared from her sight, DJ wondered whether and if she would ever see her again.

Standing by the threshold to the departure lounge, which only passengers could enter, DJ looked down at Randa, needing to memorize every nuance of the smaller woman's features. Neither woman seemed aware of the mass of travellers that passed them as they ventured on toward passport control.

"So this is it?" Denise asked.

Randa took a step closer, their bodies almost touching. "I guess it is."

"I'll miss you, Randa... really miss you."

The nurse reached out, taking DJ's hand and pulling her close until their bodies touched perfectly. "You make it sound like this is forever, Denise." Lifting up onto her toes, Randa pressed her lips upon Denise's and the poet responded in kind. Caressing the blonde's lips with her own, she soaked in Randa's essence and implanted every detail of her touch and scent into her mind.

A long moment later DJ moved away and wrapped her arms around Randa, pulling her in close. She closed her eyes, squeezing them tight against the tears that lay just beneath her surface.

"I love you," Randa whispered.

"Goodbye, Randa." Stepping backwards she looked into

confused green eyes.

Randa attempted to speak but the call for passengers taking her flight once again sounded through the airport speakers.

A chilled silence passed between them, one that words could no longer ease. Denise stepped backwards, distancing herself from the desire to join Randa on the plane and go back with her to America.

Why do I feel that I'll never see her again? "Don't forget to give your mother my best wishes for a speedy recovery."

Randa nodded, saying nothing as she backed her way into the corridor. Denise watched her closely, easily spotting the tears shining brightly in her eyes. She lifted her hand and waved, moving her fingers in a slow movement.

"I'll miss you." She mouthed and watched as Randa was engulfed into a crowd of departing passengers and disappeared from sight.

The hollow sounds of the front door slamming shut ricocheted throughout the empty house. Then a lonely silence followed, settling over every vacant, soulless room. Denise stood by the door, keys swinging limply in her left hand. They hung precariously from her middle finger and in one small movement, fell un-noticed to the floor. The poet moved forward, taking reluctant steps until she entered the living room.

Still scattered across the floor lay Sara's possessions but DJ's eyes moved instead to the rug by the fire, the last place she and Randa had made love. Taking a seat facing the rug, Denise stared into the cold grey cinders within the hearth. The fire had long since burned out and only flimsy ashes remained.

Mind wandering, Denise thought back to Randa's words after the phone call from her aunt Jo. For a moment it seemed like Randa had wanted Denise to go with her but she appeared to have a change of heart. The poet didn't know what had caused such a speedy u-turn in her request but she hadn't even had time to consider the possibilities before Randa changed her mind. There was however one fact that DJ was sure of, that having known Randa for the length of time that she had, she knew the blonde nurse always expressed her desires openly. Unlike her own self-conscious self, Randa wasn't usually afraid to speak her mind.

Leaning back into the comfortable settee, Denise's eyes moved up to the mantle, studying the carriage clock upon its shelf. The clock was a gift to Sara when she retired from teaching and her aunt had always given it pride of place as a centre focal point in the living room.

Denise closed her eyes, remembering the expression on Randa's face as she entered the corridor that led to passport control. Her confusion was clearly evident and DJ could almost sense Randa's fear and insecurity. The dejection Randa felt was unmistakably visible and DJ realised that Randa **did** want her to go with her and it was only the nurse's own insecurities about how Denise really felt that had caused her to withdraw her request.

DJ leaned forward as a bolt of stark clarity rumbled through her. *And now my own stupid, unfounded apprehensiveness has ruined it all! I was so afraid to lose her that I went ahead and did it anyway!*

"Oh god," Denise exclaimed. "What have I done?"

Chapter 29

Randa replaced the phone on its base and wondered for at least the hundredth time that week why Alexander Graham Bell's invention wasn't working for her. After the tedious and long flight from England followed by the 2-hour drive from San Francisco, Randa's first thought on arriving home was to call Denise. She could admit to herself that the reason wasn't just to comply with DJ's request that she let her know of the nurse's safe arrival. Randa needed to hear the poet's voice, needed to hear the low timbered tones that raised her spirits and libido every time she heard them.

That's what Randa wanted. *But like Grandma used to say, ' people in hell want ice water and they're just as likely to get it'* thought the blonde. Denise had never answered. In the beginning Randa assumed she had merely missed the poet, that maybe she was out working in the garden or walking. When Randa called at a time when she knew Denise should be inside, she thought possibly the poet was working on her book with the phone turned off so as not to be disturbed. Those thoughts sufficed for the first ten or so phone calls. After that, excuses were harder and harder to come by.

In an attempt to assure herself of the poet's physical well being, Randa placed another international call. After finding out that "Information" was called "Directory Inquiries" in England, the nurse was able to come up with Diane's number. Sara's friend answered on the third ring.

"Hello?"

"Diane? Diane, it's Randa."

"Oh, Randa, how are you dear? How is your mother? DJ told me she had been injured and you had to return to America. I was so sorry to hear it."

"You've seen Denise then? I was trying to reach her, but I guess I keep missing her when I call."

"That's odd, I know she has been home. She told me she hadn't been out much when I saw her two days ago at the cemetery. She was making arrangements for Sara's headstone and asked me to meet her and help her pick one out."

"Was she...did she look okay?"

"She looked a little tired, dear. I guess that's understandable what with losing Sara and all. She certainly has been through quite a bit in the last few months."

For a moment Randa thought that perhaps Diane had hit upon the problem, that Denise had withdrawn for a while trying to recover from the blow of Sara's death. It didn't explain why she wasn't answering the phone though.

"Well, thank you then, Diane. I was just a little worried I suppose. How are you doing?"

"As well as can be expected. Sara being gone is still a bit unbelievable. I'll be watching something on one of the soaps we fancied and I'll think to myself, 'I have to talk to Sara about that' and then the realization strikes me again."

"Oh, Diane, I'm so sorry. Listen, if you ever need anything, please let me know. I would love to hear from you anytime." Randa gave the woman her address in the States.

"So you aren't coming back anytime soon? That's a shame; I thought you and DJ had become close while you were here. I could tell in her voice that she misses you."

A small flicker of hope sparked within the nurse. "Well, my plans are a little...uncertain at the moment."

"I understand." There was a short silence on the line. *"I hope things work out for you, Randa. DJ needs you in her life, Sara said that to me more than once."*

Randa smiled at that. "Thank you for telling me, that means a great deal to me."

"You meant a great deal to Sara, my dear, and she was rarely wrong about people." After a few more minutes exchanging news of the small town, Randa and Diane said good-bye. Relieved as she was about Denise's physical health, Randa couldn't shake the feeling she was being avoided and she didn't know why.

After the phone call, Randa found herself gazing out the window of her living room. She was so lost in thought she almost missed the thump-thump of her mother entering the room on her crutches. The nurse turned to see the older woman

307

settle herself a little awkwardly on the couch.

"Mom, do you need a hand with anything?"

"No, I'm okay. Did you notice how much better I'm doing with the standing and sitting thing? Those hours working with the physical therapist are paying off."

"Yeah, I see that. It's still a little rough around the edges, but you're doing good." It was true, Janice Martin was doing better. The bruises were turning an ugly yellow from their original purple and the many small cuts from flying glass were healing. Soon an occasional headache from the concussion and the cast on her left leg would be the only reminders of the accident on that foggy night.

"I think I'm doing better than you are, Randa." The nurse looked at her with surprise and her mother laughed. "You may be grown up, Randa, but you're still the child I raised. I know every one of your looks and this is one you picked up from your father." At the mention of Leonard Martin, a brief shadow crossed her mother's features but passed quickly. "It was the look that said, 'I have a problem that no one can help me with.' Do you know something though? Talking about it usually did help."

The blonde thought about it for a moment and moved to take a seat beside her mother on the couch, careful not to put pressure against any injured areas.

"I guess I do have something I need to talk to you about, Mom. It's about what happened when I went to England." At her mother's nod, Randa continued, "You know about Denise and how we met and what happened to her aunt. It was horrible to watch her dying slowly and in the manner that she did. But in spite of the sadness all around us, Denise and I...well maybe just I...I..."

"You fell in love with her," Janice finished for her daughter.

The nurse's jaw dropped and her mother laughed once again. "Every look, remember? Your dad had that same look and I thank God he never lost it in the nearly 30 years we were married. I noticed the look the first moment I saw you in the hospital. Oh, you had that nurse's face on too but there are some things you can't hide from a mother. I just wondered when you would get around to telling me who it was."

"You aren't shocked?"

"I'll tell you the truth, Randa. When you first told your father and I that you were dating women as well as men, I was shocked. You said you wanted us to know first before any ugly comments could be made to us. There were a few by narrow minded fools, but the toughest things to deal with were in my own mind," her mother confessed.

"I worried that you would be hurt by thoughtless remarks. No one wants to see her child hurt. Then I was a little selfish and I thought I might never have grandchildren to love and spoil, but Randa my biggest worry was the same one all mothers have. It was the worry that you would never find that someone special to spend the rest of your life with. Have you found that person now?"

"I hope so, Mom. I mean, I know so for me but I'm not sure what she's feeling. I only know for me that this is the person I've waited my whole life for. She's warm, sensitive and deeply caring. She's passionate, talented and modest enough that she would never let you know any of those things. I think she's so used to being a private and introspective person that she doesn't know how to let what she's feeling show."

Randa looked her mother. "I told her I love her and I feel that she loves me but she's never said that. Now that I'm back here I feel a gulf has grown between us that has nothing to do with miles. I've tried to talk to her but she doesn't answer the phone. I can't let this be over, Mom. I know what I feel and this feels like forever to me."

Janice Martin's eyes glittered with unshed tears as she brought her daughter close for a comforting hug. "That's all I wanted to know, Randa. If she's the one then I'm happy for you. If you love her then I'm sure I will too. What are you going to do about the distance you're feeling now?"

"I don't know yet. Maybe I have to let her be sure about things and make the next move, but that's going to be hard. I've done everything I know how to show her how I feel. I just don't know." Randa pulled back from her mother.

"I do know I need to take a short nap before my shift tonight on the network. Working fulltime again feels strange. Thank God Derek could give me the hours. My bank account is totally deflated. I couldn't go to Sacramento, much less to England now."

Janice laughed and let her daughter go. "I'm going to

answer my e-mail while you sleep. I haven't kept up very well since my accident I'm afraid."

Neither have I thought the nurse as an idea popped into her mind.

Randa logged off from the Brightwood network for her lunch break. Instead of wandering out to the kitchen for food she booted up her own e-mail account on the computer. Taking a deep breath she began to type.

Dear Denise,

It's been a while since we connected this way but I seem to be having some difficulty reaching you on the phone so I guess this way will have to do. I've been home for a little over a week now, as you know. Mom is doing better and moving with less pain. I'm working fulltime again and I'm trying to catch up on all the chores that were neglected while I was gone. You would think with all this to keep me busy that I wouldn't miss you so much. I do miss you though, every second of every day.

I miss talking to you and laughing with you. I miss walking into your study and seeing you at work with those little silver glasses perched on your nose. I miss the way your incredible blue eyes darken when we make love and the way you hold me afterward. I go about my business in this world but nothing is the same without you.

Do you want to hear something funny? I meant it when I asked you to come to the States with me. When you hesitated in your answer I took it to mean you weren't sure about us, so I took it back. The funny part is; I *am* sure about us so I want you to know the invitation still stands and always will.

Please talk to me. I love you very, very much.

Randa

Randa hit the send button and the e-mail headed on its way.

It's up to you now, Denise

The air was cold, dank and the atmosphere held a chill that had nothing to do with the temperature. It was dark and although a small light hung from the robustly constructed wooden beams it didn't seem to penetrate every nook and cranny of the wide attic space. In far corners, large spiders were barely distinguishable in the dimly lit loft space though their presence did add to the general 'spookiness' as Denise had often called it, of the storage room.

Hardly being able to stand upright due to the low slant of the house's roof, DJ stooped forward as she moved carefully through the attic. She had just placed down the final box containing 'Sara's stash' after having decided not to sort through the abundance of items until she felt more emotionally inclined to do so. Other matters were waging a veritable war inside her head.

Stepping carefully over the mismatched boards that she had laid herself years before, and was now dubious of the workmanship, DJ stopped by the first box near the roof hatch. Beside the box was Sara's old typewriter. It was a Royal desktop and was over sixty years old, but Denise remembered how she had used it to learn to type many years ago. It was also the first typewriter she had used when she started writing and she now wondered how she ever survived without her computer! Crouching down the poet ran her fingers over the small circular keys delighting in the memories the action triggered. She remembered the time spent with Sara as the older Jennings woman had taught the younger how to touch type. She smiled as she recalled the wonderful feeling of pride she felt when she realised she was able to shut her eyes while typing her name. Denise was no more than fourteen years old at the time.

Casting her vision away from the typewriter, DJ looked

into the box beside her. Just under the containers lid she spotted the wooden box containing Sara's pack of Tarot cards. The poet pulled the deck out and placed their wooden box upon the floorboards. Lifting the small container's lid she pulled out the deck of rectangular cards. Denise twisted her body, turning around until she was facing the light, providing her with enough brightness to be able to study the pictures upon the cards in the shadowy attic.

Suddenly from down in the main part of the house she heard the sound of the telephone ringing. DJ froze, wondering again just who it could be and hoping that it wasn't Randa. She literally hated the thought that it was the blonde and that she was ignoring her. Even though she needed, more than anything, to talk to her and hear her voice, she couldn't. The poet realised she was standing at a vital crossroad in her life and knew that until she made a series of important decisions she felt she could never give Randa what she needed. What they both wanted.

Eventually the ringing stopped and the house was once again bathed in silence. The trouble was that it was the silence that the poet hated the most. Denise acknowledged that the past few months had been the most turbulent in a long, long time, probably since her parent's horrific death, but the lonely silence that now accompanied her was something she was unable to get accustomed to. DJ had always been under the misconception that she enjoyed her solitude but when faced with absolute seclusion she realised it really wasn't what she expected or wanted. What she wanted now was Randa.

Looking down at the pack of cards the tall woman crossed her legs as she began to shuffle the deck. Recalling in her mind the many times she had watched Sara use the cards, Denise mimicked her aunt's actions. Closing her eyes she held them and thought of a question just like Sara did, *what part in my life will Randa play?* Then when she was ready she lay out three cards, the past, present and future. Her brow crinkled in confusion as she looked at the layout in front of her.

"Well if I had any idea what these meant I might have my answer... idiot!"

Shaking her head Denise scooped up the cards and placed them back in their box before putting them into the larger container. *If I have time maybe I will go and find out. I bet the net will have some information about it!*

Bracing her hands carefully upon the sides of the loft hatch, Denise swung her legs around until she sat with the back of her calves against the attic's ladder. Moving forward she stepped quickly down the silver ladder and hopped down from the fourth rung. Landing just outside her study the poets eyes naturally moved to her computer. The screensaver was playing as an assortment of dancing snowmen paraded around the screen. Randa had downloaded the program over the Christmas period and she had been loath to remove it. Deciding she would find out what her cards meant, DJ walked into her study and sat down in the comfortable leather chair. Activating the screen she quickly connected to the 'net' and was surprise to find she had yet more mail in her inbox. She had only just deleted the large amount of SPAM she had discovered before she ventured into the attic.

With a curious frown and a slight hope and inkling as to just whose name she would find, Denise accessed her inbox. Instantly she recognised Randa's name and the fluttering of nervousness inside her stomach turned into, as Sara had called it, "a stampede of fairy elephants!"

Without a second thought and driven by the need to make the only contact she felt able to do so at that moment, Denise opened the mail. With bated breath the nervous poet carefully read through Randa's words and when she had finished she did it again.

Randa's need to reach out was clear and the sentiment expressed was more than enough to embed the nurse even further inside the poet's heart. Unfortunately it didn't dissolve the rampant insecurities that plagued DJ's mind. With caution she replied:

Randa,

Sorry you were unable to get through to me but I have been very busy. I've had a lot to sort out in my mind; work has dominated much of my time and a couple of days ago Diane and I went to choose a headstone for Sara.

Glad to hear your mum is doing better though; I hope she continues with a speedy recovery.

Well I am sorry I can't talk with you longer but like I said, I am really busy at the moment.

Look after yourself Randa, and I will hopefully talk to you soon,

DJ

Not even giving herself time to read over the words she knew were about as cold and detached as she did indeed feel at that moment, Denise sent her reply and quickly shut down the computer.

With a heavy heart and a feeling of utter resentment toward herself and her own cowardliness, DJ left her study, jogged down the stairs, grabbed her coat and left the house.

She didn't know how it happened, but her aimless walk around the outskirts of the village had brought her to the local park. Standing at the wrought iron gates Denise looked into her sparsely populated surroundings and decided to enter. Walking through the black iron archway, DJ made her way to one of the side footpaths and followed the winding trail until she reached the back of the park. Ahead of her she spotted her bench. It seemed like a lifetime since she had been to her place of solitude and contemplation. To be exact it was the day she had first taken Sara to the doctor.

Reaching the edge of the woodland area, Denise stepped under the shade of the trees and walked toward the bench. It seemed just as abandoned as it always had. The weeds were a little higher around the sides and the paint seemed a little more faded than before. Unfastening the buttons of her black denim jacket, the poet took a seat on the left hand side of the bench and looked out across the grass. Brightly coloured flowers were very much in bloom portraying an exuberance of life before her. In the gentle spring breeze long stemmed yellow flowers swayed gently against each other.

To her right and in the far distance, Denise could just make out the children's play area, a large square shaped section of the park covered by wood chipping for safety. DJ was just able to see the small forms of boys and girls as they spun around on the roundabout and climbed up a large structure only to glide down the silver tinted slide. The sheen of the metal captured the glare of the mid afternoon sun.

Leaning against the triple rungs of the bench's backrest, Denise stretched out her legs, crossing them at the ankles. She took a deep breath, capturing the scent of the fresh blossoming flowers. The sweet aroma filled her lungs.

Closing her eyes she thought back over the past few months. She would have never thought the events in her life would have taken such a drastic turn. So much had changed, and yet within her mind some things remained very much the same.

"I had always heard this was one of your favourite hiding places!"

Surprised by the familiar voice, DJ opened her eyes with a start. Beside her sat Diane wearing an amused smile. The poet was amazed that she hadn't even heard her approach.

"Di, what are you doing here?" she asked.

"Looking for you," the old woman replied. "You weren't answering your phone and I recall Sara often stating that this place was one of your little hideaways so I thought I would chance a guess."

The poet smiled. "Good guess," she nodded, "So how are you?"

"I'm doing okay, thank you." Diane moved a fraction closer to the poet. "I've spoken to Randa," she said and noticed DJ's slight jump at the mention of the nurse's name.

"You... you have?"

With an affirmative nod, Diane looked out across the park. "She is worried about you and to be perfectly honest... so am I."

DJ shrugged. "I'm fine. No need to worry."

Diane levelled DJ with an even stare. "If your aunt hadn't pre-warned me of what just might happen after she passed then I might well believe you. As it turns out I was forewarned of this possibility and therefore I have a message from Sara that she made me memorise."

"Really?" Denise asked in surprise.

"Really!" Diane pulled a piece of paper from her brown

315

leather purse. "Unfortunately my memory is not what it used to be these days so I decided to write it down." She unfolded the paper. "Do you want me to read it?"

DJ nodded readily.

Slipping on a pair of small round spectacles Diane began.

"Though a small part of me does hope you will never have to hear this and you will have already realised the facts I am about to bestow upon you... I actually like the idea of still being able to pass on my little pearls of wisdom from beyond the grave."

The poet had to smile at that; it was so much Sara's sense of humour.

Diane continued. "*I think it is about time I enlightened you with a few cold hard facts, DJ. You may be my niece but what I tell you is in no way my biased opinion. I've watched you grow. I've seen you blossom into the stunning woman you are today, yet you never grew out of your desire to stay out of the social eye. DJ, you are a beautiful, intelligent and caring woman who has so much more to offer this world.*

" Nelson Mandela once repeated a famous quote that stated, 'our deepest fear is not that we are inadequate. Our deepest fear is that we are powerful beyond measure. Who are you not to be Brilliant, Gorgeous, Talented and Fabulous?' 'Because my niece, you are all of these things and it is about time you stood up against yourself and took what it is out of this life that you want. And most importantly, DJ, most importantly of all you must follow your heart... always."

Re-folding the slip of paper, Diane placed it within DJ's hand and pulled the spectacles from her nose. She looked expectantly up at Denise to find teary blue eyes gazing out across the horizon. "DJ?"

Blinking, Denise looked back at Diane. "Follow my heart?"

The old woman smiled and nodded. "What is it that you truly want, DJ?"

There was no delay in her answer. "I want Randa."

"Why?"

"Why?" the poet asked, "Because she is the most amazing person I have ever met. I love the way we laughed together. The way she would walk into a room and my insides would quiver. I adore her smile and reassuring touch. I loved the way she spoke my name and how I could feel her eyes upon me when I was working. I love her," she said simply feeling glowing warmth at her admission.

"Then tell her."

"It's not that easy."

"Isn't it"? Diane asked. "Why?"

DJ searched her mind for her answer but for the first time ever she was unable to reply. *What is stopping me?*

"Remember Sara's words, DJ, and remember what she always told you... 'Your auntie is always right'!"

Both women chuckled.

"Don't ever be afraid to be who you are. You have the power to obtain whatever it is in this life that you want." The old woman paused for effect. "Take It."

DJ looked down at the slip of paper Diane had placed into her hand and a beautiful smile graced her features. She placed the paper into her pocket as she said, "And if I want Randa then I should...?"

"Go get her!"

Looking back out over the greenery of the park, Denise felt a new confidence swell within her. "You're right!"

Rising to her feet, she held out her hand and helped the other woman to stand beside her. "So... would you like me to walk you back home?" she asked.

"Well yes... that would be nice, thank you." Diane hooked her arm around DJ's offered elbow and they started a slow gait along the path. "Why the sudden rush to leave? Somewhere you have to be?" she asked with an intuitive sparkle in her light brown eyes.

"Yes," DJ replied with assurance, "I'm going to America."

Chapter 30

Randa reached over to the remote control and turned off both the VCR and the TV. She had finally finished the last taped episode of "ER" and was caught up on the series again.

It's the only show that has a fairly accurate portrayal of nurses she thought. *We aren't doctor-chasing bimbos that cling like barnacles to the nurse's station while gossiping about the latest hospital fund raiser and we aren't saints with hearts of gold who can miraculously heal with a comforting touch either. We're just human beings like everyone else trying to earn a living under some pretty trying circumstances.*

Climbing down from the mental soapbox, Randa cast about for something to do. Like always, after her shift on the Brightwood Network, she had slept for a while during the day. Now, at close to one a.m., she was wide-awake with nothing to do. Her mom had turned in around eleven o'clock, reminding Randa she had promised to stop by her condo in the morning and check on things while Janice had her physical therapy session at the house. Both women knew it wouldn't be long before those sessions would be completed and the older woman could return to her home as the doctor had promised a walking cast and a cane within the next week or so.

Randa thought back to her conversation with her mother that very afternoon. The nurse had just gotten out of bed and stumbled to the kitchen for a cup of tea. She squinted as she looked out the kitchen window into the bright early April sunshine.

Noting the buds on the peach and apricot trees, she thought to herself, *I guess spring has sprung. Whoopee.* Unable to muster much enthusiasm for the greening of the world, she ran a hand through her unruly blonde locks and made her way into the living room with a mug of English Afternoon tea. Her mother was sitting on the couch reading a book with her leg propped up on a pillow. Spying her daughter's sleepy eyes, she gave a little laugh.

"I see you still aren't a morning person, no matter how late in the day it comes."

Randa gave a small grin and took a sip of the hot, sweet liquid in her cup. "I probably wouldn't be up at all except I hate to waste a day off, even if I can't see it yet." She took a seat on the opposite end of the couch and noted the book in her mother's lap.

"What are you reading? Get something new off the web?" Randa's mother had become quite adept with the computer and now shopped more online than at the mall. Her skill came in handy now that her mobility was limited.

"Nope, just something I pulled off your bookshelf. I'm kind of surprised because I'm not usually one for poetry too much but this isn't half bad. It could use a few more rhymes though. I guess I'll always be a 'Roses are red' kind of person, but I can admit *Derbyshire Dreams* is pretty good. A little racy in spots, too." Janice stopped here as she saw her daughter staring at the book with skin paler than it had been a few seconds before.

"Randa? Is something wrong? What is it, honey?"

Randa debated within herself for a moment but knew instinctively her mother could be trusted. Looking up into her mom's worried face, she told the only part of the tale about Denise that her mother didn't know.

'Do you remember when I told you Denise was self employed and did work on her computer?" Janice nodded. "Well, that's not quite the whole story. The truth is Denise does use the computer, but she uses it to write. She wrote the book of poetry you're holding. She wrote that one and two other books of poetry as well. It was how I first came to know about her. Well, know about D Jennings, not Denise even though D Jennings and Denise are the same person except I didn't know it at the time. Does that sound as confused to you as it does to me?"

Randa's mom said nothing for a moment, seemingly trying to untangle the strings of the nurse's explanation. Finally she picked up the book and turned it over to the back cover to study the fuzzy picture of the poet's back.

"Not very photogenic is she?" was her mother's only comment. This made Randa laugh and snapped her from the melancholy caused by looking at the only connection she seemed to have with Denise at the moment. Setting her teacup on the end table, the nurse made her way to her desk. Opening a drawer, she pulled out Denise's portfolio of unpublished poems. She opened it and removed a photograph. It was one of the pictures she had taken of Denise and Sara in the living room of their home at Christmas.

Walking back to the couch, Randa handed the photo to her mother. "Oh, I don't know, I think she's pretty damn cute."

"Holy cow!" Janice exclaimed getting her first look at the poet. "Wow, what lovely blue eyes. She's gorgeous, but you didn't tell me she had gray hair." Randa laughed again at her mother's teasing.

"That's Sara with her. At least that's Sara the way I want to remember her. I don't want to remember her as she was at the end, that's not what she would have wanted either. She was an amazing woman, Mom, you would have liked her."

"I'm sure I would have, Randa. From what you told me, it seems like she was a very special lady. I think you were lucky to get to know her."

The nurse nodded her agreement. "I was, Mom. I'm even luckier to know her niece. She has a lot of Sara's character in her."

"Maybe that's your answer then. Maybe the character Sara instilled in her over the years will let her overcome the hurting and loss and let her see the love she has for you."

"I hope so, Mom. God, how I hope so."

Randa broke from her recollection and stood up from the couch. Stretching her petite frame to her utmost, she let her eyes be drawn to the computer sitting like a beacon on the top of her desk.

You've been avoiding it all day. Get a little backbone now and go check the e-mail. How bad can it be? If there isn't a reply there then it's no change from the hundred phone calls you tried. You're just back at square one again, that's not so horrible.

Mustering her courage she walked slowly to the desk and booted up the computer. Hooking up quickly to the net she accessed her e-mail account. Crossing her fingers as the inbox popped up she scanned the list quickly. A wave of relief washed over her as she recognized Denise's e-mail address. Clicking on the poet's name, the message was displayed.

As Randa read down the brief message, the wave of relief became a cold slap of reality. She couldn't believe the same person who had written the poems that touched the nurse's soul could write something so distant and unfeeling. Randa examined the e-mail again, looking for any signs of hope. Finally, she spotted something.

'I've had a lot to sort out in my mind.' What does that mean? If she's still thinking about us then maybe she hasn't decided against pursuing this relationship. And here she says 'I'll be talking to you.' Maybe she does want to talk this over with me and maybe she has been really busy like she says. Even to a mind grasping at straws those arguments sounded flimsy.

With a sigh, Randa hit the reply button.

Dear Denise,

That was as far as Randa got before her heart broke and she put her face into her hands and sobbed.

It was sometime later that Randa managed to bring her ravaged emotions back under control. She shut her computer down, not finishing or sending Denise a reply to her message. She retrieved the photo of Denise and Sara she had left out earlier after showing her mother. Looking at the picture and the happiness in the poet's eyes, Randa wondered if she would ever see that look again. As she replaced the photo in the binder, a small scrap of yellow paper showed from behind the last page in the portfolio. The last page had only been an index of the poems and the nurse hadn't noticed the folded piece of yellow tablet paper before. Obviously, the page had been torn from the tablet, thrust into the portfolio and forgotten. Taking the paper out she carefully opened it up to reveal Denise's writing. Well, not writing so much as doodling, all styles of script with little pictures of hearts and flowers. Over and over the same word was repeated, covering the page almost completely. The word was "Randa".

321

It was true to state that from the moment Denise had come to her subtle yet life-changing decision her confidence had grown immensely. Along with that confidence came the absolute clarity that the poet would do whatever it took to be with Randa and keep the nurse in her life. That decision in itself brought up a whole new set of issues and one point in particular in which DJ had made a life changing resolution.

Sitting in the lounge with a small writing pad resting upon her thigh, Denise jotted down a series of imperative notes. Choices had been made and all that was left for her to do was put her plans into action. It was going to be a new experience that was for sure. For a start she wondered how other people would take her news and decided she might as well start to find out.

Moving from the armchair, Denise walked out into the hallway and picked up the cordless telephone. With a surging confidence and assertion in her actions the poet dialled the familiar number, waiting patiently for the line to be answered.

"Hello, this is Carl..."

The poet interrupted quickly, "Hey, Carl it's DJ listen..."

"Whoa, whoa," Carl stated, cutting Denise off suddenly, **"Where the hell have you been? I have been trying to get a hold of you for days now, woman."**

DJ sighed and moved into the living room, holding the phone in the crook of her neck as she re-took her seat in the armchair and picked up the note pad. "Sorry, I've been a little out of sorts. Anyway I'm ringing you because I have a proposition." She dangled the pad from the tip of her fingers and swung it unsteadily side to side.

"Uh huh!" Carl's voice sounded suspicious. **"I have told you before, DJ, I'm a married man! I don't think Chris would be too happy if..."**

"Carl!" Denise shook her head, "I am serious here."

The editors voice turned just as serious. ***"Okay."***

Leaning back into the armchair, Denise looked down at her notepad. "First of all I was wondering how things were progressing with the book going to print and what would be the possibility of you being able to get me an advance copy?"

"How advance?"

"No more than a week from now?"

"Are you kidding?" Carl screeched.

Denise rolled her eyes as she said, "I know it's kind of a push..."

"...Kind of!"

"...And," DJ continued unperturbed, "I know I am asking a lot, but everything has been sorted, the cover chosen, blurb, introduction and what have you is all written... so with a push it could be done!"

"This is a lot you are asking, DJ," Carl said. *"Why on earth 'are' you asking by the way?"*

"It's a lot to explain right now, Carl." Denise leaned forward in her chair as a flutter of nervousness made its presence known in her stomach, "But what if I make it worth your while?"

"I'm listening."

Denise took a deep breath as she said, "What if I give you the one thing you have been striving for... the one thing you seem to think would cause a sensation?"

After a pregnant pause Carl asked, *"You mean you want to reveal your identity?"*

"In a way. I mean I want to include a personal dedication in the book that will leave no doubt as to who I am. I think venturing into the public eye would come part and parcel with that."

"Oh my god!"

Denise smirked.

"Are you serious?"

"Am I ever not serious, Carl?"

"Why... I mean, why now? What's happened to drive you to this decision? What kind of dedication?"

DJ removed herself from the chair and made her way into the kitchen. Picking up the kettle she checked the amount of water inside and after deeming it 'enough' she placed it back upon its base and switched it on. "I've made a few decisions in my life, Carl. I realised that I can't go on the way I have and I need to make some changes. And the kind of dedication I want will be a thank you to two very important people in my life."

The editor was silent for a moment as he processed the information. *"I am presuming one of these people would be*

323

Sara?"

"Yes."

"And the other person?"

"That would be Randa."

"Randa? Who's Randa? I don't think I..." Carl paused as he quickly searched his mind. *"Hold on, you mean Randa the nurse? The American woman who took care of Sara and was with you at the funeral? The cute blonde?"*

DJ had to smile. "That would be her."

"If you don't mind me saying so, DJ, I couldn't help but notice you both looked very 'close'. Is there something going on between the two of you?"

"Yes."

"Yes? What... that's it? Yes? So you are an item?"

"We were... maybe still are... hopefully... it's complicated. That is why I need you to do this... huge favour for me." Denise opened a wall cupboard and pulled a yellow mug from the lower shelf. "It's important, Carl. It will probably affect the rest of my life and I want to do this right. So, what do you think?"

A considerable silence was her reply.

"Carl, are you there?"

"Yes... I was just sitting down."

The poet frowned as she said, "I presumed you already were."

"I was," Carl replied, *"But I just had to get up and do it again!"*

DJ frowned.

"So let me get this straight. D Jennings is not only going to come out into the open and reveal her identity... but she is also going to 'out' herself... literally?" The excitement was clear in the editor's voice.

Denise nodded. "That's about the size of it."

"Oh my god!" Carl exclaimed, *"Oh my GOD! This is great... this is going to be huge. Wait until Chris hears about this, she will be astounded. You will have to do a lot of publicity, interviews in magazines and on the TV. You know they have discussed you a lot on that program 'The Open Book'! You will venture into a whole new market too..."*

"Whoa, calm down, Carl. I'm glad you like the idea but right now I need to know whether you can grant my request?"

"Without a doubt... yes! DJ, are you really sure about this... I mean not that I want you to change your mind but really... are you sure?"

"I am very sure, Carl. Some things in life are more important and I intend to show one very special person just how important she is to me." The kettle boiled and Denise placed a fruit teabag into her cup before filling it with boiling water. She placed the kettle back down and added a spoonful of sugar. "There is one more thing though."

"What is that?"

"When the advanced copy of the book is done I will be going to America... hopefully for a little while..."

"What?"

"I will of course return for the books release and hopefully announce my first novel under my own name."

"What? Novel?"

Denise wondered whether Carl was losing his comprehensive vocabulary. "I have just about finished it and you can have it when I collect the book. Damn thing practically wrote itself. I don't think I have ever written anything so fast before but I think you will like it. It's a comedy." Lifting her mug, tea bag still inside, Denise carried it back out into the living room and sat down in the armchair. She looked down at the notepad.

Again silence reigned down the phone line.

"Carl?"

"Just tell me now whether you have any more surprises up your sleeve, DJ." The editor sighed dramatically as he said, *"and here was me thinking it was going to be a typical boring day!"*

"Nope, that just about does it for now. I will be in to see you tomorrow, Carl."

The man sighed. *"Okay... oh and what about the dedication?"*

Holding her cup with one hand, Denise prodded the teabag still floating inside. She looked down briefly at her pad. "I have it written down and I will bring it in tomorrow. I would like it printed in my own handwriting."

"Well being as though you have very legible handwriting I think that will be okay."

"Great." Denise smiled in relief, "See you tomorrow then,

Carl."

"Always a pleasure and revelation, DJ, see you later."

The poet pulled the phone from the crook of her neck and disconnected the line. She grinned to herself, pleased with her decision and hoped she could get her hands on the advanced copy of the book as quick as possible. As soon as she had that, she intended to call Randa.

It had taken six days for DJ to receive her advanced copy. Six long, impatience filled days in which she had done nothing more than make arrangements for the house and its bills while she intended to be away, all being well that was. She had still to ring Randa and was more than a little unsure about what exactly she was to say to the blonde. Still, she was adamant that nothing was to get in the way of what she wanted. That was of course if Randa still wanted her. A small part of the poet hoped Randa hadn't bothered to check her e-mails but reality stated that was very unlikely.

Whenever uncertainty would rear its devious head Denise would just sit back and read the message Sara had left her. She carried the slip of paper around in her back pocket like a crutch that helped her whenever she doubted herself. The poet found a certain comfort and reassurance in the words that she had never experienced before and it gave her the courage to make the decisions that loomed ahead.

Sitting in her bedroom near the edge of her bed, DJ looked down at the two objects in front of her, the cordless phone that she had taken from the base down stairs and the advanced copy of her new book. It wasn't a soft back copy like she hoped; instead it was the hardback leather bound edition as that was easier for Carl to obtain. Running her fingers over the gold writing upon the black leather, Denise felt the difference in this volume of work. She opened the first page and instantly sought out her dedication, recognising her handwriting and signature at the bottom that revealed her full name. The poet took a deep breath with the feeling that she was approaching the end of an era.

Just before Denise had ventured upstairs with the book

and phone she'd had a call from Carl. The editor has just finished reading her new novel and seemed extremely excited about its prospects. He felt he needed to call and let her know just what he thought of the manuscript before he showed it to his wife who, he was sure, would love it too.

That had pleased DJ immensely. She was more than relieved that her friend liked it; after all she had spent all of her free time, and not so free time, writing it. Dedicating so much time to the book and neglecting her own needs had caused a disagreement between her and Randa. She was thankful Randa had the ability to make her see sense in the way she had, even if it had meant provoking their first argument.

DJ smiled as she recalled how those feelings of anger had more or less dissipated from the first moment their lips had touched. *What is it about her that makes me forget just where or even who I am?* Determined that even if it took her the rest of her life, she was going to find out, DJ picked up the cordless telephone and dialled the international number. Her stomach quivered with apprehensiveness as she waited for the line to answer.

"Hello?"

Denise frowned at the unknown voice. "Um... hi... hello, could I speak to Randa please?"

"I'm sorry but she's at the gym this morning." There was a short pause. *"Would I be right in guessing that by the English accent I must be talking to the infamous Denise Jennings?"*

She wasn't sure why but DJ didn't like the sound of the word '*infamous*'. "Yes it is," she replied cautiously. "Is that Mrs. Martin?"

"It is," replied the friendly voice.

"Oh." DJ looked around her bedroom as if needing guidance. "Could you tell me when she might get back?"

A moment of silence ensued before Janice Martin next spoke. *"I think she'll be back in about an hour but I must warn you, Denise, she's still very upset. She read your last e-mail and although I have no idea what it was that you said to her she seems so deflated at the moment. I love my daughter, Denise, and I know for a fact that she loves you but..."*

"... And I love her." Denise interrupted. "I can understand why she feels the way she does after that but it really wasn't me. I was going through a rough patch and needed time to work things out. The truth is that I love your daughter, Mrs. Martin, and…"

"That's wonderful, Denise, but I really think you need to tell her that. Oh and just for the record… call me Janice."

DJ smiled. "Okay but only if you call me DJ!"

"DJ it is."

"Great." Denise sighed. A plot started to formulate in her mind as she gazed down at the leather bound anthology. "Listen, Mrs.… I mean Janice. I have an idea. I would really like to surprise Randa and I have a plan I would like to carry out if you would be willing to help me."

"If it means my daughters happiness I would be more than willing to help." Janice replied.

"I hope it will." DJ said as she and Janice Martin began their scheming.

Chapter 31

Randa's mother wasn't all that old so she didn't think it could be Alzheimer's. She had stopped taking any pain medication a week ago so she didn't think it was the Codeine. Something was definitely strange though; Randa could feel it. Janice Martin hummed a lot and hugged her daughter a lot, for no apparent reason.

Maybe she found a boyfriend on the Internet Randa mused then felt a twinge of pain at the thought. *Wouldn't that be ironic? Mom finds someone just as I seem to be losing someone.*

Her mother didn't seem to change her routine though so Randa just decided to watch and say nothing. Saying nothing was something the nurse was becoming quite good at. As the days passed she seemed to withdraw from people a little more. She turned down invitations from friends and resisted her mother's attempts to get her out of the house and back into her usual routine. Randa resumed going to the gym but just couldn't bring herself to start socializing again. There was only one person she really wanted to socialize with but that person didn't seem to want to be with her.

After four days of her mother's odd behavior, Randa's curiosity got the better of her. It was the nurse's day off and she had decided to ask her mom why she seemed to be so giddy.

Yep, giddy is the only word for it. She just seems so happy. As down as Randa was, her mother's mood was infectious. It wasn't in the nurse's nature to mope and when she found her mother in the living room singing along with Tony Bennett on the stereo, she had to smile.

"The great love story has never been told...before...but now...now it can be told," Janice Martin warbled. Randa recognized the tune her parents had called "our song" for as long as she could remember. In the time since her father had died, she didn't remember her mother playing it. Randa didn't know what had made the difference but was glad for whatever it was.

"Hey, Mom, you're in a good mood these days. Come on, what gives?"

Her mother was the picture of innocence. "I'm sure I don't know what you mean. I didn't think you were noticing anything anyway. I thought you were a little too busy being the eighth dwarf...Sulky."

The nurse chuckled. "I've got no comeback for that one. You're right, I know. I need to accept what will never be and move on." She gave her mother a smile that didn't quite reach her eyes. "Good try though on changing the subject. Almost worked, too. Come on; tell me what's got you so happy. Maybe I can borrow a cup of it?"

"Randa, you're my favorite daughter." She paused here as Randa rolled her eyes. "Okay, my *only* daughter but you have the most active imagination of anybody I ever met. It's spring, I'm healing and I'm finally off those blasted crutches. What's not to be happy about? You young people and your fascination with angst! I'll never understand it. In my day, being happy just to be happy was good enough. It's a lesson some would do well to learn."

Randa had to laugh at her mother then. "Message received, General Martin! Commencing attempt to be happier!"

"Very good soldier, I wouldn't want to have to have you flogged," her mother returned playfully as she made her way to the couch. Settling herself back into the cushions she picked up a book and started to read as Randa went to the desk to look at the day's mail. Shuffling through the envelopes quickly her heart sank a little when no evidence of Denise's precise script showed itself.

No phone call, no e-mail, no letter thought the blonde as she kept her back to her mother, not wanting her to see the crestfallen look she was sure was once again on her features.

From behind her, her mother suddenly said, "That's awfully nice." Randa turned in her chair and asked her mother, "What's nice?"

"The poem I just read. Your friend sure has a way with words."

Randa furrowed her brows in confusion. "You mean Denise? She looked at the book her mother held. "That's not one of Denise's books. Believe me, I know what her three books look like and that isn't one of them. Where did you get

that one anyway? I don't recognize the cover."

"It was just something I came across. Listen to this poem, it's sort of sweet," her mother said.

"I didn't know I loved you
Until you left me
Stealing away the sunshine
That shone so unexpectedly in my life

Alone once more I was gripped again
By the cold clutches of loneliness
Its icy fingers tight around my heart

Without you there was no warmth
No happiness
And no reason to smile

My world filled with only darkness
An eternal night
A lonesome torture

Indescribable longings
That only you can tame
Overwhelm me until I am blind

I seek only you
The light that can free me
And I beg for your forgiveness

I claim no self worth
But I offer you my one possession
My eternal love

Yours to control
I place my fate in your hands
And offer you my lasting devotion
Forever."

Randa listened and her eyes glistened at the beauty of the sentiment. It had been a while since someone had touched her heart that way with poetry. In fact, there had only been one person who had been able to touch her heart like that. The nurse's face was the very picture of bewilderment.

"You're sure your friend didn't write that, huh? Okay, if you say so," her mother commented. "I just thought that from the dedication that it was her." Janice held the book open to the page she referred to.

Randa leapt up from the chair and went across the room to her mother. "Let me take a look at that." She took the book from her mother's hands and scanned the words on the page.

For the first time ever I would like to dedicate this anthology to two very special people. To Sara Jennings, my aunt who passed away quite recently. She encouraged and supported me throughout my life and I will never forget her.

And to Miranda Martin, who stole my heart as she so freely entrusted me with hers. I love you Randa and I pray that you will allow me to spend the rest of my life proving to you just how much.
Denise Jennings

Randa's mouth dropped open as she read Denise's heartfelt words. Closing the book, she scanned the cover. " 'Connecting Hearts: a collection of poems by D Jennings'. I don't understand. I…"

Looking at her mother in puzzlement, she said, "Mom, you…"

"Are going to be late if I don't get moving," her mother said. As if on cue, a car horn outside honked somewhat impatiently. "That will be your aunt Joann, I'm going to spend the weekend with her."

Randa's mother took a small bag from behind the couch and moved toward the door. As she pulled the front door open she paused a moment to smile back at her daughter. "Have a lovely time, Randa." Randa could only stand there stunned.

Her mother passed through the door and said, "Hello, DJ."

The velvet tones Randa knew so well replied, "Hello, Janice. Tell Joann thanks so much for the ride."

"I will, DJ. See you in a few days."

Then the tall, beautiful poet stood in the doorway. She

dropped her suitcase on first spying Randa who was still rooted to the same spot in the living room. Searching blue eyes locked onto overwhelmed green ones

"Randa..." the poet began, but then her voice faltered as she waited for a reaction from the silent nurse.

"Randa, I'm so..." Denise tried again, but was interrupted by a petite blonde launching herself into the poet's arms and placing a searing kiss on her lips. The book of poetry lay forgotten on the living room floor as two souls erased the hurt, loneliness and searching of a lifetime through that kiss.

Breaking the kiss, Randa felt her knees buckle a little at the intensity of the emotion running through her. Immediately, Denise increased her hold on the love of her life.

"Easy there, I have you." The poet smiled down at Randa.

"And you always will," was the reply as Randa brought her lips to Denise's once again.

The measure of uncertainty DJ felt as she approached Randa's door had been tantamount to the sensations one would experience before facing a military firing squad. Unsure of how Randa would feel about the way she had acted and responded to her, Denise had rehearsed countless speeches in her mind knowing she would do anything to win the blonde. Unfortunately after deeming each of them unworthy she had focused her mind instead on the scenery around her. Randa had told the poet about her home many times and it was nice to be able to see the landscape in person, even if her mind was occupied with another more important issue.

Now, standing in the doorway to Randa's home with the blonde's body literally moulded around her own DJ knew that whatever she had done must have been right. The overwhelming sensation of relief that flooded through her body was only just outweighed by the absolute completeness she felt in holding Randa once again.

With one hand firmly supporting Randa's back and the other moving up to cup the blonde's face, Denise softened the kiss. Moving away from her tempting lips, she looked down into Randa's misty gaze and smiled as she wiped a tear from the nurse's cheek.

"Sorry it took me so long to get here."

The poet looked to her left as a slight breeze wrapped itself around them. "Do you want to shut and move away from the door?"

Without saying a word Randa nodded and reached out, pushing the door closed. Taking the poets hand in a reassuring grip they made their way further into the living room. Denise took in her surroundings before her eyes turned solely upon Randa. The nurse still held her hand firmly.

Not knowing how else to begin the many words that were floating around her mind, DJ blurted out, "Surprise!"

"You have no idea." Randa replied as she gazed at the poet. "I feel like I should pinch..."

The nurse looked away and DJ noticed fresh tears shining in Randa's eyes. Her heart lurched as she realised the hurt she must have caused her. Squeezing her hand she reached out and placed her fingertips on the side of Randa's chin, drawing her attention and watery gaze back upon her.

"I'm sorry," she whispered.

The nurse shook her head. "It's okay"

"NO... it isn't, Randa. It's not hard to tell that I hurt you and just the thought that I caused you any pain... it's ..." Denise looked away, studying the floor beneath them in thought. "I'm sorry."

A long stretch of silence passed between them before Randa spoke. "Denise?"

Returning her gaze DJ stepped forward and cupped Randa's face in both hands. "Randa... I love you. I love you so much that I can't imagine one more minute of my life without you in it."

"Oh god," Randa whispered as she released a choked sob and her head fell upon DJ's shoulder. "You don't know how much I've wanted to hear you say those words, Denise."

"Well that's good," DJ, replied as she stepped backward and ducked her head to capture the nurse's gaze, "because I'm never going to get tired of telling you." She watched Randa closely as she noticed a mischievous gleam in the nurse's eyes.

"Tell me what?" Randa asked and DJ smiled.

"Hmm? Oh um... I can't remember now."

Randa laughed and swatted the poet's stomach with the

334

back of her hand. DJ chuckled as she pulled the blonde in close and wrapped her arms around the smaller frame. "*Now* I discover she has a violent streak," she exclaimed. "It doesn't matter though, I still love you." Leaning forward DJ took Randa in a long kiss. Lips parted as searching tongues reconnected and caressed each other lovingly.

Suddenly, DJ felt Randa tense slightly and the poet pulled away looking into confused green eyes. "What is it?" she asked, fearing the worst.

"Denise... the dedication."

"Did you like it?"

Randa pulled away as a serious expression crossed her features. "Well yeah but..." taking the poet by the arm, Randa led her over to the sofa. She sat down and DJ followed suit. "Denise, what you said... I mean... Denise you revealed yourself; I don't understand why... I thought that..." Randa studied the poet intently. "Why?"

"Why?" The poet echoed.

Nodding, Randa looked into DJ's eyes. "You... it's like you gave up your world. That balance and anonymity that you worked so hard to maintain."

"My world." Denise shook her head with a wry smile. "Randa, if I stayed in that world I knew I could never truly be with you; not the way I wanted and not the way you wanted me to."

"So you did this for me? I was your reason?"

"You were my main reason. I did have a long talk with Diane also but apart from that there was one slightly, maybe selfish reason for me doing what I did."

Randa frowned in question and so DJ continued.

"I thought... and hoped that maybe a famous writer might have a little more clout. Say for instance... if I decided that I might want to live over here... I think I might have more of a chance if I was somebody with a name, so to speak."

"To be over here?"

"To be with you," DJ said. "If you do still want me that is. I mean I know we do have a lot to discuss and there is a lot to consider. You have a house here and I have one back in England but... Umpf"

DJ suddenly found herself pushed back against the sofa as one ecstatic nurse climbed into her lap, lips firmly attached to her own. DJ sunk into the kiss, pushing her hands up Randa's back as she caressed the flesh under the blonde's top.

"Does that mean yes?" She asked, pulling away breathlessly.

"What do you think?" Randa replied.

"Well..." Sliding forward with the blonde still sitting on her lap, DJ rose to her feet and Randa wrapped her short legs around her waist. "I'm not sure. I may need to do a little more... delving."

"Oh?" Randa wrapped her legs tighter around DJ. "What did you have in mind?"

"You," stepping forward DJ held Randa against the wall. Their movement caused a framed picture to sway precariously from its hook, "and the many different ways I plan on making love to you."

Without waiting for a reply DJ leaned forward, pressing her lips upon Randa's neck as she planted a trail of small kisses along the soft, inviting flesh. Randa groaned as she felt the poet sucking on her pulse point and instinctively she pushed herself harder into DJ's body.

Ensuring that Randa was safe, DJ moved back slightly and Randa dropped her feet back onto the floor as their lips reunited for a searing kiss, mounting in passion and intensity. Randa's hands started to move searchingly over the poet's body, reaching her shoulders where she pushed DJ's fleecy red jacket from her back and it fell discarded upon the floor. Once done she pushed her hands under DJ's white tank top, desperate to search out the soft warm flesh.

As she pulled away, DJ's hands fell to Randa's shirt where she quickly started to pull upon the small buttons. As each fastener was released she pressed a kiss upon the revealed flesh until she reached the valley of the blonde's breasts.

"Randa?" she mumbled.

"Hmm?"

"Where's your bedroom?"

"Sod the bedroom." Randa replied she pulled the short white top from the brunette's body.

With a small chuckle DJ pulled away from Randa's chest. "Either you have been in the UK for too long..." releasing the last button she pushed Randa's shirt from her shoulders and looked down at the firm breasts encased in a lacy black bra, "or

I am beginning to rub off on you." Leaning forward she pressed her lips upon the rise of Randa's breasts.

The blonde closed her eyes as her head fell back against the wall with a slight thump. "Maybe to the first one..." she breathed, "but as for the second... I *really* like the idea of that!" DJ unhooked the bra and Randa moved her arms, assisting in its removal.

With an arched brow and a small smirk, DJ unhooked and removed her own bra before pressing their body's together. The feel of hot flesh connecting as aroused nipples pressed into each other caused both women to groan wantonly. DJ braced one hand upon the wall as she held Randa close with the other; their lips met and parted in unison as their tongues fought to taste and memorise every nuance of their lover. Thighs parted and slipped between each other as a slow grind commenced.

"God I've missed you so much!" DJ breathed as she reluctantly pulled away. The feel of her desire mounting caused the seam of her jeans to rub agonisingly over her swollen centre.

"Missed you too..." Randa mumbled as her lips sought out and tasted the poet's flesh. Travelling across broad shoulders she then moved down toward full breasts. DJ moaned as she felt one nipple then the other encased in a blaze of wet heat and a talented tongue. She held Randa's head close, looking down at the blonde locks among her fingers as she urged Randa to continue. She felt eager hands move down her stomach and slip into the waist of her jeans where Randa pulled at the metal buttons, releasing each one with a swift tug.

As she felt Randa's hand move into her loosened jeans, DJ pulled away gently from Randa's insistent mouth as her own lips descended upon the blonde's body. Cupping a breast in each hand she hovered over Randa's left breast before taking the rigid nipple into her mouth. The sensation of the swollen nub against her tongue forced a passion filled groan deep from within the poet's chest and her other hand increased its massaging of the right nipple as she rolled the distended bud around her thumb and forefinger. As she continued, Randa's grinding movements against her thigh increased, urging DJ to amplify her attentions.

After long moments she pulled away and straightened her stance, looking down into Randa's hazy gaze. DJ could feel her

337

heart hammering in her chest as her body pulsed with swelling desire.

"Denise... please," Randa groaned.

"Tell me," DJ stated as her hand moved to cup the nurse's behind and pull her close, pressing herself against Randa's heated centre. Even through the material of Randa's sweats and her jeans she could still feel the incredible heat the blonde emitted.

"I need more."

As they kissed again, DJ pushed her hands into the waistband of the nurse's trousers and slowly began to push them down her body, moving away from Randa's lips as she followed the direction of her hands. With a light thud she fell to her knees, her vision upon Randa's glistening folds and the scent of her desire.

"Oh God," she whispered as her head fell against the pit of Randa's stomach and she helped the nurse step out of her trousers.

Randa gripped DJ's shoulders. "Please, Denise."

Gently nudging Randa's legs further apart DJ moved her head toward Randa's centre, unable to resist the desire or her lover's pleas. Looking up at the now naked body and into darkened green eyes she speared her tongue forwards and teasingly moved it along Randa's swollen centre. The nurse groaned breathlessly as her head once again fell against the wall. Unable to keep eye contact she clasped her hands around the back of DJ's head, ensuring the contact.

DJ whimpered, unable to hold back her own desire at the sheer feeling and taste of Randa. Having the blonde hold her in a vice like grip against her mound only served to fuel her own passion and she squeezed her thighs together in an attempt at relief. Unfortunately her restricting jeans provided little respite in her current position.

Avoiding the place Randa wanted her most, DJ's tongue slid around her folds at a tormenting slow pace until Randa grasped her head and started moving against her.

"Denise... please... I want you inside me."

Not wasting any time and urged on by Randa's desperate movements, the poet entered Randa as she took her swollen bud into her mouth, teasing it with agonising strokes.

She pumped her fingers inside Randa, moving in a

twisting motion that she hoped would increase the blonde's pleasure. As she felt her nearing the edge she changed the gentle movement of her mouth to a hard suction, pulling on the swollen bud until the blonde cried out in a much-needed release, calling the brunette's name over and over. She thrust against the poet as DJ moved with her, increasing her sensations.

As the waves eased, DJ slowed her movements in time to catch the blonde as she slid weakly down the wall and landed softly upon DJ's lap.

The sound of harsh breathing filled the heated air. Denise pulled Randa tight against her, the blonde's head resting upon her shoulder as she moved her hand reassuringly over her sweat soaked back. After a long moment Randa pulled away, her breathing less erratic.

"I think I like this new you!" She stated with a dreamy smile.

"I like this new me too!" DJ replied. She looked seriously into heavy lidded green eyes. "So I guess I am forgiven for my behaviour?" She pouted hopefully with wide blue eyes.

"I forgave you as soon as I saw you standing on my doorstep."

"Ah." DJ smiled winningly as she moved her hand seductively over Randa's chest. "So... being as how you like this new me so much... how about exploring *me* a little further!" she waggled her brows mischievously.

"Hmm." Randa slid backward and moved from DJ's lap. Rising to a standing position she held out her hand and pulled the poet up beside her. "Depends what you have in mind."

"Preferably something that involves me wearing even less clothes?" She looked down at her loosened jeans.

Randa grinned as she stepped forward and took DJ into her arms. "Sounds good to me, but I think there is something I need to tell you first." She lifted up onto her toes and kissed Denise softly. "I love you too!"

Stepping back she slapped the poet playfully on her backside. "Last one to the bedroom has to make the other breakfast tomorrow morning," she yelled and took off through the house.

"Oh that is so not fair!" DJ groused as she followed Randa in hot pursuit, "You know where you are going."

"Then you can win tomorrow's race." Randa stated over her shoulder as she burst into her bedroom.

DJ followed close behind and grabbed Randa just short of reaching the bed. Lifting the blonde into her arms they landed on the large double bed in a collapsed heap. DJ moved to swiftly straddle the nurse. "I like that."

"What?" Randa asked breathlessly.

"The thought of you and me and tomorrow… lots of tomorrows."

"I like it too."

"So…" DJ pressed a gentle kiss upon Randa's lips. "Does that mean you and me are now a 'we'?"

Randa responded in kind as her lips caressed the poets. "Yeah!" she said, "It's always been forever for me."

"Me too," the poet replied with a grin.

Randa arched her eyebrows as she delivered a look of complete disbelief. Denise fluttered her eyelashes innocently before both women collapsed with laughter and Randa rolled the taller woman onto her back.

"So that's what all of your dramatic moping was about, huh?" she said as she prodded DJ's chest.

The poet caught the offending finger with her left hand. "Well I admit that I may have acted a little…" she pursed her lips in thought, "uncertain… self conscious… scared… maybe a little dramatic…"

"… A little?" Randa asked

DJ glared but continued. "But I always knew you were the only one for me!"

"Good save!"

DJ grinned. "Thanks it took me thirty two years to get this good!"

"Well…" Randa started, "How about you show me how good you are in other areas?"

The brunette grinned as she reached out to pull Randa closer. "My pleasure!" she replied as she yielded to her lover, safe in the knowledge that no matter what tomorrow held - they would always face it together.

The End

340

About the Authors

Val Brown is a healthcare professional with many years in Nursing. Her current job takes her to all parts of the United States.

Writing was only just a fantasy until she met a certain British poet online and started a writing partnership and friendship that has led to the publishing of this first novel.

Though she enjoys exploring and traveling, family and friends will always be her main interest.

MJ Walker lives in a small, rural village in England.

She was first published as a poet at age seventeen in the United States followed by her inclusion in many anthologies in her native country. Through her offerings on the web, MJ met and teamed up with Val Brown, an American nurse.

She is a part-time numismatist and currently studying Journalism.

A Sneak Peek

Coming later this year from **D2D**....

The sequel to Connecting Hearts by Val Brown and M J Walker:

Family Connections

The petite blonde wandered out the back door and stood on the porch, looking around with satisfaction. The camellia bushes were rife with blossoms and the newly planted pines were thriving. The small vegetable and herb garden was already providing fresh produce for the table and the yard was neatly manicured. The crowning glory to the scene though was a single perfect English rose.

An English rose by the name of Denise Jennings Randa thought. As if on cue a tanned arm showed itself from the depths of the large freestanding hammock situated under the shade of one of the large oak trees in the backyard. An equally tanned hand curled palm upward and the index finger moved rhythmically in a beckoning manner.

Randa laughed and walked to the hammock where a very contented Denise Jennings swayed in the light summer breeze. Randa was struck yet again at the sheer loveliness of her lover and partner. The tall firm body, black hair and magnificent blue eyes were a combination that would always cause the blonde's heart to beat just a little faster.

"Nurse Martin! Nurse Martin!" Denise's voice cut through Randa's assessment and she locked gazes with the woman who had come to be her whole world in the space of less than a year. Denise made her voice faint and pitiful. "Nurse Martin, I believe I have become frightfully dehydrated in your absence. I thought you were just going inside to get some water."

Randa rolled her eyes and chuckled, "Oh, brother! That's laying it on a bit thick don't you think?" She held up one of the bottles of water she had been carrying and announced to an imaginary crowd, "And the award for best performance by a poet in a hammock goes to…Denise Jennings!" She reached out to award the bottle to Denise and shrieked as she found her arm grabbed and her body hauled into the hammock where she ended up nose to nose with the dark haired beauty.

Denise smiled into Randa's eyes and said, "I'd like to thank all the little people who made this award possible." Tilting her head slightly she was able to bring her lips to the waiting ones of the nurse. Both women sighed as the soft exchange ended. "Thank you, little person," Denise murmured.

Randa smiled. "You'll pay for that 'little' remark later; remind me in case I forget." Now it was Denise's turn to laugh as she wrapped her arm around the blonde and drew her closer.

"Do I still have to pay if I tell you I wasn't thirsty for water but for your company? There is nothing lonelier than a two-person hammock with only one person in it. What kept you anyway?"

"I got the water and put on a little extra sun block because some of us don't tan up to the color of an English walnut," she grinned, "but on the way back I had to stop and look around here for a minute. This place is gorgeous and most of it's because of you. You really have a green thumb you know."

"Yeah, it was one of the things I got from Sara." Both women were silent for a moment as they were caught up in individual memories of Denise's wonderful aunt who had passed away in March from Amyotrophic Lateral Sclerosis. Her illness had brought Randa and Denise together and her death had nearly split them apart. Their love had survived the storm though and they had ended up together just as Sara had hoped.

"I still miss her," Randa said quietly.

"Me, too," returned the poet. "It gets easier all the time though to think of her and only remember the good and happy times.

You've helped me do that, helped me to keep her memory alive without all the pain I had after she died." Denise deposited a warm kiss on Randa's forehead and looked lovingly into her bright green eyes.

"It's my distinct pleasure, Ms. Jennings"

"Not yet but definitely later, Ms. Martin." A small gust blew up and rocked the hammock gently and the women relished the feeling of gentle movement and holding on to one another. They had only been living together a little over two months and things had gone relatively smoothly. There were the usual adjustments to be made when any two people started sharing the same living space. Denise was a roll the tube of toothpaste up from the bottom kind of person and Randa was a squeeze it in the middle kind.

Randa wasn't sure what made living with Denise the relatively easy thing it had been. That they were deeply and totally in love wasn't even a question. The nurse thought it was more likely the fact that they were friends before the romance happened and nothing that had happened since then had changed that fact. *We have so much more between us than just sex* the nurse thought. *Not that the sex isn't great, mind you.* Randa snuggled deeper into the poet's embrace as the flower scented breeze moved the hammock gently again. The contentment that welled up in her soul was spoiled only by a thought that had been plaguing the nurse for weeks. Her brows scrunched together in irritation.

"Stop it," Denise said. The voice caused a pleasant burr in the chest Randa had her head on.

"Stop what?" Randa returned.

"You know what. You're thinking about it again."

"Was not."

"Yes, you were. I can always tell. First your eyebrows scrunch up, then your whole body becomes tense and finally you get a death grip on me if I'm anywhere in your general vicinity," Denise explained. She looked down meaningfully at the nurse's arm that had been casually draped across her middle and was now doing a pretty good imitation of a vise-grip.

"Sorry," Randa squeaked and loosened her hold on the taller woman. "I'm not sure why this is bugging me so much. It didn't bug you, did it?"

"Nope. It was just another day. Maybe you should stop

thinking of it as June 29th, another day that will live in infamy."

"Maybe," Randa said but sounded doubtful.

"Maybe you should think about something else entirely," the poet purred.

"Any suggestions?"

"Plenty," Denise mumbled as she moved her head to begin a delicious nibbling of the nurse's earlobe. Randa gave herself over to the wonderful sensations created by her partner and resolved to not think about it for the rest of the afternoon. *Not going to think about it at all, not a single thought.*

"You're doing it again," Denise laughed and soon had the nurse laughing with her. Then the poet returned her attention to the neglected earlobe and Randa was able to forget for a little while that she was about to turn thirty.

Watch our website for the release date
www.limitlessd2d.net

Order These Great Books Directly From Limitless, Dare 2 Dream Publishing		
The Amazon Queen by L M Townsend	20.00	
Define Destiny by J M Dragon	20.00	
Desert Hawk by Archangel	15.00	
Golden Gate by Erin Jennifer Mar	18.00	
Love's Melody Lost, 2ndEd. by Radclyffe	18.00	
Paradise Found by Cruise and Stoley	20.00	
Spirit Harvest by Trish Shields	15.00	
Storm Surge by KatLyn	20.00	
Up The River-out of print **...While supplies last...** by Sam Ruskin	15.00	
Memories Kill By S. B. Zarben	20.00	
Fatal Impressions by Jeanne Foguth	18.00	
	Total	

South Carolina residents add 5% sales tax.
Shipping is $3.50 per book and will be via UPS.

Watch for more and upcoming titles:

Visit our website at:
http://limitlessd2d.net/index.html

Please mail your orders with a check or money order to:

Limitless, Dare 2 Dream Publications
100 Pin Oak Ct.
Lexington, SC 29073
Please make checks or money orders payable to:
Limitless.

Order More Great Books Directly From Limitless, Dare 2 Dream Publishing

Title	Price	
The Amazon Queen by L M Townsend	20.00	
Define Destiny by J M Dragon	20.00	
Desert Hawk by Archangel	15.00	
Indiscretions **By Cruise**	18.00	
A Thousand Shades of Feeling **by Carolyn McBride**	18.00	
The Amazon Nation **By Carla Osborne**	20.00	
Spirit Harvest by Trish Shields	15.00	
Encounters, Book I By Anne Azel	22.00	
Encounters, Book II **By Anne Azel**	25.00	
Memories Kill By S. B. Zarben	20.00	
Deadly Rumors by Jeanne Foguth	20.00	
	Total	

South Carolina residents add 5% sales tax.
Shipping is $3.50 per book and will be via UPS.

Watch for these and more upcoming titles:
Visit our website at: http://limitlessd2d.net

Please mail your orders with a check or money order to:

Limitless, Dare 2 Dream Publications
100 Pin Oak Ct.
Lexington, SC 29073

Please make checks or money orders payable to:
Limitless.

347